I Think
THEY
LOVE
YOU

Also by Julian Winters

YOUNG ADULT NOVELS

Running with Lions

How to Be Remy Cameron

The Summer of Everything

Right Where I Left You

As You Walk On By

Prince of the Palisades

ANTHOLOGIES

Out Now: Queer We Go Again!

Up All Night

Black Boy Joy

Fools in Love

Eternally Yours

Cool. Awkward. Black.

The Grimoire of Grave Fates

Writing in Color

Firsts and Lasts

Mermaids Never Drown: Tales to Dive For

I THINK
THEY
LOVE YOU

Julian Winters

ST. MARTIN'S GRIFFIN
NEW YORK

First published in the United States by St. Martin's Griffin, an imprint of St. Martin's Publishing Group

I THINK THEY LOVE YOU. Copyright © 2024 by Julian Winters. All rights reserved. Printed in the United States of America. For information, address St. Martin's Publishing Group, 120 Broadway, New York, NY 10271.

www.stmartins.com

Design by Meryl Sussman Levavi

The Library of Congress Cataloging-in-Publication Data is available upon request.

ISBN 978-1-250-32624-9 (trade paperback)
ISBN 978-1-250-32625-6 (ebook)

Our books may be purchased in bulk for promotional, educational, or business use. Please contact your local bookseller or the Macmillan Corporate and Premium Sales Department at 1-800-221-7945, extension 5442, or by email at MacmillanSpecialMarkets@macmillan.com.

First Edition: 2025

1   3   5   7   9   10   8   6   4   2

For the ones who've had their hearts broken
and dreams deferred—I hope you never stop
giving yourself second chances

Have enough courage to trust love one more
time and always one more time.

—*Maya Angelou*

I THINK
THEY
LOVE
YOU

Prologue

When it comes to celebrating life's biggest moments, Denz has seen it all.

Themed birthdays and anniversaries. Graduations to retirement parties. The engagement to wedding day to baby shower or, on occasion, a luxurious soirée welcoming the happy couple's first pet.

Yes, a "pawty."

Event planning is his family's legacy.

And at twenty-one, he's also witnessed every version of a behind-the-scenes disaster that comes with those big moments. The ruthless arguments over a party budget. The melting sweet-sixteen cake after someone used sparklers instead of traditional candles. Multiple doggy ring bearers ruining pristine wedding dresses. That awkward moment when the drunken father of the bride—because, of course, her family *insisted* on an open bar—gives a speech about how much he hates his new son-in-law in front of two hundred reception guests.

Any event involving two families interacting for the first time is typically a disaster in the making.

Which is why Denz is very casually doing breathing exercises in his boyfriend's Toyota Corolla. He refuses to lose his shit in the middle of a parking lot in Athens, Georgia. So what if his own Big Moment is approximately one hour and ten minutes away.

He's *chill*.

"Okay," Bray is saying as he climbs back into the passenger seat while juggling two large cups and a bag overflowing with food, "I got us a ton of options."

Denz exhales one last time. Outside, The Varsity on West Broad Street stands out in a pop of white and red against the gray December sky. They're only five minutes from the University of Georgia's campus. He can turn around. Spare them both this whole first in-person encounter.

But then his gaze falls on Bray. Honey-brown complexion stained a bright pink from the cold. A wool beanie hiding his dark buzz cut. That perpetual boyish look in the corner of his brown eyes. His goofy expression.

"Two slaw dogs," Bray lists off. "Double bacon cheeseburger. Triple burger. Fries. Chicken nuggets. Two fried peach pies. Varsity Orange for me. Frosted Orange for you."

"Sorry." A smile teases Denz's mouth. "Are we driving to Atlanta or *Nebraska?*"

"Road trips require supplies."

"This—" Denz waves a hand at all the food unloaded in Bray's lap. "—is a feast!"

"So . . . should I have got more nuggets? Onion rings?"

Denz cranks the heat to help settle Bray's shivering. "Not if you plan on kissing me later."

"A fair trade."

Denz ignores his sarcasm. He watches Bray stab a straw into his cup. The way his leg bounces. All the anxious energy pouring off him like a dog shaking raindrops from its fur.

He's seen this side of his boyfriend before. At swim meets where Bray hasn't placed less than fourth in a race all season. Before a test Bray's obsessively studied for.

The other day when Denz suggested they go home *together* for winter break this year.

"You're nervous," he comments.

In less than two hours, Bray's meeting Denz's parents for the first time.

"I'm not," Bray insists. He rips open a ketchup packet with his teeth, building a hill to dunk his fries in. It's the only way he can eat them.

"They're gonna love you."

"I know." Bray doesn't look very convincing while slurping his orange soda. "You're the one shitting his boxers. I saw that face you made at the gas station. When your mom called." He imitates an expression that's somewhere between a cat puking and a puppy straining to poop.

Denz chucks a fry at his forehead. "I didn't look like that."

"You did. It was cute."

"I'm fine."

"Really?" Bray's eyes sweep suspiciously around. "Did you stress-clean my car while I was ordering food?"

"No?" He did. A little.

"You know they're not gonna judge me by how many protein bar wrappers or empty water bottles I have on my floor mats, right?"

Denz does. And Bray's right—he *is* on edge.

It's been building for a week. His crankiness after every call or text from his parents. And, fine, maybe he *guided* Bray's six-foot-one frame into a nice pair of black jeans and a hunter-green sweater instead of the joggers and SpongeBob hoodie he planned to wear. Maybe Denz is dressed in a Burberry cardigan, tailored charcoal slacks, and a new pair of leather oxfords.

The first impression needs to be perfect.

Denz has never brought a boyfriend home to his parents. Someone he's been dating for over a year. Someone he's said "I love you" to. He wants everyone in his family—especially his dad—to feel the same way he does about Bray: like he's The One.

"Hey," Bray says after Denz almost chews through his thumb cuticle. "Promise I won't make you look bad today."

"I wasn't worried abo—"

Bray's narrow-eyed glare cuts him off.

Fuck. He doesn't mean for Bray to feel like *he's* the issue. He's not. Denz's sisters already love him. They met over the phone months ago. Since then, Denz has caught Bray exchanging memes and GIFs with his younger sister, Nic, online. And Kami, his older sister, calls just to discuss what's happened on their latest reality show obsessions.

The problem is the rest of Denz's family.

He's used to their high expectations. Their infatuation with public approval. Anyone associated with the Carters, including who Denz dates, needs to meet certain standards.

Case in point: the Kenneth Carter Rite of Passage test. Denz knows it's coming. His dad's private interrogation of any potential partner his children bring home. It's never malicious. But Denz doesn't want Bray to suffer through it either.

Also, he secretly wants to keep this version of his life to himself.

In Athens, he's not Denzel Carter, son of a *Forbes* Most Influential CEO. No one cares about his family's net worth. How messy his apartment is. If he shows up to class wearing the same coffee-stained T-shirt he had on two days ago, his short 'fro unbrushed. Here, he can idle in a near-empty parking lot and not worry about some photographer seeing the glob of mustard on his boyfriend's chin.

Denz isn't ready to give any of this up yet.

"Um." Bray pops a chicken nugget in his mouth. "Are we skipping the holidays?"

"What?"

"We're not moving."

"I'm getting there."

"You know performance anxiety is real." Bray finally wipes his chin. "I'm not rushing you. Dad and I aren't very religious anyway."

Grinning, Denz says, "But you have *traditions*. Like making hot apple cider Christmas morning."

"Watching *The Grinch*. Animated only."

"In your pj's!" Denz is fond of the Rudolph-onesie selfie Bray sent him last year. He can't wait to unzip it in person.

"I'm starting to think Dad likes you more than me."

"Impossible," Denz says.

Bray stuffs his mouth with fries instead of responding.

Another thing Denz feels guilty about: he's already met Dr. Emmanuel Adams. Bray eagerly introduced them when his dad visited at the end of last semester. Denz was so nervous going to shake Emmanuel's hand, he knocked over his iced latte. A milky brown flood across the coffee shop floor. Thankfully, Emmanuel laughed instead of demanding Bray break up with him then and there.

Emmanuel has become a regular fixture in Denz's life now. Random check-ins. Pep talks before exams. Inviting Denz to join his weekly Scrabble nights with Bray.

"He's excited to see you," Bray says.

"Maybe we should spend the whole break with him?"

Denz chugs his milkshake. Is brain freeze a valid enough excuse for missing dinner with his family?

"No way." Bray signals toward the back seat. Carefully nestled between their luggage is a white box from No Crumb Left Behind, Athens's best bakery. Inside, half a dozen chocolate-chip muffins await Kenneth. "These are your dad's favorite."

Bray's great at remembering the smallest detail from a story you tell him. Keeping a mental log of all your favorite things. He never forgets the stuff you hate either, like onions on your burger.

"He'll live," Denz grumbles.

"Then who will eat them, my tiny muffin?" Bray leans in for a ketchup-sticky kiss that Denz almost rejects.

He *hates* pet names.

Denz inhales again. He's hit with the scent of greasy fast food and the horrendous Snowflakes and Sweaters car freshener Bray loves. Underneath, the heady aroma of Bray's coconut bodywash soothes him.

"I need a minute."

To convince myself I'm not making a big mistake, he thinks, but doesn't say.

What if his parents *don't* love Bray?

Denz shakes his head. That's not a thing. He won't let it *be* a thing.

He cranes over the center console to rest his forehead against Bray's. "I'm gonna rip that stupid sweater off you with my teeth."

"Is that before or after I meet your parents?"

"In between?"

Bray shrugs. "I don't know. There might not be time. I'll be pretty busy wooing your mom and impressing your dad."

"You don't have to do that," Denz lies. "He's just a dad."

"There's a video of him hugging Idris Elba on *Good Day Atlanta* all over the internet," Bray deadpans. "He's not *just a dad*."

Denz lets Bray feed him bites of burger. He's not wrong about Kenneth. Denz just doesn't want to admit it out loud.

"I'm gonna convince your entire family I'm the greatest boyfriend ever," Bray tells him.

"It'll only be my parents, Kami, and Nic. Mikah too, but he's not hard to impress. Being a baby and all."

"No aunts or uncles? Cousins?"

"Nope." Denz steals the aux cord to plug his phone in. No way he's suffering through another one of Bray's true crime podcasts while driving. "Auntie Cheryl and Uncle Tevin are in LA with Jordan while he's on winter break. Auntie Eva's at Uncle Orlando's family's villa in Puerto Rico. Gone until after New Year's."

Denz planned it this way. Less prying questions and unfiltered commentary from extended family.

Bray asks, "What about your mom's family?"

"Too spread out across the country."

Bray looks slightly relieved. Like he was secretly dreading having to talk to that many people at once. Denz grew up around large group settings, either from family gatherings or the company's year-round events. Bray hasn't. He prefers nights in to parties overflowing with strangers.

Denz drums his fingers on the steering wheel. Scrolls through his playlist. Turns the heat down, then up. It's one dinner. One winter break.

"Denz." Bray's voice is restless. "You're not backing out, are y—"

"*No.*"

"Good." He kisses Denz. Soft, punctuated. "I want to meet your family."

It hits like a shock wave. A ripple in Denz's gut that might not ever subside. Bray's not intimidated. He's confident. He *wants* this to happen.

Over the console, Denz grabs Bray's hand. He squeezes three times. Their secret code: *I love you.*

"Promise not to regret this," Denz requests.

"I survived Nic's commentary on my music *and* movie taste," Bray reminds him. Denz groans. *Why are all thirteen-year-olds such feral creatures with strong opinions?* But Bray smiles sweetly. "How bad can your parents be?"

Denz cackles. He hits Play on his phone. Lorde's "Royals" thumps through the speakers as he finally throws the car in reverse.

"You have no idea."

But Denz does. He *knows* his family. They'll fall helplessly in love with Bray the same way he has. It's inevitable. Destiny on the fringe of being fulfilled.

What can possibly go wrong?

-1-

Five Years Later

Denz has a *few* regrets.

First, being too distracted to notice the uneven sidewalk as he sprints from the parking garage. No one's around to see him trip. Or hop backward to recover the loafer he lost. It doesn't matter because he's still late. Still on hour twenty-five of an unforgivable hangover from the annual 24 Carter Gold New Year's Eve celebration.

His second regret: gulping down lemon drop martini number four just before midnight on Saturday. When it comes to alcohol, Denz is far from a lightweight. But he barely got out of bed yesterday. He also forgot to set his phone's work alarm.

Halfway there, he pauses to fix his loafer. He ignores the fact that he's wearing two *different* socks. That his dark slacks are wrinkled. At least his sweater's not inside out.

It's a cool January morning. Atlanta's skyline is a tangled ribbon of blue and gray. Working the day after a holiday should be illegal. Denz doesn't care that their Monday staff meeting has been pushed back an hour. He'd prefer to be in bed instead of looking like a breathless, uncaffeinated mess while jogging through 9:00 A.M. foot traffic.

"You're late."

Outside the glass building housing 24 Carter Gold's offices, Kami watches Denz stumble to a stop.

"Wasn't timeliness one of your New Year's resolutions?" she asks.

"Was it?"

He can't remember. This—among many reasons—is why Denz limits his drinks at work functions. He tends to make very regrettable declarations to his older sister after a second martini.

Denz yawns into the crook of his elbow. "How the hell are you so put-together this early?"

Her naturally curly hair is sleeked into a tight bun. She's wearing pearl earrings and a beige Givenchy trench over a teal high-neck dress.

"I'm raising a six-year-old," Kami reminds him. "I've been up since the ass crack of dawn learning about thousands of butterfly species from his iPad." She sighs. "Did you know there are over seven hundred species in the US alone?"

Denz beams. "Mikah's a genius."

Kami tilts her head to inspect him. "The real question is why do you look like a gay Carlton from *The Fresh Prince?*"

"I do *not*," he argues. His snug Ralph Lauren cable-knit sweater with a white oxford underneath isn't *that bad*.

Kami smirks. "If you're auditioning for the only Black guy in a Lifetime Christmas movie, then sure. You look incredible."

"I hate you."

It's not true. For most of his life, Denz has semi-idolized Kami. Not quite as much as their dad, but a respectable second.

"Shall we?"

The moment Kami's heels click against the lobby's marble floors, all eyes lock on her. Near the elevators, three interns whisper excitedly. She doesn't even notice the attention. From 8:00 A.M. to 5:00 P.M., Kami's all business.

"By the way," she says, eyes lowered. Her phone chimes away as she types. No doubt she's replying to emails that piled up over the weekend. Anything that lands in Denz's own company inbox after 3:00 P.M. on a Friday goes unanswered until he's at least caffeinated the following Monday. Maybe later. "The social media numbers from Saturday are looking exceptional. The best yet."

"Did you expect anything less?"

When Denz came on as an events coordinator, 24 Carter Gold's social media presence was a LinkedIn page, a Facebook account, and an irregularly updated Twitter feed. Fixing the company's nonexistent digital footprint wasn't one of his job functions, but Denz couldn't resist.

Relentless dedication is Kami's thing. Social media is his.

He did a complete digital rebrand. Diversified the platforms they used. Captured perfect candids at events. Spent weekends creating video content around the city. Tagged partnered companies for greater visibility.

Three months and ten thousand new followers later, his dad offered him a salary bump and an extra job title: social media *director*.

Now, he's an integral part of the annual NYE party's success. While Kami, an events manager, handles the planning, Denz is the energy behind promotion. Personalized hashtags. Persistent reminders. Reshares from celebrities and his own public account, which has—not to brag—over eighty thousand followers alone.

In a family full of overachievers, he savors having a way to stand out.

"Five-star review from TFW," Kami notes as they climb on the elevator.

"Not bad," Denz says. The Final Word is a mildly reputable gossip site. He leans in a corner with Kami. Her eyes are lowered again, a soft smile tucked into the corners of her mouth. A hand shields her screen as if she's watching porn, but Denz knows better.

He whispers, "It's *him*, isn't it?"

Kami elbows him hard. Her eyes flit around. The interns are busy on their phones, finished silently worshipping her. It doesn't stop Kami from blushing, which isn't noticeable since they share their mom's rich brown skin. But Denz can tell by the way she bites her lip.

He's never met Kami's secret boyfriend. The one she's been dating since early November. The reason Denz spends at least one evening every two weeks babysitting his nephew. The most he's gotten out of Kami is a first name.

"So . . ." He nudges her arm. "How's Suraj?"

"We're not discussing this."

"Fine. Just give me a last name."

"You're not cyberstalking him, Denz."

"Wouldn't dream of it."

He already tried. Kami's hyper-curated following list consists of relatives, random college friends, and their favorite coffee shop. Not a single Suraj.

"I don't know why you won't tell everyone," Denz says, his voice still lowered. Not even Nic knows this mystery boyfriend exists.

Kami locks her phone, flexing an eyebrow at him. "*You* don't?"

Denz grimaces. Being a Carter is a full-time job. Thanks to the company's continuous growth—last October, they hosted the Obamas' anniversary party—the public's expectations of them have been consistently high. The spotlight is always on. Then there's the familial expectations, *especially* from the aunties.

What college they attend, their career aspirations, wardrobe, friend groups, who they're dating. Every detail is up for dissection and approval.

No one has let Kami forget her last relationship, with Matthew, Mikah's father. The man she delayed finishing her degree at Emory University for. The asshole who left when she was six months pregnant for "better" acting gigs in Canada. To date, his biggest role has been Sullen Bad Boy in a forgettable teen drama that Denz didn't hate-watch in the dark.

(He did.)

His own dating life is purposely nonexistent. Nothing resembling a relationship. All his casual hookups come with preestablished rules:

No sleepovers. No repeats. Absolutely no meeting his family.

Exhibit A: the hipster white guy Denz traded mutual blow jobs with in an upstairs VIP bathroom during the NYE party. Denz can't remember his name, but he was taller than Denz's five foot nine. Oh, and *dimples*. He might've worked in talent relations? Sound and lighting?

Either way, it was work-related head.

When Dimples started asking too many personal questions afterward, Denz politely kissed his cheek and slipped back downstairs. He never gives anyone the opportunity to decide whether the *real* Denz is worth sticking around for. Not since college.

But Kami deserves a second chance at love. To ignore what the other Carters think.

"You know—" Denz starts.

Kami's murderous glare stops him. He doesn't turn twenty-six until July. He wants to live long enough to see what this whole quarter-life crisis thing is about.

The elevator doors open on the sixth floor, revealing the bright, open space occupied by 24 Carter Gold. It's equal parts professional and inviting. Behind the front desk, against a lilac wall, individual vanity bulbs spell out CARTER. White concrete floors contrast with the gold-and-orchid furniture. Beyond the lobby are glass-walled offices with framed partitions. Farther down, the expansive conference room sits opposite Kenneth's office.

The staff happily buzzes around. It's as if Denz is the only one fighting a lingering hangover.

He yawns again. "God, I could go for a latte. And a muffin."

"When are they arriving?" Kami asks.

"When is *what* arriving?"

"The muffins."

He blinks at her.

"Denzel Kevin Carter," she hisses, "please tell me you didn't forget to order pastries for the staff meeting. It's *your* Monday."

He throws his hands over his face, groaning. Fuck his life. Another failed reminder.

"It's fine," Kami says in that voice she uses when things are decidedly *not fine*, but she has a plan. She waves at Jordan, their cousin and her assistant. "Crema isn't far. Order online. An intern can pick them up."

"I'm not letting an intern fix my mistake," Denz grunts. Besides, he can't afford for anyone to forget his dad's favorite chocolate-chip muffins. He'll never hear the end of it. "I'll pick them up."

"The meeting is in thirty minutes."

"I'll drive fast." He opens the coffee shop's mobile app. "Stall for me?"

"How?"

"Show off Mikah's school pictures again?" Denz jams the elevator's Down button. "You did theater. Do a monologue from *Romeo and Juliet*. Ooh! Tell Dad about Sur—"

Kami clears her throat as Jordan approaches.

Denz pastes on an innocent smile. "You'll figure something out."

The elevator doors close on her shouting, "Hurry back! And stay out of trouble!"

He grins smugly. It's just muffins. How difficult could that be?

Crema of the Crop is one of Denz's favorite places in the city. Exposed brick walls. Ebony-stained hardwood floors. Pendant lighting shining on the abstract art mounted on the walls as soft, chill music plays overheard. Air spiced with espresso and freshly ground coffee and sugary pastries.

Six customers are between Denz and the front register. The late-morning rush has arrived. He decides to kill time by checking his socials.

His account, @notthatdenzel, started off as a hobby. A much-needed distraction from the unexpected broken heart that came with his BA in communications. Subconsciously, Denz always knew he'd end up at 24 Carter Gold. That didn't stop him from working hard to prove his position was *earned* and not solely nepotism. But social media was his fun weekend activity . . . until it wasn't.

He didn't anticipate the influx of followers. Sponsorships. Paid advertising gigs. Something he could make a small profit from. He'd just wanted out of his own head.

The line edges forward.

Denz scrolls to his last post: a shirtless, fresh-out-of-the-shower photo of him holding up a new energizing face wash. Short, textured sponge curls still damp. Unshaven jawline. It's not supposed to be a thirst trap, but the droplets of water slipping down his brown chest *might* suggest otherwise.

He ignores the comments. The usual pile of "hero" and "legend" and "icon." Words Denz has never associated with himself. Exceeding "good enough" has always been his goal. Anything else is a bonus.

Over the café's music, names and drink orders are called. Soon, he's face-to-face with the college-age girl behind the register. Her name tag reads *Sophie,* with a smiley face in the *o.* She's absurdly cheery for a Monday.

"What can I get you today?"

"I have an online order for 24 Carter Gold," Denz says. "Assorted muffins."

"Oh, you're Kami's little brother!"

"I'm *Denz,*" he corrects, trying to mirror Sophie's perkiness.

"Cool. We're finishing that up. You can wait at the end."

Denz shuffles over. Behind the espresso machines, two baristas cue shots and craft perfect cappuccino foam. One is a tall, middle-aged woman with an armful of colorful tattoos. The other, Matty, is a classically handsome white guy with freckles and sandy hair. He's still newish at Crema, but Denz has already introduced himself.

Intimately.

Denz turns away before eye contact is made. He's halfway through reading TFW's review when he hears, "Darjeeling tea with light milk and honey for . . . Braylon?"

The phone almost slips from his hands.

Denz's head snaps up. It's impossible. Matty didn't just say—

"Darjeeling for Braylon?"

"Over here!"

And, fuck, there he is, cutting through the crowd—Bray Adams. Standing in Crema's lobby, not London, where he's supposed to have been for the last three and a half years. Since graduation from UGA.

Denz almost doesn't recognize him. Broad shoulders hugged by a gray cardigan and white button-up. Traces of dark stubble lining his sharp jaw. Tight curls peeking from beneath a knit beanie. Everything about him, down to his honey-brown skin, is . . . *wow*.

Denz swallows hard.

Fuck, no. That's not how this works. He's imagined this moment a dozen times. When . . . *if* Denz ever ran into the ex who ripped his heart into confetti, Bray wasn't going to be hotter than before he moved to another continent. And Denz would be in his ultimate revenge-sexy form, not wearing unmatching socks with his jaw on the floor.

Bray takes the cardboard cup. "Cheers!"

Denz doesn't know whether to direct his rage toward Matty's blushing face or Bray's ridiculously defined cheekbones. He opts for none of the above. It's time to leave. He can suffer through a month's worth of his dad's ridicule if it means—

"Denz?"

Shit. Did he really waste his three-second escape window thinking about stupid muffins?

When Denz turns, an uncertain smile sits on Bray's mouth. "'Ello there."

The light British accent prickles the hairs on the back of Denz's neck. He hates it. "Hey!" His laugh comes out like a gasp. "It's . . . you. Bray."

"Oh, it's Braylon. Not Bray."

"What?"

"I go by my full name now."

Denz forces himself not to scowl. For nearly all of college, he was Bray. Three of those years, he was *Denz's* Bray.

The memory blossoms across his brain like a summer sunset:

It was mid-May in Athens. An overcrowded, run-down two-story house off campus. A graduation party neither of them should've been at. But, as a freshman, Bray was already fully dedicated to his swim teammates, even the seniors who were leaving. And Paolo, Denz's roommate, convinced him to come celebrate his older sister's newly received finance degree.

In his first year, Denz had done a spectacular job of avoiding parties. Staying out of the spotlight. Being . . . normal. He hadn't missed much. Nothing but flat beer, bad music, and a severe lack of interesting conversations.

And then he saw him. Prickly buzz cut, shy smile. Warm brown eyes watching Denz from across the room.

Denz stared back. It was that careful, curious gaze only queer people know. The one used in public when you're deciding if the other person is trustworthy. If entering their space is safe. Three songs later, Denz went to introduce himself in a semi-dark corner.

And promptly spilled his watery gin and cranberry on Bray's T-shirt.

"Denz. Your shirt." He winced. "Fuck, I mean . . . I'm Denz. And I ruined your sh—"

After a scratchy laugh, a low voice made of velvet said, "Is Denz short for something?"

Denz smirked, suddenly calm again. "Maybe I'll tell you one day."

"One day?"

"Are you going to tell me your name?"

Another laugh. Another wave of tickling heat spreading up Denz's neck. He'd blame the alcohol but that was all over the other boy's shirt now. A deep maroon spot contrasting with his full pink lips.

"I'm Bray."

"Short for?" Denz prompted.

"You first."

Denz snorted. "Come on. *You* bumped into *my* drink"—He'll never admit how the scandalized, amused gasp Bray released in that second almost made his knees weak. *Almost.*—"so, you owe me!"

Bray leaned in. Their knuckles brushed. The corners of his mouth twitched as he whispered, "Maybe I'll tell you. One day."

The memory hangs like a raindrop suspended by a spiderweb in his head now.

Their start. His ending.

"Braylon," Denz repeats, mashing the name around his mouth like a baby trying beets for the first time. "You're here. In America. Since . . . ?"

"A bit over a year now."

Over a year. Denz doesn't know why it stings. Why he even cares. Braylon is nothing to him. An ex, another man Denz has no attachments to.

"Welcome home," he says sharply.

Braylon's response is swallowed by ice crunching in the blender behind the bar. Who needs a coffee-flavored milkshake this early?

"What?"

"You look—" Braylon stops, cheeks hollowing. Denz waits for him to finish. He looks *what*? A mess? Like a cat run over twice by an eighteen-wheeler? Braylon clears his throat. "Do you work around here?"

Denz almost rolls his eyes.

"At 24 Carter Gold. I'm an event coordinator."

"*Oh.*" Braylon tilts his head. "Your dad's company."

"Yup," Denz says, faking a smile to cover his irritation. "Four years getting a degree just to end up a cog in the family machine. I'm living the dream."

"I didn't mean—"

Matty cuts in. "Bakery order for Dense!"

"It's *Denz*," he corrects, snatching the large box of muffins from Matty's bony fingers.

"Oops. Sorry, I forgot," Matty says, holding up apologetic hands while looking anything but. "Kind of like you forgot to call me three months ago. You know, after we—"

"Thanks, Matty!"

Denz is so done. The morning's already been too long. He doesn't need to add "one-night stand publicly humiliating me in front of my suddenly back-from-the-dead ex" to his list of New Year's failures.

He glares at Braylon. "And how's *your dad?*"

The iciness in Denz's tone doesn't match the fondness he feels when thinking about Emmanuel. All the lunches on campus. Virtual Scrabble nights. But there's a spreading coldness in his chest when he thinks of his last memory of Braylon's dad. The one where Emmanuel told Braylon to pursue a public relations job at a high-profile media outlet in London. The one where he convinced his son not to wait on Denz. To move on.

Will you come with me? To London?

Braylon's offer echoes in Denz's head. He never got to give an answer. Braylon left without him. Because of his dad. Because Denz . . .

Denz exhales, waiting for an answer.

Braylon's face hardens. "He's dead, actually."

This time, Denz does drop his phone. It thuds against the bar. Cheeks burning, he chokes out, "Your dad—what?"

"Died," Braylon confirms. "Nearly two years ago."

Denz goes numb. He scrambles for the right words. Something better than "sorry for your loss," because that's so generic, so empty. But his brain doesn't work quick enough. This awkward, mortifying moment stretches far too long.

Braylon sighs. "We don't have to do this."

"Okay," Denz scrapes out.

He tucks the muffin box under one arm. Retrieves his phone. He doesn't know why he backs away slowly like any sudden movement might cause Braylon to change his mind. It doesn't happen. On the way, Denz almost collides with a customer before walking right into a water bottle display.

Plastic scatters across the floor. Denz shrugs unapologetically in Matty's direction before giving Braylon one last stare. "So. Um. I should. And. See you?"

Braylon's lips finally part. "Oh, Denz—"

Nope. He can't stay around to hear whatever Braylon's decided to say. Denz kicks several bottles in his scramble out the door.

In his car, he tosses the muffin box into the passenger seat. Ignores the texts from Kami asking where the fuck he is. He desperately tries to erase the last ten minutes from his memory.

Forehead against the steering wheel, he whispers to no one, "It's not too late to start the new year over again, right?"

-2-

"What took so long?" Kami hisses as Denz slides into the chair next to her, fifteen minutes late. He nudges the muffin box to the center of the conference room's walnut-finished table. A peace offering.

At least the meeting hasn't started yet.

"Was there a problem?" Kami persists.

"Nope!" Denz rasps, throat still too tight.

What happened at Crema was bigger than a "problem." It was a whole epic-fail compilation video on YouTube. A replay of stutters and trips and what-the-fuck moments. A specific kind of nightmare where Denz's ex-boyfriend drinks tea and speaks in a British accent and is suddenly *living in Atlanta* again.

When Kami tilts her head expectantly, waiting for more, Denz blurts, "They were busy."

He can't tell her. Not yet. Considering his family stopped being Team Bray immediately after Denz recounted their breakup a week before graduation, this is one secret he needs to keep.

"What's the holdup?" He waves a hand around the room, deflecting.

"Dad's waiting on a special guest."

"Me?"

"Keep dreaming," Kami says flatly. "I don't know who. He's been on the phone since I walked in."

For a Monday meeting, the conference room is surprisingly empty. Even after the holiday. Denz does a quick head count. Out of a staff of thirty, only six seats are taken.

Jordan sits on Kami's other side, overhead LED lights washing over his warm brown skin as he scrolls through emails. Across from him, a curl of floppy dark hair falls over Eric's brow. He's studying contracts on his tablet. If anyone's capable of challenging Kami for Most Dedicated Employee, it's Eric Tran. Rounding out the staff are Kim and Connor, two thirtysomething event coordinators passing a sheet of paper back and forth. To anyone else, it might look like they're plotting the company's next big celebration, but Denz knows better. It's plans for their annual cosplay party.

At the head of the room, Kenneth Carter paces, phone to his ear.

"Of course! Your day should be flawless." He adjusts his designer horn-rimmed glasses. "We'll fix any detail you're not in love with."

Denz smiles. This is his dad at his finest. Armani suit jacket removed. Shirtsleeves rolled to his elbows. Monochromatic green tie loosened as he listens closely, occasionally dropping suggestions like it was the client's idea all along.

The icon Denz has spent decades trying to impress.

Kami elbows him. "Fifty bucks says he convinces them to go with the peonies."

Denz scoffs. "You make twice as much as me."

"Fine. Coffee? No, a latte."

"Deal."

He hooks their pinkies. Kami's midnight-blue nail polish matches the backless Valentino number she wore Saturday night. Denz predicts she'll be on top of all the best-dressed lists for the next month.

"Cuz." Jordan leans forward. "You sure about that bet?"

"You want in?"

Jordan snorts. He's a year younger than Denz, but they practically grew up together. "Thing One and Thing Two," the elders in their family called them. An unbreakable bond of pranks and video games and Monopoly, which is how Denz discovered Jordan's hyper-competitive streak. He hates losing. Any given game night would end in a thrown board or minor bloodshed.

"No, thanks," Jordan says. "I don't like those odds."

Denz turns to Kami. "Dahlias."

"*Dahlias?*" she says disappointedly.

"What?" Denz smirks. "They're versatile. Like me."

Jordan face-palms. Kami flicks Denz's forehead just as Kenneth's hearty laugh echoes in the room. He says, "Now, about that flower arrangement. I think the peonies . . ."

Denz groans, "How'd you know?"

"The Kenneth Carter playbook never changes."

It's a sad truth. Denz adores all the five-star, glamorous parties his dad throws. Nothing but the best. But not much changes from event to event. The personalization their brand once promised has become a paint-by-numbers checklist used to woo clients. He misses the old 24 Carter Gold. The one splashed across magazine covers, raving about their parties *and* weddings.

Kenneth ends his call. "Thanks for your patience, everyone." He eases into his chair. Checks his gold watch. "We'll start soon."

Denz follows his dad's gaze to the two empty chairs between him and Eric. One should be filled by—

"Don't worry, we're here!"

Auntie Cheryl glides into the room in a pencil skirt and geometric print blouse, box braids woven into a crown on top of her head. She sets two iPhones on the table before slipping into the chair closest to Kenneth. As his executive assistant, she keeps one of her devices strictly for work. The other is her personal phone. She's the family's gossip hotline, affectionately nicknamed Auntie C.C.—Carter Confidential.

"Well, well."

Denz straightens at the new voice. Strutting toward the last chair is Auntie Eva, Cheryl's fraternal twin. The ends of her auburn bob wig cut across her round cheeks. Her pleated minidress is at least two seasons ahead of anything on the Paris runways.

She's a former model turned private fashion stylist. The who's who of clients knocking at her door are pretty impressive.

Denz isn't sure why she's at their Monday staff meeting. Eva doesn't work for the company.

"Nephew?" She studies him with a sharp eyebrow raise. "Are you auditioning to be an extra in a Hallmark movie?"

"*Told you,*" Kami coughs into her hand.

"Is that . . ." Eva eyes his sweater. "J.Crew?"

"Ralph Lauren," he says proudly.

Eva sighs. "Tragic. Certainly not the *choice* Kamila's made."

A tight grin strains Kami's mouth.

"Save the family reunion stuff for later," Kenneth says. "Now that we're all accounted for: I have an announcement to make before *someone*"—He stares pointedly at Cheryl—"makes it for me."

Cheryl lifts her eyes from her personal phone, unbothered.

"And I'm sure you're all wondering why Eva's here," Kenneth continues.

Wary glances are shared around the room. Denz bites into a blueberry muffin, trying to temper the anticipation growing in his belly. His dad's dramatic pause doesn't help.

"I wanted my family present when I say this." Another breath. "I'm retiring."

It's unnervingly quiet for a beat. Kenneth reclines in his chair, smiling as if he didn't drop the most unexpected news ever. Denz, on the other hand, feels like he's been crammed into one of those T-shirt cannons, waiting to be shot out into a crowd of starving sharks.

"You're . . . what?"

"Stepping away as CEO of 24 Carter Gold," Kenneth confirms. "It's time."

Time? He's only fifty-eight. Denz isn't certain how the whole pension thing works, but he swears that's too young for retirement. And it's not as if anyone's trying to force him out. This city—hell, *the world* adores him. Step aside Nicolas Cage, Kenneth Carter is the real national treasure.

Denz's next question slips out during the congratulatory applause from the staff: "Who's your successor?"

More silence. The aunties trade whispers. Kami's curious eyes slide to Kenneth as he grabs a chocolate-chip muffin from the box. "Next week, we'll send out a formal announcement," he says. "After that, a wide search for the next CEO will be conducted."

Eric chokes on his coffee when Cheryl says, annoyed, "You can't do that, Kenny."

"I've made my deci—"

Eva cuts him off. "It's the *wrong* decision."

A mix of confusion and slow-blink shock spreads around the table. The twins are three years younger than Kenneth. That's never stopped them from acting like they were here first.

"You can't give the keys to a multimillion-dollar company— *our family's legacy*—to some stranger who sent you a résumé on LinkedIn," Eva chastises.

Kenneth chews his muffin thoughtfully. "And what's your suggestion?"

"Keep it in-house," Cheryl demands. "The next CEO should be someone who *knows* this company. Who loves it."

"Preferably a family member," Eva says not so quietly.

"That's not a requirement," Kenneth insists.

Denz picks at his muffin. He watches his dad steeple his fingers, ignoring Eva's snappy comeback. Kenneth's in the zone.

Denz is too.

The inception of 24 Carter Gold was inspired by an idea his dad had right after college. He was the King of Parties. Not keggers or the frat-house, vomiting-in-the-bushes '80s movies kind. Thoughtful, organized, full-on *celebrations* that had everyone on campus begging him to coordinate their next get-together. Denz's grandparents, a retired doctor and teacher, funded most of the start-up. Their connections provided the initial clients. When they died, their shares were left to Kenneth, the aunties, and their husbands.

What Eva said makes sense. The company should stay within the family, one way or another. But it's still his dad's decision.

"I'm not stepping away until late spring, so . . ." Kenneth pushes up his glasses to eye every face at the table. "The public search can wait. I'll take self-nominations. Everyone in this room has contributed to our current success—"

"*Everyone?*" Eva challenges, eyebrow arched.

They all know where her comment is directed: Kim and Connor, who started six months before Denz. While Kenneth is always diplomatic about his approach, the aunties are . . . direct.

Ruthless, to be honest.

"*Everyone,*" Kenneth affirms. "Any nominations?"

A hush. Denz anticipated a Carter Monopoly Night bloodbath. Who wouldn't want a shot at Kenneth Carter's throne? The second this goes public, ambitious event planners and CEO-wannabes are going to pounce. His dad is giving them first dibs, and no one's shooting their shot?

Kami's hand goes up. "I'm in."

Denz grins proudly. Kami's one of the most senior staff members. Kenneth has mentored handfuls of event managers who've gone on to start their own companies, but Kami stuck around, perfecting her craft while also elevating the company's status.

"Being CEO means a lot of hours in the office," Eva reminds her. "How will that affect Mikah?"

Kami's brow pinches. Before she can reply, Cheryl jumps in. "Kamila can handle it," she posits. "Kenny did it. And I'm a prime example of a working mother who can do it all. Right, Jordan?"

"Uh," Jordan stammers, "right, Mom."

"I wouldn't call what you do *working,* sis," Eva says dryly.

Denz winces. He's impressed by his coworkers' ability to maintain neutral expressions during the exchange.

"Kamila's a *fantastic* candidate," Cheryl asserts.

Kenneth makes a note on his phone. "Anyone else?"

Eric raises his hand, cheeks flushed. He's handsome, walking that fine line between a bookish nerd and one good selfie away from being a model. He was hired three months before Kami, fresh out of the University of Texas. Now, they're both the company's top event managers. CEO is the obvious next move for him too.

"Eric!" Kenneth's grin broadens. "Glad to see you step up for this opportunity."

Kami quietly bristles. Not because Eric nominated himself. They work great together. It's Kenneth's public approval of Eric's decision, something he didn't extend to her. When it comes to his children, excellence is the bare minimum.

Kenneth leaves space for other nominations.

Kim finishes two muffins, cheeks so full there's no way she could volunteer herself. Connor sinks low in his chair like no one will notice him. Cheryl narrows her eyes at Jordan.

"No way," he says, surrender hands raised. "I'm just an assistant. That's too much responsibility."

Denz appreciates his cousin's honesty. Jordan's barely two years out of college. Stepping into a CEO role would be a bold move. Even Denz recognizes his own weaknesses. He's a boss at the marketing side, but when it comes to performing during actual events?

He's . . . not a Kami or an Eric.

A year ago, on the morning of a major politician's luncheon, Denz failed to pay attention to the IN and OUT signs of the hotel's kitchen. He slammed right into the pastry chef carrying a four-tier cake. A buttercream nightmare. After cleaning up, he did an emergency run to six different bakeries in search of a replacement. While the guests enjoyed the variety of cupcakes he found, his dad's glare made Denz want to hide in the hotel's walk-in freezer for the rest of the event.

If prompted, the aunties could list each of Denz's "hiccups" throughout his 24 Carter Gold tenure. Which is why he nearly swallows his tongue when Eva says, "Denzel would make a great candidate!"

Cheryl chokes. *"Denzel?"*

"Me?"

"You've been around the offices since you could crawl," Eva says, undeterred by Denz's wide eyes. She turns to Cheryl. "You can't deny what he's done for the company with social media."

Warmth fills Denz's chest. Eva rarely gives out compliments.

"Posting cute photos of tablescapes online is very different from running a business," Cheryl counters. Of course. Always the other side of Eva's coin.

"He contributes more than that," Eva argues.

"My point is," Cheryl says, "we need leadership. Someone who takes life seriously—"

"Whoa," Denz interjects. "I'm a very serious person."

Cheryl guffaws. "Nephew, be honest. You don't even take your personal life seriously. I get it. You're young. Life is fun now. Why commit to anything or anyone, right?"

Denz tries not to squirm. A hush spreads through the room. No one comes to his defense. He's not sure he has the words to defend himself.

"CEO is a significant commitment," Cheryl carries on. "A marriage. You can't just log off. Avoid it when things get tough. Are you up for that?"

Denz's jaw clenches. Leena, his mom, has one unbreakable rule: *Respect your elders.* She's old-school Southern. He loves her for that. So, as much as he wants to tell his auntie—Jordan, forgive him—to "fuck off in traffic," he doesn't.

Kenneth's heavy stare lands on him. "Denzel?" He's waiting for a response.

Everyone is.

"No," he whispers, to Eva's obvious dismay.

Expression unreadable, Kenneth adds another note in his phone. "It's settled, then. The final decision on whether I promote from within or open the position to a wider candidate pool will be decided by each nominee's performance. I'll email details later." He pushes back from the table. "Let's get to work."

After the meeting, Denz is halfway to his office, staring down at his phone rather than meeting anyone's eyes—Jordan's *oof I'm glad that wasn't me* look was enough—when he remembers the muffins. He hates leaving a mess for interns to clean up. He turns back to the conference room.

The door is cracked. Soft voices escape. His dad and the aunties.

"Why would you do that in front of *my* staff?"

A sigh from Eva. "You're really thinking of bringing someone new in, Kenny?"

"I'm doing what's best for them."

Denz leans in closer, listening.

"Are you?" Eva challenges. "Is this about you and—"

"My company, my decision," Kenneth interrupts.

"Wrong," Cheryl chides. "You own the majority of the shares, but our voice matters. You can't bring in an outsider."

Denz hears his dad's frustrated exhale. Then, Eva again: "You should've told them my idea about—"

"We're *not* discussing that again," Kenneth says, tone clipped. "No weddings. I'm not going back."

"*You,*" Cheryl counters, "need to consider what will keep the company alive."

"Or the next CEO will," Eva says.

Denz's shoulders sink. *What the fuck is happening?*

"We're done," Kenneth commands, voice getting closer.

Denz scrambles away like a cat frightened by its own shadow. He apologizes to the intern he nearly knocks over and for the mess he's definitely not going back to clean up now.

On the edge of Denz's desk is a bowl of assorted candies. They're for the days he's overwhelmed by a deadline. Stressed about an event. As he fishes out a roll of Smarties, he decides today is that day. It's been two hours and he still can't get his mind off the staff meeting.

In a few months, 24 Carter Gold will have a new CEO. His family's company could be run by an outsider. What does that mean for him? What if the boss wants to move in a new direction, remove him from planning events like the annual NYE party? What if he doesn't even have a job? What if—

When he looks down, his fingertips are covered in multicolored dust and the Smarties wrapper is empty. He groans before opening Facebook on his phone.

His disdain for the archaic, information-stealing app is well known. But the company's Gen X and Millennial clientele still flock to that hellsite to voice their opinions in a nearly limitless character space. Maintaining an account is a necessary evil.

He's so distracted, so distressed, his thumb accidentally hits the blue-and-white globe icon instead of switching over from his personal profile to the company one. Hundreds of notifications drop down. The first sucks the air out of his lungs. One of those *four years ago today . . .* posts. A Polaroid of four smiling faces with Kami's looping script on the bottom of the white border:

In the photo, sandwiched between Nic and Kami, are Denz and Bray.

Nausea churns in Denz's stomach. He can hear Bray's scratchy laugh in his ear. Smell that coconut bodywash. Taste the peachy burst of champagne while kissing Bray at midnight. Feel the spiky buzz cut under his palms, the sinewy muscles along Bray's back as they had sex until dawn broke the sky apart.

It's too much. Except, the Bray in that photo isn't who Denz saw at Crema. The fucking *Braylon* with his detached expression. Cold accent and hardened eyes. So far from the man Denz knew before London.

"Ugh." Kami flops onto the chaise sofa opposite Denz. "I'm over today."

Denz is so startled, his phone flies from his hands. It lands facedown on his desk.

"Wh-what?"

Kami's suspicious gaze drifts from his face to the candy bowl. "How many Smarties have you had?"

"I'm not Mikah," he says. "I just . . . hate Mondays."

"Okay, Garfield, calm down."

Kami plucks a pack of M&M's from the bowl. "Weird meeting." She separates the candies by color before munching on a green one, her favorite.

"Can't believe Dad's retiring. I thought he'd be running this place forever."

"You did?"

"Let's be real, Kam. He's a great dad, but a better boss." Denz crunches on a new Smartie. "He sees this place more than any of us."

"True."

"No offense to Eric, but I'm glad you nominated yourself," Denz says. "You'd run the fuck out of this place."

A grin creeps across Kami's cheeks. "I have a few ideas."

Denz perks up. "Ooh. Tell me you're ready to jump back into weddings."

It's something else he can't stop thinking about—what Eva said. The missing spark around here. With the holidays over, there's at least a hundred newly engaged couples around the city, all looking for someone to plan their big day.

Kami's nose wrinkles. "Why would I want us to get back into weddings?"

"Hello! They're what put us on the map!" Denz steals a red M&M. "It's what we're known for."

"Exactly. *Known for*. The past. We're better without them."

Are they? Denz should tell her about the cryptic conversation he overheard. Kami needs to know what she's walking into.

He frowns when her hand grabs his on the desk. Great. A pep talk's incoming.

"I'm proud of you too," she starts. "For knowing your strengths. Not falling for the pressure."

Denz lifts a questioning eyebrow.

"I rarely agree with the aunties. Especially about us." She grimaces. "But I'm happy you didn't let Eva convince you to go after something you're not ready for."

"Not—" He drags his hand away. "—ready for?"

"Denz." Her voice is more annoyed than malicious. Like she can't believe she has to spell this out for him. "You're invaluable. Saturday wouldn't have happened without you. But being CEO is serious."

That word again. "Serious." Something his sister clearly doesn't associate with him. It's one thing to be doubted by the aunties, even his dad. But coming from Kami, this angers him.

"I'm as good as Eric or anyone else here," he says. "I take a lot of things seriously."

"Okay." Kami folds her arms across her chest. "What, then?"

He snatches his phone from the desk. "My brand!"

"What else?"

"Our family's legacy. Our dad's dream."

He never talks about it, but the first time Denz saw Kenneth in action went like this:

He was six years old, peeking from behind a group of cameramen and producers. A young and growing 24 Carter Gold was chosen for a segment on a reality show. *Marvelous Weddings.*

A close-up: the bride-to-be, Audrey Hudson, a certified EGOT, was sobbing on the love seat in Kenneth's office. On bended knee, Kenneth coaxed her out of the death grip of *wrong flowers, wrong dress, wrong groom.* A fairy godfather with promises of happily-ever-after and a Kleenex for her mascara-streaked cheeks.

Captivated, Denz wriggled through the production team. Right into the shot like a kid interrupting his parents' Zoom meeting.

No one screamed, "Cut!" His unplanned interruption was met with laughter. Even Kenneth grinned.

They finished filming with Denz in the thick of it, propped in his dad's lap. Watching Kenneth rescue someone's dreams from destruction. It was *Marvelous Weddings*' highest-viewed episode ever. The turning point for 24 Carter Gold. New clients poured in from everywhere.

Eventually, after dealing with one too many nightmare clients, Kenneth took wedding planning off the list of services provided. But Denz still thinks of that day. The instant he realized he wanted to be the one who changed someone else's life, if only for a moment.

Denz still hasn't reached his full potential. Hasn't made his mark in the Carter empire. This is his time.

He stands abruptly. "I may not have been around as long as you or Eric, but I'm devoted to seeing the company thrive."

"Are you?" Kami sighs. "God, Denz. You're not even committed to your own personal life. How many years has it been since you put forth the effort to be in a relationship?"

Denz didn't sign up for a surprise roasting from his sister. He needs to say something. *Anything.*

"I'm nominating myself, Kam."

He *should* stop there. But he's pissed and emotional. Of course he says the stupidest thing imaginable to reinforce his point:

"I tried keeping it low key, but . . . I have a boyfriend."

"You have a *what?*" A new head pops into his office doorway. Auntie Cheryl. *"Who?"*

"I—*ah.*"

The lie doesn't come fast enough. Denz looks between his stunned sister and intrigued auntie. This is where he yanks his foot out of his mouth. Corrects things. But if he confesses now, he'll confirm Cheryl's earlier comments about him.

Denz has been humiliated enough today.

"Boyfriend," he squeaks out. "Serious. Relationship."

Denz doesn't give Cheryl a chance to digest his stammering. He stomps out of his office. All the way to the other end of the company floor.

"I nominate myself!"

To his credit, Kenneth looks up from his desk, unalarmed.

"Nominate yourself for what? Loudest, rudest employee ever? I doubt you'll have any competition."

Denz freezes. He's in his dad's office. Along one wall, countless awards glitter in the Atlanta sunlight. Opposite the desk is the lavender love seat where Aubrey's life was changed. Where *his* life was changed.

"Son?"

Denz eyes the soft, concerned expression unfolding across his dad's face. His mind's made up. He's not letting his dad's legacy— his own legacy—die without a fight.

He squares his shoulders and says, "I nominate myself to be the next CEO."

-3-

👑 the Carter Family Group Chat 👑

Today 1:59 P.M.

Aunt Cheryl Carter
EMERGENCY! Who is Denzel's secret
boyfriend?!

Nic Carter
Denz + boyfriend? not a thing
😂 💀

Aunt Cheryl Carter
ITS TRUE!
Name? Occupation? Family history? I need deets
ASAP!

Aunt Eva Carter-Rivera
Sis please your age is showing. no one says
deets

Uncle Orlando Rivera
Ooh burn! 🔥

Nic Carter
Uncle O stop watching EASY A!

Aunt Cheryl Carter

This boyfriend better not be in the NFL. No actors or rappers either!

Nic Carter

auntie your husband is literally a music producer! 😖

Aunt Cheryl Carter

A very respected one! We don't need any more family scandals.

Kami Carter

Some of us are trying to work . . .

Uncle Tevin Williams

can someone help me find that TikTok recipe for countertop tacos? its my night to cook

Aunt Cheryl Carter

Babe not now! DENZEL. HAS. A. SECRET. BOYFRIEND.
Leena?

Leena Carter

I just want all my children happy.

Today 2:12 P.M.

Mom

Hi sweetheart! Call me ASAP!

Unsurprisingly, the news traveled fast.

Before the workday's end, everyone around the office had heard about the newest CEO candidate: *Denz*. He'd barely stepped into the downstairs lobby before Corrine, the front desk receptionist, was asking all about his new boyfriend too.

"Have a great night, C!" he'd said, cheery and fake, while shouldering out the glass double doors.

Avoiding his mom? Not as easy. She'd called the second he was outside. Like she had some kind of Parent GPS on him. Over his car's Bluetooth, he gave her quick, one-word answers before pretending to lose service in a tunnel.

He hasn't called her back.

"Okay, okay, wait, wait," Jamie says between wheezing laughs. He's a hulking figure. Six foot two, all toned muscles and wavy brown hair. "Start over. I need to hear this again."

"Again!" exclaims Mikah from his spot on the carpet, opposite Jamie.

It's Denz's turn to babysit. Kami is out with Suraj. It's not lost on Denz that the *real* secret relationship their family group chat should be focused on is hers.

He snatches a pepperoni slice from the box on the coffee table. Tonight's dinner: pizza and kiwi-strawberry juice pouches. He's truly living his best adult life.

"From the top?"

He doesn't mind recounting the last few days to Jamie. They've been best friends since age fourteen, a destined meeting at their private school, Brighton Academy. Two outsiders on a campus full of pretentious, born-rich assholes. Technically, Jamie was one of them, but he didn't act that way. He was a human golden retriever going through a rebellious-skater phase. Still new to the "established" scene, Denz was in his own preppy, sweater-obsessed phase.

(Who's he kidding? It's a full-on *lifestyle* now.)

After attending college in different cities, moving in together was the next obvious step in their lifelong companionship.

"I'm speechless." Jamie wipes happy tears from his eyelashes. "What're you gonna do?"

"Tell the truth?"

"That you *invented* a relationship to look serious for *your family?*"

"Is it that bad?"

"Should I plan the funeral now or wait until the body's cold?"

"Draw three!" Mikah shouts, smacking a *SKIP* and yellow *3* card on top of the red *8* card Jamie played a minute ago.

Whimpering, Jamie falls over. The Uno rules they're playing by are preposterous and wrong, but Denz isn't about to burst their bubble. Babysitting with Jamie is always more fun.

Their top-floor luxury apartment is cluttered by the aesthetic of two combating personalities: an HGTV DIY mood board and some *Gossip Girl*-esque fever dream. Denz is willing to overpay for all eleven hundred square feet if it means his best friend is one living room away.

"I need help," he admits.

"Is it time?" Jamie says.

"Time for what?"

"To Will Thacker your love life!"

On second thought: Denz could probably survive living alone.

Will Thacker Nights are a post-college tradition. The two of them on the sofa with thin-crust pizzas and mocktails served in champagne flutes, watching and rating classic rom-coms.

Seven words started it all: "I need to believe love is real!"

That's what Jamie yelled after one of his typical three-week relationships imploded. History shows Jamie Peters had been "in love" at least six times before that night. He demanded Denz watch *Notting Hill* with him. Two hours and too many cackles later, Denz wasn't convinced Hugh Grant's character (whom their tradition is named after) deserved a second chance. At least Jamie was hopeful again.

Secretly, Denz loves rom-com endings. The big moment where someone professes their love in the most unrealistic fashion. Proposing on an airplane. Running across New York City before midnight on New Year's. Holding a boom box over your head.

But his life isn't a movie.

Jamie says, "We'll find you a boyfriend."

"How?"

"Hire someone?"

"Too expensive." Denz folds his pizza before biting. "Also, too *Pretty Woman*."

"You're much prettier than Richard Gere." Jamie drops a *DRAW FOUR* card on Mikah's red *2*. "Dating apps?"

Denz chucks a pizza crust at Jamie.

"Momma said no food fights, Uncle Denzie!" Mikah announces. He's the only one allowed to use nicknames with Denz. He's not ashamed of the chokehold Mikah has on him.

"Hinge?" Jamie suggests. "Tinder?"

"No and hell no."

"Grindr? Ooh, Scruff?"

Denz stabs a straw in his new juice pouch, glaring. He's always avoided dating apps. Being gay *and* Black isn't the easiest thing to navigate in online spaces. Why voluntarily sign up for people to showcase their racism or fetishism while hiding behind a fake profile pic? No, thanks.

"A past hookup?" Jamie proposes.

Denz considers. It goes against all his rules. He doesn't save one-night stands' numbers or DMs. Also, what's he going to say to Tongue Ring Guy? *BTW, when you're done down there, do you have any plans tomorrow? Want to meet my family? Cool, pass me the lube.*

He shakes his head. "It wouldn't work."

Tongue Ring Guy would never survive the Kenneth Carter Rite of Passage test. To date, there's only been one man from Denz's limited pool of suitors who has.

Which, of course, is why Jamie says, "What about an ex?"

Denz almost chokes on a pepperoni. He still hasn't mentioned Braylon's return to anyone. Not even Jamie. He also hasn't been back to Crema since.

"Uno!" Mikah shouts while holding *two* cards.

Jamie face-palms. "If this little dude beats me again, I'm going to jump into traffic."

Denz snorts, tearing off a new slice for his nephew.

"Huh." Jamie rubs greasy fingers over his round chin. "What if you dated a guy in a coma?"

Their last WTN was *While You Were Sleeping*. Denz's Sandra Bullock crush is strong. But it's not altogether a bad idea. A pretend boyfriend. Someone sweet and funny that his family will instantly adore. Someone with best-friend qualities. Someone like . . .

"God bless you, Will Thacker," Denz says, "you horny-for-books hero."

Mikah tips his head back. "What's horny, Uncle Denzie?"

"A triceratops." Denz meets Jamie's eyes. "What if *we* faked it?"

"Your death? Seems excessive. We could pull it off. I've watched so much *Law & Order: SVU* lately." Jamie sighs dreamily. "I'd let Christopher Meloni step on me. He could spit in my—"

"No." Denz shivers. "What if *you* were my fake boyfriend?"

Jamie goes silent. Mikah slaps his final cards down. "I win!"

But Denz is the real winner. "Think about it. My family loves you. My *dad* loves you—"

"Like a son," Jamie says, strangled.

Denz slides off the sofa. He sits pretzel-leg behind Mikah to re-shuffle the deck. "You know everything about me. My ambitions. My past. My favorite drink—"

"Your poop schedule," Jamie adds.

Mikah giggles into his hands.

"Sure, that." Denz deals out the cards. "*We're* a perfect decoy."

"We have zero chemistry. Other than that time in high school when you tried to kiss me—"

"*You* tried to kiss *me!*"

"—while we were drunk," Jamie continues. "A hand might've innocently gone there . . . I was still figuring stuff out. You were obviously into it."

Denz can't fight off his smile. Jamie was the first person he came out to. A year later, Jamie came out as pan. He's not saying what *almost* happened between them helped Jamie understand his true self, but it was an epiphany for Denz. Sometimes, queer kids just know who their people are, even without saying it, and those family bonds can be stronger than the ones formed by blood.

"Point is," Denz says, "we'll make it work."

How could any of the Carters disapprove of Jamie? He comes from a well-known family. He's not a rando internet guy with a sketchy past. He's not a hookup who knows more about Denz's dick than his career goals. Definitely not an ex with a British accent and a tarnished history with the Carters.

Sighing, Jamie whispers, "Okay. But just until you get the job."

"Promise." Denz extends his pinkie. "Don't worry. This is gonna be easy."

Jamie hooks their fingers. Mikah joins them. Denz kisses the top of his unruly curls, chest relaxing.

He's one step closer to proving everyone wrong.

What about pet names? is not a text Denz imagined himself sending while on the clock.

Or ever.

He's on location at a chic hotel thirty minutes north of the city. The company's planning a black-tie fundraiser for underserved schools, hosted by a local NBA player. While Connor does a walk-through with the organizers, Denz gathers social media content:

The Correggio-inspired mural on the ballroom's high ceiling. Glimmering teardrop chandeliers. The proposed floral arrangements. If he sneaks a handful of selfies in the marble-floored bathroom with the gorgeous lighting for his own account, well, it's all business.

Jamie's reply comes a minute later:

Pet names?? Are we getting a doggo?? FINALLY!

Denz rubs his temple. Why is his best friend like this? He uploads a video of Connor in action before responding:

no! terms of endearment. cute nicknames

The family's probing into Denz's romantic life is relentless. Auntie Cheryl "randomly" pops up in his office to ask for a name. Kami tries to get him to crack with long stares in the elevator. Nic's outright asked via text when he decided to lock down a man. He can only ignore their questions for so long.

That's why he's spending part of his day conspiring with Jamie. They need ways to deal with the inevitable. Things like posting adorable photos on social media. Scheduled FaceTime calls while Denz is at the office. How to act in front of the Carters.

I thought you hated pet names, Jamie sends.

He does. Passionately. A side effect of the breakup with Braylon.

My tiny muffin. Three words whispered in the morning, to Denz's mild annoyance. During study breaks. Between gasps as strong hands peeled off his clothes. In his worst moments, just to make him laugh.

"Fuck," Denz hisses while staring at his phone. He's gone forty-eight hours without thinking about Braylon. He can't start now. He props one of the fundraiser invitations against an empty champagne flute. In the iridescent light, the curling gold script on the cardstock shimmers.

He gets a few shots before writing back: we need to be convincing!

They need an airtight plan. It won't be enough to *say* he's dating Jamie. To post a couple of photos online. The Carters will want in-person proof. And Jamie's one semester of acting at UNC Chapel Hill won't cut it.

Ellipses appear, then disappear.

Outside the ballroom, Denz leans against a marble column. Uniformed staff pass him in a flourish. He clocks three different guests wearing velour tracksuits right out of an early 2000s music video strolling into a meeting hall.

His phone buzzes. An email from his dad. Denz inhales sharply as he opens it.

DATE: Today, 1:02 P.M.
FROM: kennethcarter@goldencarterevents.com
TO: staff@goldencarterevents.com

SUBJECT: Future CEO Evaluation Assignments

Dear Staff,

Below are the promised assignments for the CEO assessment. Each candidate will oversee the planning and execution of a VIP event for the spring quarter, with the support of a small team. As these are two of our most valued and high-profile clients, I expect everyone to put their best foot forward.

The evaluation process will conclude March 28th. Should one candidate prove themselves a better fit, I'll introduce them as the successor at my retirement party, a public statement to follow.

EVENT: Mayor Tiffany Reynolds's Valentine's Day Gala
DATE/TIME: February 14 at 8:00 P.M.
CANDIDATE: Denzel Carter
ASSISTED BY: Connor Fisher, Eric Tran

EVENT: Emily Sedwick's Engagement Party
DATE/TIME: March 6 at 7:00 P.M.
CANDIDATE: Kamila Carter
ASSISTED BY: Kim Perry, Jordan Carter

If I find neither candidate suitable, 24 Carter Gold will announce a nationwide search for a new CEO in April.

Best of luck to all!

Regards,

Kenneth L. Carter

CEO, 24 Carter Gold

Event Planning Services

Denz skims the email twice before focusing on his section. The mayor's annual Valentine's Day gala. It's Atlanta's favorite party, an event they've organized since she took office. A cakewalk for him, honestly.

Kami has it much worse.

The Sedwicks have a long history with 24 Carter Gold. Part of

Denz wishes that was his assignment. Their previous engagement parties for the two eldest daughters made the cover of *Southern Bride*, a featurette in *People* too. It'd be the perfect opportunity for him to infuse some of the magic that made the company stand out. But the Sedwicks are also notoriously . . . diva-like. Over-the-top Southern glam on nitro. He doesn't need that headache.

While rereading, Denz pauses, frowning. Eric's listed as one of his assistants. Not a nominee.

When did he drop out of the competition? Why?

Denz makes a mental note to ask later.

Across the lobby, Connor looks at his phone before fist-pumping. Denz smiles at his Muppet-like waving.

It's down to him and Kami. He's unsure how to feel about that.

A notification chimes. The text preview startles him. It's not from Jamie.

Mom
Since you're avoiding us: dinner next Friday with
me and dad.
7 PM reservation. Kingfisher & Redbud.
BRING THE NEW BOYFRIEND!

Below the final message is a GIF of Tyra Banks shouting "We were all rooting for you!" Guilt knots in Denz's stomach. He fires off a quick response.

we'll be there!
you're gonna lose it when you see who it is

Fuck, why did he add that last part?

Two seconds later, another chime. Jamie's response: should we go on a practice date?

Near the front desk, Connor is wrapping up. Denz rushes to grab a couple more videos to edit later. He considers Jamie's idea. They're never going to fool anyone if they can't get past his parents first. A practice date would help.

He sends back, coffee tomorrow at Crema? my treat.

On the way to meet Connor, Jamie's reply lights up his phone:

See you tmrrw sweet cheeks!

"How is this so hard?" Denz groans.

"That's what he—"

"*Don't,*" Denz warns, glaring at Jamie, "finish that sentence."

Jamie shoots him a *yikes* expression. One of many today.

In the span of thirty minutes, they've managed to fumble through ordering drinks for each other, argue over what table to sit at, and knock over a large glass of water—to the quiet annoyance of the Crema staff—just trying to hold hands.

Denz has held Jamie's hand before. On drunken walks home from parties. During scary movies. That time Denz had the flu and vomited half his body weight into the toilet. But this?

This is different. It's *wrong.*

On the table, Jamie's hand looks like a dead fish in Denz's. Nothing about them says *We fucked in the car on the way here.* Or *You're all I thought about today.* It's nothing like the way his hand used to look when held by—

Not going there, he reminds himself.

Point is, these aren't boyfriend hands. It's two people trying too hard, which won't fly in front of Denz's family. In front of his dad.

Fuck, it's *hand-holding,* a basic human interaction most people learn as toddlers. Denz is more than capable of this.

"What if we . . ." He tries to rotate their palms. Jamie slurps loudly on his Berry Bliss iced tea, not even trying. "There!"

Denz has slipped his fingers between Jamie's. It's still awkward. Maybe if he strokes his thumb along Jamie's knuckles and—

Nope. That feels wrong too.

"How are you so fucking bad at this?" Denz whispers loud enough to draw the attention of an exasperated mom in yoga pants and her curious kid. He grins apologetically before shifting back to Jamie.

"Er." Thick, dark eyebrows hide under Jamie's wavy bangs.

"What?" Denz snaps.

"Why are your palms so hot?"

"My palms are not hot. They're average temperature. *Normal.*"

"It feels like I stuck my hand in a volcano."

Denz scowls. "Luckily, we don't have to hold hands the entire dinner."

Only when they arrive and leave. He's already laid out the rest of the arrangement for Jamie. Four family appearances: dinner with his parents, the Valentine's gala, the Sedwicks' engagement party, his dad's retirement celebration. Anything else can be done without physical intimacy.

God, how weird is it going to look when he kisses Jamie?

"So, how's Gigi?" he asks, instead.

Gigi is Jamie's latest ex. It's been four months since the breakup. He's been uncharacteristically single ever since. New relationships for Jamie are like Kylie Minogue songs at gay clubs—on constant rotation. He's also great at remaining friends with exes.

Denz can't relate.

"She got a puppy," Jamie says. "His name's the Hulk."

"Why?"

"It's what she used to call me—"

"*Jamie!*" Denz bites back a laugh. "Forget I asked." He's too informed about his best friend's sex life as it is.

"I thought you might want to use it as a pet name." Jamie winks over his cup.

Denz shakes his head. "What about your parents?"

A frown creases Jamie's mouth.

Jeff and Liz Peters are what Denz calls "conversational liberals." The kind that love to remind everyone they "voted for the first Black president" while never standing up to their racist, homophobic, bigoted country club friends. Who never rally against laws that affect their own son's community.

Despite his parents' overflowing wealth, Jamie never accepts their money. Instead, he works at four different bars around downtown Atlanta. His charm and loveable face make up for the fact that he's a nondrinker pretending to be a bartender.

Still, once a month, he accompanies his parents for dinner. Denz never asks why. He gets it. Everybody has that one shitty family member. In Jamie's case, it's two.

"I'm seeing them next week," Jamie says.

"I'll have *Fire Island* ready when you get home."

Jamie smiles appreciatively.

The café door swings open. Denz's eyes widen.

In strolls Jordan, phone to his ear. Denz wasn't prepared for anyone from the office to show up during his practice date. Certainly not his cousin.

Actually . . . this is perfect.

"Hey." He squeezes Jamie's hand. "Jordan's here. Let's try out the boyfriend thing on him."

Jamie's face goes pale. "He—what? I. Wait. Are you sure?"

"Of course, *honeybun*." Denz manages to not gag. "Jordan's the best test subject."

When they were teens, the three of them spent every summer together. An inseparable trio of puberty acne and late-night video game tournaments and remorseless chaos.

"No one knows us like him," Denz says.

"But . . ." Jamie watches Jordan pick up a cardboard cup at the end of the bar. "What if we can't bullshit him?"

"Then we're fucked."

"That's not the confidence booster you think it is."

"*Sweetheart,*" Denz says, head tilted, fake fondness in his voice, "we got this."

"Do we? Because I think we should—"

"Jordan!" Denz waves his cousin over.

Jordan beams as he approaches. "Fellas! What're you two up t—"

The sentence dies in a choked noise as Jordan gawks at the overlapping hands on the table. Denz beams at him. Jamie looks ready to launch himself out the nearest window.

"What, uh." Jordan blinks hard. "Is going on?"

"Nothing." Denz shrugs, casual as can be. "Just having lunch with my boyfriend."

"Boyfriend," Jordan repeats hoarsely. He clears his throat several times. "As in dating? *That* kind of boyfriend?"

"Sorry we didn't tell you sooner." Denz's attempt to stare lovingly at Jamie resembles a raccoon gazing at an unattended trash pile. "Please don't tell the fam. It's a surprise."

The "fuck me" Jamie whispers is met by an under-the-table kick from Denz.

"Wow!" Jordan's eyes shift to Jamie. "This is . . . the best news ever?"

"It is!"

Jamie's enthusiasm doesn't match the my-soul-has-just-left-my-body horror in his eyes.

"Cool." Jordan nods like an out-of-control bobblehead. "I should go. Just came to grab a gingerbread latte for my boss. Kami. Which you know, so." He tugs at his collar. "Gotta grab these bad boys while supplies last!"

Denz raises an eyebrow. He hasn't seen Jordan this excited since inhaling that batch of pot brownies Jamie baked them one summer.

"Congratulations! Love this for you two!"

Then Jordan's gone.

Denz detangles their fingers. Jamie face-plants into his forearm. He mumbles something about cardiac arrest and calling a coroner, but Denz is too busy grinning. Convincing Jordan was a solid start. By the time they have dinner with his parents, Denz and Jamie will be ready.

The perfect fake boyfriends.

-4-

Mom
Hi sweetheart. Car service is running behind.
ETA 20 mins.

Denz is fine.

He's pacing outside the restaurant. His parents are arriving in nineteen minutes. To meet his new boyfriend, who's *not here*. Who hasn't replied to Denz's six where are you??? texts. Who agreed to meet Denz thirty minutes before their reservation for one last run-through of their plan.

But it's fine.

Early January air bites at his exposed ears. Each time a new rideshare pulls up and it's not Jamie climbing out of the back seat, his anxiety spikes.

He's not backing out, Denz mentally chants. The writing on the empty sidewalk in front of him says otherwise. He calls one more time.

"Jamie Noah Peters," he hisses at the voicemail, "when I see you, I'm gonna personally feed your *peanut-butter-covered balls* on a silver platter to Pompom, Ms. Philips from across the hall's cursed terrier, and—"

"Denz?"

His spine tenses. He struggles to end the call, his hand shaking.

Even with the low, almost unrecognizable accent, Denz knows who's behind him.

He counts to five before turning.

Fading sunlight falls over Braylon's short, tight curls like a tangerine crown. Pink kisses the apples of his cheeks. His single-breasted overcoat is open, the two top buttons of his white oxford undone to reveal a distracting flash of honey-brown collarbone.

"'Ello," Braylon says first, confusion pinching the corners of his eyes.

"What're you doing here?" Denz manages.

"I work nearby." Braylon gestures behind him. "And you?"

I live *here*, Denz almost snaps. *In America. Where you left me, remember?*

"I'm—"

He looks at his phone, swearing under his breath. *The dinner.* His mind races for the best way to tell his parents Jamie's in a coma.

Braylon edges closer. "I'm glad I ran into you."

"Again?"

Braylon ignores Denz's sharp tone. "I wanted to talk to you about something."

Jesus, do they have to do this now? Denz still feels awful for not saying anything about Braylon's dad. He was caught off guard, which isn't a real excuse. It's complicated. He really liked Emmanuel, all the way up until he encouraged Braylon to break up with Denz.

His phone chimes with another update from his mom:

10 minutes away!

"Thing is"—Braylon rubs the back of his neck in that nervous way Denz remembers—"I'm doing quite well at my job. It's a non-profit. I love it there. But it'd help if we could get more support from . . . prominent figures."

"Uh-huh."

It's not that Denz is ignoring Braylon's rambling. He's multi-

tasking. Studying every new car that pulls up curbside, anticipating his parents' arrival.

"Sorry, are you listening?" Braylon asks. "I wanted to ask you
something."

"Well, *ask* then."

"That's what I was doing."

"No," corrects Denz, finally making eye contact, "you were
giving me the Wikipedia version. Just say it."

Nostrils flaring, Braylon half snarls, "Your family's company
has done loads of events with the mayor. I need help reaching
her. For a one-on-one chat. Our organization would benefit im-
mensely from her public support."

A new text from Leena: We're on the street, but Friday night
traffic!

Despite the cold, Denz's face is on fire. Still nothing from Jamie.
Braylon's talking again, but all Denz can hear is his mom's lecture after she discovers he *lied* about having a boyfriend and the
whoosh of a new email from his dad ending Denz's CEO chances
before he's even back in the car.

"Denz?" Braylon says.

Down the street, a sleek black SUV nudges its way closer.
Denz's skin prickles. It's his parents.

"Just email the company receptionist," he says dismissively.
"She'll connect you—"

"I'd rather it be you."

Denz falters. "Me?"

"Who makes the introduction with the mayor," Braylon says.
"You know me best, so."

Denz has no time to tell Braylon how wrong he is. He *doesn't*
know him anymore. The SUV is one traffic light away. He's still
without a solution to the whole missing-boyfriend clusterfuck
he's created. No one except for—

His head snaps back to Braylon. *No,* he can't. There has to be
another option, like running headfirst into traffic.

The SUV pulls up to the curb.

"Fine." Denz grabs Braylon by the arms—*When did his biceps get so thick?*—maneuvering him until they're standing side by side. While the driver opens the back door for Leena, Denz whispers, flustered, "I'll introduce you to the mayor. Whatever. Right now, I need you to smile and pretend to be my boyfriend."

"Pretend to be your *what?*"

"Have dinner with my parents and me," Denz says through a tight grin. His mom steps onto the pavement in a chic red Salvatore Ferragamo coat, Kenneth following in the same suit he wore to the office. "Act like we're a happy couple."

"You're mad if you think I—"

"*Please.*"

He flashes wide, desperate eyes. Something in Braylon's stubborn resolve fades. He forces out a painfully big smile.

"Also," Denz adds quietly as his parents give the driver final instructions, "they obviously hate you for . . . you know. So, um, make a good impression."

"Are you fu—"

"Mom!" Denz allows himself to be yanked into a lung-rupturing hug. "Missed you too."

"Is that why you ignored my calls and texts?"

Leena Carter may be inches shorter than Denz, but her no-bullshit eyebrow arch makes him feel infant-sized. They share similar features: rich brown skin, sharp eyes, a hint of dimples in their smiles. But everything about her is more pronounced, including her sidelong look as he scrambles to explain himself.

"Don't they say something about absence and the heart growing fonder?" he stammers.

Next to her, Kenneth clears his throat. "Son, what's going on?"

His stare pointedly shifts to Braylon. Leena's does too. "Wait, where's your—What is this?"

Denz inhales deeply. *So, this is happening.* "Mom. Dad." He inches closer to Braylon. "This is the boyfriend I mentioned."

Kenneth stiffens as Leena chokes out, "Your boyfriend is . . . Bray?"

"It's *Braylon*," Denz gently corrects before Braylon can. "He goes by his full name now."

"And he's back?" Leena blinks like she's involuntarily been dropped into a paranormal reality show. "In *America?*"

"Yes," Denz says. His dad's still quiet.

"And you're together—" Leena frowns. "—again? With him?"

"Correct."

"I . . . wow."

Denz fights off a grimace. With Jamie, he was better prepared. He'd mapped out the hand-holding and how he was going to laugh when Jamie revealed that watching *When Harry Met Sally* one too many times led to the inevitable between them and his mom's shock was going to be comical. His dad's eyes weren't going to be so narrowed. This long stretch of awkwardness between them wasn't going to exist.

But here it is.

To his surprise, Braylon makes the first move. "Mrs. Carter, it's lovely to see you again," he says, waiting for consent before shaking her hand. "Sorry it's been a bit."

"*Years*," Leena clarifies.

Braylon's smile brightens. "Denz is right. Absence does make the heart grow fonder." His eyes are almost soft, affectionate when they land on Denz. "I'm thankful for another shot to prove I'm worthy."

Something twists in Denz's belly. He's marginally impressed.

Braylon turns back. "I'd love to get reacquainted over dinner."

A beat. Kenneth tilts his head. Denz knows that look. He's searching for flaws, deciding whether Braylon's worth his time.

Denz is preparing for the worst when there's a shift between their hips. Braylon's cool knuckles brush against his. His hand clasps Denz's. Immediately, muscle memory takes over. Denz's fingers tangle with Braylon's, warm palms kissing in the crisp night air.

It's not weird like it was with Jamie. In fact, it's irritatingly *normal.* Denz wants to snatch his hand back.

"Mr. Carter," Braylon says, "would that be okay with you?"

Kenneth's brow knits together. His eyes don't leave their hands. Eventually, he folds an arm around Leena's shivering shoulders and says, "Sure. I could use a drink."

"Or the whole bottle," Leena mumbles.

His parents lead the way toward the restaurant's doors. It's not a *Welcome home*. An *I trust you're as serious about my son as he is about being the future leader of my company*. But it's close enough.

Kingfisher & Redbud is swimming in lush charm. All wood and stone décor. The air soaked in the lingering scent of aged wine and fresh ingredients and smoked meats. Luxurious renditions of trademark Southern cuisine fill the menu. From his parents' favorite corner booth, Denz tries to find anything to take his focus off the man sitting next to him.

God, why did he do this to himself?

At least Braylon's trying. He asks Leena's opinion on appetizers. Draws her into a conversation about her dress. He's unbothered when Kenneth's not as responsive. Braylon smiles easily, moving on to the next topic.

Colin, their waiter, arrives with a whiskey neat for Kenneth and rosé for Leena. The chef's already searing their usual meals: Kenneth's favorite cut of steak and Leena's chili-rubbed chicken.

"And for you, Mr. Denzel?"

"The gourmet burger," Denz says. He adds a nonalcoholic fizzy lemonade, though he knows he'll need something stronger by the end of the night. Too bad he's driving.

Colin pivots to Braylon. "For you, sir?"

Braylon's eyes scan the menu again. An idea hits Denz. Something he planned with Jamie. "Start him with the mixed greens salad. Light vinaigrette," he tells Colin.

"Uh . . ." Braylon tries.

"Grilled chicken for his entrée. Louisiana rice." Denz grins at his parents. Knowing his boyfriend's order will undoubtedly prove their relationship is serious.

"Excellent choices," Colin says.

"Actually," Braylon says before Colin can leave, "I have some changes."

Denz chokes on his water. "Um. What?"

In his periphery, Kenneth frowns. "I'll have the grilled Angus strip," Braylon says, his gaze flitting from Denz to Colin. "Medium well, please. No salad. Instead, an order of the salt-and-vinegar chips—sorry, the fries. Thank you."

"No problem." Colin disappears.

"My apologies." Braylon lays a hand over Denz's on the table. "I'd love to try something new tonight. If that's okay?"

Denz pastes on a fake smile. He doesn't trust himself to speak without telling Braylon how he *really* feels.

"I love your accent!" Leena says, seemingly on her way to forgiveness.

Braylon runs a bashful hand over his curls. Denz wonders if they're soft. The same texture his hair would get between swim seasons, just before he buzzed it all off again. On second thought, *no*. That's the last thing Denz wants to find out.

"It's kind of automatic now, innit?" Braylon playfully nudges Denz. He doesn't smell like coconut bodywash anymore. There's notes of freshly peeled oranges and cardamom. Just another thing for Denz to hate. "Hard not to pick up while I lived there."

"In London," Kenneth deadpans.

"Correct."

"Where you went for work." Kenneth swirls his whiskey. "After breaking my son's heart."

Braylon clears his throat. "Well. Yes."

"Did you like it there?"

"It was . . . different."

"Different, good? Different, as in the biggest mistake of your life?" He doesn't wait for Braylon to elaborate. "And the job? PR, right? Make any good connections? New relationships? Was it worth—"

"*Dad,*" Denz cuts in. It's not like he didn't expect this. But he didn't anticipate the urge to protect Braylon from it too. As much as he wants to watch Braylon squirm, he's bailing Denz out of a disastrous situation. He deserves a little slack.

For now.

"I'm getting reacquainted with your new boyfriend," Kenneth tells him.

"I know, Dad, but—"

"So, Braylon," Kenneth says, his tone casual, "what brought you back? Job transfer? New career opportunity?"

There's a long pause. Braylon traces the condensation on his glass with a finger. "Partly. And . . . my dad died."

"Oh God." Leena's hands fly over her mouth.

Kenneth shifts uncomfortably. His eyes say, *Why didn't you warn us?*

Denz mouths, *I tried to.*

"It's quite all right." Sadness outlines Braylon's smile. "Brain aneurysm. He thought it was a migraine. Went in his sleep."

Leena reaches over to cup one of his hands. "I'm so deeply sorry."

"He was an amazing man," Kenneth adds. "Very respected. I hope you know that."

"Thank you," Braylon whispers, not making eye contact with Denz. "I did. Honestly, I'm fine. That's what therapy is for."

His rough laugh is met by a grin from Leena.

Denz bites his lip. He should say something. *Do* something. He's supposed to be the supportive boyfriend, and despite all Braylon's posturing, Denz knows he can't be as okay as he sounds. It was his dad.

Instinct doesn't immediately kick in, so Denz goes with the next best thing: impulse. He rubs a hand across Braylon's spine. Hums quietly.

A phone buzzes on the table.

"Sorry," Kenneth says, standing. "I need to take this. It's Audrey Hudson. I'm planning her summer wedding anniversary celebration. Twenty years, can you believe it?"

More vibrations. "Oh!" Leena swipes her phone up. "It's time for my nightly chat with Mikah! Be right back."

When his parents are out of earshot, Denz snatches his hand away. Braylon scowls at him. "What were you doing?"

"Comforting you."

"By humming 'Fix You' by Coldplay?"

Denz sighs. "It works on my nephew all the time."

"I'm not a kindergartener—"

"First grade."

"—and have you heard yourself sing? I'm surprised Mikah doesn't have nightmares."

"Shut up."

"You're awful." Braylon's face wrinkles. "I'd rather be serenaded by Katy Perry."

Denz flips him off. He can feel himself almost smirk. "I'm trying to make this look *real*. For my parents, okay?"

Braylon says irritably, "Then try being less like Ted Lasso and more like—"

"Everything okay?"

Leena scoots back into the booth. Her curious head tilt forces Denz to toss an arm around Braylon's wide shoulders. "G-great! Perfect!"

Braylon smiles tensely, not saying a word. It's enough to ward off more questions from Leena. Soon, Kenneth rejoins the table, and the food arrives.

The waitstaff moves fast and efficiently. Plates are set. Glasses are refilled. Braylon's steaming steak and the sharp vinegary scent from his fries drag a growl from Denz's stomach. The food on his own plate is—

Not what he ordered.

"*Oh*. Um . . ."

He stares at the roasted flounder and spring salad. An overwhelming whiff of onions makes his nose wrinkle.

"That's not a burger," Braylon points out.

Through a gritted smile, Denz says, "It's fine."

"It's not," Braylon opposes. "For one, seafood makes you nauseous. Two, you hate onions. Passionately."

Denz tries to laugh. "That's a strong word."

"It's true."

Denz isn't in the mood to argue. To let one more thing ruin tonight. Except . . . something white-hot spreads through his chest. Into his cheeks. Under his breath, he says, "You remembered? About the onions and—"

"Of course." Braylon's eyes flash. "Why wouldn't I?"

Because I didn't even know your dinner order, Denz wants to remind him. *Or that your dad died. Why you came back.*

"Son," Kenneth says, interrupting his thoughts, "should I—"

"I've got it," Braylon insists. He nudges Denz out of the booth, flagging down Colin. Denz gapes at him. Braylon's all smiles and relaxed charm like he's chatting with an old friend, explaining the mix-up to Colin.

"How sweet of him," Leena whispers, impressed.

Kenneth sits cross-armed, stone-faced. It doesn't stop the smile from edging across Denz's mouth.

Well played, Braylon Adams.

"Let her decide," Leena urges after a sip of wine.

The rest of dinner has gone without incident. Denz's new plate arrived with an extra pile of hand-cut fries as well as a complimentary bottle of Clos du Temple. Leena's on her second glass. Conversations drift in and out. The latest: Nic's indecision over which college to attend in the fall.

"I don't know why she won't pick an Ivy," Kenneth huffs. "She's so smart."

"What about an HBCU?" Leena offers. "Or somewhere closer to home. Like Spelman. Agnes Scott. Emory or—"

"UGA," Denz and Braylon say simultaneously. Coincidentally. Denz's eyes lower to his half-finished burger when his mom smirks.

"She's a Carter," Kenneth says. He gulps his whiskey. "She has a legacy to uphold. She's better than—"

He cuts himself off. Denz doesn't need him to finish.

UGA wasn't Kenneth's first choice for Denz. Duke, UPenn, or even UCLA, where Jordan ended up. Notable, flashier colleges for the press to rave over. But Denz wanted somewhere he could be his true self while still remaining close enough that he wouldn't miss anything in his family's lives. Besides, he *liked* Athens.

But it wasn't what his family wanted.

His eyes cheat over to Braylon. He's watching Denz, cheeks flushed at being caught.

"Can't believe she's already off to uni," Braylon whispers. "Wasn't she just thirteen?"

"Yeah," Denz exhales.

He tries to ignore the sourness at the back of his throat. Braylon's ankle pressed against his under the table. His dad's unreadable stare drifting between them. How he never thought he'd be here again: hoping a first impression didn't mean the end of something he wants.

Six Years Ago
Junior Year—Fall Semester

"You can't hear them."

"I'm not trying to—"

At Nic's hard glare, her mouth screwed into a *you're not fooling anyone* pout, Denz shuts up. She's barely thirteen and already as intimidating as their dad. When did that happen?

He tugs on one of her box braids. "I was listening for Mikah."

Nic rolls her eyes. "Liar. He's asleep in his crib. And you're freaking out."

"I'm not—"

"Who's freaking out?" Leena asks, hovering over a fresh pie on the kitchen island.

"Denz," Nic announces, dodging the hand he tries to clamp over her mouth. "He thinks Dad's gonna murder Bray."

"He won't," Kami assures while loading the last plates from dinner into the dishwasher. "At least not until after Christmas."

Denz flips her off. He sidles up to his mom, frowning. "He won't, right?"

"I mean . . ." Leena cuts four equal slices from the pie. "When we bought this house, he specifically requested a big backyard. Easier to hide the bodies."

"Mom!"

His sisters cackle. Leena's shoulders shake as she tries to hold in her laugh. "He'll be fine." She shoves a small plate in his hands. "Eat. Enjoy being home. Your dad's harmless."

Denz wants to refute that claim. He *knows* his dad's history. Knows the trail of boys Kami's brought home that haven't lasted five minutes alone with Kenneth Carter. Bray's been gone eight minutes. It's a record Denz celebrates by forking up a giant chunk of his mom's sweet potato pie.

He misses this. The air coated in a heavy blend of vanilla and nutmeg and melted butter. His mom playing Whitney Houston— *The Preacher's Wife* soundtrack is a holiday staple—on the Bluetooth speaker. Nic wearing a mash of prints and stripes Auntie Eva would disapprove of, calling it "trendy." The sleepy bags under Kami's eyes, still adjusting to motherhood a year later, accentuated by her smile after her first bite of pie.

"Jesus, Mom, how is it so perfect every single time?"

Leena smirks. "My secret ingredient."

"Which is," Denz prompts.

"Nice try. I'm taking that to the grave."

"Come on!" Denz and Kami whine. They grin at each other. Since Nic was five, the three of them have maintained a bet on who would discover the hidden ingredient in their mom's pie first. No amount of begging, bribing, or overfilling Leena's wineglass has worked. That doesn't stop their efforts.

Nic beams. "I know what it is!"

Denz narrows his eyes. Growing up, he'd always been closer to Kami. But when she left for college, suddenly the eight-year age gap between him and Nic became nonexistent. She tells him almost everything. He can't believe she kept this secret.

Nic leans her head on Leena's shoulder. "It's love."

Denz and Kami groan. Leena hip-checks Nic away. "Nicola, *please*," she says. "I'm still not using your dad's name to get BT-whatever to perform at your next birthday."

"BTS," Nic grumbles, defeated.

Denz tugs her under his arm, laughing. Kami replaces their sister at Leena's side. Each of them chewing and giggling and talking. No expectations. No questions from the aunties or uncles about what's next now that he's only a year and a half away from graduating.

Honestly, he hasn't given it much thought. He can't imagine Bray won't somehow be a part of that bigger picture, whatever it might look like.

It's been at least fifteen minutes, he thinks. Should he . . .

"Bray's fine," Kami tells him.

Denz startles. "I know."

"So why do you look like Nic when she thinks she's found where Mom hid the Christmas gifts?"

"Hey!" Nic protests.

Denz scoffs. "I'm *chill*. Stress-free. No worries over here."

"I call bullsh—"

"Nicola Carter," Leena warns.

Nic shovels pie into her mouth. Kami guffaws. Leena's distracted enough by Whitney Houston's vocal acrobatics on "Joy to the World" that she almost doesn't notice Denz casually edging toward the entryway.

"Denzel, don't you dare—"

"Did you hear that?" He leans on his tiptoes, pretending to listen. "I'm just gonna check on my nephew. See if he needs anything."

He's out before his mom or sisters say another word.

Away from the kitchen, the house is quieter. It still hums softly like when he was a teen, holding every conversation and laugh and occasional cry in its bones, but Denz can't hear anything else. Until he's down the hall. Feet away from the room converted into a nursery for Mikah. Across from Kenneth's home office.

The light's on, door open. Gentle voices escape. A sharp squeal. Then, overlapping laughter. Denz raises an eyebrow, creeping closer, heart hammering when he almost runs into his dad exiting.

"Oh," Kenneth says. "There you are."

"I wasn't doing anything!" Denz blurts.

Kenneth smirks like he did whenever he caught Denz Face-Timing Jamie instead of sleeping as teens. "If you say so. Mikah woke up. Think he needs to be changed. Or he smelled your mom's amazing pie."

He makes room for Denz in the office doorway. Denz's mouth opens in surprise. Warmth spills through him as he watches.

Bray sways in a circle. Mikah's tucked to his chest. His tiny, tipped-back head is supported by Bray's large hand. They stare at each other, smiling.

"He's kind of surprising." Kenneth nods toward Bray, voice low. "Smart. Caring. He thinks he's funny but—"

"He's really not," Denz whispers back, way too fond.

Kenneth lets out a muted laugh. "I've met worse. Thanks to Kami. God help me when Nic starts dating."

Denz doesn't want to take his eyes away from Bray and Mikah turning in another circle. Eventually, he does. To his dad, he says, "Does that mean you approve?"

"He's . . . different."

It's not a yes or no. But Denz catches it. The little sparkle in his dad's eyes when he tugs off his glasses. It's a minor win. Good enough for him.

Kenneth claps a hand on his shoulder. "There's a slice of pie calling my name. Want me to send your sister back?"

"No," Denz says. "I've got it."

"Suit yourself. I'm pretty sure it's number two."

Kenneth's amused chuckle echoes as he disappears down the hall.

Denz waits a beat longer. His gaze follows Bray's shuffling, the way Mikah's breathing synchronizes, their smiles never breaking. He absorbs how tonight's a night of so many firsts he never imagined hours ago in The Varsity's parking lot.

How, no matter what, this is where he wants to be. At home. With his family.

With Bray.

Outside Kingfisher & Redbud, the city glitters like a smashed disco ball. Flashing streetlights wink off towering glass skyscrapers. Neon signs reflect in the tinted windows of a waiting SUV. Denz jams his hands into the pockets of his wool peacoat, puffing out foggy breaths as his mom hugs Braylon.

"Thank you for coming," she says. "We don't get out much with other couples. Or at all—" She stops short, smiling stiffly when Denz raises an eyebrow. "It was nice seeing you."

Braylon beams. "It was lovely seeing you."

"Don't keep this one out too late." She smacks Denz's arm. "We want him rested for his next big career move, right?"

Braylon nervously scratches his jaw. "Oh, um. Right?"

"Can you believe he's trying to be the next CEO of the family business?"

"Hardly." Braylon's snort is more surprised than anything.

There's a distrusting gleam in Kenneth's stare. Denz's brain scrambles for another lie, but Braylon says, "We all know how superstitious he is. When Denz really wants something, he never talks about it out loud. Bit ridiculous, innit?"

"Excuse you, I—"

"That's him!" Leena cuts in with a cackle. "He didn't change his boxers for a *week* while waiting on his UGA admissions letter."

"Mom!"

She's wrong. He didn't change his favorite *socks*, the same green polka-dot ones he wore when he made honor roll and aced his AP Lit and Composition final. He's a firm believer in routine, that's all.

"LeeLee." Kenneth touches his wife's elbow. "We should go."

After helping Leena climb into the warm, spacious back seat of the SUV, Kenneth pivots to Braylon. His mouth's a hard line.

"Just so we're clear," he begins—for a second, Denz had thought they'd avoided this moment—"I want what's best for my kids, always."

Braylon swallows.

Denz chews the inside of his cheek as the cool night air descends on them.

"I don't know what's happening between you two," Kenneth continues, "or how you ended up back together, but my son says he's serious about you."

"Mr. Carter, I—"

Kenneth holds up a hand. "I haven't forgotten what *you* did." He casually fixes his coat's lapels. Squares his shoulders. "It's going to take more than one great night out to trust it won't happen again. So, I expect to see you at the mayor's gala. All the other events too."

Braylon hesitates. "Of course."

"Prove me wrong."

Kenneth turns to tug Denz into a half hug. After, he joins Leena in the SUV. Its red brake lights disappear into traffic.

Ten seconds pass before Denz remembers to breathe. The city's loud around him. Cars pouring music into the streets. People laughing, searching for their next drink, next party, next break from a long week. Underneath it all, Denz feels like it's only him and Braylon on the sidewalk.

Brow deeply furrowed, Braylon stares into nothing. "Wow," he whispers. "I forgot how *intense* your dad is."

Denz's laugh uncoils the tightness in his chest.

"That's *every* Carter."

"He's gonna proper murder me." Braylon's eyes track a pack of college-somethings bottlenecking into an upscale bar across the street. "He'll hire a professional. An ex-CIA or former MI6 agent. While he's chatting with Oprah, someone will be fishing my body out of the river."

"He wouldn't."

Braylon whips around to face Denz. "He *hates* me."

"Can you blame him?"

Fuck. Denz didn't mean for those words to come out. Well, he did. It's not like he hasn't thought about it a dozen times tonight. But he didn't want it to be like this.

He yanks his coat closed. The cold tints Braylon's cheeks pink. Or maybe that's the embarrassment.

"Thanks for tonight," Denz says. "For—"

"Suffering through Coldplay?"

"It wasn't that bad."

"Nails on a chalkboard. Stepping on a cat's tail. Country music. All things that sound better than your singing."

Denz's lips part, ready to snap, when a crooked grin slides the left side of Braylon's mouth up. A snort shocks Denz. He shakes his head.

"Thanks for that too."

"So," Braylon says after a beat of silence, "care to explain what all of that was about?"

Denz winces at the cloudless sky. He doesn't want to discuss it, but he owes Braylon. Big. Sighing, he launches into the full story. Everything from the retirement announcement to the aunties to Kami's cutting words and nearly kicking down his dad's office door.

Once Denz finishes, Braylon says, "Hmm. Seems like quite the dramatic reaction to what your family said."

"Gee, thanks. Always nice to have you validate my stupid ideas."

"You're welcome." Another tiny smile from Braylon.

Denz lets out a smoky breath. "Sorry you had to deal with my dad's—*you know*."

"Threats of bodily harm if ever I hurt you again?"

"More or less."

"I had my own agenda."

"About that," Denz says. "You don't have to come to the Valentine's gala. The mayor's close with my family. I'll get you a one-on-one. No need to keep lying to save my ass."

He's not sure how he'll fix this shitstorm now. If his dad doesn't see Braylon again, he'll know Denz was lying. The entire family will know. But he can't force Braylon to continue pretending. Not without a good reason.

He yanks out his phone. "Let me just—"

"I'll be there," Braylon interrupts.

"You'll . . . what?"

"The gala. I'm coming."

"But my family." Denz shakes his head. "They'll have questions. A lot. If you think my dad's bad, wait until you meet my aunties."

Braylon shrugs. "I'm not worried."

Denz's eyes narrow. "Is this because you don't believe I'll get you a meeting with Mayor Reynolds?" It's not like he's the one who ghosted Braylon. Who moved to another country. If anyone should have trust issues, it should be him.

The restaurant's door swings open. A handsy couple stumbles out to their idling Bentley. The driver shuts the door before pulling away from the curb.

"I trust you," Braylon says.

Denz ignores the small spark of warmth in his chest. It's his body's natural reaction to the cold. Not those three words.

"I still want to be there," Braylon clarifies.

"Why?"

"I don't have any Valentine's plans." Denz's questioning eyebrow lift is met by an eye roll. "If you show up without your 'boyfriend'"—Braylon's air quotes are offensive to Denz—"on the most romantic day of the year, what will your family think?"

"The same as always."

Denz is incapable of taking anything seriously, including dragging his boyfriend to what is potentially the biggest event of his career.

Somberly, he says, "You don't have to—"

"We'll discuss details later." Braylon plucks the phone from Denz's cold fingers. "Here's my number. Text me yours."

Denz reluctantly sends Braylon a message: hello.

"Well, um," he says around the tightness in his throat, "see you soon?"

Braylon nods once before walking away. Denz strolls in the opposite direction. He doesn't peek over his shoulder. Refuses to check if Braylon's watching him, scowling. Or maybe smiling again.

On the way to his car, Denz does something he hasn't done in a very, *very* long time:

He saves a man's number in his phone.

"Wait! Hold on!" Jamie frantically waves his hands at the screen. Thankfully, Denz has one wireless earbud in, so no one hears how loud he is. Still, he lowers the volume on his phone just as Jamie says, "*The* Bray Adams? Ex-boyfriend Bray? Lives-in-London Bray? Your ex-boyfriend who lives in London, *that* Bray Adams?"

"That's him."

"And he just appeared out of nowhere?"

"Kind of?"

Denz props the phone against his office monitor. On the FaceTime screen, Jamie's toweling off in their apartment's gym locker room. As distracting as random appearances from shirtless men passing by or the occasional gym-bro flexing for a mirror selfie is, Denz manages to stay on topic.

This is his first opportunity to tell Jamie about Friday night.

"And he agreed to be your fake boyfriend? For dinner with your parents?"

"Something like that," Denz says with a sigh.

"Plot fucking twist."

Denz hides his amused grin behind his knuckles. It's been five days since Braylon played Prince Charming for Denz's parents. Five days since Denz found Jamie under a blanket on their sofa with red-rimmed eyes and a fumbling apology.

"I couldn't do it," he admitted. "Lying to your family. Pretending we were more than inseparable, platonic soulmates who hate *Made of Honor* with our entire existences."

(Denz *still* wants all one hour and forty-one minutes of his life back from watching that Patrick Dempsey abomination.)

Denz understood Jamie's reasoning. On the drive home, he realized his plan wasn't fair to his best friend. He'd selfishly coerced Jamie into helping him. Jamie gained nothing from lying. At least with Braylon, there's a trade-off.

"Bray the Boyfriend—"

"Actually, it's Braylon." Denz cringes. When did he become so defensive about a name he never even used until recently? "He, uh, prefers Braylon now."

Denz considers throwing his phone in the trash the moment a scandalous grin splits Jamie's face.

"So this is a thing?"

"It's a plan B," Denz modifies. "He pretends to be my boyfriend. I get him a meeting with Mayor Reynolds for his job."

"Where does he work?"

"A nonprofit."

"Which one?"

Denz bites his lip. He didn't ask. "A good one?"

Jamie towels sweat off his face, eyebrows pinched. "Where's he living now?"

"Atlanta?"

"Bro." Jamie exhales. "You haven't seen each other in *years.* Not since he bounced across the Pacific—"

"Atlantic."

"—and you haven't taken five minutes to ask him the most basic icebreaker questions?"

"To be fair," Denz starts, then stops. He's got nothing. It's not that he isn't curious about Braylon's life since the breakup. It's just that . . .

He'll never admit this to anyone, but there were nights—sad, lonely, extremely tipsy nights—where his mind wandered to the man who couldn't make eye contact with him at their college graduation. Unfortunate nights where Denz's hands almost betrayed him. Almost searched Braylon's name on social media. For a small glimpse. Not to see how great life was in fancy London, or even if Braylon was dating anyone.

Just to know he was okay.

Even now, he can't convince himself to do it. The wound feels too fresh. Why is heartbreak that one scar that never heals cleanly? It always finds a way to ache, no matter how long it's been.

"If you want this to work," Jamie says, pushing damp hair off his brow, "get to know who Braylon is *now*."

"Sounds like a scam."

"Isn't every relationship?"

Denz's face wrinkles. "What should I do?"

"Start by asking questions! Also, I suggest you two establish some rules."

"Rules for what?"

"Denz." Jamie stares at him incredulously. "How many fake-dating rom-coms have we watched together?"

At least half a dozen, and that's just the Netflix originals.

"You need guidelines," Jamie insists like some wise romance mentor and not the man whose last relationship ended over street tacos. "When does this end? Where are you going to show off your fake relationship? Physical boundaries—"

Denz snatches a pen and a pad of neon-green Post-its from his desk drawer. He pauses mid-scribble. "*Physical* boundaries? Like hugging? Kissing?"

"Yeah." Jamie waggles his eyebrows. "Is sex on the table?"

"Hell no!" Denz hurriedly lowers his voice. "No sex on, under, or *around* the table. None at all. Why would we?"

Jamie sniffs his armpits before slipping on a clover-green T-shirt, LUCKY MICKEY'S TAVERN stamped in white letters across the front. "Because you're fake-dating your ex."

"Elaborate."

"*We* were never going to have sex."

"Obviously," Denz agrees.

"But the variables have changed. You have past sexual history with Braylon. From what I remember, lots of unforgettable dicking happened between you two."

Denz is going to set himself on fire. "Irrelevant details."

Jamie scoffs. "Bro, you were a ten back then. You're a twelve now. Braylon might want to—"

"He won't." Denz pauses, considering. "You really think he might?"

"If I ran into someone I once found hot and there was a tiny possibility they were single and—" A sharp blush flares across Jamie's cheeks. "You know what? Never mind."

Denz has questions. But a loud knock at his doorway stops him. It's Kami, smiling weirdly, holding a powder-blue box.

"I'm hanging up," he says.

"Talk to Braylon! Figure your shit out! Find out if he wants to fu—"

Denz ends the call. Kami plops down across from him.

"New local bakery we're thinking about partnering with," she explains, revealing a variety of cupcakes in the box. Denz reaches for a dulce de leche. Kami starts with key lime.

This awkwardness between them is new. It's unexplored territory. Even while Denz was in Athens, he stayed in constant contact with her. They've always been on the same side of everything. Politics, climate change, which Jonas Brother is the hottest.

(It's Nick and they won't be hearing any other suggestions.)

They've never gone this long avoiding each other, including when Kami found out Denz told Jamie *and* Nic he was gay before her.

But here they are, licking frosting off their fingers in silence.

At last, Kami says, casually, "A reporter followed me into the lobby this morning." It's not a rare occurrence for someone to stop them outside the building, asking for a quote. "He tried to get on the elevator with me."

Denz snaps forward so fast, he gets lightheaded.

"What the fuck?"

"Don't worry." Kami giggles. "Corrine MMA'd his ass. She's quick for sixty."

Denz peels the wrapper off his cupcake. Anything to keep his mind off what he would've done if he saw that reporter. "What did he want?"

"Info about Dad retiring. The next CEO."

"Did he mention names?"

Denz wonders if he came up at all. If the media looks at him as a serious contender. The same way he's looking at himself.

"The aunties. Some business investor who financed a hybrid car. The Carter kids."

"What'd you tell him?"

"To mind his own fucking business."

Denz laughs. As much as he always wants to protect his sisters, he knows they don't need him. Kami's four years older. She dealt with the family's fame long before Denz recognized it existed. And Nic can throw a punch better than him.

"We missed you at Sunday dinner," Kami mentions.

Every few weeks, Leena hosts a big dinner. Despite Kenneth's insistence on hiring a caterer, she spends hours in the kitchen cooking. Uncle Orlando shows up with beer and wine. Uncle Tevin and Auntie Eva fight over their favorite sports teams. For one night, everyone's under the same roof, laughing and shouting for hours.

Denz passed on his mom's invitation because: (a) she'd expect Braylon to join and there was no way he was upending Braylon's life twice in less than forty-eight hours; (b) he was in no mood to answer the eight million questions about the "new boyfriend";

and (c) he'd promised Jamie a Will Thacker Night—*Moonstruck* and thin-crust Hawaiian pizza.

"How'd it go?"

Kami grins. "Same as usual."

"Mom yelling at Uncle Tevin for trying to help in the kitchen."

"Jordan ignoring everyone after losing during Spades."

"Uncle Orlando teaching Nic a new old-school dance," Denz says.

"She didn't know what the Electric Slide was!"

Denz takes another bite. "Mikah showing Dad his cartwheels."

"Auntie Eva hating what I was wearing," Kami says. "It was a Comme des Garçons sweater."

Denz shrugs, amused by her irate expression. "And I bet Auntie C.C. wanted updates on everyone's love life . . ." He trails off, not meeting Kami's pointed gaze.

"*Braylon?*"

He stuffs the rest of the cupcake in his mouth. Fuck, he didn't mean to go there. The family group chat has been nonstop since Saturday morning. *Thanks, Mom.* He's surprised it's taken Kami this long to bring it up.

"When? How?" she asks him. "Wasn't he in London?"

Denz swallows. "Yes. But we ran into each other. At a bar." Almost the truth. There *is* a bar at the coffee shop. Not the kind that serves alcohol, but . . . semantics. "Months ago."

"Months?" She searches his face for something, a crack in his armor. Denz clenches his ass cheeks so hard he feels it in his nostrils. "You haven't mentioned him. Or brought him around at all."

"*You* haven't mentioned or brought Suraj around."

"Fair point."

"You know how our family is," Denz says, leaning back in his chair. "Especially about *him*."

Kami nods. "You wanted time to enjoy it. For yourself."

"Y-yeah."

He hates the lying. Hates that tender piece on the inside of his heart that knows why Braylon was the worst option to begin with. Their history's too complicated. Too tangled between the Denz he was and the one he is now. It's the very reason he avoids relationships.

"Look at us." Kami smiles at him. "Two Carters with secret romances."

"Do you think Nic has one too?"

"Ha! Does the one she has with her phone count?"

"Bet the aunties and uncles have a side group chat just to talk about us."

"Wouldn't be surprised at all," Kami says before finishing her cupcake.

"It's not . . ." Denz pauses. "Weird, right? Me and Braylon?"

Deep down, Kami's nothing like him when it comes to romance. She doesn't wear her heart on her sleeve. He never caught her crying over Matthew. She probably did, but her focus and drive and one-relationship-doesn't-define-me badassery outshined any tears.

She smirks. "What isn't weird about our lives?"

He laughs hoarsely.

"Are you happy?" she asks.

God, Denz wants so bad to tell Kami he fell headfirst into this mess because he wanted *her* to believe he wasn't who everyone says he is. Because he wants to believe it too. Instead, he says, "Braylon's great."

"Good." She stands after checking her phone. "Sorry. Fourth video call this week with Emily Sedwick in five minutes."

"But it's only Wednesday."

"She's the youngest princess of a multimillion-dollar family who wants doves released during her entrance at an engagement party. Not wedding. *Engagement party.* She doesn't care about my time."

Denz chuckles. The irony isn't lost on him. Kami, who wants

nothing to do with wedding planning, has her future hinging on an engagement party. Meanwhile, Denz the Noncommittal King is pouring all his potential-CEO energy into a Valentine's gala. It's ridiculous.

Multicolored Post-it Notes hang from all over his monitor. A decoupage of reminders: *sign venue contract, call florist, schedule meeting with baker, review menu,* and *no flamingo-pink decorations*—a special request from the mayor's team.

Which reminds him . . .

"Hey," Denz says, "would you go with a DJ or a live band for the gala?"

"DJ," she immediately replies.

"Is that your event-manager answer or your secret way of sabotaging me?"

"Denz, you're not a big enough threat for me to sabotage."

"Ouch," he gasps, fake wounded. "Good luck with your call! I'm sure you'll have no problem convincing Emily to go with the *peonies.*"

He's not sure what's louder: his exploding laughter or Kami slamming the door on her way out.

Today 4:13 P.M.

we should meet to discuss things
hi! this is Denz btw in case you already deleted my number

Formerly Known As Bray
Bold of you to assume I saved it in the first place.

hahaha! were you always this funny?

Formerly Known As Bray
What would you like to discuss?

how we're gonna pull off this fake relationship?
entanglement?

Formerly Known As Bray
Sounds problematic. I have an early meeting
tomorrow. I can be free round 11.
Crema?

umm suuuuuure?

Formerly Known As Bray
See you at 11, Unknown Number that's texting
me.

-6-

Denz can't believe he's back at the scene of the crime.

What is his life now?

He finds Braylon seated inside Crema at a corner table. Slung across the back of his chair is a black messenger bag with a Skye's the Limit logo, the Freestyle Script font designed in a rainbow palette. His snug gray sweater hugs his biceps and shoulders.

Denz almost forgets how to order.

For a long moment, they sit in silence. Braylon sips his tea. Denz's left leg jogs under the table.

Shit, when did starting a simple conversation with someone who's seen you naked become the toughest part of my day?

His cheeks warm. *No, no.* His brain can't go there. But it does. Flashbacks of Braylon stretched out on his dorm bed wearing nothing but a sleepy smile, his fingers drawing lazy circles on Denz's bare shoulder, entices a twitching half erection in his slacks.

"So, uh . . ." He wiggles in his chair. "Come here often?"

Fuck, really? What's next? I've lost my number, can I have yours?

"Sometimes," Braylon says evenly.

"And you drink . . . tea now," Denz points out, because he apparently has the conversational abilities of a thirteen-year-old boy on a first date while his parents eagerly spy from two tables over.

"Hard not to get into tea while living in London," Braylon deadpans. "The company I worked for had shit coffee. The tea was exceptional. Is that a problem?"

"Nope."

Enjoy your sewage water, Denz thinks, but doesn't say.

"You're making a face," Braylon says.

"I'm not," Denz argues, clearly making a face.

"If you have a prob—"

"Let's just discuss how we're gonna *Wedding Date* this situation of ours," Denz suggests.

"How we're going to *what* now?"

"You know." Denz gesticulates wildly. "*The Wedding Date?*"

"Is that a reality show? I'm not into those."

Denz growls so deeply, Matty almost drops a mug behind the bar. Thankfully, he just got on shift. Otherwise, Denz suspects his iced latte would have an extra hint of *fuck you* in it. "Since when are you not into reality shows?" He sighs. "*The Wedding Date* is a movie. A rom-com."

"Haven't seen it."

"Of course not. I forgot you don't know real cinema. Only Marvel movies."

"Those are quality films," Braylon says. "*Captain America: The Winter Soldier* is a proper rom-com. Friends-to-lovers-to-enemies. Amnesia. Star-crossed lovers. Don't get me started on the *Captain Marvel* films. Carol and Maria obviously—"

"Boring," Denz interrupts. He gives a quick plot overview of *The Wedding Date.*

Braylon's forehead wrinkles. "But you're not paying me. Are you?"

"No!"

Something flashes in Braylon's eyes, the tiniest shift in the corners of his mouth. Denz focuses on his drink.

"We need to establish expectations. Like in the movie. We need to be on the same page."

"About how this is going to work? Between us?"

"Exactly!"

Braylon pulls a fountain pen and leather notebook from his bag. At the top of a clean page, he writes, *The Rules of Dating.* He underlines the title.

Denz blinks. "You're writing this down? By hand?"

"Why wouldn't I?"

"Hello." Denz waggles his phone in the air. "You have one of these."

"I *like* writing by hand."

Braylon squints at Denz like it's a piece of information he should remember. And he does. From semester after semester where note-taking was an essential step in how Braylon managed a 3.9 GPA as a trophy-winning student athlete. Most nights, his highlighter-dyed fingers would angle Denz's jaw for a long kiss between chapters before Braylon returned to leaving notes in the margins of thick textbooks.

Denz's own study habits were the perfect blend of stress and all-nighters. He escaped UGA with a 3.7 GPA. He's not ashamed of how.

"First," Denz says, opening a new memo in his phone. "The places we need to act like a couple. The mayor's gala, obviously."

"I suppose any event your family will attend?"

"Coworkers too." Denz lifts his eyes. "Not that you need to make random appearances."

"Where else? Hypothetically. If it'll help our causes."

"Well . . ." Denz thinks for a moment. "There's an engagement party for a well-known family. That's in early March. My dad's retirement party is later that month."

Braylon scribbles notes. His tiny handwriting is still adorable and unreadable. Denz's stomach knots at all the unwanted memories flooding his brain.

"You don't have to show up. I promised you a one-on-one with the mayor on Valentine's—"

"What if I did? Go to all of them?"

"Why would you?" Denz asks.

Braylon straightens. "One meeting with the mayor might not be enough for what I want to accomplish."

"Which is?"

"I'm organizing a function for the teens at the nonprofit. During spring break."

Denz hears Jamie's voice in the back of his head. "What do you do now?"

"I'm the program director for Skye's the Limit, an LGBTQ+ youth center." That explains the messenger bag. "I'm trying to expand our reach. Buy-in from new donors is a struggle." His mouth fights off a frown. "An endorsement from the mayor is a start, but I'm thinking bigger."

Denz nods.

"And I—" Braylon rubs the back of his neck. "—could use your help. Specifically."

"Planning the event?"

"Yes. That." The edges of Braylon's face soften. "School breaks aren't easy for these kids. No friends around. Unhealthy home situations. Loneliness. They need a safe space where they feel wanted. Celebrated."

Denz rests his chin on his knuckles. He's never heard Braylon so passionate. It reminds him of his own dad talking Audrey off the ledge on *Marvelous Weddings*.

"Also," Braylon says, "we can't show up as a happy couple on Valentine's Day and fake break up the next morning."

"Good point. When should we, uh. Call things off?"

"April sixth. After my event."

"April sixth," Denz repeats while typing in his phone. His eyes follow Braylon's hand as he writes:

#1: Pretend to date whenever in public.
#2: End Date—April 6th

"Next—" Denz has to clear his throat several times. "Physical boundaries."

"Like holding hands?"

"Yes. But, um, also . . ."

It's Denz's turn to frown. Why does this feel like some recurring nightmare? Like he's stuck in high school sex ed and instead of a carefully labeled diagram of the male body, it's *him*, standing naked in the front of the class, everyone laughing.

He whispers, "Kissing."

His family knows what he's like. Remembers how he was with Braylon. They weren't over the top with their PDA. But there was cuddling by the fireplace. Lingering stares, soft touches in public.

And yes, *kissing*. A serious relationship would require that. *Right?*

A quiet beat. "Only with verbal consent," Braylon says, his voice rough.

Without looking at each other, they both add another bullet point. Crema's eclectic music playlist shifts from a pop song to an acoustic cover of a Prince hit.

"Should we—" Denz's eyes trace from the stubble on Braylon's jaw to his bobbing Adam's apple as he slurps more tea. "—have rules about . . . other forms of touching?"

"Do you mean hugging?"

"Kinda?"

"What? Touching your back? Hand on your hip?"

"Sure?" Denz's cheeks flush. Fuck Jamie Peters for getting in his head like this. "But, well, actually . . ."

"Sex?" Braylon says flatly.

"Yes? Er, maybe?"

"Why would that be an option?"

This time, Denz's screeching "I don't know" does startle a mug out of Matty's hands.

"How would having sex in front of your colleagues—*your family*—make our fake relationship more legitimate?"

"I—" Denz stops. His brain's too preoccupied with how he's going to murder his best friend, hide the body at the bottom of Lake Lanier, move to New Mexico, and get away with it.

Braylon bristles in his silence.

"Sorry. Never mind." Denz's eyes lower. "No sex."

Aggressively, Braylon scribbles, *#4: NO SEX*.

"Anything else?"

Yeah, my self-esteem. A new life. A time machine so I can travel back to Old Denz and tell him not to talk to the cute boy with the buzz cut at a stupid graduation party.

"Jamie and I were gonna FaceTime. While I was at work," Denz says instead. "You know, so my coworkers *see* us doing couple-y things."

"I'm quite busy at work. Dedicating time for that seems counterproductive."

Of fucking course. Why did Denz think this is the same Braylon who would call him *during class* to ask about dinner or where he left his swimming goggles. This tea-drinking, scruffy-faced, talks-like-the-long-lost-son-of-Idris-Elba isn't that Braylon.

"I could," Braylon's tone softens, "text you."

"Text?"

"Yes. Like, jokes. Things to make you laugh."

Denz grins slyly. "What kind of jokes?"

"Not *that kind.*" Braylon kicks his ankle. "Don't be cheeky."

"Fine. Text, not sexts," he narrates while adding another bullet point to his list. "But we have to do social media."

"Do what with it?"

"Look like a couple," Denz says, annoyed. "You'd be surprised how invested people get watching a relationship's success online."

People like Auntie C.C., who has eyes everywhere.

"Selfies," Denz explains, "us doing normal, cute things." When his eyes retrain on Braylon, he's grimacing. As if Denz suggested mandatory matching-outfit photos.

Braylon sighs. "I prefer we not."

"Why?"

"Because I don't want to be stalked by your eighty thousand overzealous followers."

"They're harmless." Denz pauses, backtracking. "Wait, do *you* follow me?"

"What? No!" Pink spreads down Braylon's neck. "I mean, technically?"

Denz raises a suspicious eyebrow.

"It's occupational research," Braylon insists. "I like to keep up with who our teens are into. Who's trending. They're proper big fans of your content, by the way."

"Are they?"

Braylon nods. "So, I may have *perused* your account. On a strictly professional level."

Denz fights off a smirk.

So, Braylon follows @notthatdenzel. Because the teens he works with think Denz is cool, or whatever. He's not going to make a big deal about it. He's certainly not sitting taller, shoulders cocked, preening like a damn peacock.

"If it's all right, I'd like to keep my personal life private," Braylon requests.

"Okay," Denz agrees. "No selfies, face pics, or tagging you."

He can respect that. It doesn't stop him from arranging their hands next to their cups on the table. He weaves his fingers between Braylon's.

"We can still make it social media official."

After three attempts, Denz gets the perfect shot: an overhead photo of their hands bathed in a lush mix of sun and interior lighting. He adds a brief caption, some hashtags. His notifications skyrocket seconds after posting.

Braylon stares at his tea. "We probably shouldn't tell anyone about our arrangement."

"Yeah," Denz says, wincing guiltily. "Except Jamie knows."

Braylon sighs.

"But we can trust him!" Jamie is a vault of secrets. "Is there anyone you want to tell?"

Careful brown eyes study Denz. The crease between Braylon's brows deepens. "I don't really have anyone. To tell."

"Not even a best friend?"

"No."

"What about your old UGA teammates?"

They were Braylon's little Athens family. Somehow, even when he was the youngest in the group, he was always the big brother type, watching over each of them.

"Haven't kept in touch," Braylon says.

"Your roommate? Ben? Bryce?"

"*Brent.*"

"What about him?"

"He barely said goodbye when we moved out of the dorms," Braylon notes. "I bet he's somewhere in Boston or Nashville. Chugging iced coffees. Living his best finance-bro life."

"So, there's . . . no one?"

The café's music switches over to something slow, somber. Braylon's expression matches it. He swirls the last of his tea, never drinking.

Denz's next question comes out before he's thought it through:

"Who came to your dad's funeral?"

An emptiness flashes over Braylon's eyes. He blinks, resetting. "Dad's old colleagues. Neighbors. Loads of people who brought so many casseroles and cakes and—"

"Braylon," Denz interrupts, "who was there for *you?*"

The question silences Braylon. Like he's never thought about it. Never given himself permission to.

"Who was supposed to be there?" Braylon counters.

"I don't know. Didn't your mom have a sister?"

"Who lives in *Sweden*," Braylon reminds him. "Besides, she stopped being close to Dad a few years ago. She called, at least."

"No one else?"

Denz can't imagine. His family is huge, on both sides. When his grandparents died, he couldn't walk five feet without someone to hug him or brush his hair, let him sob on their shoulder.

"I didn't have—" Braylon stops. "It doesn't matter."

Somewhere in those three words, Denz thinks he's saying, *You weren't there so why do you care?*

It's probably not true. That doesn't make the thought go away.

"Only Jamie knows," he repeats.

"Only Jamie," Braylon confirms, nodding.

Denz is tempted to ask Braylon to finish his thought from a minute ago. What didn't he have? *Who* didn't he have? But that's not fair. Braylon doesn't owe him anything from that time in his life.

Just like Denz doesn't owe him anything from the last five years.

The sun's warm on Denz's cheek outside Crema. He lingers on the sidewalk while Braylon orders something to-go at the front counter. His thumb scrolls through his notifications, purposely ignoring the family group chat. His attention keeps returning to the photo he posted. Their hands look so natural.

Believable.

That's confirmed when a new comment from Auntie Cheryl pops up: five heart-eye emojis and a ridiculous number of exclamation points.

Braylon steps outside, holding a paper bag. "Sorry. Whit, my coworker, is a total badass. She's also quite grumpy if you show up empty-handed after going out for lunch."

"Relatable." Denz motions to the cup in Braylon's hand. "More tea?"

"An herbal blend."

"Ooh, there's more than one kind of dirty leaf water?"

"Has anyone told you what a dick you can be?"

"Multiple," Denz says, catching a glimpse of Matty through the window. Speaking of. "I forgot to mention earlier, but . . . I'm not gonna date or, like, *whatever* with anyone. While we're, you know."

"Fake-dating?"

Denz smirks. "You're learning."

"Me neither." Braylon tugs at his collar. "Not that I was. You know. Dating anyone."

"Atlanta men aren't as hot as the Brits?"

"Hardly." Braylon looks away. "I'm invested in my work, that's all."

"Sounds boring."

"And here I was worried you wouldn't approve."

"Always here to invalidate your love life," Denz says.

The corners of Braylon's mouth twitch higher.

"BTW . . ." Denz raises his phone to show off the various online platforms the nonprofit uses. "Who handles your social media? It's grossly ineffective."

"It's a collaborative effort!"

"Hmm. You were never good at group projects."

Denz stares at his screen. Skye's the Limit's online presence is like the vanilla milkshake of company profiles. Nothing offensive, just . . . there.

"All of you should be fired."

Braylon's laugh is a soothing noise. It hits Denz like a cold shower. Memories of nights on the grassy terrace between the Miller Learning Center and the Fine Arts Building. From talking for hours instead of sleeping. Kissing instead of studying.

It takes all Denz's focus not to shiver.

"Sorry we can't all be social media gurus like you," Braylon says.

"It's a shame."

"Our five thousand followers aren't complaining."

"Because they're either bots or people who get joy from watching grass grow."

Braylon scowls. "You little shit."

"Argh. Come here," Denz demands after one last glance at the sad grid.

Under Crema's black-and-white awning, where the natural light's better, he poses Braylon near the door. A Pride flag hangs inside the glass. The vibe of the entire block is small-town-neighborhood-tucked-inside-a-big-city realness. Wide sidewalks, whimsical shops. The perfect backdrop for a cozy movie.

Denz arranges the cup in Braylon's hand so the logo is visible. He adjusts Braylon's messenger bag too. Branding is everything.

"What are you—"

"Shut up," Denz says without any heat. He angles Braylon's jaw toward the lens. "Just smile."

He steps back. His fingers aren't tingling from the soft, bristly hairs of Braylon's stubble. That's not a thing.

With an indignant huff, Braylon follows Denz's instructions. It only takes one attempt.

"You're welcome," Denz says after AirDropping the photo into Braylon's phone. "Post this everywhere. Friendly vibes. Hot gu—"

He cuts himself off. Was he really about to say that?

"Instant reach," Denz finishes, throat tight.

Braylon's too busy staring at his phone to notice. "You're . . . good at this."

Denz's face warms. He needs to get out of the sun.

"Don't forget to tag the café," he commands. "Add the location too."

"Noted."

"My work here's done." Denz pockets his phone. He buttons his coat before turning to leave. Over his shoulder, he says, "I'll be expecting a dirty, flirty text from you tomorrow. Make it good."

The left side of Braylon's mouth edges up. "I'll try not to disappoint."

Denz walks away. If he's smiling all the way back to his car, well—it's clearly the caffeine. No other reason.

notthatdenzel started following **the.braylon.adams**

the Carter Family Group Chat

Today 3:29 P.M.

Aunt Cheryl Carter
Denzel and the ex who left him for the UK are
social media official now!

Kami Carter
His name is Braylon.

Aunt Cheryl Carter
His name is 💩 until we meet
We can't just let anyone in this family especially
not someone who ruined my nephew!

Uncle Orlando Rivera
Dramatic much, C?

Aunt Eva Carter-Rivera
Speaking of the gram . . . Nicola what are you
wearing in your latest post?
You look like an extra on schitt's creek

Nic Carter

it's called FASHUN, Auntie E! nobody calls it
the gram

Jordan Carter

Wait . . . denz and his ex? back together?

Aunt Cheryl Carter

Yes! Now it's your turn son!
Time to find a nice GF with a financially stable
family and a clean background.
A girl you can marry!

Jordan Carter left the conversation.

In his rush to fix the Jamie problem and coordinate with Braylon, Denz let one key detail slip between the cracks: *Jordan*. The same Jordan who Denz introduced Jamie as his boyfriend to.

He hovers outside his cousin's office like a wildlife observer documenting a rarely seen species in their natural habitat. The space is an effortless mix of personal and professional. A shelf of succulents. A fitted Los Angeles Lakers hat hung next to a canvas painting of Malibu Pier. On the desk, soft strains of Frank Ocean play from the laptop.

Jordan's hunched over his phone, reading intently. Denz recognizes the body language: the Carter grind.

It's been rooted in each of them since they were little: Work hard. Never settle for average. Be the best version of yourself whether you think anyone's paying attention or not, because when you're a Black professional, they're *always* watching.

Denz respects Jordan's dedication. He's not going to be Kami's assistant forever. But he misses the Jordan from swimming races in the pool. The one who challenged him to hot dog–eating contests. Who spent every summer as a kid talking about all his goals.

When Jordan got into UCLA, Denz knew that was it. He wasn't

coming back. He was destined to become a beach yoga instructor or an investment banker. Someone fully removed from the public spotlight. But four years later, he was back in Atlanta, fulfilling his role in the Carter dynasty.

After a minute, Jordan's eyes lift. "Figured you'd show up eventually."

Denz plops into the chair in front of Jordan. "What's new?"

"You tell me." Jordan flips around his phone screen. "Or should I ask the group chat?"

"Please don't."

"Nice post on your IG, by the way," Jordan says. "Have you read some of this shit?"

Denz has skimmed. There are over three hundred comments on the photo of him holding Braylon's hand at Crema. He's clocked the recurring theme: either it's *omg this is so cute!* or *who's the top?*

He grins sheepishly. "So, about the other day. When you saw me and—"

"Jamie, your *boyfriend?*"

"Yeah . . . that."

Denz sighs. He's considered lying. It's not like he's going to stop doing that anytime soon. But when he stares at Jordan, beyond the mustache and goatee, the faint lines in his forehead, Denz sees the boy who whispered in the dark about never knowing his real dad. About how much he loves his stepdad, Uncle Tevin, but there's a piece missing.

He can't lie to Jordan.

"It's fake."

"What is?"

"Jamie and me," Denz confesses. "Braylon and me. All of it."

Jordan pauses his playlist. "Is this because of what my mom said? At the meeting?"

"Kinda."

A vein in Denz's left temple is threatening to burst. After a long breath, he finally explains everything. From how it started to the levels it's reached. The more he talks, the lower Jordan's jaw drops. It's almost comical, how much more dramatic his reaction is compared to the one Jamie had.

"Shit," Jordan hisses.

"Yup."

"I get it. I'm not condoning lying," Jordan asserts. Unlike his mom, Jordan's never been into gossip. "But it's rough being us. One of the Carters. Beyond the media bullshit and all the attention. It's the family shit too."

They both laugh.

"If it'd get my mom off my back," Jordan says, "I'd fake a relationship too."

Jordan's even more low-key about his dating life than Denz. He never discusses it. The last girlfriend he mentioned was Yazzie, his high school sweetheart. No one since then. At least, no one Denz is aware of.

"Anyway," Jordan says, smug, his cherry lips lifting, "I knew there was no way you and Jamie were fucking."

"Excuse you. *How?*" Denz was very convincing the other day. He can't help Jamie has the acting range of Adam Driver.

"Zero chemistry."

"We have chemistry!"

"The *best friend* kind. Strictly bro behavior." Jordan's eyes drop back to his phone. "It'd be weird if you two were really dating."

"So weird," Denz agrees.

Those summers as teens, when Jordan spent more time at Denz's house than his own, were magical. Every weekend, he would show up with a sleeping bag and an armful of video games. Denz still can't smell freshly cut grass and chlorine and boyish sweat, and not think about his cousin and best friend. They were voted *Most Likely to Start a Fire* by his dad. An inseparable trio.

"I'm surprised you two didn't kill each other," Denz says, laughing. "You were always fighting over Mario Kart."

"Because he cheated!" Jordan sniffs indignantly.

"A likely story."

Jordan tugs at the collar of his black turtleneck. "Jamie's still single?"

Denz shrugs. "You know him. New relationship every month."

"Poor him," Jordan says dryly.

"He'll find the right one soon."

Jordan doesn't reply. Denz swears there's something anxious in his thoughtful expression. A buzzing notification forces Denz to wiggle around, unearth his phone from his back pocket. Two new texts. From Braylon.

Why should you never break up with a goalie?
Because he's a keeper.

The snort-giggle his body releases surprises Denz. He doesn't know why. Braylon's humor has always been terrible. Cheesy, actually. Like jarred, store-brand nacho cheese.

And it's a million times better than any sext Denz has ever received.

He replies, this is appalling!

And then: we need to make a small change to our rules. my cousin Jordan knows.

There's no better time than now to rip the Band-Aid off.

A bubble of a dancing ellipsis appears, then vanishes. A second turns into five. Denz can't blame Braylon for being upset. It's been less than twenty-four hours and he's already fucked up.

Finally, a new message arrives.

Sorry. Whit needed my help with something.
Anyone else? I'd like to be prepared.

Relief tingles through Denz's bloodstream. He doesn't give himself a second to question *why* he's comforted by Braylon's response. He types out a quick answer.

NO ONE ELSE! I SWEAR! NO NEW FRIENDS!

Braylon sends, Family doesn't count as friends.

Denz's eyes widen. He starts to mentally compose a scathing, funny but venomous reply when more texts from Braylon land.

Apologies. I forgot to add 😜
Was that too harsh? You're probably making a
face.

It's impossible for Denz to contain the whale-like noise his throat emits. It's horrendous and inexcusable and all Braylon's fault.

He types, *YOU ASSHOLE*, then deletes. He tries, *London should've kept you*, but that's too rude, even for him. He settles on, who are you???, then locks his screen.

Thirty seconds. Then, an answer.

Apparently your fake boyfriend, who's very busy
at work by the way.

He typed out "by the way." Denz is speechless. He's halfway through another reply when a throat clears so loudly, Denz startles out of the chair. From the floor, he spots Jordan leaning over his desk, smiling in a way that makes Denz's *eyebrows* sweat. He squints back.

"For someone in a fake relationship, you look pretty happy," Jordan comments. "You sure it's not real, cuz?"

Denz pockets his phone before standing. "That's slander. I'm leaving."

"I can't wait to read all the fan fiction about you two," Jordan says sunnily.

Denz flips him the finger on the way out. Jordan's wrong. It's *absurd*. This situationship is far from real. Denz will never let anyone in his heart like that again.

Especially not Braylon Adams.

Denz is barely settled back at his own desk when Eric knocks on his doorframe. His dark hair is unstyled. Eric isn't wearing his glasses, and Denz can see the heavy shadows under his eyes. A mustard stain stands out against his pink button-up. His usually perfect posture is slouchy.

Kenneth has remained tight-lipped about why Eric dropped out of the CEO race. Even Auntie Cheryl isn't sharing intel. If she has any.

Denz has considered asking, but—

He's never had lunch with Eric. While Denz has been out for drinks with Connor and Kim and their respective partners, he hasn't been with Julie, Eric's wife. Questioning why someone dropped out of a life-changing career opportunity feels personal on a level they're not.

Eric says, "Hey, boss."

"Don't call me that," Denz pleads.

"You don't want to manifest it?"

"No. Yes. I mean, I hate that name for someone in charge."

"Fair enough," Eric says. "I called the Rigel to set up a tour. Wanted to get an on-the-ground game plan for the mayor's gala."

Like the star it's named after, the Rigel is a monstrous but still intimate event space north of the city. It's hosted parties for the cast of *Queer Eye*, rising Hollywood stars, awards shows. Just last month, they accommodated a high-profile wedding TFW couldn't stop raving about, including a paragraph about *another* Atlanta event-planning company handling the ceremony seamlessly. Allegedly, Denz hate-read the article over muffins.

The Rigel is the perfect place to take 24 Carter Gold into its next phase.

He opens the calendar app on his phone. "How soon can we get in?"

"Never."

Denz tilts his head. "What?"

"The venue manager said the space was never confirmed." Eric pushes a curl off his forehead. "They never received a signed contract from you."

Denz's eyes dart to one of the Post-its hanging from his desktop monitor. The neon orange one. In his big handwriting: *sign venue contract.*

"Fuuuck." Bile races up his throat. "W-we'll fix that. I'll email—"

"It was due yesterday," Eric says, far too calm.

No. Denz remembers reviewing the document. Highlighting where his initials went. Double-checking the date. There was nothing more important than—

"Fucking fuck!"

Yesterday. Crema. Spending entirely too long creating a list of rules for a fake relationship. Taking that stupid photo for social media. Walking away with a cheek-aching smile.

Denz sucks in a shaky breath. "What can I do?"

He's messed up before. He's also found quick solutions. But this isn't replacing a cake with dozens of cupcakes. It's not forgetting a memory stick with the slideshow of the happy couple's dead grandparents for an anniversary dinner. He doesn't have a way out of this.

Eric folds his arms. "You could tell your d—"

"Not happening."

Getting his dad involved effectively proves Denz *isn't* ready for the CEO position.

Eric exhales, thinking. "How about someone as connected as your dad? Someone who's been in close contact with every client on his behalf?"

Denz doesn't like where this is going. "Not her," he says.

"She's your best chance."

"There has to be a better option."

"Love that positive energy," Eric deadpans. "Like it or not, she's all you got."

Denz swallows a scream. Fucking fuckity fuck of all the fucks ever given. Is this really how his dream dies? Over one stupid Post-it?

He drops his head into his hands, defeated. "Promise me,

whoever inherits this office next, you won't let them hang one of those silly 'Keep Calm and Party On' neon signs on the wall."

Eric snorts. "Quit being dramatic."

Denz comes prepared. He's ordered a slice of raspberry truffle cheesecake from his favorite Michelin-star restaurant. Slipped on a cashmere sweater over his button-up. Meditated for five minutes to get rid of any bad energy. Put on a brave face even though he's close to shitting his boxers.

He's ready when Auntie Cheryl emerges from her office, Jimmy Choo clutch bag in hand, swiftly strutting toward the elevators.

He jogs to catch up. "Auntie!"

"I'm done for the day, nephew," she says, heels clicking on the floor. "Run your new Insta-Snap-Tok idea or whatever by your dad."

"No, it's about—"

"Not interested."

"But—"

"Goodbye, Denzel!"

"I have cheesecake," he gets out before her finger can hit the down button. "Raspberry swirl and truffle sauce. Your favorite."

Cheryl's shoulders lower as she rotates around. She scrutinizes the paper bag in his hand, then his face. "What did you *do*?"

"Nothing," he answers.

"Quit the games," she says, jaw tight. "It's been a long day, these shoes are cute but *painful,* and I'm going to be late."

Denz takes her in. Her braids are woven into an elegant bun. Vintage pearl earrings complementing her understated makeup. A forest-green pencil dress under her wrap coat.

"Meeting with a client?"

"Date night with my husband," she replies sharply. "Your Uncle O got us tickets for the opening of *Chicago.* We're having dinner at Garden and Wine first."

Denz nods, impressed. Orlando is the art director for the Fox

Theatre. It's not that Tevin is incapable of planning romantic nights out. But between his studio commitments and traveling to support all his Billboard-topping artists, he rarely has time for anything above a minimal-effort gesture. Cheryl never complains.

"Spill," she sighs, annoyed, "or go away."

"I fucked up."

Her face remains expressionless, as if she's not the least bit shocked by this revelation.

"I forgot to sign the contract for the Rigel," he admits.

Cheryl studies him. Then, she laughs. It's more disbelief than mocking, but it stings just the same. "Nephew," she says mid-guffaw, "you've had some slipups before, but this truly drags the bar straight to hell."

"I know." He squares his shoulders. "I need your help."

"You need *Jesus*."

He expected that response. The aunties never play favorites. They're equally critical of Denz and his sisters. But Cheryl's already shown her allegiance to Team Kami. Still, he's not giving up.

"I can't tell my dad what happened."

"Clearly," she agrees.

"I made an error."

"A *critical* error." Cheryl rests her hands on her hips. "Denzel, you've earned your spot here. Mostly. But things like this can't happen *if* you're the CEO. You can't forget to sign off on payroll. To hand out IOUs while your staff's bills, mortgage, and childcare go unpaid."

"I wouldn't forget."

"Current evidence says otherwise," she counters.

Denz wants to fight back. He's no longer that ten-year-old boy being scolded for using his auntie's favorite Versace bathroom towel as a cape to play superheroes with Jordan. But his mom's in his head. Her unbreakable rule. He's only going to win this war by showing Cheryl respect, even when she's not offering him the same.

"What's in it for me? If I help?" Cheryl asks.

Denz lifts the cheesecake bag higher. She looks unimpressed.

Plan B it is.

"Braylon's coming to the mayor's gala."

She crooks an eyebrow up as if to say, *And?*

"I'll make sure you get to talk to him." He inhales deeply. "Alone. Before Auntie Eva."

There it is. Intrigue lights up her brown eyes. Jordan inherited his mom's incredibly competitive nature. Any opportunity to have an edge over her sister, Cheryl happily takes.

When they were dating, Denz kept Braylon away from his extended family. There was never a formal introduction. A Meet the Aunties over dinner. Is it his fault that when they came home for summer, Eva was vacationing with Orlando in Paris? Or during holiday breaks, Cheryl was visiting Jordan?

It was a coincidence. He didn't *plan* it that way . . . is the story he's been telling for years.

Cheryl's mouth twitches. "I can ask him anything I want?"

"Within reason," Denz bargains.

This is a dangerous game. Offering Cheryl the chance to conduct her own TMZ interview with his fake boyfriend. But he's desperate.

Cheryl pretends to consider. A minute passes before she opens her clutch. Two clicks later, her phone's to her ear.

"Dahlia? Hey, girl. It's Cheryl Carter over at—Yes. I'm fine. How are the kids?" She paces in a small circle while talking. "I need a favor."

Denz peeks over his shoulder. God, he hopes no one else is around to hear this. Especially not his dad.

"I know it's a"—Cheryl's eyes cut to him—"*foolish*, rookie mistake. If you help us out, I can promise a certain Grammy-winning R and B artist's son will host his sweet sixteen at the Rigel this year. Yes, Usher. You know Tevin's producing his comeback album."

Denz cringes. Great. Now he's going to owe Uncle Tevin too.

"Just have him digitally sign?" Cheryl snaps her fingers at Denz.

"You're emailing him *right now?* Thank you. You're the best. Kiss those beautiful babies for me. Bye."

"Um . . ." Denz waits.

Cheryl's lips purse. "It's done. Anything else?"

"N-no." He can barely stand upright. "We got the space again?"

"*I* got the space," she tuts. "Sign the contract. You're in the clear. For now."

The pinch behind Denz's ribs finally subsides. "Thank you, Auntie."

"Mm-hmm." She snatches the cheesecake bag from his loose grip. "I'm leaving now. Goodbye, nephew."

When the elevator doors slide open, she adds, "I hope your boyfriend's ready for me" before stepping inside.

"Me too," Denz whispers to no one. As he stumbles back to his office, his eyes are drawn to a glow. The light in Kami's office is still on.

On a quiet street, in the heart of Decatur, is the bungalow Denz spent his early adolescence in. A charming three-bedroom with creaky hardwood floors and a finished basement where he and his sisters would play hide-and-seek-in-the-dark for hours. It was chilly in the winter. Too hot in the summer. But he had his own room with *Danny Phantom* and *Teen Titans* posters.

He loved it there.

Then came the overnight buzz from *Marvelous Weddings*. A more upscale clientele meant the Carters becoming a brand. The expectations of living that followed way too soon.

Now, his parents own a home on nearly seven acres, deep in the suburbs of Druid Hills. Denz loves it here too. Fresh lilies in the foyer. The walls and furniture are in neutral colors. Seven bedrooms, a private backyard where he can dip his feet in the heated pool, watch the sunset.

It's made the cover of *Atlanta Homes & Lifestyles* multiple times. But there are moments where he misses the modesty of that bungalow. The magic of simple.

On a late Sunday afternoon, he stands inside his parents' massive kitchen, waiting for commentary on the rose-colored Canali suit jacket he's wearing. The mayor's gala is less than two weeks away. Auntie Eva took one look at his proposed outfit options and demanded an emergency makeover.

"We're not fumbling the bag because you have no style."

Now, his career aspirations have become a group project. He's confident Eva cares more about beating Cheryl than what's at stake. Still, this is his fourth outfit in the last hour.

"What's wrong with my own clothes?" he says.

"You have the wardrobe of the forgettable best friend in a rom-com," comments Jamie as he smooths Denz's black lapels. "Your clothes are the Kevin of outfit choices."

"The *who?*"

"Exactly."

Jamie's fully invested in this *Project Runway* transformation. A needed distraction. Dinner with his parents was, of course, a trash fire.

From the living room, where she's putting together his next ensemble, Eva yells, "You can't show up wearing—God forbid—something *off the rack*. You need to look like a boss."

"That's my default mode, Auntie."

"Aww," Nic says from his left. "It's adorable how much you really believe that."

She's in a Paramore T-shirt and ripped jeans, her curls braided into cornrows. He doesn't consider her a fashion expert. But on such short notice, the opinions of his sister, mom, and nephew are all he has.

Jamie turns to the judges. "Well?"

"Six out of ten," Nic says. "Four-point deduction for the model's attitude."

He's going to murder her.

"Ten!" At least he can depend on Mikah's enthusiasm.

Leena says, "I liked the blue Armani one with the gold silk tie better."

Denz shoves his fist into his mouth. He wants to hop on the kitchen island and cry.

When his parents bought the house, they hired famed interior designer Rosa Hernández for her decorative vision. But there was one room she couldn't touch—the kitchen. That was his mom's project.

Leena grew up in a smaller home. Two bedrooms for her parents, herself, Aunt Avis, and Uncle Rashad. The kitchen was their lifeline. A place to cook and dance and laugh. The second she married into the Carters, she wanted a space big enough to hold all of that and more.

The finished product is a masterpiece. All-white marble countertops, black cabinets and doors, crème de menthe walls. A walk-in pantry and wine fridge. Denz doesn't consider himself religious, but this is his family's church. His sanctuary.

Before finding an apartment with Jamie, Denz moved back home. At night, when the house was blanketed in sleep, he'd sit on the island with his phone and a jar of peanut butter. He'd study popular influencers' accounts. Find the best apps for editing photos. Cling to any interruption from the fact that he was brokenhearted.

Alone, licking peanut butter off a spoon. What *real* adults do after college.

"The jacket's nice, sweetheart," Leena says encouragingly.

"You look like a waiter," Nic notes.

Jamie yells, "Auntie E, it's a big no!"

Under the hiss of a garment steamer and bags being unzipped, Denz hears Eva snapping instructions to the two assistants she bullied into working on a Sunday. "It's from *Target*? Burn it. Give me the Milan suit."

Leena pops a grape in her mouth from the bowl she's sharing with Mikah. "What's Braylon wearing?"

Denz loosens the top button of his shirt, stalling. That's something he should know, right? What his fake boyfriend's sporting to the biggest Valentine's event in the city?

Nic's eyes widen. "You don't know what *your own boyfriend* is wearing."

"Who cares?" Eva's head appears in the kitchen entryway. "It's *Denzel's* night. Braylon's arm candy."

"He's more than . . ." Denz stops when Eva raises a sharp eyebrow. Right. Braylon hasn't won *everyone* over yet.

"At least you two get to spend the most romantic night of the year together," Leena says.

Since Kami returned to work from maternity leave, Leena's volunteered to watch Mikah on event nights. But her absence started before then. She hasn't been to a party in years. Once 24 Carter Gold stepped away from weddings, holidays became their busiest times. And Kenneth never takes an event off.

Denz's parents never spend Valentine's Day with each other.

"Almost finished with look number five," Eva announces.

Leena rubs Mikah's curly 'fro. "Come on, baby. It's movie time."

Kami's started introducing Mikah to all the age-appropriate Studio Ghibli films. It's his mission to force anyone in his vicinity to rewatch them with him. Denz has seen *My Neighbor Totoro* an obscene number of times.

Jamie follows them out. Denz is alone with Nic. She pokes one of her lemon-yellow nails in his chest. "You're hiding something."

"Am I?"

"I know what's going on."

"You . . . do?" Denz stammers.

She eyes him, distrusting. "When Kami dropped Mikah off, she was *happy*. Walking-on-clouds happy. Getting-dick-regularly happy."

"*Jesus,* Nic! That's our sister."

"She's clearly in love. Just like you."

"I'm not—" He sputters. "I mean, *she's* not. In love. It's nothing."

"Bullshit." Nic taps the end of her nose. "I'm observant. Perceptive."

"Really getting all the mileage out of those SAT words, huh?"

A wry smile crawls over her lips. "Kami's got a man. She acts the same way you do whenever someone mentions Braylon."

"I don't act a . . . way," he says defensively.

"I'm not like the others. I don't have issues with Braylon." Her eyes soften. "I . . . missed him."

Denz's stomach twists guiltily. Nic didn't have the simple life he had before the Carters became a brand. She was born into constant public attention. As a result, she's always kept a small, tight-knit circle of friends. Somehow, Braylon made it into that group of people she genuinely cared about.

"Even after the breakup," she says, "I always thought he was the Peeta to your Katniss."

"The *who* to my *what?*"

"The One, genius!"

Funny thing is, Denz did too. A long time ago. It's silly to believe a first love is going to be who you spend the rest of your life with. That only happens in Reese Witherspoon movies. But the summer before senior year, Denz let himself dream: Sharing an apartment with Braylon after graduation. Coffee in bed together. Walks around the city. One day, falling to bended knee and proposing.

A Hallmark Christmas movie happy ending.

Then came Braylon's *Come with me? To London?* Emmanuel suggesting Braylon leave Denz behind when he took too long to give Braylon an answer.

"The One" is a concept Denz is no longer subscribing to.

"Nephew!" Eva says. "We're ready for you!"

He pastes on his best I-don't-hate-this smile. To Nic, he whispers, "Was the blue suit *that* bad?"

"You looked like the genie from *Aladdin*."

Fuck, he needs to find a better support system.

-8-

Today 10:58 A.M.

Formerly Known As Bray
How do astronomers organize a party?
They planet.

you thought this was FUNNY?

Formerly Known As Bray
Sorry. It's been a busy day at work.
I'm not on top of my game.

you can make it up to me tomorrow

Formerly Known As Bray
Wow! How did I get such a generous fake
boyfriend?

luck i guess

Denz can't believe he's working his lunch hour. He blames Auntie Eva. And his mom. Jamie and Nic too. Valentine's Day is fast approaching, and Denz can't let *anything* ruin the mayor's gala.

Including what his fake boyfriend is going to wear.

So, one quick Google search later, he's standing in front of a two-story building wedged between a small art gallery and a custom T-shirt printing shop. The exterior is white stucco with tall windows. In black lettering, surrounded by a rainbow circle, the sign reads, SKYE'S THE LIMIT.

On the double glass doors leading inside, a message awaits:

For the ones like Skye . . . you'll always belong here.

Denz smiles.

Sunlight washes across the interior. Pastel furniture is angled throughout the open space. A rainbow river painted on the cement floor winds through a collection of cubicles. Beyond that, hints of a lounge area, stairs, and an elevator.

Denz knows most of the colorful flags hung on the walls: pride, transgender, bisexual, pan, ace. There are a few he doesn't immediately recognize. A lavender, white, and dark green one. Another made up of oranges, reds, and pinks. A yellow flag with a purple circle.

He's met by a pretty, twentysomething Black person with a Skye's the Limit lanyard. The badge says WHITLEY, SHE/HER. Her sparkly blue nails tap against a defined bicep.

"Can I help you?"

Denz's eyes search around. Why didn't he text or call ahead? What if Braylon's not here? "I'm looking for—"

"Denz?"

The voice comes from one of the cubicles. Then Braylon strides cautiously into the lobby. He grips a mug of steaming tea.

Denz waves awkwardly. "Surprise?"

Braylon blinks owlish eyes. Whitley has one of those *should I call 911 or just pepper-spray his ass?* expressions. Denz is equally intimidated and awed.

"Sorry. Um, this is Whit." Braylon gestures toward his coworker, who may or may not be ready to take Denz down with a move she learned in a self-defense course. "And this is Denz. My . . . boyfriend."

A tiny, weird zip of heat runs through Denz's chest at that last word.

"Nice to meet you," he says to Whit.

She cocks her head. "So this is the guy that has you smiling at your phone like an idiot?"

Smirking, Denz says, "Well, this is new information."

"It's *false* information." Braylon clutches his mug tighter. "Shouldn't you be at work? Planning the gala?"

"That's why I'm here. I'll explain later." He turns to Whit. "Now, on average, how often is he smiling at his—"

"That's quite enough," tuts Braylon, stepping between them. Denz shrugs. "Hungry?"

The other part of the reason he's here is their earlier message exchange. By the sheer volume of emails Denz has gotten over the last few days, he can tell Braylon's pouring all his energy into the spring break day party. In college, between managing classwork, swimming, and a boyfriend, Braylon often forgot to eat if Denz wasn't there to remind him.

He's not saying he drove twenty-three minutes in traffic out of *concern* for Braylon's poor nutritional habits. He's simply performing his fake boyfriend duties.

"You want to have lunch?" Braylon frowns. *"Here?"*

"I do."

"And you won't mind if I work while eating?"

"Not at all. I need to answer emails about the gala, anyway."

For the most part, he's got everything under control. The mayor's staff seems happy. Eric and Connor have his back. He hasn't forgotten to triple-check all his Post-it Notes. But he keeps waiting for Auntie Cheryl to show up and reveal he's really three cats in a trench coat pretending to be an adult.

An hour or two away from the office can't hurt.

"I'll order delivery." Denz stretches onto his toes to search the cubicles. "Which one's yours?"

He offers Braylon a giant, billboard-ready grin. Whit appears thoroughly entertained by the exchange. A beat passes before the left side of Braylon's mouth ticks up.

"Actually, delivery sounds great."

"Let me get this straight, you eat these"—Denz lifts a fry—"with vinegar now?"

"They're quite good!" Braylon plucks one from his drenched pile. When he pops it in his mouth, chewing widely, Denz gags.

Braylon's cubicle can only be described as systemized mayhem. It's big enough for a desk, a rolling office chair, and two standard chairs for visitors. Piled in the empty seat next to Denz is a coat, scarf, and a stack of folders. Books and papers are everywhere else, just like Braylon's old dorm room. All that's missing is Denz's gray UGA sweatshirt.

They've been working and eating for thirty minutes now. Denz answers emails. Braylon runs through his list of what's needed for the day party. Things like vendors, donors, decorations, permits to host the event outdoors. The last five minutes, however, have been dedicated to Braylon's questionable condiment choices.

"Try one," he requests.

"I'd rather drink bleach." Denz dips a vinegar-free fry into his ketchup. "It's bad enough I'm voluntarily eating this trash, anyway."

Since he'd inconvenienced Braylon with his spontaneous appearance, the least Denz could do was order delivery from The Varsity. He has many regrets.

"You used to love their food," Braylon comments.

"False." Denz sips his Varsity Orange milkshake. "I *tolerated* it because you loved their food."

"Is that how you remember it?"

"Of course. Sophomore year, right?"

The corners of Braylon's mouth twitch.

Nothing happened between them at that graduation party when they were freshmen. Denz had only hooked up with one other guy before then. An encounter he didn't even initiate. And Braylon wasn't out yet. His anxious jumping at every new voice, thinking it was one of his teammates, didn't lift Denz's confidence.

By the end of the night, they parted ways without exchanging numbers.

Then came fall semester, sophomore year. A serendipitous

encounter at Miller Learning Center. Denz reaching for the same book as the man he thought he'd never see again.

A fumbled smile as he said, "Hi. Again."

Braylon's stuttered, "I-I'm out now. Can we go somewhere and talk?"

Denz didn't hesitate.

The red VARSITY sign on West Broad Street was a beacon. Denz wasn't a fan of their very average food or atmosphere. But in a corner of the parking lot, he found new things to love—the crush of orange soda and mustard and tingling pressure from Braylon's kisses.

He remembers it like this: a prickly buzz cut under his palms. Shaky hands tugging at his shirt. Even clumsier fingers unzipping his jeans. Hot breaths along his bare abdomen. A tentative tongue, lips closing around him.

An effortless first encounter? Not even close. But it was more than enough for Denz.

Too much, actually. Now, he's discreetly crossing his legs. The heat in his belly climbs fast into his cheeks. It doesn't help that his eyes can't tear away from Braylon licking malt vinegar off his fingertips. Denz clears his throat.

"So, what else has changed? You know, about you?"

Braylon tilts his head, confused.

Denz motions to the soggy fries. "This. The accent. Your hair. Tea—"

"What's wrong with tea?"

"You used to love Americanos!"

"In college, yes."

"Sorry to disappoint you," Denz says, agitated, "but that's the only Braylon I know. Not by choice."

A pause. Braylon frowns. "What about you, then?"

"What about me?"

Braylon crosses his arms. Denz doesn't *stare* at the shape of those biceps under his black Henley. He merely makes a mental note to hit the gym soon.

"When did blue become your favorite color?" Braylon asks.

"It's not."

Braylon gestures to the navy-and-white-striped Fendi sweater Denz is wearing. "You wore the same color to dinner with your parents."

Out of all the disastrous things from that night, Braylon remembers *that?*

"All my other shirts were wrinkled" is Denz's only defense.

"And the other day? At Crema?"

Denz scowls. "What's your point?"

"I should know these things about you," Braylon reasons. He rests his elbows on the desk, leaning forward, subjecting Denz to infuriatingly nice collarbones. "We can't convince anyone we're dating if I don't know what you like or hate now."

Denz's sigh echoes.

They're alone in the center. Whit left to run errands. Denz watches the door, thinking.

The second he was permanently back in his family's orbit, Denz had to change. Everything down to his wardrobe shifted. He was Denzel Carter again. He had an image to present. Who he was in Athens isn't who he was expected to be in Atlanta.

Thing is, he's never had to share those differences with anyone before.

"I hate wine," Denz admits.

"Have you—"

"Don't tell me I haven't found the right one yet," Denz interrupts. "I've tried them all. Perks of the job. It's a waste of time."

"Incorrect, but fair."

"Roller coasters make me sick now," Denz says. "It's . . . not pretty."

"Devastated we can't fake-date at Six Flags."

Denz hates how easily his own mouth mirrors Braylon's smirk. "Avocado on toast is overrated and trash."

"Wow. How can your opinions continue to get worse?"

"I contain multitudes."

"You contain rubbish," Braylon counters.

"Also . . ." Denz ignores Braylon's indignant expression when he plucks a single, drippy fry from his pile. "People who wear socks in bed are monsters."

He chews vindictively, frowning even though—*fuck him*—the vinegar's sharpness with the fries' saltiness is delicious. God, he's never telling anyone.

Braylon coughs. "Would that be before or after . . ."

Denz waits for him to finish. Spots of color flood his cheeks the second Whit marches back inside, ducking into her own cubicle, phone to her ear. Braylon chugs the last of his Varsity Orange, gathering their garbage.

He says, "Would you like a tour?" his previous sentence forgotten.

Afternoon sunlight glitters in from the floor-to-ceiling windows on the upper level. Beyond the sizable meeting table, a small study area, and rooms dedicated to mental health counseling is a corner office with a BORN THIS WAY rainbow flag on the door. Engraved on the gold plaque is:

NORA BRIDGER
FOUNDER & CEO

"She's on a trip to California," Braylon explains. "Business stuff." He doesn't elaborate. Denz doesn't ask any questions.

The buzzing phone in his back pocket alerts Denz that, technically, lunch is over. He should return to the office. But he's too captivated by Braylon reciting the nonprofit's history. He decides to record a video of Braylon talking about the fenced-in recreational space behind the building. The minute-and-ten-second clip reveals one important detail to Denz: this is where Braylon's meant to be.

He's a leader here.

Denz wonders if anyone at 24 Carter Gold sees him that way.

If that same fire is in his eyes when he discusses social media numbers and company buzz and what he wants their next steps to be. If anyone thinks of him as the next Kenneth Carter. Can they picture him sitting at his dad's desk? How would *Chief Executive Officer* look under his name in an email signature?

Does anyone see him as a man on the verge of greatness?

Kami's the strategist, the press darling, even when they try to break her. Nic is the rebellious prodigy, who never lets anyone see what cards she's holding. Denz is . . . the fun one. But does enjoying life mean no one will ever view him as a leader?

It's all he thinks about when they're downstairs again. "And don't mess with the espresso machine," Braylon is saying in the hybrid lounge/kitchen, a shared space for staff and the teens, "or Whit will properly end you."

"It's true!" Whit shouts from her cubicle.

Braylon stage-whispers, "Once, she made an intern cry. Over not cleaning it properly."

"And I'd do it again!"

Denz laughs.

"Oh," he says, remembering why he's really here, "what're you wearing to the gala?"

Braylon leads them back toward his cubicle.

"A suit? Something . . . black?" Braylon pauses, a knot between his eyebrows. "Should I wear a bow tie?"

Denz can already hear Auntie Eva the moment Braylon walks into the ballroom: *A basic, boring black tux on the biggest night of your boyfriend's career?* He doesn't need that kind of stress in his life.

"Don't wear red. Too cliché," Whit warns from somewhere near the front.

"What are your measurements?" Denz unlocks his phone. If he hurries, maybe Eva can work another *Devil Wears Prada* miracle.

"Why?" Braylon crosses his arms, clearly aware of what Denz is attempting. "What are *you* wearing?"

Denz hasn't decided. He's leaning toward the Mikah-approved

ivory single-breasted Tom Ford blazer with coral slacks. "I have options," he tells him, swiping through outfits on his phone. "Nothing gray or black or—"

"Boring?"

"I-I didn't say that." If he stammers, it's not because Braylon's firm chest is suddenly pressed against the wings of Denz's shoulder blades. His chin hovering over Denz's taut shoulder.

"Your face implied it."

"That's harsh."

Braylon swipes back one photo. "The maroon. Not as flashy as everyone expects the Carters' Golden Boy"—he ignores Denz's offended gasp—"to look, but I like it."

"You do?"

Braylon never answers. A cacophony of voices comes through the front door. Five teens in scarves and hats and heavy coats. They toss garments around like this is home. Conversations abruptly change directions, one after another, until eyes fall on Braylon and Denz.

"Holy sh—" A Black girl with lavender knotless braids cuts herself off. "Is that hashtag notthatdenzel?"

"Kennedi," a freckle-faced white boy with multicolored braces hisses. "There's no way Denz Carter is—"

Denz grins, waving.

"Patrick, it's him," Kennedi squeals. She smacks the shoulder of a lanky brown-skinned boy next to her. "Malik, weren't you just watching that video of him talking to LeBron and—"

"Quite the scene you've caused," Braylon whispers to Denz.

Denz doesn't go rigid at the ghost of warm breath against his ear. His stomach doesn't knot, and his cock certainly doesn't plump up just a little. He's a twenty-five-year-old adult with self-control.

"Denzel Carter," Braylon announces, edging away, "please meet some of the teens I work with: Kennedi, Patrick, Quinn, Malik, and Rowan. They're in a work-study program, which is why they're not in class."

Denz slips on his most charming, effervescent smile.

"Hello."

Instantly, a dozen questions are launched at him. Things like: How much is he paid for ads? What free stuff does he receive? What equipment does he use? Is he related to Jay-Z and, therefore, Beyoncé?

He laughs, answering one at a time.

When Rowan, a short nonbinary teen, asks, "How do you know Mr. Adams?" Denz hesitates. In his periphery, Braylon's frozen.

"College," Denz says.

"We have—" Braylon rubs his jaw. "—history."

"That means sex," Quinn stage-whispers.

The group giggles, waggling their eyebrows. Braylon face-palms. Denz fights off a snort, absently moving an inch to his left.

Closer to Braylon.

He doesn't notice it at first. Braylon's arm sliding around his waist. But as more questions pour in, he inhales notes of cardamom, feels protective fingers on his hip, hears the rasp of laughter somewhere above him.

"That's quite enough," Braylon says, stepping back.

Is it? Denz thinks, until he realizes Braylon's talking to the teens.

"You lot have work to do, correct?"

"Okay, Mr. A," Malik concedes. His gaze shifts to Denz. "You'll come back, right?"

Denz glances up. He forgets to be angry about the height difference between him and Braylon, too caught on the question in those brown eyes.

Will you come back?

"Uh, yeah," Denz stammers. "Definitely."

Several texts are awaiting Denz when he's outside. All from Eric ranting about a Real Housewife who's furious she was left off the mayor's invite list. As if anyone's forgotten the *married politician* she drunkenly flirted with at the last party she attended.

Denz adds a reminder to call her later.

The afternoon breeze kisses pink into Braylon's cheeks. The same shade of his bow-shaped lips. Denz's eyes linger for a second. Then five. He should go.

Problem is, he's not sure how to say goodbye?

It was one spontaneous lunch. It's not like he needs to hug Braylon or kiss him on the cheek. No one's around to see them together.

"That was fun," Denz gets out.

"Even being forced to eat food from The Varsity?"

"'Forced' is a strong word," Denz says, jamming hands into his coat pockets. "Coerced, maybe."

Braylon bites his lower lip. A flash of white teeth that used to leave gentle indentations around Denz's nipple. God, he needs to go.

"Well," Denz tries. "I won't keep you. I have extra work now that we didn't get much done."

Braylon sniffs. "Are you calling me a distraction?"

"I'm saying get your ass inside before you catch the flu." Denz exhales a plume of white smoke. Braylon's slipped outside with only a beanie on, no coat. "You can't have the flu with my big day around the corner."

"*Your* big day? That's not very boyfriend-like."

Denz unhappily tilts his chin up. *"Ours?"*

"Better." Braylon grins. "Next time, I won't be so chatty. We'll work at separate cubicles."

Next time. Is that an open invitation? Denz wishes Braylon's face wasn't so enigmatic.

"Cool." Denz coughs. "I'm just gonna—"

"Wait."

Braylon edges closer. Denz can smell a hint of vinegar as he exhales. His warmth is overpowering, his soft palm grazing Denz's cheek, his thumb stroking over Denz's upper lip.

"You have—"

An unprovoked rush of muscle memory overtakes Denz. He

steps onto his toes. His hands instinctively rest on Braylon's chest for balance. His head tilts. He's ready for . . .

"—ketchup. Right here," Braylon finishes, pupils widening at Denz's sudden proximity.

At Denz being inches from his mouth. From *kissing* him.

"Shit!" Denz stumbles back. "I shouldn't have—"

"No, no. It's fi—"

"Sorry. Oh fuck. I'm so sorry."

"Denz, are you—"

"Going," he rushes out before Braylon finishes. "Bye!"

In the safety of his car, heat blasting, fingers gripping the steering wheel, Denz replays the last two minutes. From *I'm just gonna* to *Bye!*

Every painful second.

He anticipates a text from Braylon. Any moment now. An official ending of their agreement.

When the message never arrives, Denz slumps in his seat. Calm seeps into his bones. Reality slowly shifts from the margins into focus.

Somewhere in those two mortifying minutes, he *thinks* Braylon Adams said it was fine that Denz almost kissed him.

-9-

Mayor Tiffany Reynolds's yearly Valentine's Day gala is a glamorous, unforgettable spectacle.

Only a hundred tickets are made available to the public. Another hundred are reserved for the mayor's family, close friends, staff, and some notable singles. At her heart, she's like Kenneth Carter—a determined matchmaker. More than once, she's attempted to set Denz up. He always declines in favor of his true soulmate: top-shelf vodka.

But tonight, Denz has an actual date. An exceptionally *late* date.

The step-and-repeat outside the Rigel is a who's who of celebrities and athletes and political influencers. Denz doesn't spend much time there. No one's noticed he's alone either.

Coming out at an early age means the media doesn't care about his love life unless he's making out with an attractive model or there's a scandal involved. He's at that age where he's still a hot topic in the gossip columns. However, in queer years, he's teetering on the edge of being aged out for the young, sparkly, freshly out gays that gossip sites like The Final Word love to write about.

He's okay with that.

The Orion Ballroom is a sleek space with lofty ceilings, four bars, and wall-to-wall screens featuring immersive artwork. The crowd quickly fills up empty tables and the expansive dance floor. Eric convinced Denz to hire DJ Apollo rather than a live band. A cycle of love-adjacent themed songs vibrates through the ballroom.

Currently, it's Lady Gaga's "Bad Romance."

Apropos for the way Denz feels about his situation.

He distracts himself by inspecting the details: cascading strings of black and red rose petals suspended from the ceiling. Cupid ice sculptures bookending the bars. Trays of champagne flutes with wild hibiscus flowers floating inside. The room's centerpiece—an eight-tier red velvet cake. Staff blurs by him in white tuxedo jackets, wearing crimson-and-gold domino masks.

What's a party without a little drama?

The atmosphere is magnetic. Laughter and music and bottles continuously popping. He captures it all for the company's social media.

"You really pulled it off," Kami comments when he pauses at one of the bars. Her lavender, one-shoulder minidress has gold foil designs all over it.

"Did you doubt me?"

She sips her wine, shrugging.

"You did," Denz accuses, smiling. "What? You thought I'd hire a magician? Have a clown make terrible balloon animals?"

"A bounce house would've been a hit with this crowd."

He doesn't disagree. The current tide of young actors and reality stars jumping around to the Darkness's "I Believe in a Thing Called Love" is just shy of ridiculous.

"Admit it." Denz bumps her shoulder. "I'm damn good at this."

"I'd pay you to plan Mikah's seventh birthday party."

He laughs, ordering a glass of water from the nearest bartender. Deep down, Denz knows it's her pride talking. His success could potentially end a dream she's had for years. He hates that winning means his sister loses.

At least one of them will carry on the family's legacy.

"Is Suraj coming?"

"No," Kami says flatly. "I'm working."

"You're *drinking*."

She takes another languid sip. "An essential part of managing you on event nights."

"I don't need babysitting," he says defensively. "It's all under control. My checklists are flawless." He downs his water. "You're avoiding the question. It's *Valentine's*. Your boyfriend should be here."

"*Lower your voice.*" Kami's eyes dance around the ballroom, as if that word—"boyfriend"—could summon the aunties. "Who said we're using official titles?"

Denz shakes his head. "You've been hiding him from our family for months. If that isn't a boyf—"

"Where's *Braylon?*" she counters.

Denz looks away. The last texts he got from Braylon, over forty minutes ago, were equally chaotic and apologetic:

Sorry. Running late. We had a bowling day for
the teens.
Showered and changed. Sorry again. Leaving
home!
Loads of traffic. Will be there soon. Very sorry!

Denz slaps on a big, fake smile. "He's coming. I can't wait. I miss him."

"Calm down, Ryan Reynolds," Kami says, giving him a weird look. "We get it. You love Blake."

Denz squawks but his comeback is intercepted by Jordan appearing at their sides. He swipes a champagne glass, shouting, "On your six!"

Kenneth breaks through the crowd in a striking Stefano Ricci tuxedo. On his arm, in a sleeveless red gown with a tiered skirt, is Mayor Reynolds.

Jordan squares his shoulders. Kami smooths down her dress, eyes twinkling. That's when Denz notices the photographers trailing the mayor. Well, fuck. He rests his empty glass on the bar before turning on his own practiced charm.

"The Carter Trio," Mayor Reynolds says. She's a tall, curvy woman with fawn skin and a freckled face. A glimmering tiara sits atop her teased hair. She hugs Kami, then Jordan. "Denzel, this party is heavenly. People can't stop talking about it."

"Anything for you, Mayor."

"Oh, *please*. Call me Tiffany."

Denz grins but doesn't cross that line. Not with his dad watching nearby. "I'm glad you're enjoying yourself," he says over a Maroon 5 ballad.

"This might be the best V-Day gala yet!"

Very cautiously, Denz glances to her left. He waits for his dad's approving smile. It's more of a stiff nod.

"Thanks for fixing that last-minute menu catastrophe," the mayor goes on.

Denz freezes.

Hundreds of emails were exchanged over the last month. He answered a dozen this morning alone. But in all the *do we really need a meeting for this?* messages, he doesn't remember approving a menu alteration. It's been set since last week.

He tugs at his collar. "Um, no problem?"

"I'm so embarrassed. My team forgot to include my husband's lactose intolerance in the dietary restrictions list," the mayor says.

"Oh, yeah." Denz swallows bile. He can sense his dad's heavy stare on him. "All fixed."

"Justin loved the broccoli fritters," the mayor tells him.

"Amazing, right?"

"And the tomato basil bruschetta."

"Who doesn't love a great bruschetta!"

Denz needs to find out who handled this oversight without letting *him* in on the issue.

"Justin's been asking all night," the mayor continues, "for the crispy baked asparagus fries recipe. The ones with the—" She pauses, hands on her hips while watching Denz sweat.

"The, uh," he stammers.

"The spicy garlic aioli," Kami proposes. "Remember you had me taste-test it?"

Denz nods robotically. "Yes. You did."

"They were phenomenal," the mayor says.

As Jordan segues into a conversation about the specially crafted cocktails for the night, Denz shoots Kami a grateful look. She changed the menu. He's happy that one more tiny fuckup hasn't ruined his chances. But he's humiliated and angry too.

How did his team miss this? How did *he*?

"Denz," Mayor Reynolds says when one of her staffers tries to drag her away to meet a senator's daughter and her girlfriend. "Check in with me before the big speech, okay?"

"Of course."

She disappears. Kenneth tugs Jordan aside, whispering instructions Denz can't hear. He whips around to Kami.

"How could you?"

"What?" she whispers.

Denz matches her volume: "You didn't consult with me before intervening with *my* event."

"Is it my fault I'm BCC'd on all communication from the mayor's people? There wasn't time to ask your permission," she reasons. "I did what was best for the company."

"Next time, don't treat me like I'm five. I'm an *adult*."

She guffaws. "Then stop acting like—"

"Are you two okay?"

When Denz turns, Jordan's gone, but Kenneth isn't alone. Cheryl's there in a shimmery minidress. Eva's gold-leaf hairpiece complements the Aphrodite-inspired gown she's wearing.

"What a star-studded party, Denzel," Cheryl says. "Was that *the* Malcolm Givhan from By Invitation Only by the hors d'oeuvres?"

Denz grins smugly. "Maybe."

"He never comes to our events."

"You two look . . ." Eva scrutinizes them. "What's a word below 'lovely'?"

"Decent," Cheryl suggests. "Theme appropriate, though."

Denz bites his tongue. *Sorry we can't all be attention-seeking like Uncle Tevin in his all-white ensemble, Auntie C.C.*

"Denzel," Eva exhales. "I thought we agreed on the Tom Ford jacket and red tie?"

They didn't, technically. And, well . . . Denz isn't dressed in the Paul Smith maroon suit with matching loafers because of what Braylon said the other day. But he's not-*not* wearing it because of that either.

"I didn't want to outshine the host."

"At least the party understands the assignment," Eva notes. "You have a lot to live up to with your event, Kamila."

Kami manages a tight, calculated smile.

"Where's your date, Denzel?" Eva searches the crowd. "Is it over already?"

Denz flinches. "No—"

"Don't worry, nephew," Cheryl cuts in. "In case your . . . *boyfriend* decides to ditch you for another country again, we have a plan." She gestures toward the other end of the bar where a man chats with the bartender.

He's handsome: fair sepia complexion, a perfectly styled pompadour. Any other night, Denz would be locked in an unoccupied office, learning what's under that jade suit, but he's not interested. Frankly, he's scared to question *why.*

"His name's Javier," Cheryl tells him. "Javi for short."

Kami says, "Doesn't he work for Elite Events?"

"Keep your enemies closer, Kamila," Eva replies.

"Sorry," Denz says, incredulous. "Did you invite a man who works at our *competitor* as my backup date?"

"We're looking out for you!" Cheryl's sympathetic eyes say, *because things didn't work last time.*

Denz doesn't need the reminder. Or a plan B. "I'm good. My relationship's good," he says firmly. "Braylon's just—"

Very, un-fucking-believably late.

"I'm here!"

A body nestles into Denz's side. He wills himself not to gasp at Braylon's freshly shaven face. His strong jaw under the ballroom's lighting. How his shoulders look in the Boss tuxedo

Denz suggested he wear. Those apologetic eyes staring back at him.

"Happy Valentine's Day." His fingers squeeze Denz's hip.

"You too," Denz whispers.

"Sorry I'm late," Braylon says, smiling dreamily. "Can I make it up to you?"

"Sure?"

He doesn't mean to answer with a question of his own. It's just that—*Jesus*. The sincerity in Braylon's voice is next-level acting.

Jamie could never.

A pair of throats clear noisily.

On cue, Braylon turns, hand extended. "Apologies. Aunt Cheryl and Eva, correct?" He smiles at Kenneth next. "Lovely to see you again, Mr. Carter."

"You *finally* made it," Kenneth says.

"Traffic was an absolute nightmare," Braylon explains while kissing Kami's cheek, half hugging her. "Beautiful as ever, Kami. I've missed you and Nic. Is she here?"

"It's a *school* night," Kenneth grunts.

Kami says, beaming, "She's dying to see you."

"I can't wait to see her."

"So." Eva sizes up Braylon. "You're Denz's boyfriend."

"Boyfriend the sequel," Cheryl corrects over the thrum of a Whitney Houston cover of "Higher Love."

Denz sighs. *Here we fucking go.* But Braylon's warm, unbothered laugh sings above Denz's grim thoughts.

"Yes. I suppose it is a part two."

"There won't be a trilogy," Eva bites.

"I should hope not," Braylon says earnestly. "We're quite serious about each other."

Cheryl cocks a hip. "And how did you two get back together?"

"We, uh."

Denz can't answer quick enough. They never rehearsed their fictious backstory. Not like he had with Jamie. His parents didn't ask at dinner either. Now, he's without a lie that'll not only convince the aunties, but Kami and his dad too.

"Shockingly enough," Braylon starts, "it was at a Halloween party."

"At a bar," Denz jumps in.

Braylon nods. "I'd got quite pissed on tequila. We've all been there, right?"

"Unfortunately," Eva confirms under her breath.

Next to her, Kenneth remains expressionless.

"I'd run across Denz's socials before," Braylon continues. "I'm a program director at an LGBTQ+ youth center. It's important to know what queer influencers interest them."

"You saw one of my videos," Denz inserts, trying to keep up.

"Yes. I found out we were both at—"

"The Velvet Room."

"And I DM'd you like a right git." Something flashes in Braylon's eyes. "I was too intimidated to approach you."

"Because you left him for London," Cheryl suggests, an edge to her voice.

"Sadly, yes." Braylon doesn't shrink under the aunties' challenging glares. He's not overwhelmed by Kenneth's presence either. His focus lands back on Denz. "But I walked up to you. I said the music was too loud and—"

"We went to the patio," Denz says.

"You laughed when I spilled my drink."

"You ruined my shirt just like I ruined yours when we first met," Denz confirms, as if any of this actually happened. "I asked you to walk around downtown with me."

"I bought you a s'mores doughnut because—"

"I'd never had one."

The room drops away. No spinning lights. No Taylor Swift's "Love Story." Only Braylon and him, standing on a city corner under a streetlamp. Awkward smiles and unexpected laughs and never needing words to fill up the space between them.

"We talked for hours," Braylon almost whispers. "Made up for lost time."

Denz inhales shakily. It's not real. He went to a Halloween party at the Velvet Room. Posted about it on social media. But after two hours of mingling and cheap drinks and disinterested flirting with strangers, Denz went home.

Alone.

But, somewhere in his belly, he wishes this is what really happened.

At his side, Kami hisses, "Fuck me."

Yeah, Denz thinks. He grimaces. *No. Absolutely not.*

"Sorry," he says, tugging on Braylon's hand. "My boyfriend's dying to meet the mayor. Big fan. Enjoy the party!"

The dance floor's crowd swallows them up. With all the gyrating bodies, Denz is forced to squeeze Braylon's hand tighter. He ignores the indignant yelp from behind him, too frustrated to care.

How could he let that happen? Giving Braylon permission to tell their fake reunion story. Sure, it was sweet, endearing even. But it was too perfect. *Doughnuts?* Please, everyone knows Denz is a muffin man. The aunties are probably having a cackle while dissecting every silly, incorrect detail Braylon put in there.

Denz might drink himself into a real coma before the night's over.

"Would you slow down."

He barely hears Braylon's gruff voice over Prince's "Kiss." Denz stops abruptly, spinning around to growl, "What was that?"

Braylon's eyes widen. "What. Was. What?"

"*That.*" Denz gesticulates toward the bar. His dad and Kami are gone, but the aunties are still there, watching like vultures zoned in on a decaying body. "The whole—you know!"

"I have no clue what you're talking about."

"The *story*, Braylon," Denz snaps.

"Wait." Braylon shakes his head, disappointed. "You're upset because I saved you from making an utter arse of yourself in front of your family?"

"Stop talking like Hugh Grant. I was gonna improvise."

"You were going to fail."

"Thanks for the vote of confidence."

Braylon glowers. "What was wrong with what I said?"

Over Braylon's shoulder, Denz clocks Eva being hauled to the dance floor by Uncle Orlando. Cheryl's clutching her phone, thumbs at the ready to transcribe the latest entry in the *Keeping Up with the Carters* group chat.

Pasting on a sparkling smile, Denz says, "You were too perfect. It was like a fantasy date recap on *The Bachelor*."

"And that's a bad thing?"

"You've seen that show, right?"

"Of course. It's all Kami and me talked about." Braylon steps closer. "Sorry if my attempt to help you land a promotion by pretending we magically fell back in love came off as cheesy."

"Like a jar of Cheez Whiz." Denz's shoulders droop. "And we're doing this for you too."

"Are we? You still haven't held up your end of the deal."

"You'll meet the mayor."

"When?"

Denz strains to hold his grin. To not shove Braylon into the champagne tower. He wishes Braylon would stop staring at him like that. With his stupid, pouty mouth. The one Denz almost kissed the other day.

A Rihanna song he's heard a hundred times before comes on. Denz remembers this:

January, sophomore year. Sitting in the passenger seat of Braylon's Corolla, fingers tangled over the center console. The low hum of the radio. Braylon singing along with Rihanna while staring at him. Denz refusing to get out of the car, even though he was late for class, a constant rotation of *I never want to say goodbye to this boy* in his head.

Now, Braylon grumbles, "Can't believe I'm apologizing for being the Prince Charming you asked me to be."

Denz sighs out, "You're right."

"I . . . am?"

"I'm not holding up my part. Would you like to meet Mayor Reynolds?"

A pause. Braylon's eyes narrow suspiciously.

"It's not a trick question," Denz grunts. "I'm not going to trip you or anything."

"I know."

"Then what?"

The edge to Braylon's face softens. "I'm thinking about what I want to say to her."

Denz recognizes all the little tics. Like that night in Braylon's car, right before he met Denz's parents. He considers offering a suggestion, maybe an opening line, but decides on a different tack.

He threads his fingers through Braylon's. Refuses to acknowledge how *effortless* the movement is.

"Come on. I'll do the talking."

Soon, they're in the mix of Mayor Reynolds and her team. Denz turns on the Carter charm before introducing Braylon. He talks up all the work the nonprofit's doing for Atlanta's queer youth. Some of the goals Braylon mentioned at the center. The mayor listens intently, and Denz doesn't release Braylon's hand until he knows he has her.

He steps back.

"Mayor—I mean, Tiffany," Denz says with a practiced laugh, "could we get a photo?" His phone's already in hand as her assistant begins to protest. He pleads, "For the teens?"

The start of a dimple appears in Mayor Reynolds's cheek as she sidles up to Braylon, shooing the anxious assistant back.

"You know I love the kids."

Nervously, Braylon rests an arm around her waist.

It's the perfect shot. The popping red of the mayor's gown with the sleek black of Braylon's tux. Her tiara glimmers. Braylon's smile glows, his attention fully focused on the camera.

Denz sends the image to their text thread. He watches Braylon talk animatedly with his hands. Mayor Reynolds nods, beaming. A warm feeling spreads in Denz's chest that he tries to blame on the alcohol. Except, he hasn't had any.

Maybe it's how successful the party is. Or that intense sensation of accomplishing more than one goal. Knowing he did something good for someone.

He doesn't want to dwell too much on it.

When the mayor's impatient staffers give the universal *wrap it up* signal, she graciously waves at Braylon. "I'll be expecting an email with details about that event soon!" she yells while being escorted away.

Braylon stumbles over to him, eyes glassy.

"That . . . just happened?"

"It did," Denz confirms.

"You don't understand," Braylon says. "I've been chasing her for *months*. No response to emails or phone calls. Total silence. But we just spoke for five minutes." An indecipherable glint flashes across his eyes. "Denz, *you* . . ."

Denz waits. Again, Braylon leaves his last sentence unfinished. But he squeezes Denz's hand firmly.

Denz is *not* blushing at the touch.

"Big deal," he says. "I made an intro. It's nothing."

Braylon's gaze catches on something behind Denz. "Your dad," he whispers, ducking his head, "is watching us."

"Ah." Denz could tell that Kenneth still wasn't convinced by their act. He says dismissively, "You know how he is. Not as easy to win over as the others. Kind of stubborn."

"Like his son."

"Don't make me regret what I just did for you."

"No, no. I wouldn't dare." Braylon chews the inside of his cheek. "Should we, um, give him more proof?"

"What do you mean?"

"Well." His eyes sweep Denz's face. "Should we kiss? To prove earlier wasn't simply a show?"

"Oh," Denz says hoarsely.

Should they? It might help. Denz is supposed to be concentrating on the party. He's here to impress his dad with his leadership abilities, not make out with his—unreasonably hot—fake boyfriend. Though, with Braylon's face so close, he's finding it harder and harder to reason against the idea.

"Are you okay with it?" he asks, low, unsure.

"It's in the agreement."

It *is* in the agreement:

> #3: Kissing is allowed, but only with verbal consent.

Denz swallows, palms sweaty. "Is it okay if I kiss you? For, like, evidence. Or whatever."

Wide brown eyes darken. This was a mistake. Braylon's suggestion was a joke. He doesn't actually *want* to kiss him. And Denz should have never—

Braylon's lips are on his.

He's *kissing* Denz.

At first, it's awkward. Noses colliding, foreheads knocking. Denz is eager to make it look cinematic, to fool everyone into believing they're in love, but this is all wrong.

Until Braylon leans into it.

His hands cup Denz's cheeks. The new angle eases a sigh from Denz's lips. His knees shouldn't be unsteady. This kiss is nothing like their first one at The Varsity. That was reckless and fun and real.

This is . . . a performance.

A fucking Emmy-worthy one.

A sly flick of tongue. The soft skin where stubble was. Pressure that tingles from lips to spine to toes.

Denz pulls away, heartbeat erratic. He refuses to assess Braylon's expression. Pick it apart to see if he felt any of what Denz just did.

"Okay," he croaks. "The mayor's speech. I need to. Er, get onstage soon."

Where the hell was Connor with an itinerary and a credible excuse for Denz to walk away?

Braylon's mouth twitches. Denz doesn't stay long enough to see if it's a smile or a frown. He rushes to the corner where his team is staged. Denz gives himself thirty seconds to find his chill. Eric passes him a bottled water, not saying a word.

When Denz unlocks his phone to review his speech notes, the first thing that appears is the photo of Braylon standing tall in his tux, smiling right at the camera.

Denz can't help grinning back.

-10-

Denz is too busy after Valentine's Day to think about . . . other things.

Things like tripping and almost falling off the stage before introducing the mayor at the gala.

Things like watching Uncle Tevin drunkenly convince half the guests to join him in doing the Cupid Shuffle after the speeches.

Things like The Kiss.

The work doesn't end after the last toast, and the venue is cleaned and the reviews from "Denzel Carter's biggest night yet"—as stated on TFW—pour in. On Monday, the follow-up emails begin. Assignments for his dad's retirement party land in his inbox before 10:00 A.M. Getting an early start on finding a band, bargaining with the photographer for a better rate, coordinating the guest list is key.

By Friday, he's buried in new tasks.

There's no time for freaking out over nothing. The Kiss is in the back of his mind. It's the Florida of his thoughts—he knows it's there but refuses to acknowledge it.

Except when he checks his social media. After exiting the Orion Ballroom's stage, he wrangled Braylon into taking a photo of their clasped hands next to a half-eaten slice of red velvet cake. The comments are nonstop.

@yessskstew: we love to see gay men happy and committed! who is he? #cute ♥♥♥

@denzelcarterstans: omg did u give him ur other cake later???

It's fine. He's still a perfectly functional adult. Until his phone buzzes with a new text from Braylon.

On a scale from 1 to 10, you're a 9.
And I'm the 1 you need.

Denz can't stop the snort that escapes him. It's fucking *adorable*. He never expected Braylon to follow through so thoroughly on this part of their agreement.

Braylon never misses a day. Always has the daddiest of dad jokes. Denz almost wants to tell him that he doesn't have to put in this much effort. He doesn't have to make Denz smile like this— big and cheek-aching, eyes scrunched. But he doesn't want it to stop either.

He immediately texts back: do you steal all your material from Russell Brand?

Braylon's reply hits a second later: No. James Corden. He's funny, right?

you can't be serious, Denz sends.

Deadly.

Denz's monitor chimes with a new email: a list of caterer suggestions from Eric. He's supposed to be working. Which he will . . . just as soon as he sends one more message to Braylon.

did i tell you kami has a secret boyfriend?

I think the rules state you're not supposed to
TELL people if it's a SECRET.

Once Denz replies to Eric with the name and contact information for the caterer from his parents' last wedding anniversary— the one his mom couldn't stop raving about—he texts, fine. dont get mad when i dont share any embarrassing pics from his archaic facebook with you.

I won't. Because then he'd still be a SECRET.

Denz's email chimes again. He texts, you're no fun.

It's two minutes before Braylon's next answer comes in.

You're a dreadful brother and fake boyfriend.

Denz laughs so loud, he doesn't hear the knuckles rattling against his office door. Eric steps inside, eyebrows high on his forehead. Denz knocks over his candy bowl trying to recover.

"I was just about to—"

"Your dad sent me," Eric interrupts. He loosens his tie, his expression grim. "He wants to talk to you. Sounds serious."

Denz's gaze leaps to his monitor. The last unread email isn't from Eric. It's from Kenneth Carter, the subject line in all caps.

MY OFFICE NOW

It's 3:52 P.M. when Denz slides onto the lavender love seat in his dad's office. Thick, battleship-gray clouds gather outside the windows. In the distance, the early rumbles of thunder. It matches the sound of Denz's heartbeat. Silence stretches like taffy as he watches his dad roll up the sleeves of a rose-pink shirt from behind his desk.

Kenneth clicks away at his keyboard.

Denz resists his left leg's urge to jiggle. Other than during meetings or at events, his dad's not a big talker, a trait none of his children inherited. However, when he's this quiet, it's never a good sign.

Two more clicks. A curious hum.

Denz stops breathing.

"'A visually stunning atmosphere, from the custom Love Potion martini to the ballroom showered in glitter following inspiring speeches in support of local charities,'" Kenneth reads from his monitor, pushing his glasses up. "'Mayor Reynolds's annual Valentine's Day gala was a dazzling, not-to-be-missed celebration. On a holiday soaked in over-the-top commercialism, the gala managed to impress its hundreds of guests with the right hint of magic thanks to Denzel Carter, from premier event-planning company 24 Carter Gold. Reynolds eagerly credits Mr. Carter for delivering the electric pulse to a night meant for hearts of all kinds.'"

Denz rubs his knees anxiously.

"A review from Malcolm Givhan," Kenneth says, pointing at the screen, "in By Invitation Only."

By Invitation Only is the *People* to The Final Word's *US Weekly*. Equally reputable, depending on the kind of content you're looking for. Personally, Denz is way more into "Who Wore It Worse?" than "The 40 Most Beautiful Atlantans Under 40," but whatever.

A smile pokes at the corners of Kenneth's mouth. "They haven't reviewed one of our events in *three years*."

Denz knows. Getting Malcolm to even glance at one of his emails was a week's worth of work.

"Nice job, son."

The knot between Denz's shoulder blades begins to fade. It's been nonstop around the office for almost two months. The beginning of the year is always busy for them—everyone needing to celebrate something after coming off several of the biggest holidays for proposals. He hasn't had a moment all week to recap the mayor's party with his dad.

"Thanks," Denz says, sitting taller.

"The numbers on socials look good too." Kenneth rocks back in his chair, tugging off his glasses. "I've been waiting for things to slow down so we can talk."

"Dad, are things ever slow?"

"Never." Kenneth rests his glasses on the desk. Folds his hands. "Your boyfriend made quite the impression on your aunts."

Another thing Denz knows. Auntie Cheryl didn't even wait until Sunday morning to spam the group chat with her review of Braylon.

Tall! Handsome! Intelligent! she wrote. *Works at a nonprofit for*

LGBTQ teens. Perfect for the family image. Better than the other sketchy guys Denzel's been seen with.

"Eva didn't hate what he was wearing," Kenneth jokes.

"And . . . you—?"

Denz leaves room for his dad's thoughts. The sudden tension in his jaw is the only answer Denz needs.

"I didn't call you in here to talk about him," Kenneth says. "The gala was one of our best showings in a long time."

Denz nods. He hasn't given himself a minute to take in the success. His first major solo event. "A dazzling, not-to-be-missed celebration," apparently. Hearing the review read by his dad, in the office where all his dreams began, where his next dreams are forming, is a euphoric kind of high he never imagined reaching this young.

"And yet it was almost a complete disaster," Kenneth goes on with a deep frown. "You failed to read the email about the mayor's husband's dietary restrictions."

Oh, hello Other Shoe. Thanks for finally dropping.

"About that," Denz attempts. "I—"

Kenneth cuts in. "You clearly weren't the one who handled the issue. Thankfully, nothing awful came of your mistake."

"Did Kami tell you?"

She's the only one who knew, he thinks.

"What? No." Kenneth scowls. "You thought I didn't catch on at the party? That I'm unaware of what's happening at my own company? Out of everyone here, Kami would be the *last* person to sell you out."

Denz bites the inside of his lip. He's an asshole for assuming his sister would do that. Even though she *did* go behind his back to fix things.

"What had you so distracted?" Kenneth asks, sighing. "Your relationship?"

"No." Denz can't explain the slight edge in his tone. His defensive posture. "It's not Braylon."

"I didn't say it was *him*."

Denz tries not to crumble under the weight behind that one sentence.

"Dad, it was one mistake."

"One mistake can cost you clients," Kenneth says, frustrated. "Thousands of dollars. Your reputation. *Someone's health.* More importantly, the trust and belief of your staff."

Denz doubts a bad case of diarrhea or bloating is going to influence how Kim, or an intern, looks at him, but he doesn't voice that aloud.

"Being in charge means taking every small, simple, tedious detail seriously," Kenneth tells him.

"I know that."

"Do you?" Kenneth challenges. "Having Carter as your last name won't save you when you mess up."

"I don't need it to," Denz says quietly.

Kenneth exhales like someone who's spent an entire day in shoes two sizes too small and has had enough. "Son, I've had amazing clients. I've also had plenty who used any excuse to shit on all the hard work we've put into this world."

Denz's knuckles ache from squeezing his fists so tightly. He stares past his dad. To the charcoal sky outside.

He thinks about his favorite 24 Carter Gold event:

His parents' fifteenth wedding anniversary. He was ten, watching everything through the gilded banister of a rented mansion. His mom's dream was to have the Cinderella-inspired wedding reception they never got the first time around.

His dad didn't disappoint.

He remembers lush gowns and crisp suits. Dancing and drunken giggles and a table full of pumpkin desserts. The sparkle of his mom's "glass" slippers matching the one in her eyes. Heady magic sprinkled in the air. The thud behind his tiny rib cage as his dad handled every second with a seamless energy, wanting nothing more than to leave a lasting impact on everyone's memories.

Denz saw himself being that great one day.

Today's not that day.

"This is my legacy." Kenneth rubs his temples. "It's the livelihoods of the family I've created here. Stepping in as CEO is a promise to the shareholders. A commitment to your staff. To yourself. Is that something you can handle?"

A growl wakes behind the clouds. Thin raindrops slice down the window. Denz forces his own tears to stay behind his eyelashes.

He's not going to cry. Not here. Not in front of his dad.

His boss.

In an eerily calm tone, Kenneth says, "You're young. I was too when I started. Grow from this mistake. Be the kind of leader you were born to be."

He waits for Denz to nod.

Denz does.

"And if you can't handle it," Kenneth says, frowning, "then step aside for someone who's ready."

His words reverberate alongside the doubt Auntie Cheryl voiced outside the elevators when he forgot to sign the venue contract. The ones from Kami over a month ago. Haunting reminders of the kind of Carter he keeps failing to be.

Denz stands, dazed. "I won't let you down, Dad," he says, barely keeping his voice in check as he walks out.

"God, today's the worst!"

The last voice Denz expects to hear at 4:57 P.M. is Kami's. He's standing in front of the elevator. His phone vibrates with a notification. Probably another text from Braylon that will go unread. He hasn't bothered responding since walking into his dad's office.

The snarling thunder outside is as loud as Kami's heels when she stomps up to him. He's not in the mood to talk. If only the damn elevator would reach their floor faster.

Kami whips out her own phone. She types away.

"Ugh. Emily fucking Sedwick."

Clearly, she *is* in the mood to chat. Denz pointedly stares at his shoes.

"She's the worst of the sisters," Kami proclaims.

"Hmm?"

He only half listens to her rant. Something about Emily wanting an early 2000s boy band to reunite for one night only and perform the song her NFL-defensive-lineman fiancé proposed to her with. Denz isn't surprised. He met plenty of kids like Emily at Brighton. The "money is no object" kind that think the world revolves around their parents' enormous bank accounts.

The opposite of Jamie.

Denz isn't naïve, though. More than 50 percent of 24 Carter Gold's clients are like the Sedwicks. They're also the reason he's wearing Armani loafers and is one elevator trip away from slumping in the heated leather seats of his BMW.

It's a lot to reconcile with, and Denz is too focused on hiding the tears sticking to his eyelashes.

"She wants me to pull off an honest-to-God Santa Claus miracle too," Kami continues, snapping her tan trench closed. "Snow in March. In *Atlanta*. Create a winter wonderland for her first dance with Warner."

Outside of his NFL ties, Warner's family is also loaded. Shocking. Denz jams the down button once more.

"Who does that?" Kami huffs.

"A Sedwick," he finally replies.

"A fucking Sedwick." Kami's phone pings. "Emily's drama can wait. I'm taking Nic early prom gown shopping. Wanna come with?"

Denz hesitates. *Is the elevator broken?*

"Promise no more work talk," Kami says, elbowing him. "Come on. It'll be fun."

Denz tries to sigh but his sinuses ache from all the sniffling. At least he hasn't cried yet.

"Hey." She pivots in his direction. "What's up?"

"Nothing."

"You're lying."

"I'm good," he strains.

"If your definition of 'good' is one Adele song away from destroying a tub of Gooey Butter Cake from Jeni's Ice Cream in one sitting, then yeah, you're perfect."

Denz tips his head back, exhaling. "Allergies."

Instantly, Kami reaches up to rub his bicep.

"Allergies" was their secret code as kids. Whenever one of them was so angry, so crushed by a comment from the aunties or uncles or even their dad, but didn't want to cry in front of anyone, they'd whisper that word. Their protective walls went up after that. Denz would sing so loud, no one could hear Kami's quiet sobs. On his bad days, she'd pass him her designer sunglasses to hide his damp eyes.

Nic's never needed a code word. One lethal look, and everyone knows to leave her alone. Even Denz is frightened of how cold she can be when pushed too far.

"Dad?" Kami whispers.

He carefully nods.

"We've been fighting all week," she says, sympathetic. "He's not a fan of my ideas for the engagement party."

"Ideas like—?"

He wonders if Kami has changed her mind. If she's starting to see things like Eva does. Like *he* does. Going back to their roots—wedding planning.

Kami grins. "After the toasts, I thought we should offer a lucky guest the opportunity to throw Emily in front of a MARTA bus."

Or maybe not. A laugh hangs in the back of Denz's throat, but the tears threatening to spill out silence it. His lips manage to twitch upward.

"It's nothing personal, Denz. Dad means well."

"I can't tell."

"We're never going to do things like him."

"I don't want to be *like* him," Denz says stiffly. "I want to be better. I want to be good eno—" He stops before the last word comes out.

Kami's soft eyes say she already knows. "Letting him get the best of you isn't how you win this game."

"Is that what it is?" He finally laughs, a wistful noise that carries in the silent offices. "A goddamn game? Me versus you? Some sort of *Mad Max* shitshow where we tear each other apart for their pleasure?"

"It's not like—"

"You didn't have to save me at the mayor's party."

"Of course I did."

"I would've figured it out."

"It's *the mayor*. Not some rich, pretentious family of ungrateful assholes in a city full of rich, pretentious, ungrateful assholes." She frowns. "Our reputation was on the line. If you look bad, we both look bad."

"We're not the same."

Kenneth made sure he knew that earlier.

"We're *Carters*," Kami reminds him. "That's all the people dying to apply for this job care about."

"Whatever." He stubbornly looks away.

"Denz," she tries, her voice gentle. "It's not a competition."

"It *is*. And I don't want to lose. This is my dream."

"It's mine too. But for different reasons."

"What's that mean?"

"It means . . ." Kami pauses, chewing her lip. "It means I don't think we're in it for the same thing. I know you. We grew up across the hall from each other. I wonder if . . ." She releases another breath, her eyes searching his face. "If it's my dream and your fantasy."

The sting from holding in his tears is almost too much now.

Quietly, she adds, "I'm trying to help you."

"I don't need it!" Denz hates how screechy his voice is. Hates the way Kami backs away, confused and wounded.

"Wait, Kam—"

"I forgot a . . . thing. For Nic. In my office," she stammers. "Get home safe, okay?"

Denz doesn't know how to reply. He doesn't have to. The elevator doors slide open. He climbs inside, alone. Kami remains in the same spot, unmoving.

He pretends the shine in her eyes doesn't mirror his own. After all, it's only allergies.

11

It's been forty-eight hours since the meeting with his dad, and Denz is good.

He's great.

He's—

"Okay, enough," Jamie says, standing shirtless over him. Denz is sprawled on the sofa clutching a bag of white cheddar popcorn. He hasn't moved, other than for a bathroom break, in nine hours. The sun's on a weekend-long retreat, the clouds outside thick and gray. His current situation feels earned.

Judging by the muffled lecture coming from the 5 O'CLOCK BREW T-shirt caught around Jamie's head, he disagrees. The black shirt is one size too small. It's uncertain if that's by design or from Jamie's inability to follow basic laundry instructions. Wavy hair sticking up everywhere, he says, "You've been like this for two days."

"Like what?"

"Like a puppy who's waiting for their family to pick them up from the doggy hotel after a vacation, but they never do because they died in the zombie apocalypse."

"That was . . . specific."

Jamie scratches his scruffy jaw. "What happened?"

"Nothing," Denz lies. "Rough week at work."

Jamie scoots in close to Denz on the sofa.

Denz loves this about them. How they've never required space to be comfortable. Neither has ever subscribed to toxic

masculinity bullshit. Cuddles should be a mandatory requirement for any friendship. Honestly, it should have been far easier
for them to fake-date one another.

"The CEO thing?" Jamie asks.

Denz exhales into a nearby throw pillow, nodding.

"Want me to call out sick?" Jamie offers. "We can have a
WTN."

"Watching *The Proposal* won't fix my problems."

"I was going to suggest *Neighbors*."

"That's not a rom-com."

"Blasphemy!" Jamie squeezes Denz's ankle before standing
again. "Zac Efron and Dave Franco's characters were unquestionably boning. At the very least, trading blow jobs. That's why
Zac's character is such a prick in the sequel. Jobless and dickless."

"The perfect storm."

While Jamie fixes his untamed hair, Denz tosses a handful of
popcorn in his mouth. "What happened to you Friday night? I
thought you were off?"

Jamie pauses his grooming, cheeks flushed. "Oh, I went to
a . . . basketball game."

"Is that a joke?"

Jamie averts his eyes. "The Atlanta Eagles are very good this
year. They're going to the playoffs."

"Atlanta *Hawks*," Denz corrects, squinting at him. "You hate
sports."

"I literally work at three sports bars."

"Where you've been banned from touching any remote for
switching the games to *House Hunters* reruns."

"People need to know the value of a housing budget and a
qualified real estate agent," Jamie argues. "I'm saving marriages."

"I doubt that."

"Anyway . . ." Jamie drops to his knees, searching under the
coffee table for his door keys. "I don't *mind* basketball. Sometimes.
Jordan invited me."

There's a beat. Jamie bangs his head on the table. Cautiously, he peeks from behind Denz's empty water glass like a mouse hunting for food.

"That's cool, right?"

When they were younger, seventeen to Jordan's sixteen, Denz would sometimes wake up to find Jamie and Jordan whispering and giggling. Fighting through another round of Mario Kart. He was never jealous of their connection. His cousin *and* his best friend getting along? It was the best.

But after Jordan left for UCLA, the trio reverted to a duo again. They never really got back to status quo. Denz chalks it up to getting older. He can't remember half his high school class-mates, despite how often Facebook tries to remind him.

He's happy they're hanging out, even if it's without him.

He shrugs. "Jordan needs friends."

Something weird passes over Jamie's face. He blinks it away. "You sure you don't want me to stay home?"

"All I need is this." Denz raises his popcorn bag. "If you're not spending Sunday nights with a hard lemonade, junk food, and watching a Netflix docuseries, you're doing adulting wrong."

"You forgot a vibrator."

"Stay out of my room!"

Jamie jiggles his keys. "Fine. Our next WTN is a Jane Austen adaptation. *Persuasion.* It's a rom-com."

"I'll be here." Denz waves a dramatic arm at the sofa. "Living my best life."

Except, when Jamie's gone, even with the TV droning and the balcony's French doors cracked to let in the soft drumbeat of raindrops, it's too quiet. Denz's mind drifts. To his dad's office. His awkward conversation with Kami. All the way back to Auntie Cheryl's words at the beginning of the year.

You're young. Life is fun now. Why commit to anything or anyone, right?

He was so confident they were all wrong. No one understood him or his dreams. How he's always wanted to be the hero people look up to.

But does Denz really know how to *be* a hero? A role model? As great as his dad?

On the coffee table, his phone buzzes. A text notification. He stares at the name—Formerly Known As Bray—for a long second. All weekend, he's thought about texting Braylon. But when he's in his head like this, he's no fun to talk to.

Braylon's not obligated to deal with Moody Denz. Not anymore.

Another text. Denz considers leaving it unread until tomorrow, when he's less grumpy or sad or covered in white cheddar cheese dust. But he can't help himself.

Formerly Known As Bray
I have an idea. I might need your help again.

> sounds dangerous. should i contact the white house? parliament?

Formerly Known As Bray
Don't be rude.

> sorry thats my default mode
> whats the idea?

Formerly Known As Bray
Are you interested in "coaching" the STL staff on proper social media content?

Denz squints at his screen. First off, he's *offended* by the very violent quotes around "coaching." As if what he does isn't real.

Secondly, he has zero time for anything extra outside of concentrating on his dad's retirement party. He just had his ass handed to him two days ago for less than 110 percent dedication to the company's future. He can't possibly help Braylon.

Dusting his hands on his T-shirt, Denz prepares a diplomatic response. Except, his thumbs hover over the keyboard instead of typing. He imagines Braylon on the other side of the screen. That little knot between his brows. Teeth worrying his lower lip.

Braylon's been aggressively independent most of his life. A

product of his mom dying young and Emmanuel's attempts to balance work and raising his son alone. He hates asking for help.

This isn't easy for him.

Denz considers his approach. He's not fast enough.

His screen lights up with a FaceTime call from Formerly Known As Bray.

He freezes.

Why does a video call with his fake boyfriend feel oddly intimate? It's not like he's stretched out on the sofa, naked. Not like Braylon hasn't *seen* him naked before.

Wow. The excited stir in Denz's basketball shorts feels like being thirteen again. Between that, and his phone's noisy *deet-deet-deet*, Denz ends up panic-answering.

"Hello?"

He's met with a crooked view of Braylon's kitchen. There's a cutting board, slices of cheese, and a loaf of bread. The background noise is a familiar combination of soft music and a sizzling pan.

Offscreen, Braylon yells, "One moment!"

With a curious grin, Denz asks, "Are you . . . cooking?"

"Yes. Sorry. Ow!"

Braylon's face finally appears on-screen. He's far from the brow-furrowed, nervous man Denz was picturing minutes ago. Instead, he's unshaven, curls rumpled, smiling sheepishly. When he steps back, he's wearing a wrinkled white T-shirt. Everything about his appearance is cozy. Like *he* hasn't spent the entire weekend having an existential crisis.

Must be nice.

"I'm making a sandwich."

"A sandwich," Denz repeats.

"It's an incredibly delicate process," Braylon tells him. "Texting was a nightmare. I called to explain my idea."

Denz rolls onto his back, holding his phone above his head.

"I'm listening."

Please don't be something like lip-synching to Ariana Grande.

"Hold, please." Braylon disappears. "Fucking bacon grease! How dare you?" He peers back into the camera. "Are you laughing at me?"

"N-no," Denz says around his choked giggles. "What kind of sandwich are you making?"

"French toast grilled cheese, of course."

"You—what?" Denz yelps when the phone slips from his hand, smacking him in the face. Switching back to his side to avoid a concussion, he glares at Braylon. "You're cooking *that* sandwich? With me on the phone?"

"Is there a problem?"

Denz swallows the *fuck yeah* he wants to yell, replying, "No" without a hint of longing in his voice.

In college, neither of them were experts in the kitchen. Denz mostly lived off microwavable foods. If it wasn't on the coaching staff's approved meal list, Braylon didn't know how to cook it. But his one specialty was the French toast grilled cheese. Two slices of warm, egg-and-cinnamon-soaked, pan-fried bread stuffed with Gruyère cheese and bacon, the sandwich finished with a light drizzle of maple syrup.

It was the best thing Denz has ever eaten.

He misses the *sandwich*, not the way Braylon would cook one for each of them, brushing greasy kisses along the side of Denz's neck afterward.

"So, uh." He coughs. "Your plan?"

"You mean my brilliant idea?"

"Yes, that. Whatever."

Denz watches as Braylon switches between flipping bread and talking. He wants to create video content for the nonprofit's socials. Friendly staff intros spliced together with day-to-day activities. Rapid-fire Q&A stuff, a tour of the facility. Unfortunately, Braylon also proposes a dance video, but to Perfume Genius, not Ariana.

To his own surprise, Denz *likes* the concept.

"I can only Google so much on how to make relatable and

informative content," Braylon says, lifting his phone. "I need an expert."

"Wow. Is that a compliment?"

"Is it working? Would it help if I said please?"

"Only if you get on your knees too." Heat flares under Denz's cheeks. He didn't mean for it to sound so . . . suggestive. He almost drops his phone again, stammering, "What I meant to say is—"

"You're into groveling?" Braylon flexes an eyebrow.

"Are you kink-shaming me?"

"I'm asking if you'll help me with another project. *For teens.* You're the one being inappropriate."

He's close to apologizing, until Braylon's lips twitch like he's losing a battle with a laugh. Denz snorts out, "You asshole."

"Is that a yes?"

"It's a *maybe.*" Denz bravely rolls to his back again. "Approval pending."

He lets the silence stretch between them like the low-hanging clouds outside. "Is this another attempt to impress your boss? For the promotion?"

"Something like that."

"You still haven't told me much about it."

"It's all, er . . ." There's the nervousness Denz was expecting earlier. Braylon clears his throat. "What did you say? *Pending.*"

Denz crosses his ankles. Outside of the introduction to the mayor and providing general help with the spring break day party, he's been too preoccupied with his own responsibilities to truly assist Braylon. He can do more. *Needs* to do more. He'd still be outside Kingfisher & Redbud, explaining to his parents why he lied to impress them, if it wasn't for Braylon.

When this is all over, Denz wants Braylon to accomplish his goals. Get whatever he needs to move up. Even if it means Denz's own situation is . . . well, *pending.*

It's too quiet.

Braylon says, "Everything okay?"

Denz stares off to the open patio door. He listens to the rain's soft rhythm. He's never been good at talking about his failures with others. Not even Kami or Nic know the darkest parts of his brain. But it'd be nice to talk to Braylon about what happened.

Like they used to do in Athens.

In the achingly vulnerable hours of an early morning or a drowsy midnight, they'd whisper their secrets to each other. Braylon's struggles as a student athlete. Denz's battle with family pressure. The grim days when Braylon missed his mom. Their dads.

After the breakup, Denz locked away that part of himself. He only shares the bare minimum now. What's necessary.

But, fuck, he misses it.

"You know," Braylon starts. Denz's gaze drifts back to the screen. The background's shifted from the bright kitchen lighting to a standing lamp, the back of a smoke-gray couch. A living room like the one Denz is sulking in. "We don't have to discuss it."

"No. Um. I don't mind."

Braylon's attentive eyes encourage him to continue.

He wiggles into the permanently dented spot from Will Thacker Nights. He tells Braylon about the meeting with his dad. Not catching the email from the mayor's team. The weirdness with Kami. He rambles until his throat goes dry.

Braylon's expression remains thoughtful from start to finish. He never makes Denz feel like the complete failure everyone else projects on him.

"You know," Braylon says again, "I've heard the cure for a bad workweek is French toast grilled cheese."

Denz's stomach grumbles. "Too bad I never learned the recipe."

"You could come over? I'll make you one."

"You don't have to do that."

"I want to."

Denz bites his thumbnail. Is he really considering this? Driving to Braylon's apartment in the sad, soggy weather for a *sandwich*?

He glances at the white cheddar handprints covering his shirt. His big toe wiggles out of a hole in his sock. He doesn't want to think about the last time he showered.

"I don't even know where you live."

Almost instantly, Denz's phone vibrates—a text with Braylon's location.

"See you in thirty minutes?" Braylon says.

"Forty-five."

The least he can do is change his shirt. Brush his hair.

Braylon ends the call. It's a long ten seconds before Denz scrambles off the sofa.

First stop: the bathroom to wash the stupid smile off his face. No one should ever be this ecstatic about a sandwich.

Six Years Ago
Sophomore Year—Spring Semester

Denz imagined cooking with his boyfriend in his studio apartment would go like this:

Hand-holding at the nearest supermarket. Wearing matching aprons while mixing ingredients. Dancing around the kitchen to soft music. Sharing long kisses over savory French toast grilled cheeses as a movie—preferably not another superhero one—played in the background.

Instead, the sky cracked open and unleashed a mid-May downpour the second they stepped outside Publix. His marble countertops are covered in spilled ingredients. Aprons are replaced by wrinkled T-shirts. Wet feet mean no dancing, and a Marvel movie booms on the living room's flat-screen.

But then there's Bray, leaning against the stainless steel fridge.

Bray in Denz's worn-soft UGA sweatshirt and a pair of low-slung lounge pants decorated in strawberry frosted doughnuts, his swim season buzz cut growing out.

Bray, dark eyebrow arched as he says, "I said add a *dash* of cinnamon."

"I did!" Denz's gaze dips to the bowl between his hands. Floating above the whisked milk, salt, sugar, and eggs is a thick layer of brown. "Sort of?"

"You're a disaster."

At home, Denz's mom is the cook. Whenever she visits her family in Ohio or Arizona, his dad has a personal chef on standby. With almost two years of college under his belt, the best meals Denz can create on his own either involve pressing the right function on a microwave or sliding a frozen pizza in the oven.

Bray steals the bowl away. "Back to square one."

Their forearms brush. Something like lightning sticks in the space between them. Dopamine colliding with nausea, a feeling Denz hasn't escaped for *months*.

Jamie calls it "the honeymoon phase."

Denz disagrees.

Through his open balcony door, the storm's become a drizzle. Snarling thunder is now the soft drum of a baby's heartbeat. Earthy scents blend with the smokiness from the bacon sizzling on the four-top range. Bray whisks fresh ingredients in a new bowl. Denz's eyes trace over the apartment.

It only took a 3.6 GPA, and some very unsubtle begging, to convince his parents to pay for this off-campus space after freshman year. His dad suggested a bigger, lavish town house. Denz wanted something *normal* like their old bungalow.

The compromise is eight hundred square feet that's unintentionally gone from his to *theirs*.

His latte next to Bray's iced Americano on the coffee table. His hamper overflowing with Bray's swim jammers. The bathroom counter crowded with his skin care products and Bray's shaving kit. Half the fridge occupied by Bray's precooked meals and smoothies.

It's the same in Bray's dorm. Denz's hoodies on the back of a chair. His favorite earbuds lost in the sheets.

Their lives bleeding together.

"Are you paying attention?" Bray asks.

"Yes," Denz says, indignant. If only there wasn't that inch of visible skin where the hem of Denz's too-small sweatshirt rides high on Bray's hip to distract him. He lingers on the stretch of hairless, honeyed skin.

"*Denz.*"

He startles. A smirk plays at the corners of Bray's mouth, as if he *knows* what Denz is thinking. Innocently, Denz says, "What's next?"

"Can I trust you to cut the bacon?"

"Can't be that hard, right?"

"I don't know." This time, Bray's eyes lower. "You tell m—"

"*Don't,*" Denz warns, "finish that sentence."

Bray laughs. In the kitchen, he moves with the same fluidity as when he's underwater—smooth and graceful. From the stove to the counter, scooping bacon onto paper towels. It's like he *belongs* here.

That thought is so scary, so intense, Denz doesn't realize he's grabbing the nearest knife from the wrong end until he almost slices off his thumb.

"*Shit.*"

"Careful," Bray says, alarmed.

"I'm fine."

"Sorry," Bray whispers into his neck. "I'm being a dad again, right?"

Over time, Denz has learned Bray goes full parental mode around people he cares about. Kami says it's the Capricorn in him. After a tough meet or over holiday breaks, Bray's the first in the team's group chat checking in, reminding everyone to drink water and be safe.

It's kind of adorable.

"Professor Adams," Denz says, putting on his best schoolboy face, "if you teach me how to cook your world-famous French toast grilled cheese, I promise to be a good student."

"You're a monster."

"I know."

Together, they cut the bacon into neat slices. Unpack the Gruyère cheese from the shopping bag. Bray instructs Denz how to layer everything on the brioche bread.

"Where'd you learn this recipe?"

"As a kid . . ." Bray pauses. "My mom used to make these for me. All the time."

There are parts of each other they've learned through hints. Abridged references with key details left to be filled in later. Things like Bray's mom dying from cancer when he was seven.

He rarely mentions her without a thickness to his voice, a shift in his mood. Denz never pushes him. It's a mutual understanding since Denz doesn't always freely offer specifics about his own family. At least, nothing that can't already be found through a simple Google search. They tread lightly, only taking what the other gives.

Today, Bray's ready to share.

"My dad tried so hard to replicate the recipe after she died," Bray says, his limbs gradually loosening. "But he's so bad in the kitchen. Like you."

Denz pinches his hip but doesn't interrupt.

"It was a lot for him," Bray says. "Missing her. Being Mom and Dad for me. After a while, he gave up on the sandwich. I was eight."

As much as Denz hates how over-the-top or unbearably rigid his parents are, he can't imagine growing up without either of them.

"I went years without it. My favorite comfort meal." Bray carefully dips a sandwich in the batter. "Then, one day, I found an old notebook in a kitchen drawer. You know, the one you throw random shit in?"

Denz laughs. The Junk Drawer, an affectionate term his mom used at their bungalow. The place for Tide pens and scissors and that phone charger you swore you lost years ago.

"It had all my mom's recipes. Including this one."

Bray lowers a sandwich into the pan.

"I was fourteen?" He tips his head back, thinking. "I messed up so many times. But I got the hang of it."

"That's why you want it to be perfect?"

Fondness sits in the corners of Bray's smile. "It's like she's here with me anytime I make it just right."

Denz gets that too. He's tried imitating his mom's sweet potato pie, to disastrous results. But there's something about peeling the potatoes' softened skin. Adding the spices. Watching everything blend together in a stand mixer.

It's like she's next to him.

While one side of the bread browns, Bray says, "I make them for Dad. When he's too busy with work to think about food. Or when he's sad and doesn't want to talk." He's sheepish when he adds, "But no one else. Not until you."

Denz tries to break that down into small, digestible pieces. He doesn't want it to be so big. So overwhelmed by how easily this has happened in less than a year.

Bray ducks his head. "Sorry, I made this weird, didn't I?"

"No, no," Denz rushes out. "Not at all."

He's not sure what else he wants to say, so he doesn't.

After the first grilled cheese is finished, Bray guides Denz through the process. He's forcibly quiet as Denz builds a lopsided sandwich. Accidentally drips batter on his bare feet. They're hip-to-hip, Bray smiling goofily as Denz plops the egg-soaked bread into the pan. In the background, a bluesy Elvin Bishop song plays in the Captain-Doctor-Incredible-Panther-Man movie: "Fooled Around and Fell in Love," one of Kenneth's favorites.

Denz catches himself humming along.

"And now . . ." Bray twirls the spatula like a master chef pandering to a live studio audience. "The flip technique."

"You can't be serious."

"There's an *art* to this."

Denz snatches the spatula away. "I can handle it."

"Go ahead, Bobby Flay." Bray gestures widely toward the stove. "Show me your skills."

Denz rolls his eyes. He's flipped pancakes before. Technically, he was in the kitchen where *Uncle Orlando* flipped pancakes. It still counts. He just needs the right angle of approach.

His first try nearly tips over the pan.

Bray snorts.

"Shut it," Denz hisses.

By the fourth attempt, he manages to flip the sandwich. It lands with a splat, uneven but mostly intact. He whoops.

Bray eyes the blackened bread. "You burnt it."

"I like it crispy."

Bray leans down to kiss the top of Denz's shadow-fade haircut. "Nice try. Four out of ten."

"God," Denz says, laughing, "you're lucky I love you."

He freezes. Back stiff, knees locked, mouth hanging open as the spatula slips from his hand, clattering on the hardwood. It's not nearly as loud as the expression on Bray's face.

"You . . . what?"

"It was the song!" Denz splutters, panicked. "I mean, what I'm trying to say is . . ."

What *is* he trying to say?

He can't possibly love Bray. It's only been eight months. This is his first *real* relationship. It's supposed to take longer to say those words. Isn't it?

There's a ringing in his head—an obvious warning.

"The sandwich," Bray blurts.

"The . . . sandwich?"

"Burning," Bray says, coughing. "The sandwich is burning!"

Oh. That shrill noise is the smoke detector. By the time Bray's fully opened the balcony door and dropped the frying pan into the sink, three things hit Denz at once:

One, he literally almost set them on fire.

Two, he's one more incident away from losing his parents' security deposit.

Three, Bray isn't going to say those three words back because Denz is an impulsive idiot who needs to find a fucking *filter* and—

"Are you okay?"

The voice comes soft and steady, startling him. A thin haze of smoke hovers between them. He stares at Bray's concerned face.

"Yeah?" He blinks. "Just spaced out, I guess."

Bray cuts off the stove. "So, about what you said . . ."

Oh no. That's how all "you're sweet, but I don't feel the same" speeches start. Is he really going to get dumped over charred grilled cheese?

Bray says, "I love you, too."

"Er—what?"

"I've been wanting to say it for weeks." Bray smiles, rubbing the back of his neck. "I thought it was too soon? But it's *not.* For me, anyway. Then I thought you'd freak out. Which, um, are you?"

He's rambling, shifting from foot to foot.

Denz can't help himself. He kisses Bray so hard and unapologetic and *deep*; he thinks he might drown. Maybe he already did, eight months ago.

A year ago, when he caught this shy, goofy, buzz-cut boy at that party.

Maybe this is all Denz wanted from today: a smoky kitchen, a stupid Marvel movie playing in the background, Bray wearing his sweatshirt, kissing the words "I love you" into soft lips until they're swollen.

"One more thing," Bray says. "You're never allowed near the stove again."

12

Unsurprisingly, Braylon's apartment is minimalism on level ten.

The patio door is open. Below, through a gauzy blanket of fog, downtown Decatur restaurants and shops glow. The living room feels simultaneously empty and inviting. The plush-looking sofa from their FaceTime call. A wall-mounted flat-screen hovering over a game console with neon green and blue wireless controllers. Piled on the coffee table are paperbacks, folders, a closed laptop—organized chaos reminiscent of Braylon's cubicle.

But it's nothing like Braylon's old dorm.

Denz hates how his brain works. Hates that tiny, electric ache behind his ribs. *Why* is he here again? He inhales. Bacon grease and cheese and cinnamon.

After leaving his shoes by the door, Denz finds himself sitting on the kitchen bar, watching all the action unfold.

"No stools yet. Sorry about that," Braylon comments. Barefoot, he shuffles around. The same white T-shirt from earlier complemented by a pair of gray sweatpants sitting low on his narrow hips.

Denz tries not to stare.

"Picking some up soon," Braylon continues. "Thanks to you."

"Me?"

An embarrassed smile unfurls over Braylon's mouth. "Remember when you called me out for not chatting up any of my old teammates?"

Denz grimaces. "I didn't mean—"

"No. It's true." Braylon laughs while hand-drying a pan. "Remember Lyle Ng?"

"Of course."

Denz liked all of Braylon's teammates. Mostly, anyway. They were the perfect mix of loud and funny and softhearted. No one was ever a homophobic asshole after Braylon came out. Or when he introduced Denz as his boyfriend at a group pizza night.

But Lyle was his favorite.

He put extra care into looking after Braylon. He had a habit of dragging Denz into every group conversation as if he understood any of their references or jokes. Like he belonged there.

"I emailed him," Braylon says while gathering ingredients. "We're going to set up a time for him to come by soon. Properly catch up."

"Aww. You're learning to play nice with other adults."

Braylon ignores Denz's sarcastic grin. "Since this is your fault, you're helping me pick out bar stools."

A flicker of heat attacks Denz's cheeks. He looks around. Is he the first person Braylon's invited over? Has Whit been here? Also, was that a subtle invitation to spend an afternoon furniture shopping with Braylon?

He says, "IKEA challenge accepted."

When he starts to scoot off the counter, Braylon stops him. "No. Stay there." A gentle smile creases his lips. "Maybe you'll learn something this time."

"Doubt it."

"At least try?"

Denz pretends the softness in Braylon's voice isn't unnerving. "Whatever," he says, inventorying the kitchen.

Very few dishes sit in the sink near his hips. There's an apron on a hook outside the pantry. A spice rack beside the four-top electric stove. Rows of Tupperware with prepped meals fill the stainless steel fridge.

"You cook more."

"I lived *alone* in London," Braylon says. "Couldn't survive off takeaway forever."

"It's not a bad life."

Braylon raises a suspicious eyebrow. "I take it you still don't cook?"

"You want me to buy a million ingredients? Follow a recipe? *Sweat?* And for what?"

"Nutrition," Braylon suggests dryly. "A lovely meal."

"That's what delivery is for."

Braylon shakes his head, amused. He works methodically. He fills small gaps of silence with naming all his favorite dishes to cook and the complicated ones he's still trying to master.

Denz tries not to stare at the flexing cords of muscles in Braylon's forearms as he whisks the batter. It's nothing he hasn't seen before. Except, in the kitchen's bright lighting, on a rainy night that leaves everything sluggish and dreamy, he's spellbound.

"Are you okay?"

Denz jumps. He recovers before falling into the sink. On the other side of the counter, with a wraparound Union Jack design, is a mug of cold tea.

He wants to smash it.

"Tell me about London," he requests, instead.

"What about it?"

"Did you like it there?"

"Yes." Braylon lays the first slice of bread in a pan of sizzling butter. "Loads of beautiful, historical places to visit."

"Okay, *Downton Abbey*, chill."

Braylon smacks his knee with the spatula. "Shut it."

"What else?"

"Food was good." Braylon rests his hip against the counter, thoughtful. "Some of it was a bit dodgy. Have you ever had Marmite?"

"No."

"Don't. It's quite tragic. You deserve better."

Despite his best efforts, Denz grins. *"And?"*

He hates the affection in Braylon's voice as he rambles. The way his eyes glaze over, almost euphoric, as he describes places, the weather, getting lost in Soho. But he can't stop the questions from bubbling up.

"Were the people nice?"

"I got on with my coworkers. People 'round my flat were kind." Braylon flips the bread. "London's like any other city. Always nice places where you can walk down the street freely. Then there's the people who think *we* don't belong." He presses his forearm to Denz's—two shades of brown skin. "Racism doesn't have a favorite city. It loves them all."

Denz hums sadly.

"Was there, um . . . a special someone?"

A long pause. Braylon rubs his chin stubble, considering. How could anyone in London *not* instantly fall in love with him?

"*Oh!* Yes."

Braylon snatches his phone from the counter. Denz regrets ever asking. He's not ready to see a dozen sweet snapshots of Braylon and some British guy who probably looks like a young James Bond.

"I had a cat."

Denz tilts his head. "A . . . cat?"

"British Shorthair." Braylon flips his screen around. "Her name's Fluff the Magic Kraken."

She's a ball of dusky white fur. Cute, but clearly irritated in every photo.

An unexpected laugh chokes Denz. "You named your cat *that?*"

For the first time, he notices the knot in his sternum has loosened. *So, no boyfriend. No attachments. No lovesick fling waiting for him to come back.* Denz can work with that.

"She was lovely. Quite beastly too," Braylon says. "She didn't care one bit when I left her with a neighbor to move back here."

"Jesus, *shut up.*" Another laugh. "You sound like John Boyega."

Braylon flips him off.

"London changed you," Denz notes, not maliciously. Simply a fact. "Even your clothes are—"

"What's wrong with my *clothes?*"

Denz tugs at the collar of Braylon's shirt, willing himself not to focus on the brief appearance of collarbone. "Y'know other colors besides gray, black, and white exist, right?"

"Says, Mr. I Only Wear Blue."

Denz inspects himself. *Well, shit.* He's wearing the sweater from dinner with his parents.

With an incredulous huff, he says, "You're different. I'm not."

"Bullock—" Braylon cuts off when Denz raises an eyebrow. "I hate you."

They grin at each other, but Denz's fades too soon. He whispers, "You even changed your name."

He's not sulking. Or pouting. Spulking?

Braylon lifts the sandwich onto a plate. Cheese oozes from the sides. He drizzles the bread with maple syrup.

"Bray is what my mom called me," he says. "When she was . . . alive."

Denz has only ever seen one picture of Elyse, Braylon's mom. The same one framed on an end table in the living room. She's twentysomething with large hazel eyes, heart-shaped lips. In her arms is a napping, curly-'froed Braylon. He's four years old in the photo.

"My dad named me Braylon." He exhales. "Mom shortened it. She thought people would mispronounce it otherwise."

"Oh." Denz never knew that.

"Even after she died, I let people call me Bray," Braylon admits, softer, sadder. "But when Dad passed, I realized I didn't love that name. I just wanted to hold on to my mom. Keep as many parts of her around as possible." Another pause. "And now I don't have either of them."

Denz's fingers flex on his thighs. He wants to touch Braylon. Is he allowed? Is that something only reserved for a *real* boyfriend?

Not some asshole who guilt-trips his ex for wanting to be called by his actual name.

He swallows, unsure of what to say next. Maybe that's the thing about death. Maybe words, no matter how sincere and perfect, are never enough.

A brief emptiness shadows Braylon's face. Like this apartment. Like his life since graduating college.

He laughs, bitterly. "I didn't have 'becoming an orphan before twenty-five' on my bingo card. Cheers to therapy." He passes Denz the plate. "Found a lovely therapist. She's helped loads."

"Sounds nice."

"It is." Braylon smiles. Small and lopsided, but it's there. "What about you?"

"What about me?"

"*Please.* You're different too."

"'M 'ot," Denz says through his first bite.

"Hell no. The heir prince to the 24 Carter Gold empire doesn't get to come to my flat—"

"Apartment."

"—insult the way I talk, my exquisite taste in clothing," Braylon continues, pulling a chilled bottle of water from the fridge for Denz, "and not acknowledge his own issues."

After a sip, Denz says, "I have none."

"Fuck off." Braylon guffaws.

"No. Seriously. I'm perfect."

"Since when did your life become so obsessively about a *job* that you're miserable?"

"I'm not miserable." Denz sighs. "Fine. I'm not *always* miserable."

"Only on rainy Sundays?"

"Or when someone claims *Captain Whatever* is one of the greatest rom-coms ever."

"*Captain America: The Winter Soldier,*" Braylon corrects, offended. "And it bloody well is. Fight me."

"Or when," Denz says, face wrinkling, "he puts *vinegar* on his fries."

"So, basically, all the time."

"I didn't come here for a character assassination."

"No?" Braylon smirks.

"I'm here for *this*." Denz aggressively chews another bite. He eyes Braylon with extreme contempt, all the while melting inside at the grilled cheese's flawless execution. It's criminal how Braylon is still the one person who knows what he needs the most.

"Why do you want to be CEO so bad?" Braylon inquires.

It's a question he should have an automatic response to. Things like *Money and prestige. To prove the aunties wrong. It's a lifelong career goal.* But that's not the answer Denz gives.

"This company—what my dad's done—is why my family has *anything*," he says. "It's why I am where I am."

Denz spent 90 percent of college avoiding the spotlight. He didn't want to be *on* twenty-four-fucking-seven. When asked, he never went into deep detail about his dad's company. It's not like Braylon couldn't see it whenever they visited home. How, outside of Athens, being a Carter was Denz's entire world.

Back then, he didn't know who he wanted to be outside of that. Now, he does. He thinks. He hopes.

"All my life, I wanted to be my dad."

Braylon's seen the *Marvelous Weddings* clip. Knows that part of Denz's backstory. He decides, in this tiny kitchen scented with bacon and butter and a hint of cardamom, to tell him more, finally. How he's determined to make the impact Kenneth has on other people's lives. That losing the one thing that gave him purpose as a kid feels like drowning.

His constant fear of being . . . *enough.* For everyone.

He whispers, "Do you know what it's like to be so scared you're going to fail that you constantly fuck up anyways?"

"Um. 'Ello." Braylon snorts. "I'm the gay son of an *art curator* and a first-gen Nigerian American *doctor*. My whole life is a severe case of impostor syndrome. But you're not a fraud, Denz."

"How do you know?"

"Because I've been there. Been *you*."

Denz leaves room for Braylon to continue.

"I followed my dad's dreams for me," he says, taking his eyes off Denz to wash dishes. "Moving for a job. Starting a new life. I thought I was making him proud. Doing what he expected of me."

Denz chews instead of commenting.

"I was wrong."

Under the lights, Braylon's face sharpens. His nostrils flare. That sad gleam returns to his eyes.

"I learned a lot about myself in London." His gaze doesn't waver. "But I—"

Denz holds his breath.

But he what? Regrets leaving? Wishes he would've given Denz more time to make a decision? Should've ignored Emmanuel's advice? He wants to apologize?

"I would've done it differently," Braylon says. He dries his hands on a towel. "I wish I could tell him how I felt back then. How I feel now too. But he's gone and . . ."

Silence. Another unfinished sentence.

As Braylon puts away dishes, Denz says, "I really liked your dad."

"He was a complicated man." A wistful smile nudges Braylon's lips. "But he loved you too, Denz. Truly."

Denz looks away. He doesn't want to give in to his thoughts. The guilt he feels for still being a little angry with Emmanuel, even in death.

"Maybe this is your chance to do things differently," Braylon suggests. "What do you want for yourself?"

"I—" Denz stops short.

He's known since the moment he put on his graduation robes where his future was headed. Before that, too. Like freshman year when he picked his major. Or when he was ten, watching his parents' second chance at a dream wedding reception. As a six-year-old, witnessing his dad save Audrey Hudson's big day.

But he never bothered to ask if it was what *he* wanted? Is Kami right? Is this his fantasy, not his dream?

"I don't know," Denz confesses. "Guess I haven't changed that much."

Braylon doesn't argue with him. Instead, he slots himself between Denz's knees.

Their eyes meet. Denz inhales peeled oranges and cardamom. His tongue absently flicks over his lips.

He doesn't know the proper etiquette for having your ex-now-fake-boyfriend's hips bracketed by your knees. His hands rubbing your thighs. He'd check Reddit if all his brain power wasn't already rerouted to his rapidly rising dick.

"Actually, I'm not so different either." Braylon smiles wickedly. His hands inch higher. "There are certain things I still . . . *enjoy.*"

Denz can't simultaneously focus on breathing and staring at Braylon, so he chooses the latter. Who needs oxygen anyway?

Ivory light halos Braylon's messy, dark curls. Hunger creeps into the corners of his eyes. He leans in. Warm breaths ghost across Denz's lips. Then, prickly scruff scratches down his cheek as Braylon bypasses his mouth.

He hovers in the space under Denz's jaw to whisper, "Can I kiss you . . . here?"

Denz grips the counter's edge. "Y-yes."

The pressure is feather-light, then gone.

"And here?" Braylon's mouth rests against Denz's Adam's apple. Denz barely responds before lips open around the cartilage. The kiss comes with a hint of teeth.

At the base of his throat. "Here?"

"Sure." Denz clenches all his muscles as Braylon lingers, his tongue tracing. Fingers dance along Denz's hips but never stay for long. Just enough to create a ripple of goose bumps across Denz's skin.

"What if I kiss you—" Braylon's head dips. "—here?" He tugs at Denz's sweater, exposing his collarbone.

"I, uh." Denz gasps. "I wouldn't mind."

"Are you sure?" Braylon skims his mouth along the bone's shape. "Because I can—"

"*Please.*"

Braylon complies enthusiastically. His tongue glides across the surface. Numbness tingles into Denz's fingertips. He's gripping the counter too hard. His thighs tremble as Braylon presses into him to taste more skin.

Each kiss comes with an arch of Denz's spine. Every *yes* or *more* that crawls up his throat, he swallows back.

Braylon grabs his hips. Yanks him forward. He positions Denz close enough to nip at the tendons along his neck, returning to places he's already been, renewing the tender soreness under Denz's skin.

"What about h—"

"God, yes. Just do it."

Denz hates Braylon's laugh against his damp throat. He wants more teeth, less talking.

Braylon tugs his sweater up. "What if I kissed you here?"

"*Hnngh*" is all Denz can reply with when Braylon tongues one of his nipples. It'd be embarrassing if he wasn't so impressed with his ability to form any noise as Braylon delicately kisses the other side of his chest. He's aware of the thumbs slipping into the waist of his jeans.

The fingers playing with the button.

"Denz," Braylon breathes against his sternum. "I have another question."

A hand strokes the line of Denz's cock behind the denim.

He practically yelps. "*Shit*, what?"

"Can I kiss you," Braylon pauses, looking up through his eyelashes, "down here?"

Either the thunder's returned or Denz's heart's about to combust. He bites his lip hard, unsure how to answer. Their arrangement has rules.

Something-something about sex, right?

"What about the no-sex rule?" he manages, thighs spreading.

"This isn't sex."

Denz laughs, head tipped back. "It's literally called *oral sex*."

"I call it a blow job."

"Same difference."

"Technically, not." Braylon exhales contently when it's Denz who undoes the button, yanks at the zipper. Together, they work his jeans and boxers to his ankles. Braylon crouches, tongue sliding over the unshaven hair under Denz's navel. "Sometimes I call it head."

"S-same . . . d-diff—"

Denz gives up after Braylon's teeth pinch the valley of his hipbone. Dizziness overtakes him. More kisses smooth along the sensitive skin on the inside of his thighs. He can't breathe. Then, Braylon's mouth dips into the dark hair surrounding Denz's cock.

"I love watching your toes curl when I—"

Instead of finishing, Braylon swallows half of his erection in one go.

Denz dissolves into nonsensical words and noises.

In college, Braylon was clumsy and self-conscious about sex. Denz was his first *everything*. But each time brought out an eager, more determined Braylon. A renewed need to find ways to leave Denz speechless.

Now . . . he's deliberate and thorough. Fucking godlike. Denz doesn't want to think about where he learned any of this. *Who he's practiced on.* To stop himself from screaming, he says, "I hate tea."

Braylon sinks lower.

"I hate vinegar on fries."

Soft kisses tickle from the base of his cock to the tip.

"Union Jacks." Denz fights the compulsion to grab the back of Braylon's head. To keep him in one place. "Stupid Big Ben. The 1975. Wembley. Buckingham fucking Palace—"

Braylon's mouth slides off. The noise his throat makes is somewhere between a groan and growl.

"Are you quite finished?"

Almost, Denz thinks. He makes the mistake of looking down. Staring into wide, blown-out eyes. A slick pink mouth hovering above his shiny cock. Braylon's left hand is braced against the front of his own joggers, palming his hard-on like he's on the edge too.

It's enough to undo Denz.

"Um, yes?"

"Good."

With zero hesitation, Braylon takes him fully. He doesn't choke. There's no pause for adjusting. Only a throat swallowing. Warmth and velvety softness and *holy shit.*

Denz can't watch anymore. He can still hear it. The slurping. Braylon's hand moving faster along his own erection. The tiny, eager noises he makes around Denz's dick.

Like he can't get enough.

It's an overstimulating hurricane that leaves Denz shivering. Against every shred of will he has left, Denz's toes curl. He hisses a "fuck the monarchy" before going boneless on the countertop.

He barely has the energy to lower his eyes again.

The sight sets another wave of trembles through him:

Joggers pooled around Braylon's thighs. A tight fist around his flushed, wet cock. Tremoring shoulders. Swollen lips letting out hot, choppy breaths as he comes. His expression is as blissed out as Denz feels.

Maybe Braylon hasn't changed that much after all.

-13-

"Don't panic."

Denz has whispered those words ad nauseam for the last five minutes. Exhaling, he grips the sink. His legs are still shaky. There's a dull ache in his lower back from arching so hard. Shiny beads of cold water drip down his cheeks to his jaw as he stares at his reflection in Braylon's bathroom mirror.

He's fine.

So what if his ex-now-fake-boyfriend just gave him the best orgasm he's had in years.

So what if said ex-now-fake-boyfriend also came simply from pleasuring Denz.

It's okay. *They're* okay. Maybe.

He didn't stick around long enough to check. As soon as Braylon unpeeled himself from Denz's thighs, Denz hopped off the counter, asked where he could clean up, then penguin-waddled through the bedroom to the bathroom. He didn't pull up his jeans and boxers until the door was locked.

All signs of being perfectly fine.

His eyes scan over the items neatly arranged on the sink: shaving kit, electric toothbrush, a fancy citrus deodorant next to a small bottle of hair-and-body oil that, based on a brief sniff, has warm, spicy notes.

Explains the orange and cardamom, he thinks, and immediately shakes his head.

Jesus, what the fuck is he doing? Denz came here for a *sand-*

wich. To discuss his work issues, figure his shit out. Not to creep on body products. Definitely not to get a blow job from the man who's faking a relationship to help Denz land a promotion.

He splashes more water on his face.

He's done things like this before. Quick, messy hookups. He's ducked into enough dark rooms or sketchy bathrooms. Done the occasional walk of shame. He can march right back into the kitchen and be the same chill Denz he was before coming here tonight.

No attachments, right?

He stares at his reflection one last time.

"*Please* don't panic."

The curtains in Braylon's bedroom are peeled open. A bluish glow from the late night's sky washes over the silver-and-white bedspread, the two end tables, a dresser. His walk-in closet reveals a monochrome wardrobe. Even his sleepwear, neatly folded on the edge of the bed, is gray, black, and white. Another reminder that this isn't the Braylon from UGA with lounge pants or boxers decorated in bright, ridiculous designs.

The room's only pops of color come from a series of paintings forming a panoramic view of a beach. Ocean blue-greens and sunrise pinks.

Denz studies everything from the bathroom doorway. The cleanliness. No dirty socks or forgotten sex toys lying around. The one stray item is a sweatshirt peeking from beneath the bed. It's gray with red lettering across the chest, a size too small for Braylon.

Denz's sweatshirt.

Suddenly, a voice to his right says, "'Ello there."

Braylon leans in the bedroom's entryway. *Shirtless.* "Sorry," he says when Denz startles. He holds up his crumpled T-shirt. "I was gonna toss this in the hamper. Kind of, uh. Got some of my, er. Your, um . . ."

In the dimly lit room, Braylon's blush is neon pink.

"Come?" Denz suggests, arching an eyebrow. "Jizz? Spu—"

"Are you quite finished?" Braylon groans. "Yes. My shirt is ruined. Happy?"

Is Denz? He's *amused*. Still three seconds from having a gay panic attack. Maybe even a little turned on again? (Seriously, it's been a long time since his toes curled like that.) But is happiness sitting on the edge of everything he's feeling?

"I can have it dry-cleaned," he offers. "Or buy you a new shirt."

"Unnecessary."

Braylon steps fully into the room. Beams from the bathroom's lighting dance over his chest, every definition in his abdomen. He's gorgeous.

Denz might die.

Braylon signals behind Denz. "Also, I sort of need to . . ." All his fidgeting pulls a smile from Denz's lips. "Uh, mouthwash. For the . . . I got some of your—"

Until that.

In the unexpectedness of clothes coming undone and lingering kisses and, well, *the toe-curling blow job,* Denz hadn't realized he came in Braylon's mouth. Hadn't given it another thought, too caught up in watching Braylon's euphoric expression.

Braylon must notice his mortification. "Oh God, don't make that face," he says. "It wasn't terrible."

"It wasn't terrible?" Denz repeats in an octave only dogs can hear. Braylon might as well have said, *I've had better. Two out of five stars. Would not recommend to others.*

"Could we not?" Mild frustration shadows Braylon's expression. "I'd just like to clean up a bit. If that's okay with you."

It's not a question.

Carefully, Denz switches places with him, refusing to flinch when the bathroom door closes. He should go. They had a laugh. The sandwich was as delectable as he remembers. And he's not as stressed about work.

That's all he came here for. The *other stuff* was a bonus.

A history of hookups has taught him to never stay afterward. According to Braylon, they didn't break any of their agreement rules. It was a quick, harmless blow job. Denz isn't reinventing his own rules about no attachments, either. There's absolutely no reason to wait around for the awkwardness to ruin things.

So why is he sitting down on Braylon's bed? Why's he reaching for the sweatshirt? Why is he sniffing the soft cotton, like his scent could possibly linger after all these years?

The bathroom door swings open.

"Oh."

Braylon, still shirtless, blinks at him.

"Is this mine?" Denz doesn't want to assume. Half of Braylon's wardrobe in college was UGA apparel. Perks of being a student athlete. But the answer Denz is expecting comes in the guilty twitch of Braylon's mouth.

His next question slips out before he's thought it through. "Did you keep it all this time?"

Braylon coughs. "Yes."

Quiet crawls between them. Denz considers Braylon. His wiggling toes on the carpet. The slow rise and fall of his chest. It's as if he's building the courage to confess something.

Denz waits.

Braylon finally says, "I needed something to remind me of home while I was in London. You always left it behind in my dorm."

"Or you'd *steal it* from mine."

Braylon rolls his eyes. "Anyway. While I was packing, it was right there, and I took it."

"You took it," Denz repeats. Startling warmth snakes up the back of his neck.

"You should take it back," Braylon says. "It's yours."

"No," Denz says faster than he expects.

Maybe it's the late hour. Maybe it's Braylon's wide-eyed, embarrassed face. Whatever the reason, Denz likes the idea of leaving a piece of himself in Braylon's apartment.

In his life.

Which is something he'd do with an actual partner. Not an ex *pretending* to be his boyfriend.

"Keep it." Denz drops the sweatshirt on a corner of the bed. "I'm too busy to have it saged and exorcised of all the London demons."

Braylon crosses his arms, unconvinced.

Denz tries not to stare at the dusting of hair growing between his pecs. After a long beat, he says, "This isn't going to get weird, right?"

He can already picture the uncomfortable texts they'll exchange next week.

"Because I gave you head?"

"Well," Denz starts, "I mean—"

"Or because you didn't reciprocate?"

Denz's eyes grow cartoonishly wide. "I—shit. You surprised me. I—"

Braylon snorts loudly before he can finish.

Oh. Denz flips him off.

"No weirdness," Braylon says, still half laughing. "It was just a blow job. That's all. You were tense. Had a shit week. Orgasms release endorphins, and I need you at the top of your game for my idea to work. You're still up for it, right?"

Denz nods. "I'm in."

He'll schedule a follow-up email. Send out a Google calendar reminder. Later, though. Right now, he needs his eyes to stop tracing over Braylon's chest. The soft smile pushing at his cheeks.

How the hell does he look so sweet after having Denz's dick in that sinful mouth?

"I should get home. Work tomorrow morning," Denz says because, if Braylon asked, he'd unquestionably stay the night.

"Okay," Braylon says.

"Okay," Denz echoes, not even a little disappointed. "So . . ."

His brain once again dances around how to say goodbye. A

hug? A fist-bump and "thanks for the sandwich and next-level blow job"?

He settles on, "See you soon. For more, um. Fake boyfriend things."

At the front door, he adds, "Thanks, Braylon" with a genuine grin that refuses to fade, even after he steps into the cool, damp night.

By midweek, Denz is in full event planner mode. No email goes unanswered. He drains his phone's battery talking to vendors and caterers. Schedules meetings with Eric to discuss floral arrangements, menu ideas, the entertainment. Uploads detailed notes on his dad's party into the cloud with backup copies stored on his desktop.

He never leaves the office before 5:00 P.M. Sometimes, later.

Denz manages to juggle three things at once—the retirement party, Braylon's spring break event, and their plans for fixing Skye's the Limit's social media. It's like being in college again, his blood mostly composed of energy drinks and whatever's fast and easy to eat.

He loves every second of it. But there's still one item left to address.

"What's this?"

Kami stares suspiciously at the lemon poppy seed muffin Denz places on her desk.

"A peace offering," he replies.

"Are we fighting?"

"I don't know." Denz flops dramatically onto the comfy chair in her office. "I thought we were?"

"Why?" Kami's gold bangles slip down her wrist as she tucks a curl behind her ear. "Because you had a meltdown last week?"

"I didn't have a—" Denz sighs. "Fine. I was being a brat."

"You had your reasons."

"I didn't have to take it out on you."

"No, you didn't." Kami bites into the muffin, obviously waiting for more of an explanation.

Denz doesn't have one yet. He's still processing it all. The conversation with their dad. What Kami said. The things Braylon said too.

(The things Braylon did. Which he's not thinking about. Except, occasionally, his brain *goes there*.)

Kami clears her throat.

Shit. Was Denz daydreaming about grilled cheeses and velvety lips on his neck while in his sister's office? He's truly fucked up.

"I want this as much as you," he blurts, cheeks hot. "To step in as CEO. Keep our family name where it belongs." He tugs his collar away from his damp neck. "Sometimes, I'm in over my head. I know. But this isn't a fantasy for me. It's a goal."

Kami's shoulders straighten. The deep plum shade of her Ted Baker Michahd pencil dress accentuates the ruby undertones in her complexion. Denz recognizes the thoughtful look in her eye.

Of the three of them, Kami's always been the most driven. Just like Nic's the brains and he's the life of the party. It's never been a competition with his siblings for who can stand out the most. And out of everyone in his life, Denz is certain his sisters want the best for him. They're never afraid to be unapologetically honest with him.

Kami finishes her muffin before she says, "Okay."

"Okay?"

"Yes, dork." She dusts crumbs into the empty wrapper. "Let's show everyone whose fucking name belongs on this company."

Denz's grin matches the one on Kami's mouth. His eyes dance around the office. Her latest vision board is pure chaos. Scattered photos connected by red dry erase marker lines. It's like a murder wall.

"Is that—" Denz's eyes narrow on something in a far corner. "—BASE jumping?"

"Warner's idea," Kami says with a long exhale.

"Jesus."

"*Emily* wants to arrive by helicopter. Her ideas are a carbon copy of what her sisters did, but bigger in the worst ways."

"Remember when Taylor arrived in a carriage like Cinderella?"

"Or Madisen's musical entrance like Belle from *Beauty and the Beast?*"

"That's why Emily wants snow in March?" Denz snorts. "Going for Elsa from *Frozen* vibes?"

"She's insufferable. I like the challenge, but it's so much drama for an *engagement party.*"

"Imagine planning their wedding," Denz says.

On top of the eight million things on his to-do list, he's also been keeping tabs on 24 Carter Gold's competition. If Denz wants to prove he can take the company to the next level, he needs to know what the enemy is doing. Elite Events and Something Blue Enterprises get their biggest social media numbers from weddings. Huge, flashy affairs. That's how they stay so close to the top.

"Do you think Auntie Eva might be right?" he asks.

"Hmm?"

"You know." Denz gestures toward the whiteboard. "Getting the company back into weddings. Re-creating the buzz we once had."

Kami's nose scrunches. "Are you still on that?"

"It's not a silly idea."

"Wedding planning is the worst."

Denz barks out a laugh. "How would you know?"

By the time Kami finished her degree at Emory, settling into life as a single mom with a newborn and even more expectations, their dad had fully severed ties from wedding planning. They started small again. More intimate connections with their client's vision for a perfect event rather than what would land them on the cover of *Southern Bride.*

"I saw what it did to Dad and Mom back then," Kami says matter-of-factly.

They don't talk about it often. The behind-closed-doors arguments their parents had in Denz's early teens. All the tension from the company's rapid popularity. Paparazzi waiting outside restaurants. The juxtaposition between their camera-ready faces for a Christmas spread in *Simply Southern* magazine and the long, awkward silences over family dinners.

The topic of their parents' almost-separation sits in a dark corner of their history. Next to Kami and Matthew, Auntie Eva's first failed business venture, the way Denz's grandparents forced Auntie Cheryl to end things with Jordan's dad for the sake of the "family reputation." But the ripple effects are always felt.

Even now.

Still, Denz can't help saying, "It'd be different this time."

No matter who wins, Denz and Kami will have each other's back. They can ease into wedding planning. A new client every few months; rekindle that magic spark that made them who they are.

"The company's fine," Kami says. "We're good."

"But we could be better."

"Yeah, and my brother *could* bring me better muffins," Kami teases, tossing the crumpled wrapper at him. "Sometimes, things don't need drastic changes to be better. Subtle tweaks. Remembering what made it great in the first place."

He fake-yawns. "Boring!"

"Anyway, how's Braylon?"

A familiar tingling sinks into Denz's cheeks. Memories rush him: kisses against his throat. Calculated fingers tickling along the inside of his thighs. Braylon coming apart seconds after Denz did.

"Oh, um, good?" He shifts anxiously in the chair. "Alive?"

"Wow." The smile on her lips is peak Auntie Cheryl after discovering a new piece of gossip. "You're *smitten*. You've got it bad, Denzel Carter."

Yeah, no. He doesn't.

"So," Denz says, by way of deflection, "when's Suraj proposing? Isn't it about time?"

"All right." Kami shuffles the papers on her desk. "You're excused. Go away."

Denz wishes his thoughts would go away that easily. Things like maple syrup drizzled on brioche bread. The pleasant burn of stubble against his chest. His old sweatshirt, the one Braylon's kept all these years. The unnerving number of times his mind drifts back to one silly night while he's having an afternoon espresso or answering an email, pacing around the parking garage three times looking for his car before realizing he's on the wrong level, is absurd.

Which is how he ends up at Twist-n-Salt, another one of Jamie's bars, with a bowl of nachos and whatever drinks his best friend slides in front of him.

The bar's vibe aims for upscale chic, but lands somewhere left of an elevated Applebee's.

First, the visual nightmare of neon signs hanging everywhere. Then there's the tacky upholstery on the booths. The wobbly high-top tables. Christmas tinsel on the shelves of alcohol bottles behind the bar. Denz is certain the staff left that up out of pure spite rather than negligence.

"Okay," Jamie says between customers, resting his elbows on the stained-wood bar. "Tell me how it happened."

Denz picks at his nachos. The cheese is radioactive orange and, despite what the menu advertises, the soggy jalapeños are from a *jar,* not fresh.

"Again?"

Jamie grins. "I need to get inside your head to understand."

Denz doubts that. They've traded sex stories before. He's heard all the messy details of Jamie's first time. In return, he overshared about that one hookup who was fiercely into foot play and dirty talk.

But this is *Braylon*. Fake-boyfriend Braylon. There shouldn't be a sex story about him, at least not a recent one.

Denz sloshes his drink around. It's a suspicious shade of purple.

"I went to his place for a grilled cheese. We talked about London. I word-vomited about my stressful week at work—" He clocks the sharp eyebrow raise and makes a mental reminder to apologize for not coming to Jamie first about his problems. "Blah, blah, blah. He thought a blow job would calm me down—"

"And it did!"

Denz refuses to agree.

"And then," Jamie says eagerly.

"I found my old sweatshirt under his bed," Denz says.

Jamie considers this, the neon pink NO PLACE LIKE HOME sign above his head shining across his furrowed brow. He steps away to refill someone's beer, mix a martini for another customer. When he returns, Jamie smiles and says nonchalantly, "Sounds like nothing to me."

Denz winces at his next sip. It tastes like berry-flavored toilet bowl cleaner. Also, did Jamie not hear a word he said?

"Nothing?"

"You were upset," Jamie says. "He gave you comfort head. Happens all the time. Especially with boyfriends."

"We're *not* boyfriends." Denz buries his face into his hands. After a beat, he hisses, "We're only doing this for my family. It's not real."

Jamie pops a cheese-soaked nacho in his mouth. "Is Braylon freaking out?"

Denz pauses. "No?"

Braylon's perfectly normal. He still emails new ideas for the spring break party. Texts his awful "boyfriend" jokes that Denz finds himself laughing at in the middle of meetings with Eric. Nothing out of the ordinary. Maybe that's why Denz's brain is mush.

Does he *want* Braylon to act differently? To show the slightest hint of awkwardness about what happened?

"It was good, right?" Jamie asks.

"No comment."

"You needed to de-stress," Jamie notes. "It's not like you're getting dick regularly."

"I get dick," Denz argues.

"Doesn't sound like it to me," a middle-aged white man wearing a mesh trucker cap and far too much flannel for March says from two stools over. "Another Guinness, J."

Before Denz can react—or scream—a waitress sidles up with a tray of empty glasses. "Yeah, sorry sweetie," she says, tucking a strand of overly dyed blond hair behind one ear, "but the way you're acting, seems like that orgasm was long overdue."

She ignores Denz's unhinged flailing while offloading her tray. "Can I get a round of Fireball for table seven?"

"You mean the Jamie Peters Special?"

"No," she grumbles, not in the mood for Jamie's offbeat charm. "Fireball. That's it. Don't make me cut you."

Jamie salutes her.

Blondie Waitress pivots to Denz with a sympathetic smile he wants no part of. "Work stress is the worst, hon. Get a vibrator. Saved my life."

Then, she's gone.

Denz wants to know when his sex life became a group project. He watches Jamie refill Flannel Guy's beer before pouring whiskey into five new shot glasses. Reluctantly, Denz sips his lavender-hued cocktail.

Fine, Jamie—all of them—*might* be right. What happened with Braylon did feel good. Incredible. And he's been less tense around the office ever since. But was it *just* the blow job?

"Stop!" Jamie smacks Denz's hand. "Don't do that."

"Do *what?*"

"Get all in your head. It makes you look constipated."

"Fuck you." Denz laughs, ignoring the fact that no one's said that to him since college.

Since Braylon.

Jamie wipes down the bar and adds, "It's not the end of the world. You have what? A month left of this? Enjoy it." He lowers his voice. "If one of my exes agreed to fake-date me and was that good with his mouth, I'd find out what other things we could fake-try while we still had time."

"Anyway," Denz says, shaking his head. "I didn't come here to talk about . . . *that.*"

"Like hell you didn't," Jamie says, snorting.

"I wanted to officially invite you to bartend at my dad's retirement party," Denz says louder. "We could use the extra hands."

It's not the *only* reason he's offering Jamie a gig. Dinner with his parents was, as expected, a disaster. Jamie's not answering any of their calls. That also means his bank account's a little tighter. Even through his post-toe-curling-orgasm haze, Denz still notices the way Jamie's being fiscally cautious, but he knows his best friend never accepts handouts, no matter how sincere they are.

"So . . ." Denz chews another sodden nacho. "Want to come party with the Carters?"

"Do I get my own staff?"

"You'll be *on* a staff. It's an open bar. You'll split tips."

"Do I have a say on wardrobe?"

"If you want to suffer Auntie Eva's vengeful wrath, then sure." Denz tugs out his phone. "All-black dress code. No T-shirts. *Nice* jeans."

"Do I at least get a drink named after me?"

Denz tosses a jalapeño at him.

Jamie shakes it off. "Everyone's going to be there? Aunts and uncles?"

"Unfortunately."

"Nic?"

Denz points an accusing finger. "You two better stay at least ten feet from each other. You're like Owen Wilson and Vince Vaughn at parties."

"She's the Vince."

Denz grins. "Obviously."

"And what about . . ." Jamie dries the same spot on the bar over and over. "Jordan?"

"Why wouldn't he be there?"

Jamie doesn't answer. He fixes an apple martini that's a shade too green for Denz's liking before passing it off to a waiter. "Okay, I'm in."

"Perfect." Denz chokes on another sip. "Bro, this is *awful*."

Jamie guffaws. "Too late. You already hired me. No take-backsies."

Denz sighs, unsure what he's going to regret more: hiring the world's worst bartender for the biggest night of his family's life or the hangover he's going to have tomorrow morning.

Most likely, both.

"Are you quite sure," Braylon is saying, his voice low and awed, "this is an *engagement* party?"

"More like an engagement *extravaganza*," Denz says.

He's been to two of these before. First, at fifteen, for Taylor's fairy-tale soirée at a hilltop Italian villa outside Atlanta. Then, when he was eighteen, for Madisen's enchanting celebration on a lush peach farm. But *this?* Nothing compares to what Kami has pulled together.

The company has rented out the entire Atlanta Botanical Garden for Emily and Warner. Behind a roped-off area, photographers stand ready to capture the latest arrivals. Ten-foot arches wrapped in fairy lights create an entrance into the gardens. And against the fiery rose skyline, the lights look like stars suspended by a god's hand.

"This is an experience," Braylon comments.

Denz turns. The glowing archway has nothing on Braylon in an ivory blazer and midnight-black button-up, his curls neatly styled. His tie—a startling bloodred—complements his honey-brown skin.

The absolute nerve of Braylon Adams to show up looking like the promising beginning of a dream has destabilized Denz's concentration.

"We should," he attempts. "We need to, uh . . ."

Braylon dips his head to whisper, "Plan?"

They agreed to meet early. Strategize. It's their first appearance together since the gala. Their last real chance to win the Carters over before his dad makes a final decision. Tonight needs to be perfect.

Yet, the one brain cell Denz has left is so focused on how soft Braylon's lips look from this angle, he forgets to nod.

"Should we—" Braylon's eyes trace Denz's face. "—go about it the way we did on Valentine's?"

"You mean argue about *The Bachelor* in front of everyone?"

"No, you git. *Improv.* If we're asked any questions."

Denz tries to form a response, but Braylon reaches up. His thumbs brush lint from Denz's lapels. It's infuriating, the way his body stiffens and relaxes at the same time.

"Save it for the pictures, losers."

Kami appears from around a corner in a sleeveless, Catalina-blue drape-front dress with gold heels. Her hair's elegantly pinned up, showing off her heart-shaped face, her pearl necklace.

"Quite stunning, Kamila," Braylon says by way of greeting.

"Not trying to outdo the guest of honor, are you?" Denz teases.

"Wouldn't dream of it." Kami smirks. "You two look . . . cozy."

Denz is spared from giving a stammering, pathetic response. Soon, Jordan hustles up, speaking breathlessly into an earpiece. He has a tablet tucked under one arm, a phone in hand, and the eyes of a man seconds from cracking.

"Guests are mingling. Tables are set. Tech check is good," he rattles off. "Kim says appetizers are ready. Sedwicks almost here."

"My dad?" Kami asks while procuring the phone from his shaky grip.

"Arrived ten minutes ago."

"Entrance music?"

"Fixed," Jordan swears. "Warner's request for Black Eyed Peas 'I Gotta Feeling' has been nixed."

Braylon looks mortified.

"Wonderful." Kami types out an email before eyeing Jordan. "When was the last time you hydrated?"

"Two hours ago?"

"Water. Now," she instructs. "Deep breaths, J. We've got this."

Jordan nods before grinning. "Damn, you're good at this." He double-times it back in the direction he came from.

Kami stares blankly at her phone.

Denz stands back, trying to filter his expression. It's not that he hasn't seen Kami in action. He's been by her side enough times to know she's all business, never rattled. But it's different now. Her *name* is on the line.

Underneath all the poise and elegance, Denz can see the 5 percent of fear that she's not enough, a feeling he lives with twenty-four-seven.

"You two," Kami says, back in command mode, "photos, then inside for dinner and speeches."

Denz tenses.

On Valentine's, he didn't have to worry about couple-y red-carpet photos. He was running the show. Braylon was late. He's been lucky that the press hasn't given much attention to his social media posts featuring Braylon's hands. Only his followers have.

If he poses for the photographers with his "boyfriend" by his side, they'll be trending by morning. Braylon's a private man. Always has been.

Denz promised not to cross that line.

"Lovebirds?" Kami inspects them. "Something wrong?"

"Could we," Denz says way faster than he expects, "skip the step-and-repeat?"

Kami tilts her head.

Something prickly and familiar sets into Denz's bones. He hasn't felt it since college. When his family wanted to know everything about his new boyfriend and Denz wanted nothing more than to protect this *thing* he had with Braylon.

"I mean, I look great, but . . ." He waves a hand in Braylon's direction. "I don't want this guy feeling *average* standing next to me."

"How dare you," Braylon huffs.

"Truth hurts."

"He looks amazing," Kami argues.

Denz gives his sister a long look. "Kami, *please*. Just this once?"

She scrutinizes him for a beat, then pivots in the opposite direction. "Follow me."

Walking through the gardens is like stepping into an Alice in Wonderland daydream. The centerpiece is a wide stone fountain. Sitting on the water's surface are lush green swirls of grass and colorful petals. Guests mingle over champagne, surrounded by towering lawn structures shaped like the Mad Hatter's hat, the Cheshire Cat, the Dormouse. Tea candles light a path to the main banquet table where Emily and Warner are sandwiched between family and friends.

"No doves? Helicopter entrances?" Denz asks.

Kami's mouth pinches. "We compromised."

"Do I want to know?"

"Nope. You'll see later."

The music's soft, an effortless rotation of current pop hits and country classics. People drift from the manicured lawns to the dinner area. Virginia bluebells, specially flown in, sprout from vases on each table. Not a single peony in sight. Denz is impressed with Kami's dedication to throwing the Kenneth Carter playbook in the trash.

Denz's stomach clenches. By the bar, his dad is watching closely. The tension from their office talk hasn't faded.

An unexpected hand rests against the small of Denz's back. He gazes up at Braylon, catching the pointed look he directs toward the bar.

A resigned sigh leaves Denz's lips when he notices the aunties and uncles joining his dad. "Ready to face the wolves again?"

"Wolves? Hardly." Braylon scoffs. "They're pups. I haven't yet shown them my teeth." He flashes his canines, winking.

Denz laughs. "Who the hell are you?"

"What?"

"You're just . . ." Denz shakes his head. He tries to stomp out that warmth spreading in his sternum. "Nothing."

"We can avoid them a bit longer," Braylon offers, rubbing the knot from Denz's trapezius. "If you want?"

"Yes, please."

He lets Braylon guide him away. The sea of faces is a strange mix of Warner's rowdy teammates, B-list celebrities, and the political types. Denz is accustomed to entertaining this crowd, but he forgets how weird it must be for Braylon. He doesn't show it, chin lifted until they're at Kami's side again as she animatedly gives instructions to her team.

"No problem," Jordan says.

"Kami, *sweetie!*"

Emily Sedwick, looking like an Amy Adams Disney princess in an off-the-shoulder, tear-drop-blue ball gown, approaches. Her gold hair is spun up with flowers. She squeezes Kami's hands like she's being chased by an evil witch—or a rabid future mother-in-law.

"Save me," Emily pleads theatrically. "Work your magic."

To her credit, Kami's smile doesn't falter. She goes full event manager mode, beelining through the crowd with Emily in tow.

Denz is praying for whoever crosses her tonight.

Someone at the head table clinks a fork against a champagne flute.

"Maybe we should," Braylon says, minty breath brushing Denz's cheek, "find our seats?"

"And a lot of alcohol," Denz advises.

Kami has arranged a table for just the three of them. Far from the aunties and uncles and their dad. His sister works in mysterious, benevolent ways.

When the speeches start, it's very apparent the booze was flowing long before the Sedwicks arrived.

Mr. Sedwick jokingly recounts threatening Warner's life

during their first meeting. Mrs. Sedwick dedicates her three minutes to a dead relative, which leaves everyone cringing. Taylor and Madisen regale the guests with their own engagement party stories before breaking into an off-key rendition of "I Say a Little Prayer." It's all downhill from there. Denz orders two lemon drop martinis just to survive.

Halfway through a story from Warner's fourth-grade teacher, Denz pokes Kami's shoulder. "Hey."

"Hmm?"

"Do you think the aunties had anything to do with our event assignments?" As Kami's confused eyebrows lift, Denz adds quietly, "Think about it. You got an *engagement party* even though they love to bring up what happened with Matthew. And Valentine's Day went to me, the one who's never had a man they approved of."

"They like Braylon."

Denz shoots her a *do they really?* look.

She snorts. "It's a coincidence."

"It's a *conspiracy.*"

"You're giving them far too much credit."

"Whatever," Denz grumbles. He's not sure if it's the sweetly romantic ambiance. Or maybe the alcohol. Whatever it is, his next question comes in a nervous whisper: "Did you ever, like, picture yourself at one of these things?"

"What do you mean?"

"I don't know." He does but is too embarrassed to say it. "If you had one of these parties for yourself, what would it be like?"

Kami thinks. "Hypothetically?"

"The most hypothetic of hypotheticals."

"I'd want simple. Nothing like this. More . . . *personal.*" He can tell she's imagining it. Her eyes sparkle as she says, "Mikah's favorite mini cheesecakes. A live band playing the songs me and my fiancé fell in love to. No speeches because, hello, have you met *our family?*"

Denz bites his knuckles to stifle a laugh.

"I'd want Nic to recite a poem I wrote for him," Kami goes on. "We'd be somewhere intimate and comfy, like Mom and Dad's backyard."

Denz smiles harder.

Kami's eyes flick to a tipsy Emily. "And I'd wear something less . . ."

"Flashy?"

"Gauche."

Denz almost loses it. Kami rotates to face him. "What about you?"

"What about me?"

Her gaze slides to Braylon, who's dutifully listening to Warner's high school football coach recite how he set them up. When Denz doesn't follow, she hisses, "*Seriously?* As much as you harass me about Suraj, you never thought about your own relationship?"

Denz wants to give Kami the easy answer: *No. Never again.* He believed in The One once. He'll be damned if he gets burned twice.

A beat passes.

In his periphery, Braylon's chatting with Kim and Connor at the table next to theirs. Denz wants to hate how gorgeous he is. His stupid, sometimes British, accent. Everything about this version of Braylon. But he can't.

To Kami, Denz says miserably, "Sometimes."

Kami squeezes his hand on the table like she knows whatever he's not saying. How could she? Even Denz can't figure out what's happening in his head these days.

Eventually, the speeches end. The music is cranked up. Denz relocates to the bar. He watches the world's most rhythmless dancing over another martini. On his right, Kami triple-verifies the checklist on her phone. She has the feral look of a woman desperate for a glass of wine and an excuse to kick off her heels. That's his cue to step in.

But she turns to Braylon and says, "You know what I could use?"

Braylon raises a curious eyebrow.

"A dance."

"I'd love to," Braylon says as Denz stares, wide-eyed.

"Wait, what the—"

"Fantastic," Kami cuts in, side-eyeing Denz before grabbing Braylon's hand. She leads him to where couples are swaying near the fountain.

Denz blinks. There's a sudden tightness in his chest as Braylon twirls Kami around. A burn in his belly that can only be the alcohol when Kami tosses her head back, laughing. From here, their banter appears natural, as if they haven't missed a beat, even though it's been years since they interacted like this. It's everything he and Braylon haven't been so far: *effortless*.

"Wow," Jordan says, sidling up. "He looks happy."

"Who?" Denz whispers.

"Braylon, obviously."

Denz can't take his eyes off them. Braylon's clumsy attempt to dip Kami. The way they keep tripping over each other's feet.

"Bet he's missed this. Being around us," Jordan comments.

Denz gives a sharp laugh. "Why would he?"

It's ridiculous. Their family's chaotic. There's never a moment off. Why would anyone voluntarily be a part of this?

Jordan shrugs. Then, the corners of his mouth lift. "I don't know, cuz. Probably the same reason you look so jealous watching them."

Denz wheezes. *Jealous? Of what?* He doesn't care that Kami's giggling into Braylon's chest. The stupid grin Braylon's wearing.

Jordan swigs his vodka soda with lime, eyeing him with a devious interest that should only be reserved for Auntie Cheryl, not his favorite cousin.

"I don't—I'm not." Denz shakes his head. "It's *fake*, remember?"

"Sure." Jordan pats his arm. "Keep telling yourself that."

And Denz does. While finishing his drink. For the long minute he catches the aunties whispering to each other, studying Braylon and Kami from a few feet away.

It's what he needed. For them—and his dad—to fall in love with Braylon again. To believe their lie.

What he really needs is more alcohol.

Denz flags down a bartender. He drowns all the weird thoughts preventing him from doing what he's here to do—be a supportive brother, look like a confident and competent future CEO—in a highball glass of top-shelf vodka with a cute lemon wedge. He's okay.

He's—being knocked sideways by a breathless Braylon.

"Um, are you drunk?" Denz says, annoyed. "I'm trying to—"

"We're in trouble."

Denz takes him in. Wild eyes, sweaty brow, cheeks darkening by the second. "What's wrong?"

"My boss is here."

Denz's forehead wrinkles as if to say, *And?*

Of course, Braylon's panicking. Just like in college. Every test and essay, swim competition, silly fight with Denz that turned out to be an excuse for great make-up sex.

Denz probably shouldn't be thinking about that right now. Probably shouldn't be ordering a new drink either. But, well, here he is.

"Listen," he says after a sip. "The Sedwicks are entitled asshats, but they're also very generous with their donations. Tax write-offs. Good press. All that jazz."

Braylon frowns. "I've never lied to my boss before."

"You've never faked a sick day?"

"I don't *fake* sick days," Braylon snaps.

"Only relationships, huh?"

Admittedly, Denz *enjoys* the flash of annoyance in those brown eyes. The hint of canines when Braylon's seconds away from growling. He wonders what Braylon might do with that mouth if . . .

Oh God. Why doesn't anyone ever water down the liquor at these things? Denz is one gulp away from tipsy.

He shakes it off. "Just go talk to her."

"She's busy talking to *someone else.*"

Denz follows Braylon's eyeline to an older white woman with grays streaking her businesslike blond bob. She's like any other guest here. But next to her is—

"Fucking fuck of all the fucks," Denz says under his breath.

Why? Why does his dad have to know everyone in Atlanta? Why is he escorting Braylon's boss in their direction?

"What do we do?" Braylon asks.

"Change our names?" Denz suggests. "Find a couple of bodies in the morgue that look like us, stage a fire, fake our deaths, then use all my frequent flyer miles to relocate to Antarctica?"

"Excuse me, *what?*"

"Drink this," Denz instructs, passing off his glass to Braylon. There's no reason to panic. This is Denz's area of expertise. Lying under pressure. "Follow my lead."

"Isn't that how we ended up—"

Denz grabs Braylon's free hand. Squeezes three times like they used to whenever the other was on the verge of a meltdown. Braylon's face softens.

"We good?" Denz asks.

Braylon chugs the vodka, nodding.

"Here they are."

Kenneth strides forward in a navy velvet Giorgio Armani tuxedo jacket. An Auntie Eva pick from New York Fashion Week. "Son, I was just having the most *fascinating* conversation with Nora Bridger," he says, too boisterous. "Who just happens to be your boyfriend's boss."

Denz grins tightly.

Up close, Nora resembles a young Helen Mirren. Short, elegant yet not impersonable. Her wrinkles somehow elevate her beauty. The black gown she's wearing has understated lace details. Her warm smile is inviting in a way Denz appreciates.

"I wasn't expecting to see you tonight, Braylon," she says.

Braylon tugs at his collar.

"He's here with my son, Denzel," Kenneth jumps in.

"Oh, I know you very well," Nora says a little too cryptically for Denz's liking.

"You do?"

"You're the one all the teens at the center adore." Nora turns to Braylon, ecstatic. "He's @notthatdenzel, right?"

"The one and only."

A wave of unexpected endorphins from Braylon's endearing tone assaults Denz.

"I invited him to help out with our socials, remember?" Braylon says.

Nora nods like it's gradually coming together. Her eyes lower to where Denz is still holding Braylon's hand. "I didn't know you two knew each other . . . in that way."

Kenneth's mouth puckers.

Blush reddens Braylon's face. "Well, yes," he stammers. "Thing is—"

Denz clears his throat. "Nice to meet you, Nora. I'm Denzel Carter," he says smoothly, extending his other hand. "Event coordinator and social media director for 24 Carter Gold." He swallows. "Also, Braylon's boyfriend."

Braylon squeezes his hand three times.

"*Oh.* Boyfriend?" Nora blinks.

"Yes."

In his periphery, Denz can see his dad carefully observing their interaction.

"He never mentioned dating anyone. Not that I'm privy to that kind of information about my staff. I figured with the kind of attention your family gets . . ." Nora's voice drifts off.

Braylon coughs hard.

"We've kept it low-profile," Denz explains. "For our careers. Braylon talks nonstop about his goals for Skye's the Limit."

Nora smiles proudly.

"And Denz is vying for CEO after I retire this month," Kenneth adds. His suspicious eyes continue to roam over them.

"Wonderful!" Nora claps. "The company's in great hands. Braylon's also up for a promotion. Lots of responsibility. A *big move* too."

Denz squints when Braylon laughs sharply. Whatever questions he has about Braylon's reaction are derailed by Nora asking, "How long have you two been together?"

"October," Braylon mumbles just as Denz reflexively says, "Early January."

They both freeze, mouths open.

"I mean," Denz stutters.

"It's kind of," Braylon attempts.

Nora tilts her head, confused. Kenneth rocks on his heels in that impatient way Denz recognizes from childhood.

With a deep breath, he collects himself.

"January, officially. After the holidays. But we started seeing each other again around Halloween." An unhealthy amount of sweat dribbles down his spine. "It's a funny story."

Denz recounts the same reunion story Braylon told on Valentine's Day. He recites what he remembers. The party and the doughnut, their long walk through the city. He clocks the unanticipated tenderness shifting through his dad's features, as if he's really *hearing* the story this time. Like he believes it.

"A second-chance romance," Nora gushes. "How beautiful."

Kenneth nods his approval.

Denz feels his heart slow to its normal, steady rhythm.

As one song fades into another, Braylon says, "I don't mean to be rude, but I've yet to dance with my *gorgeous* boyfriend." His eyes land affectionately on Denz. "I'd hate to waste such a lovely party."

Nora says, "We'll talk more at the offices."

Braylon ushers him toward the fountain. On the way, he

steals a shot glass off a waiter's tray, wincing as he downs it in one swallow.

Denz laughs.

Unfortunately, their dancing is like two plastic Ken dolls shoved together. Middle-school-level awkwardness. They fight over who should lead, then who *shouldn't* as they collide with more than one couple.

"Have you always been this horrible?" Braylon asks.

"You're no Usher, either."

"You're like a drunk Ewok."

Denz rolls his eyes. "Has anyone ever explained to you what *rhythm* is?"

After the first chorus, a miracle happens. Braylon's hands settle on Denz's hips. Denz's arms lock around his neck. They're buzzed, stepping on each other's feet, but it works. Somehow, it feels like . . . *them.*

Braylon's soft baritone voice sings, "And you take me the way I am."

"Oh my God." Denz cackles. "You know the *words?*"

"It's a good song!"

Evidently. It's been played hundreds of times during engagement announcements, wedding receptions, and romance movies Denz has seen. But this is a startling revelation. After so many years together, Denz thought he knew everything about Braylon. But he guesses that's the thing about great relationships:

You can spend a lifetime with someone, and they never fail to surprise you with another side of themselves.

Long fingers squeeze his waist. Denz's eyes lift. "Thanks," Braylon mumbles. "For what you did back there."

"It's in the agreement," Denz insists. "You lie for me. I lie for you."

"You do realize how problematic that sounds, right?"

"Tell that to Margaret Tate and Andrew Paxton."

"Who?"

"From *The Propo*—You know what? Never mind."

In the distance, something that sounds like an unhinged lawn mower cranks up. Then, out of nowhere, Denz sees them.

Snowflakes.

They twirl in the air. Fall gently on tables. Across the guests' faces. Gleeful laughter erupts, the Sedwicks cheering drunkenly. As Emily tries to gather white flurries on her palms, Kami stands proudly in the background.

So, this is her surprise. She's a fucking genius.

Denz looks back to Braylon. Tiny flakes catch on his eyelashes. The dizzying mix of vodka and nostalgia has words leaving Denz's lips before his brain can parse them.

"Can I ki—"

Braylon's mouth meets his, cutting him off.

It means nothing, Denz tells himself.

The pressure Braylon applies. His own shaky exhale. The tongue teasing his lips apart. His fingers grazing the short hairs at the base of Braylon's neck. He adds it all up and it equals *not a single thing.*

He pulls away first, half shouting, "I'm drunk!"

"Me too," Mr. Sedwick says as he staggers by.

Braylon dusts snowflakes from his curls. "I'm quite out of it myself." His nose scrunches, like he's contemplating the last two minutes with extreme regret. "Probably best not to drive home tonight."

He's right. Denz could call a rideshare. It'd be expensive and, on a Saturday night with traffic and construction, the gardens are at least a forty-five-minute trip for him. Over an hour for Braylon. In the morning, Denz would have to get a way back to pick up his car, but—

"Maybe we should get a hotel?" Braylon blurts.

"Together?"

"Yes. No. Same hotel. Maybe the same room? But separate beds."

Braylon's scrambling somehow takes the weight off Denz's chest.

"There's a couple nearby," he says. "I could get us a company discount."

Braylon takes a wobbly step back. "So, shall we?"

Why not? Denz can't imagine things getting any worse than everything else that's happened tonight.

-15-

"One bed."

Denz has repeated the same two words for a full minute.

They're in the lobby of the Mélange, a five-star luxury hotel within walking distance of the botanical garden. It's almost 10:00 P.M., and Denz regrets not planning this better.

Braylon paces behind him, phone in hand. His shoes clacking across the beige-and-green onyx marble floors doesn't take Denz's mind off what the front desk manager just said.

A room with one bed.

It's not the worst thing. He's shared a bed with Braylon before. Of course, they weren't exes then. Back when they treated the queen-sized bed in Denz's apartment like their own personal Naked Cirque du Soleil performance. But none of that's happening tonight.

Except . . . there's the kiss they shared less than an hour ago.

No. Out of the question.

"You're sure there's *nothing* else available?"

Kiana, the very patient night manager, whose hand keeps twitching like she might stab Denz with a letter opener, smiles tightly. "That's correct, Mr. Carter. We have one room left. A deluxe with a gorgeous city view and a king-sized bed."

"No room with double beds?"

"No, sir."

"How about a rollaway bed?"

"No, sir."

"A nice ottoman with extra linen?"

A wild look crosses Kiana's dark brown eyes. "No, Mr. Carter. One room left. One king-sized bed."

He groans, almost face-planting on the counter. "What about—"

"It's *fine*," Braylon interrupts. The giddy buzz from the alcohol and dancing has faded. In its place, a grumpy, scowling beast. He holds up his phone. "I checked. Nothing in a twenty-mile radius."

"Maybe we should try outside the city?" Denz suggests, one eye twitch away from frantic. "I'll get us a car. A limo. We'll go to a nice—"

"*Denzel*," Braylon says tightly. "Everyone's booked. We're already here. Let's just . . . stay."

Denz sags against the counter.

"As I said when you arrived," Kiana chimes in with the slightest hint of exasperation behind her tone, "it's the NBA playoffs. The Miami Heat and all their fans are in town. And Ed Sheeran's performing all weekend at Mercedes-Benz Stadium."

Which explains the blend of hipsters and people in jerseys spilling into the streets.

"What about," Denz says, way too hopeful, "a suite?"

He's not against booking the top-floor presidential. Hell, if it means he can sleep in a bed on one end while Braylon's at least fifty feet away on the other, he'll buy out an entire floor.

"Well . . ." Kiana grins, typing away. "We do have one last city-view, deluxe room with a king-sized bed available."

Braylon smacks a credit card on the counter. "We'll take it."

"Perfect. I just need a form of ID to put on file."

Before Braylon can fish his license from his wallet, Denz tugs out his own, along with a black AmEx company card. "Our room and whatever else we want is on the CEO."

Although this isn't technically a "business necessity," Denz is positive his dad won't mind. Or he'll find a way to bribe Auggie in accounting so Kenneth never finds out. Most likely the latter.

Braylon doesn't fight him.

A few keyboard clicks later, Kiana hands them key cards and a complicated list of directions to their room. Braylon suggests Denz go up and order room service, since the selection of food at the engagement party hardly soaked up any of the drinks they shared, while he runs to grab essential items.

Denz's feet hurt, he's still half buzzed, and in no mood to argue.

"Enjoy your stay!" Kiana chirps, and Denz follows up with an unflattering smile before getting lost *twice* looking for the elevators.

As promised, the view is breathtaking. Countless skyscrapers shimmer with artificial light. Centennial Olympic Park's colossal Ferris wheel glows in purples and blues. Atlanta is a field of glittery neon, and Denz watches from a glass tower.

The room itself is an opulent mix of ivories and grays. The flat-screen is a black mirror reflecting everything back at him: touches of gold and emerald in the furniture. The plush highback in a corner. A small paper bag with the Mélange's logo.

Maybe stopping in the hotel's shop for a couple of . . . *incidentals* of his own was a little presumptuous?

Denz paces the geometric-patterned carpet. He glances at the bag. Shakes his head and paces some more.

This is ridiculous. It was a couple of drinks. One dance. A spontaneous kiss. Fine, two kisses, counting the gala. Oh, and the blow job on Braylon's kitchen counter.

It all means absolutely *nothing* in the grand scheme of things. Denz needs to chill.

On his third lap of the room, his stomach makes a very unpleasant noise, so he orders a little of everything from the room service menu. Braylon returns just as the food arrives. He disappears into the bathroom with a large plastic bag from a nearby pharmacy.

Denz sets everything out picnic-style on the bedspread: a buffet of quesadillas, a bowl of mixed berries, one personal pizza, both seasoned and sweet potato fries, and chocolate-chip cookies.

"Sorry, are you wasted or high?" Braylon asks when he flops onto the bed.

Denz pops a berry in his mouth. "Both."

Braylon's shrugged out of his suit jacket. Slipped off his shoes and socks. Ditched the tie, undone the top two buttons of his shirt.

Denz tries not to stare. Reflexively, his eyes drift to the paper bag and—

Nope. He can survive one night.

He grabs drinks from the minibar—lemonade for himself, water for Braylon—before sitting pretzel-legged on the bed, keeping a manageable distance between them.

They fight over Netflix. Braylon rejects a holiday rom-com starring an actress Kami's friends with. Denz vetoes anything where half the movie's plot is just things exploding.

"How about *My Best Friend's Wedding?*"

Braylon swipes a fry. "Never seen it."

"How?"

"No interest."

Denz waves a dismissive hand. He's already embarrassed for him. "It's decided," he says, clicking Play. There's no way he can allow Braylon to live such an unfulfilled life.

Pizza in his lap, Denz shushes Braylon when the opening song begins.

Sharing a room with his ex isn't as weird as Denz imagined. Midway through Julia Roberts's elevator panic attack, they sit shoulder-to-shoulder against the headboard. Braylon demolishes the seasoned fries, a handful of berries, one of the cookies, but doesn't touch anything else. Denz doesn't complain. More for him.

It's not exactly a WTN—he wouldn't dare betray Jamie like that—but it's *fun.*

Braylon laughs hysterically while Cameron Diaz sings karaoke.

He squeezes Denz's hand when the wedding party sings "I Say a Little Prayer" because, yup, the Sedwick sisters totally stole their act. After Julia Roberts kisses Dermot Mulroney, they pause for a ten-minute rant from Braylon.

"The *audacity*."

When the credits roll, Braylon asks, "So, after all that, she ends up with her gay friend?"

Denz falls halfway off the bed, laughing.

He sends a check-in text to make sure Kami got home safely. After confirmation, his eyes scan over Braylon. He's frozen, watching previews for related movies on the TV.

"My dad would've loved that movie."

Denz lowers his phone.

"Sorry." Braylon's best attempt at a smile fails miserably. "I keep bringing him up—"

"No," Denz interrupts. "I don't mind."

Braylon sighs. "He was a bit of a disaster."

Denz's wide-eyed expression tugs a fond guffaw from Braylon.

"He was the smartest man in just about every room," Braylon goes on. "But he was a shit cook. And he cheated at Scrabble."

"I knew it!"

"He threw himself into a million projects. Never finished any. Like painting his office. Building a birdhouse. Cleaning the attic." Braylon pauses, chewing the inside of his cheek. "Me."

Denz bites his thumbnail.

"Sorry. That sounded unfair?"

"I get it," Denz tells him, far too aware of what it's like to be the son of someone constantly trying to make you into the better version of themselves.

Braylon drags a hand through his curls, releasing another sigh. "He loved movies like that. Mom did too."

"Then how'd you end up with such poor movie taste?"

Braylon tosses a sweet potato fry at his cheek.

"No, seriously," Denz says. "Why do you hate rom-coms?"

"The endings are so trite. So predictable."

"That's what makes them great," Denz nearly shouts. "I know I'm gonna feel good at the end. That I'll have something to hope for. I need to know that, despite how shitty this world is, there are moments in life where it's all worth it."

Braylon watches him intently.

"The best part is," Denz continues, "even if you know the ending, if you predicted how the couple is going to get there in the first five seconds, the journey is never the same. How we get there is always, *always* different."

He shyly lowers his eyes. He's never said that out loud. Not even to Jamie during a Will Thacker Night.

Another fry bounces off his forehead. Braylon grins before standing to stretch. Denz doesn't linger on the strip of exposed brown skin from his shirt riding up.

"I need to shower," Braylon says, yawning.

After plugging his phone into the charger, he pads to the bathroom.

When the door clicks shut, Denz springs from the bed. He shakes out his hands. What is he doing? Gushing like a schoolboy about why he's obsessed with rom-coms? And to his ex, of all people? The one who left him heartbroken? Also, what was up with that little nervous smirk Braylon gave him before disappearing?

Behind the door, the water sprays loudly against the tiles.

Ten feet away, Braylon's *naked*.

Impulsively, Denz cleans up the wreckage of their food. Straightens the bedspread. He adjusts the dimmer switch, leaving the room lit by the TV's glow, then thinks better of it, cranking the lights to maximum voltage. He's not going for intimacy. But there, on one of the floating bedside tables, is the brown shopping bag from the lobby.

The little reminder of where Denz's head was two hours ago.

"You keep looking at that bag."

Denz swallows down a yelp. He didn't hear the door open. How long was he in his own head again? His attention snaps toward the bathroom. Steam billows out and—

Fuck.

Braylon towels off his curls in the doorway. Water droplets drip from his jawline to his collarbone, slivering down his abdomen. He's only wearing a pair of white boxers. Damp hair leads from strong thighs to toned calves.

"Either there's a ticking time bomb in there—" Braylon eyes the paper bag. "—or it's dessert, which I hope you plan on sharing." His tongue flicks over full, pink lips.

Denz's stomach flips in a very inhuman way.

"Neither?"

"That's disappointing. The dessert part, I mean." Braylon motions behind himself. "Do you need to—?"

Denz sucks in a sharp breath. "Brush my teeth," he gets out. "And, like . . . get ready for bed. To *sleep*. In the bed. Nothing else." He feigns a loud, obnoxious yawn. "Wow, I'm so exhausted."

"All yours, then."

Denz shifts anxiously around Braylon. He almost slips on the condensation-slick floor before kicking the bathroom door closed. With a shaky hand, he wipes the fog off the mirror, glaring at his reflection.

"Reality check," he whispers to Mirror Denz. "You've seen him half-naked before."

Mirror Denz looks incredulous.

"Damn it, he's had your dick in his mouth," Denz grumbles. "The bed is huge. Sleeping next to him is *nothing*."

Again, Mirror Denz fails to agree.

On the gray marble counter are rows of products. Not the freebies hotels provide. Instead, there are different deodorant brands. A brand-new toothbrush next to two toothpaste options. An unscented travel lotion with, according to the ingredients, shea butter and green tea.

Denz is caught off guard by his own helpless smile.

Braylon took the time to search out a variety of toiletries for him to choose from. Because he knows Denz hates complimentary hotel products. Or has breakouts from their generic ingredients.

It's enough for him to strip down to his boxers. He washes his face with the matcha hemp cleanser Braylon selected. Brushes his teeth. Throws up finger guns and winks at Mirror Denz before exiting the bathroom.

He finds Braylon sitting on the edge of the bed. In his lap is the bag from the hotel shop.

"Oh."

Braylon's eyes trace from Denz's toes, upward. They stray on his hips, the hair along his stomach, his chest muscles. He whispers, "It's, uh . . . not cheesecake."

He empties out the contents. A box of condoms. The world's most overpriced travel lube bottle.

Denz wants to throw up, scream, and set the entire hotel on fire. Embarrassed, he rubs the back of his skull. He forces himself to maintain eye contact as he says, "So, earlier. While you were gone. I was thinking—"

"Your first mistake."

He ignores the sarcastic twist to Braylon's lips. "Between the party and, I dunno," he manages, sighing. "We kissed. And it was—good?"

The corners of Braylon's eyes crinkle a little.

"Then, I thought, well . . ." Denz's nose scrunches. *"Whatif-wehadsex?"*

It tumbles out in an unintelligible whoosh. Five words crammed into one.

The silence is expected.

Braylon, doubled over laughing, is not.

"Okay," Denz says, even more flustered. "Thanks for confirming I have the worst ideas."

"N-no, that's—"

"Enjoy the bed," Denz insists. "I'm just gonna go drown myself in the shower."

Strong, determined fingers wrap around Denz's wrist before he can stomp away. He staggers backward. Braylon steadies him.

He catches Denz between his knees. His amused brown eyes stare up at Denz.

"I thought the same thing," Braylon says.

"You . . . *did?*"

"The party. The thing with my boss and your dad. Dancing. The kiss." Braylon's chin dips. "Me and you and sex. Tonight."

Denz isn't exactly speechless. He's just not sure how things like vocabulary and sentences work anymore.

"So we're clear," he begins, "you *want* to have sex?"

Braylon winces, then nods.

"With me?"

Another painful nod.

"Right now?"

"Preferably after you stop being a twit," Braylon huffs.

"I mean, sex is great, but being a twit is—"

"Are you quite finished?"

Denz swoops down for a kiss, not bothering to ask. Another rule broken.

Their mouths crush together. It's slow, unlike his heartbeat. He groans as fingers find the grooves of his hips. His palms follow the path of stubble to soft, warm cheeks. He arches unapologetically at the noise Braylon makes deep in his throat.

Impatience takes over. Recklessness too. Teeth catch Denz's bottom lip. A delicious ache. "Yes" spills out so easily, he swears it comes from another room.

Braylon lifts him off the ground. He tosses Denz on the bed. Muscle memory kicks in as Braylon crawls on top of him. Legs instinctively spread. Braylon's hips roll and . . .

Oh. Braylon's so hard.

Denz is too. His hands scramble over the sinewy back muscles. He doesn't know whether to push or pull but his head's spinning. Shallow pants escape his mouth as Braylon pins his wrists to the sheets.

He stares down at Denz, a hunger darkening his eyes.

"For the record," Denz says, "this was all my idea. The sex and the kissing and—*argh*, why aren't we doing more of that?"

"You're insufferable."

"Yeah, yeah, back to the kissing part."

But Braylon doesn't move. His gaze dips to where the condoms and lube lie beside Denz's head.

"I'm on PrEP," he says, fast and nervous. "And I haven't had sex with anyone in . . ."

Denz tries not to react to that pause.

"A long time."

"Good to know," Denz breathes out. He's fighting the urge to do the math on "a long time." "Me too. On PrEP. I guess I should've mentioned that. The other night when you . . . well." The heat in his cheeks is unbearable. "And the other partners thing is, um— complicated?"

"Matty at the café?"

"I—"

Braylon shakes his head. "Never mind. I don't want to know."

Denz's mouth clicks shut. Okay, good. He doesn't have the mental capacity to explain his sex life since their breakup. Not with Braylon on top of him, the firm shape of his dick trapped behind cotton boxers pressing needily along Denz's inner thigh.

"I still want to use condoms," Denz says. "If that's all right?"

Braylon's shoulders relax. "Of course."

Denz isn't ready for how quickly Braylon scurries off him. Kicks out of his boxers. For him hovering over Denz again, naked. His thick erection bobs from a nest of neatly trimmed dark hair, a stark contrast from the very shaved groin Denz remembers from college.

Jesus, he's not gonna make it to the next step.

Braylon tugs at the waistband of Denz's boxers. His eyes ask, *Can I?* and Denz nods, lifting his hips. When he's nude, Denz pushes his head into the pillows. He lets Braylon study him with pupils blown wider and darker than a solar eclipse.

"Okay?" Denz asks.

"Quite."

His hands slide up Braylon's chest. He thumbs brown nipples. Relishes the euphoric hiss Braylon releases. All his nerve endings catch fire as Braylon falls on top of him. He hitches his legs up and Braylon's hands reach under to cup his ass.

Instinctively, he clenches around nothing.

"You're so— Fuck." Braylon meets every one of his impulsive thrusts. "I want you so much, I—"

Denz pushes Braylon's shoulders until he can see his face. His fingers skim a prickly jaw. "Shut your *Bridgerton* mouth and—"

Braylon kisses him roughly.

Everything behind Denz's eyelids explodes.

They move like that for minutes. Kissing. Rotating their hips so their erections meet over and over. Denz's belly is wet and sticky. He doesn't think either one of them can last, but—fuck every-thing—he wants them to.

He wants . . .

He jerks out of the kiss, gasping. Braylon watches him with flushed skin.

"Can we . . . ?" Denz starts, wiggling until he's no longer ten seconds from ruining a pretty hot moment. "I mean, how are we gonna, *y'know*."

Braylon smirks, and Denz wants to punch him.

In college, someone always initiated this part. The fucking. They were both versatile, so it was never a fight over who was what position. Usually, they went with whoever started the touch-ing, the kissing, undressing. But Denz doesn't know if Braylon's still that way.

If that side of him has changed too.

"I don't mind being the—" He stumbles with words. "If you're not into . . ."

Wow, when did he turn into a sixteen-year-old virgin? He's literally had sex on a public bathroom counter. Why can't he say top or bottom?

Something flashes in Braylon's eyes. Gracelessly he says, "I'm still both. So. Well. Whatever you prefer?"

"Do you want to—"

"Not if you'd like to—"

"Well, I thought you might since—" Denz gestures to himself, pushed against the mattress, Braylon braced on his elbows above him. It's impossible not to get distracted by the way the muscles in Braylon's forearms flex.

"What if that means—" Braylon cuts himself off, blushing again.

"Come on now." Denz grins. "Don't threaten me with a good time and then go shy."

Braylon's dramatic huff ghosts minty breath against Denz's lips.

"What if I wanted to ride you?"

Denz's brain goes offline. When he finally manages to reboot, blinking out of a daze, he says, "Yeah. I'm good with that."

Everything in his head moves at light speed. He's no help with the condom. Braylon pinches the tip, slowly unrolls the latex down Denz's aching cock. With a steady hand, he applies a generous amount of lube. He leans up to coat himself.

Denz wants to offer assistance, if only to see what his fingers across Braylon's hole does, but he's drunk all over again. Caught in a wave of intoxication as Braylon repositions himself. His body welcomes Denz like the sand embracing the tide.

Their next kiss is deep and thorough.

Denz's gasps are a verse. Braylon's whimpers are a bridge. Their moans build to a chorus, echoing noisy half sentences they'll never repeat in the daylight.

It's easy to fall back into a routine. Denz's hips lifting and falling. His fingers stroking Braylon's spine. Braylon's hands splayed on either side of Denz's head as he rocks down smoothly. Sweat slicks their skin, adding to the symphony their bodies create.

Denz's eyes slide shut. He can't watch Braylon's expressions. The blissed-out one. Hard lines melting into soft ones. Instead, he listens for cues: the mewls and hitched breaths and, "Deeper, yes, *there*."

He obeys.

Braylon arches into a perfect bow. He squeezes and relaxes, his rhythm never faltering.

How is he still so great at this?

Denz focuses on lasting a minute longer. Then three minutes. Five. Whatever it takes for Braylon to reach that point where he bites his lip hard. Shivers while falling apart on Denz's cock.

He doesn't know when Braylon notices how on edge he is. When his tempo slows. When he leans close enough to skim their lips together in an unsealed promise.

"Hey."

Denz peeks one eye open. "Ugh. Yeah?"

Braylon grins. "You can."

"Can what?"

"You know."

Denz exhales a laugh, shaking his head. "You can't say it, can you?"

Braylon narrows his eyes. He whispers sternly, "Come inside me, *Denzel*."

That's it. Denz blacks out. One day in the future, someone will tell him how loud he whined. Kissed his name off swollen lips. Cupped Braylon's ass, held him in place, and sank deep into him until it felt like endless warmth surrounded his whole body.

Someone will tell him how Braylon shivered. Describe the extreme reverie in his expression when Denz came undone underneath him. How long it took him to catch his breath, smiling against Braylon's shoulder.

One day, he'll remember it all and wish he didn't say, "I really need to pee" immediately afterward.

-16-

Denz should've stayed in the bathroom longer.

After discarding the condom, a quick pee, washing himself up, and running a face cloth under warm water for Braylon, he returns to the bedroom and stops short.

Lying on his side, on top of the covers, Braylon smiles lazily. The electric blues and purples from the city melt across his sweat-slick skin. His head's propped up by one hand, curls disheveled. The other hand is cupped over his groin. He can't hide his erection.

"Fuck," Denz hisses.

Braylon chuckles. "Think we just did."

"No, I mean." He shakes his head. "You didn't get off."

In all the messy kisses, frantic movements, the orgasm stretching through his skin until he was certain it'd rip off, he didn't pay attention to Braylon's needs. Denz came, then ran off to the bathroom. He's an asshole.

Braylon shrugs. "No worries."

"Hell no." Denz marches over to the bed, dropping the cloth on the sheets. He crouches over Braylon. "We're fixing this. Now."

Braylon laughs into a kiss. "What'd you have in mind?"

Denz draws back, thinking. There are so many options. So many things he hasn't done to Braylon in *years*. He could jerk him off. Swallow him to the root like Braylon did at his apartment . . .

No. He wants something else.

For Braylon, but also selfishly for himself.

He flops back into the place on the sheets he was five minutes ago. Big mistake. He scoots out of the sweaty-damp spot. Lower lip between his teeth, Denz eases his knees apart. He tilts his hips up, hoping Braylon understands.

A wildfire spreads across the sepia in Braylon's eyes.

"Are you sure?"

Denz nods. "Mostly? Only 'cause, like. I ate all that junk during the movie and—"

Suddenly, the last piece clicks like a LEGO into place. That's why Braylon only ate the seasoned fries. A handful of berries. One cookie. The reason he requested water instead of tea or more alcohol from the minibar.

He'd secretly planned to bottom all along. The bastard gave Denz an option knowing damn well what he wanted.

A tentative smirk pulls at Braylon's mouth.

"I hate you," Denz says, half laughing. "Yes. I want you to fuck me."

"Fine, fine. If you insist."

"I do. That is, if you don't mind . . ." Denz trails off, too embarrassed to admit he's nervous. Not about the sex. But how his body might react.

Braylon cups his chin, thumb stroking high on his cheek. His other hand tears another condom from the strip. Finds the lube.

"I'm quite sticky and sweaty," Braylon begins. "Could use another shower." He curls forward, pressing a kiss to the corner of Denz's mouth. "I'm not worried about what happens. It's natural."

Denz's fingers twist into the sheets.

Braylon's so close, his voice gentle. "I'll go slow," he promises.

The soft, downy hairs on his legs tickle the back of Denz's thighs. His hand slips from Denz's jaw to his chest, riding the current of his accelerated breaths. All of Denz's nerves connect to the eagerness blackening Braylon's eyes.

"You don't have to. Go slow, I mean. I've done—"

He doesn't want to finish that sentence.

An unreadable expression circles Braylon's face, then it's gone. He nods once.

"We'll go at your pace," he says, serious.

Those words massage the tension from Denz's chest. Ease the fears tightening his stomach. He allows Braylon's slick hands to shift his thighs wider. His eyes flutter shut at the cold press of lube against his hole. He trembles around the first finger, then the next. The shaking doesn't let up until Braylon whispers, "I think you're ready," and Denz's entire body screams, *YES*.

"Please."

"Tell me if it's too much," Braylon says against his jaw.

Denz exhales tightly when the head nudges in. A long beat passes before his body adjusts.

"It's not," he gasps.

"Good." Braylon's smile is imprinted onto the side of Denz's neck. "Because you feel fucking *incredible*."

Denz isn't sure if it's the huskiness of Braylon's voice. The way he cages Denz in. Sucks at Denz's jumping Adam's apple. Meets every one of Denz's groans with a chest-deep grunt. Moves at a pace that's so painfully gentle, it's frustrating.

Whatever it is, Denz prays it never stops.

"Ah-*ah*."

"All right?" Braylon asks between measured thrusts.

"Mm-hmm."

Denz doesn't trust himself with actual words, too afraid he'll shout things he can never take back, no matter how hard he tries. So, he savors the chest kisses. Allows Braylon to yank him back on his thick cock.

Braylon never asks him to be quieter. To stop swearing at the ceiling. To be anything but himself. No, he offers Denz a crinkle-eyed smile that's bare and frighteningly boyish like they are back in those first months together in Athens.

"Still okay?"

Denz exhales out, "Yeah," instead of the more colorful responses his brain had in mind.

"I can—" Braylon's hips draw back.

"No," Denz says more urgently than he planned to. "Deeper."

"Okay, but I'm gonna—"

"I know."

He can tell by the way Braylon's nose scrunches. The tight corners of his mouth. The cords of his biceps going taut. Denz knows the signs. He wants to stop them . . . just a few more minutes.

Thing is, Denz typically likes sex this way—fast. Over before it starts. Unattached orgasms are easier to walk away from. Strictly a physical thing. When it's about getting off and not making a memory, he can handle that.

What he's struggling with is how he wants Braylon to change the angle. Test Denz's limits. He doesn't want quick. He wants rough fingers pinning his hands above his head. He wants their shared panting, his toes curling into the sheets, the pleasant ache in his lower spine from arching so hard to meet Braylon's thrusts.

He wants Braylon to make him beg.

He's achingly hard again. Just the feel of his erection flopping against his belly, the tip wet and sensitive, is too much and not enough.

"One more minute."

Braylon's shoulders tremble.

"Stay there. Another second."

"Denz, you—"

"*Please.*"

Braylon whines but obeys. He gives and Denz takes. Then, Denz squeezes around him and Braylon's quaking, biting his bottom lip hard enough to draw blood. His eyes are wide and blissed out, but so focused on Denz's next command.

"Come," Denz says, shuddering. "I've got you."

And Braylon does.

Denz wraps his legs around stuttering hips. He grins into

the crook of Braylon's neck as everything comes in a thirty-foot wave, crashing around them.

Not once does he bother to come up for air.

Morning arrives too soon.

Ribbons of orangey sunlight burst through the windows. Sunrise burns against Denz's eyelids. He regrets not closing the curtains. Then he remembers what happened last night and . . .

That's fantastic. All of Atlanta saw him having sex. *Twice.*

His phone vibrates on the nightstand. He checks his notifications. Six texts from Jamie, two from Nic, and another hundred or so from social media. He's hungover, a pounding headache trying to crack his skull in half. Denz doesn't have the energy to explain to his best friend why the hell he didn't sleep in his own bed last night.

Instead, he scrolls through social media.

It's the usual. Followers tagging him in photos, DMs about promotional opportunities he'll respond to later, and comments galore. People are still obsessively liking the Valentine's Day post. It's up to fifty thousand likes. No one knows who the mystery man is yet.

He stifles a laugh as he reads their theories.

Behind him, Braylon snores quietly.

Denz takes in the moment. Their bare feet poking from underneath the rumpled bedspread. Braylon's hand resting on Denz's naked hip. He snuffles and exhales into one of the hotel's expensive pillows. It should all be so weird—having a man in bed with him after years of ducking out the second the condom's off—but it's not.

It's oddly comfy.

He knows in his core that, at any second, the bubble could burst. It's *going to* burst. That's how these things work.

But not yet.

A ridiculous idea crosses his mind. He edges down the cover. Wiggles backward in Braylon's direction. Rolls painstakingly slowly onto his back before opening his front-facing camera. He holds the phone high.

From this horrible angle, Denz is bleary-eyed, face unshaven, hair wrecked from Braylon's hands. He can't tell if that's lube or *something else* tacky against his chest. Braylon's equally unkempt, a deep pillow crease in his cheek, but he still manages to look angelic.

Denz can't stand him.

He adjusts the view until everything except for Braylon's arm is cut from the frame. An acceptable post-sex, morning selfie.

"Whatever you're doing," Braylon grumbles, then yawns, "could you please do it a bit quieter? My head's pounding and I might puke all over you."

"Wow. Charming."

"It's what I excel at." Braylon yawns again, louder. "Charm and getting absolutely *wrecked* over two drinks."

"Lightweight."

"Your mother."

Denz gasps, fake affronted. Braylon laughs into his shoulder. The heat, the closeness, the soft hair on Braylon's chest grazing his bicep, makes Denz acutely aware of his morning wood.

Why is his body like this?

With one eye open, Braylon squints at him. "Are you taking a selfie?"

"No. Yes. Maybe?"

"Of us?"

"No," Denz sputters. "I wouldn't do that without your consent. It's just me . . . and your arm? No face."

"And did you get my *arm's* consent?"

Humiliation heats up Denz's skin. Braylon snorts, pressing his nose to the tendons between Denz's neck and shoulder. "Here. Let me."

"You don't have t—"

"Gimme."

They fumble the exchange. Denz almost suffers *another* phone to his face, but Braylon catches it midair. His wingspan is greater—fucking six-one giant—so he reaches above them. He blindly snaps off a few photos with his face hiding in the crook of Denz's neck. Something ripples in his stomach when Braylon's lips brush under his jaw.

He examines Braylon's work. "These are terrible."

Braylon peels himself away. "They're *art*."

"Fuck, you're awful at this."

"I'm not!"

"Yes, you are. Your ancestors are offended. Have you never taken a selfie before?"

A sudden urge to kiss Braylon's pouty mouth rattles Denz. Scratch that. He's going to be the one throwing up last night's food.

"C'mere," he demands.

After too much effort and groggy complaints from Braylon, Denz rolls to his side. He convinces Braylon to spoon him. A hint of relief comes when he realizes he's not the only one with a sleepy erection. Denz poses Braylon's hand against his chest. Fixes the bedding until it only covers his lower half.

The shot is captured in one attempt:

Denz, shirtless on his side. Braylon hidden except for his arm; long fingers curled around Denz's scruffy chin. Sunlight washes over them in the perfect shade of orange.

He captions it: *morning cuddles*. Adds the sleeping-face and smiling-with-three-hearts emojis.

"You're okay with this?" Denz double-checks.

His first two posts were tame. Small hints to tease his followers. But *this* . . .

The gossip blogs will certainly smell blood in the water. At least it'll push the narrative for his family.

Braylon stares at the photo for a long minute. "Yes," he whispers.

"I won't tag you," Denz promises again.

"I know."

And that hint of confidence, of the trust in Braylon's voice, wakes a smile from the corners of Denz's lips. He posts, then tucks his phone under a pillow.

A beat passes. Braylon doesn't move away. There's a distinct nudge between Denz's thighs, behind his balls, that encourages his own half-hard cock to life.

God, he could go for another round.

No. Last night was . . . they were drunk. It was a one-time—two, actually—thing, but that's all.

He does his best to slide into Now Denz. The one who doesn't do sleepovers. Who never saves numbers, never repeats. Never, ever gets attached. He shakes off the ghost of College Denz because that version was uncertain and got his heart shattered.

That Denz wouldn't last five seconds as head of 24 Carter Gold.

He needs to crawl out of bed. It's time to get dressed. Order a car to drive him back to his own. Also, he should check in with Kami. Offer to help her with any of last night's wrap-up like a responsible future CEO would.

With the engagement party out of the way, his dad's retirement event is all that's left before the next successor is chosen.

Now, more than ever, Denz needs to focus.

But the moment he turns to face Braylon to tell him this, the words dry up in his throat.

He's caught on the shadowy bristle along Braylon's jaw. Warm skin soaking up the light. The sleepiness in his brown eyes. Even this Braylon, with the curls instead of a buzz cut, quiet smirk instead of a loud, infectious grin, the heavy brow of someone who's experienced success and loss and life in another country, looks at Denz like he's still that boy in Athens pretending to know what the fuck he was doing.

"Do you think," Denz pauses, swallowing, "I can do it?"

"Do what?"

"Run the company. Be the boss. Carry my dad's legacy."

"Do *you?*"

Denz knows what the aunties think. What his dad thinks. What Kami thought—or maybe still *thinks*, he's not sure. But right now, he only cares about one person's opinion.

"I want so bad to do what my dad's done for others," he says.

"Sometimes, I think I can be just like him. *Be good enough.* And then . . . I don't know." He shrugs half-heartedly. "No one else sees that in me."

Braylon props his cheek on his knuckles. He stares down at Denz.

"Then I look at you and see so much confidence," Denz says, quieter. "I know I keep saying this, but you're different. It's not a bad different. Anymore."

"That's a compliment, right?"

"A fact." Denz's tone is a weird tangle of envy and fondness when he says, "You look like you belong at Skye's the Limit. Nora believes in you. I saw it last night. You don't need me to get that promotion."

He smooths the wrinkle from between Braylon's brows.

"You're great on your own, Braylon. People love you."

"They love you too," Braylon counters.

Denz laughs bitterly. "They love who they see online. Or at parties. My family loves when I don't fuck anything up."

He throws an arm over his eyes, groaning. Soon, fingers wrap around his wrist, tugging. Denz is forced to look up at Braylon's deep scowl, his narrowed eyes.

"The people who *matter* love you for you."

Denz inhales.

"I believe in you." Braylon's mouth slowly stretches upward. "You're great on your own too."

Denz follows the stream of careening sunlight over Braylon's face. The clarity in his expression. Once again, he's chosen his ex to spill his guts to over everyone else in his life. He should probably analyze that. But his stomach chooses now to growl angrily, and Braylon shakes with laughter.

"Shower and breakfast then?"

"Okay," Denz agrees, relieved. He can't spend another minute in his own head.

His gaze drifts down the bedspread. The very naked parts of them are still hidden. He doesn't want to take any chances on his dick being reenergized by showering *with* Braylon, so he suggests, "You first."

Groggily, Braylon crawls from their one-night-only cocoon. He stumbles to the bathroom. Denz's eyes linger on his hairy legs, the shape of his ass until the door shuts.

Fist to his mouth, he moans.

This is why their agreement had conditions. Preventive measures. Now, it's like all the rules are nothing but blurry, Rorschach inkblots, open for varied interpretation.

He reaches for a distraction. His phone. Something to keep his mind off the noise of the shower water hitting the tiles. Of Braylon standing, naked, under the hot spray. Of . . . Braylon, in an off-key voice, singing the song they danced to last night?

"Are you fucking kidding me?"

Denz hurls a pillow at the bathroom door. Braylon's voice gets louder.

Fine. Maybe it can't hurt to blur the lines some more.

Denz leaps out of bed. Sprints into the foggy bathroom. He kisses the surprised yelp off Braylon's lips. He maneuvers them both under the waterfall spray. Braylon's body instantly responds, and Denz doesn't recall a rule about hand jobs in their agreement.

The lines need redefining anyway.

the Carter Family Group Chat

Today 10:33 A.M.

Aunt Cheryl Carter
KAMI MADE THE FRONT PAGE OF SOUTHERN BRIDE!

Aunt Eva Carter-Rivera
Correction: THE SEDWICKS made the front page of Southern Bride's BLOG.
Denzel was featured in BY INVITATION ONLY.

Aunt Cheryl Carter

Kami was in the background! Their writeup
mentioned the company 6 times!
Whats your point, E?

Aunt Eva Carter-Rivera

That you're wrong.

Aunt Cheryl Carter

Its still great publicity!
Meanwhile our nephew is posting thirst traps in
bed w his BF

Nic Carter

auntie please dont use the words "thirst trap"
when talking about my bro
its gross & he could never

Aunt Cheryl Carter

Its all over Facebook!!! Taking attention away
from Kamis big night

Aunt Eva Carter-Rivera

He's in a serious relationship that's getting good
buzz.
Isn't that what you wanted??

Aunt Cheryl Carter

I didn't want to see our nephew's nipples on
dlisted's twitter!

Nic Carter

[Tatianna from drag race choices.gif]

Leena Carter

It's Sunday morning. Y'all need Jesus.
Going to ask my bible club to send an extra
prayer up for each of you.

                        *   *   *

"Tell me more."

Denz should be at his apartment, resting. Tomorrow starts the final leg of the CEO race. He should be napping on the sofa. Or cleaning the bedroom he didn't sleep in last night. Instead, he's on an outdoor patio at Buttermilk & Jam, a swanky café in Buckhead, feeding his mild hangover with cornbread muffins and coffee.

Spring always comes early in Atlanta. February has barely vanished before lush greens return to the trees, the air scented in blooming flowers, trenches and boots shed for shorts and sandals.

Overhead, delicate white clouds float in a rich cornflower-blue sky. Dozens of red umbrellas shade the patio. Denz rolls up the sleeves of his somewhat wrinkly white oxford.

Across from him, Jamie waits impatiently.

He's been recapping the engagement party. The gorgeous setting and awful speeches. Running into Braylon's boss. The part about one too many drinks, carefully leaving out the kiss. He's just started on Kiana, the front desk manager, when Jamie says, "So, when did you two fuck?"

Denz spits out his coffee.

It's a slow brunch crowd. The closest customer, a fortysomething man, is too engrossed in his laptop to care. That doesn't stop Denz from kicking Jamie under the table.

"We didn't have—"

"Oh, you definitely did." Jamie laughs. "Your clothes are wrecked, you're obnoxiously giddy, and you keep watching your phone like Juliet waiting to hear from Romeo."

It's not true. Denz can't help if the aunties are feuding in the family group chat. Or that his notifications have been out of control ever since posting that morning selfie.

But, like, *maybe* his eyes go there once or twice, expecting a text from Braylon.

After leaving the hotel, they shared a light breakfast. They ate in an easy silence, ankles brushing, eyes lingering a second too long. Denz kept waiting for the awkwardness to appear. It never came. Not even when the car service dropped them off at the botanical gardens.

They didn't kiss goodbye. But Braylon's pinkie remained curled around Denz's until they were forced to walk in opposite directions toward their cars.

So, it's not Denz's fault he's anticipating an *I'm home* message from Braylon to pop up on his screen. He's simply being thoughtful.

"You're doing it *again*."

Denz snaps to attention, almost knocking over his mug.

Jamie leans forward and says, in a conspiratorial voice, "Was it good?"

"No, stop."

"I knew it!" Jamie's grin widens. "British dick is amazing."

"He's from *here*. Dunwoody."

Jamie pushes his wavy bangs back. He's in a tight-fit black V-neck and skinny jeans. He reaches for one of Denz's muffins as he says, "Irrelevant. You two finally boned. You're happy. What's there to complain about?"

Wow. For once, Denz *doesn't* have anything to complain about.

The sex *was* good. And it wasn't weird afterward. His family's still buying into the whole fake relationship. The company's trending, whether from Kami's successful event or his photo with Braylon, Denz doesn't care. He's content.

"Well?" Jamie prompts.

Denz smiles fondly into his coffee. "It's . . . nice."

His phone chimes on the table. It's not another social media alert. Or an update in the group chat. It's also not the *I made it back to my apartment safely, thanks for the great night* text he's forecasting in the most nonchalant, zero-fucks-given way.

But it is a message from Braylon:

> Is your name Earl Grey?
> Because you're definitely a hot-tea!

This time, Denz snorts so hard, he sees stars. Another text bubble appears under the last. Denz bites his lip, watching the floating ellipsis.

I'm home by the way, Braylon sends. The party was wonderful. You looked great.

He fights off another stupid grin.

you werent a bad date, he texts. 8 out of 10.

Braylon's response reads, You're too kind. I'll do better next time.

Denz starts to type out a *thank you for the body-tingling orgasm in the shower earlier* but thinks better of it. Some thoughts should stay in the drafts.

"*Ohmygod*, please stop," Jamie begs, startling the phone from Denz's hands. He locks the screen before Jamie can read anything.

"Hmm?"

"Whatever your face is doing right now is gross," Jamie says. "I can't handle how cute you two are."

"It's *fake*, asshole."

"Oh. Okay." Jamie stares at him, eyebrows lowered like he's unsure if they're speaking the same language. "Of course. Totally fake."

Denz is about to ask what's happening with Jamie's tone when a throat clears. A short, stout woman with stringy red hair stands over them, her deadly glare directed at Jamie.

"Jamie Peters," she hisses. "You're on the clock."

"Um, hi, Georgina." Jamie winces.

"What're you doing out here for an hour and ten minutes?"

"Bussing tables?"

"While sitting down?"

"Yes." Jamie does his best to sit taller, but it's more of a raised slouch. "The lower elevation helps me focus?"

Georgina rolls her eyes. "Get your ass back to the bar. Amber's drowning. A party of twelve ordered Long Islands and appetizers. Go before I fire you and rehire you next weekend for the St. Paddy's Day crowd!"

Jamie scurries away from the table.

Before Georgina joins him, she points a stern finger at Denz, cheeks burgundy. "Don't think your food's on the house either. I expect a big tip. Tell your mom I said hello. And let your dad know we're serving those tomato and goat cheese quiches he loves again."

Denz smirks. He tugs out his wallet, forgetting all about Jamie's cryptic expression or replying to Braylon's last text.

It's time to go home.

-17-

Kenneth Carter loves a themed party.

This year's annual New Year's Eve bash is Cinematic Beginnings.

The Belvedere Ballroom, inside a downtown Atlanta hotel, is decked out glamorously: soft gold lighting and champagne-colored decorations. Professional hair and makeup stations in the corners. Black-linen-covered tables with mini Oscar statues holding peonies and popcorn-filled film canisters and Polaroid instant cameras. Marquees hang over the bars advertising theme-appropriate cocktails. A red carpet leads to the dance floor.

It's so corny and extra.

Denz's thoughts are confirmed by the movie *New Year's Eve* projected on one of the far walls. Tonight's also very on brand for one of his dad's events.

After an hour of mingling, Denz escapes the main floor. Fuck, he hasn't missed this. The life he has to lead as the son of Kenneth Carter. All the endless smiling and handshakes and boring conversations with VIP influencers. College has spoiled him.

At the bar, he procures a tray of drinks and a slice of silky chocolate espresso cake. Then, he's on an elevator to the private second floor. Away from the noise.

Closer to the *real* reason he's here.

"This is . . . bananas."

Leaning over the half wall to watch the socializing below, Bray looks equally awed and terrified. He doesn't fit in with this crowd. Not in a suit borrowed from his dad, his fresh buzz cut barely hiding how soft and boyish his face is. But Denz loves how out of place his boyfriend is. An old pair of Jordans in a closet full of glass slippers.

He loves that Bray's *here*. In his world. For the first time.

To Bray's left, Nic smirks. "This is *average*," she says over Out-Kast's "Hey Ya!"

"Really?"

"*Please.*" Nic is at least eight inches shorter than Bray, but she still manages to look down at him when she says, "Wait until you see the birthday parties. Or Valentine's. The mayor goes all out." She rolls her eyes. "God forbid another Sedwick gets engaged. Those are intense."

"*Who?*"

"Listen, junior." Nic pats the back of his hand. Denz swears there's a sixty-year-old hairdresser trapped inside his sister's body. "This is who we are. This is your life now. Parties. Smiling twenty-four-seven. Pretending to like strangers. Having people go through your trash to see what you ate for lunch."

"They do *what?*" Bray goes pale.

"Enough, Nic." Denz wedges himself between them. He passes Nic a highball of pineapple juice. "Stop scaring my boyfriend."

She steals the cake slice, grinning. "Not my fault he's weak-minded."

"I'm not—"

"Jesus," Denz says, interrupting Bray's protest. "You're just like Dad."

Through a mouthful of cake, she says, "Thank you."

"That wasn't a compliment."

"Neither is your face in this lighting."

Denz chokes on a laugh. He's *definitely* missed Nic. He pivots to Bray. Hands him a rum and Coke. "Drink," he instructs.

Bray does, whispering, "Who are the . . . Sedwicks?"

"Nobody important," Denz asserts before downing his lemon drop martini. "Doing okay?"

He recognizes Bray's restlessness. How pinched his face gets. The sheen of sweat on his forehead. That same nervous Bray he saw across the room almost three years ago. The one who tries so hard to look comfortable at parties.

Denz considered turning down his dad's invitation to bring Bray. It's not as if Denz wanted to show up either. But Bray insisted. Last New Year's was spent with Emmanuel. Plus, after their final winter semester of hell at UGA, they needed this.

"I'm fine," Bray says.

"Liar," Denz teases. He loosens Bray's poorly knotted tie.

"At least the aunties aren't here," Nic says.

Denz sighs. *Thank you, Uncle Orlando, for wanting to reignite the fire in your marriage by taking Auntie Eva to Fiji for the holidays. Also, thanks for inviting Auntie Cheryl and Uncle Tevin along.*

He's pretty sure Bray wouldn't survive a party as big as this *and* that introduction.

"How's your dad?" Bray asks.

Denz leans his elbows on the half wall, sighing.

"Busy as ever."

In the sea of bodies and overflowing champagne flutes, Denz easily finds his dad. Grape bow tie matching his pocket square. Classic Ralph Lauren tuxedo with tails. The one man in the room who moves from conversation to conversation with relaxed shoulders and genuine enthusiasm. Everything Denz fails to imitate at these parties.

They haven't had five minutes to talk all night. But at least he knows Denz is here. At least he's already given his smile of approval to Bray.

Bray bumps his shoulder. "Is this what you're going to be like? After we graduate?"

"Hmm?"

"You know." Bray nods toward the stage, lowering his voice to say, "Like your dad."

"Oh, no. I don't want this."

Bray's lips quirk in bemusement. "Then what?"

Denz's face wrinkles. "It's not *exactly* what I want. I don't know. It's complicated." He sips his martini. "It's New Year's Eve. Don't make me think tonight."

There's something unreadable in the corner of Bray's eyes. He doesn't press. But Denz can see the questions forming.

"Besides . . ." Denz licks sugar from the rim of his glass. "My dad loves his company."

"It's his fourth child," Nic confirms.

"He'll never retire."

"Nope. But I'm quitting," Kami says, appearing from nowhere in a floral embroidered Zac Posen minidress. She swipes the last glass from Denz's tray—a white wine. She's halfway through before adding, "Dad's so stubborn. This band is awful. And I hate these shoes."

Nic points to her own feet. A pair of leather Superstars. "Always come prepared."

Kami flips her off. "I don't want to be an event manager anymore," she complains. "Eric can have it."

Somewhere below, Eric Tran is following their dad, checklist in hand, sweating through his suit.

"You're doing fine," Denz tells her.

"I'm serious. I'm quitting." Kami whips out her phone. "Emailing my resignation now."

Denz plucks the phone away. "No, you're not."

"Don't make me hurt you."

Denz edges away. He doesn't think his sister will punch him. He just wants to make sure she doesn't toss the rest of her wine on his velvet dinner jacket, is all. "Kam," he says calmly, "you're not quitting. This company will collapse without you. You're too good. One day, you're gonna throw a party a million fucking times better than this. It's one night. Chill."

Kami inhales deeply, the tension leaving her jaw.

Bray steps forward. "You know what you need?"

"More wine?"

"Stronger booze?" Denz offers.

"An edible, a new family and career, a decent man—"

"A dance," Bray says, cutting Nic off. He extends a hand to Kami, beaming. "C'mon."

"Bray, you dance?"

"A little," Bray replies as Denz barks out, "Hell no!"

Ignoring him, Bray loops an arm with Kami. He escorts her toward the elevator, winking at Denz over his shoulder.

"Okay," Denz says in one long breath. "That's happening."

"Don't be jealous," Nic tells him.

"I'm not," he snaps.

He's not. A minute later, he's not leaning over the half wall, glaring down at the crowd. The band covers an old Justin Timberlake song, "SexyBack." Kami's head is tipped back, cackling. And there's Bray, buzz cut and ill-fitting suit, *twerking* like a hamster on MDMA.

"What the f—"

Denz cuts himself off, howling.

Bray, who hates parties, who never wants attention, who moves like a superhero movie actor trying to be a dancer, is rolling his hips in the middle of the dance floor. Rotating spotlights catch on his grin. He's off beat and doesn't care. He spins Kami until they're both dizzy.

He has *fun*.

"Wow," Nic says, "when's the wedding?"

Denz's head jerks in her direction. Bad move. The alcohol's starting to settle in his system. "Excuse me?"

"Uh, your face whenever you look at him?" Nic's eyes slide to where Bray is. "Bro, you're gone. Down bad. Crazy in love like Bey."

He squints. "What do you know about love? You're *fourteen*."

"Clearly I know more than you."

"Hush." He snatches her glass, sniffs to make sure the bartender didn't accidentally slip her any gin. "I'm not—we're not. We haven't . . . fuck. We're still *young*."

"So? Dad proposed to Mom at your age."

He knows. And as much as Denz wants to be like his dad, he doesn't want to *be* him. He wants slow. Time to figure his shit out. Bray does too.

What's the rush?

Without thinking, his eyes find Bray again. Animated and laughing. So *beautiful* while dancing with Kami. His smile pushing into his cheeks, eyes crinkled. And Denz wants to wake up to that.

Tomorrow. And the day after. For the next few months while they finish their degrees. Years from now, too. For a limitless number of mornings until he forgets what life was like before this silly boy smiled at him from across a party.

He loses himself in the thought. Loses track of time until his dad's on the stage, giving a speech. Until Kami shoves a flute of champagne into his hand.

Until Bray's warm against his side again.

Until Nic squishes the four of them together, Bray using his ridiculously long arms to snap a Polaroid.

And Denz was so wrong. Bray *does* fit in. Right between the Denz from Athens and the Denz who lives here, with his sisters, two worlds finally connected.

The countdown starts. He hears the chorus of screams from below. The shouting from Kami and Nic. It's all white noise. Never quite as loud as Bray's question from earlier:

Is this what you're going to be like? After we graduate?

What? Happy? So in love, it might kill him?

Fuck, he hopes so. He really does.

"This is the *Titanic*," Eric says, glasses crooked, hair wrecked. His sharp cheeks are as pink as the linen button-down he's wearing. The lack of a belt is clearly from running late this morning rather than a casual style choice. "It's the *Titanic* and we're the band who decided playing music to keep everyone calm was smarter than abandoning ship."

Denz grins from his desk. "It's not that serious."

"We're *drowning*."

"We're looking for a new DJ," Denz corrects.

The one they hired for the retirement party pulled out. Turns out performing a live set in Palm Springs for an up-and-coming teen actress's spring bash is a bigger priority.

"And the florist?" Eric says through clenched teeth.

Denz scans his computer monitor. Despite his and Kami's extensive efforts to organize the flower arrangements, Kenneth still found a way to request peonies. *Classic.* He's already drafting a compromise his dad will probably reject.

"On it."

He makes a note about replying to Auntie Cheryl's demand to extend the family speeches from five minutes each to fifteen. There's only so much alcohol the guests can handle. He reviews his to-do list while Eric continues to mutter nonsense under his breath.

T-minus ten days until the party.

Nine days until his dad makes his decision.

It's only Wednesday and everyone's on edge. Toy soldiers wound too tightly. No one knows what'll happen at the start of next month. Who their next boss will be. Is it him or Kami?

Neither?

"We're sinking and playing *Mozart*," Eric continues to grumble, "and no one's throwing us a fucking life jacket as we're going down."

"Stop being dramatic, Kate Winslet," Denz says, smirking.

Eric pauses his pacing, head snapping up. "Wait," he says, brow furrowed. "When did you become me? When did I become you?"

Denz laughs.

Since being promoted to event manager, Eric's always been on top of his game. Backup plans for the backup plans. He's not the kind of person who has meltdowns over people named DJ Allegro bailing for a weekend in the desert.

"I don't know." Denz shrugs. "I guess I'm—"

"Content" almost slips out his mouth. It's not the right word. More like confident. He doesn't feel like he did two months ago. Like his entire career was hanging by a string of fairy lights from a skyscraper on a windy day.

The buzz about Kami's event is growing, but the talk around the gala hasn't died down either. He's still in this.

"I'm ready," Denz says.

His phone lights up on the desk. He already knows who the new notification is from:

Formerly Known As Bray.

Fine, the fact that Braylon believes in him *might* be that extra boost he needed.

Denz sucks in his lower lip before a smile can fully form. He refuses to acknowledge the skip of his heart. The way his belly dips and flips.

Their texting is nonstop. FaceTime calls too. Mostly discussions about Skye's the Limit's upcoming party. Things like sponsors and donations and Braylon spending way too much time on video apps discovering new dances to impress the teens with.

Every morning, Denz finds himself standing with Kami outside the lobby elevators, yawning into the crook of his elbow, searching for a new reason to message Braylon. He counts down the hours until Braylon's lunch break. Or when he'll video-call Denz to ramble while cooking in his kitchen.

But it's Not. A. Thing.

"You're . . ." Eric narrows his eyes. "Ready?"

Denz nods.

Eric watches him a minute longer. "Okay," he says, smiling just a little. "We're not gonna drown, boss."

"Don't call me that."

Eric ignores him. "Should we work on the music problem?"

"Now?"

The panic begins to return to the corners of Eric's eyes.

"*Ugh.* Fine. I have an idea of who we can contact." Denz

checks the time on his phone. Notices the unread message from Braylon. He forces the grin from his traitorous mouth. "We'll talk after lunch."

Today 11:46 A.M.

Formerly Known As Bray
Why is there a photo of you nearly shirtless in an
article for Business Today?
[link attachment]

> DENZEL CARTER: The Future of Atlanta's Social
> Scene?
> hahahaha!
> that photos from a year ago BTW
> silent auction for the trevor project
> are you secretly googling me?

Formerly Known As Bray
You wish I was "googling" you.
Nice write-up, lack of clothing aside.
Loved the bit about your dating life and the
cheeky photo of you having
lunch with some bloke downtown.

> another old photo
> are you jealous?

Formerly Known As Bray
Please. He hardly looks like fake boyfriend
material.

> he kinda looks like you
> the jawline. complexion. big hands.

Formerly Known As Bray
Slander! We look nothing alike!

> article says he's the "mysterious loverboy from
> Mr. Carter's Instagram"
> 100K likes on that post btw

Formerly Known As Bray
You must be so proud.
Are you free Thursday evening?

for???

Formerly Known As Bray
Film festival. Work thing.
I could really use an excuse to leave early.

this isnt in the agreement so youre
paying for dinner

Formerly Known As Bray
Of course.

Denz almost doesn't hear it: the hushed, anxious voices.

He's too busy smiling goofily, eyes glued to his phone screen as he walks toward the elevator. At least two interns pirouette around him. He half apologizes all while rereading Braylon's last texts. He's stuck on: *You wish I was "googling" you* and *He hardly looks like fake boyfriend material.*

Was that flirting? *Is* Braylon jealous?

The questions churning in his head are interrupted by Auntie Cheryl's voice coming from around the corner.

"I heard him on the phone. Kenny's not convinced."

"But the V-Day gala was a hit." That's Auntie Eva. "And you said Kamila's party was getting tons of coverage."

"It *is*. She killed it."

"So, what's the problem?"

"I couldn't hear the rest of the call. Maybe he wants bigger?"

Eva sucks air through her teeth. "You mean he wants them to do things the way he has."

Cheryl doesn't disagree.

Denz stops short, ducking behind an empty cubicle. He strains to hear their conversation over the noise around the offices.

"Denzel won't burn this place to the ground. That's the last thing he wants," Eva insists.

"Well, Kamila's vision is fresher than Kenny's."

"But will she consider going back to—"

Cheryl cuts her off. "No. Kenny's right. Just because the wedding planning we did in the beginning helped *you* launch your styling business—"

"And look where I am now."

"—doesn't mean it's going to change the company's *future*. We need to keep giving clients that personal experience."

"What's your plan, then?"

The low, frustrated exhale Cheryl releases sends a chill through Denz. She always has a plan—or a scheme. It's where he gets it from. But he can tell she's struggling, which only heightens his anxiety.

Kami's not enough. *He's* not enough. So, what now?

"I don't know," Cheryl finally says. "This is my *life*, Eva. My son's life."

"It's Kamila and Denzel's life too."

"One of them better step it up," Cheryl demands. "Put on a show Kenny's so fucking impressed by, we don't lose our family legacy to some incompetent, wealthy white man who throws millions into a company just to watch it fold for a tax write-off."

The elevator dings.

Whatever's said next is swallowed up by people shuffling off. Casual greetings exchanged. The aunties stepping on. Denz hovers low until the doors close again. He tries to swallow the bile crawling up his throat.

"What're you doing down there?"

He yelps, then falls over at the sound of Kami's voice. She stares down at him, hands on her hips.

"Nothing!" he lies.

"You know what? I don't want to know," she tells him as Denz staggers to his feet, dusting off his slacks and straightening his shirt. "I need a favor."

"What kind?"

"I need you to babysit Mikah on Thursday, after school."

Denz's mouth quirks. "Whyyy?"

Kami sighs in that *you already know why* way, but Denz doesn't relent. If he's bailing her out, he wants specifics.

"To spend more time with—" Her eyes dart around, making sure no one's in earshot. "—Suraj. All the Sedwick planning. This CEO stuff. Making sure I don't forget to feed my own son. His residency—" She pauses when Denz's grin widens, realizing she's accidentally shared another Suraj detail she hasn't mentioned before. "I need to give some attention to my relationship."

"Relationship?" Denz squeals quietly.

She swats his shoulder, hard. "Yes, okay? I don't want my boyfriend to feel the same way Mom did."

Denz chews his lower lip. Those memories of the arguments and silence and so-close-to-crumbling between their parents move like ghosts in Kami's dark eyes. It's another reason why he never commits to anyone. Other than the whole "ditched by the love of my life for Jolly Ol' England" thing. It's hard to balance such a demanding career and a relationship.

But if Suraj means that much to her . . .

"Are you free?" Kami asks.

"Maaaybe."

The thin veil of patience on Kami's face is quickly dissipating. "You owe me, Denz."

"Are you resorting to *blackmailing* now, Kamila?"

"If it means I can have at least three hours with Suraj? Then, yes." She runs fingers over her pearl necklace. *"Please?"*

"Fine. Uncle Denzie to the rescue."

She tugs him into a hug, whispering, "Thank you," then disappears into her office.

Denz opens his message app, smiling. He fires off a quick text to Braylon:

> change of plans . . . wanna play sick for the
> film festival to hang w me & my smart amazing
> loveable nephew?

-18-

Denz's apartment kitchen is larger than the one he had in Athens. Endless countertop space, shiny appliances, and a window above the sink that faces a nearby park. It's also less lived in. Everything has that new or barely used gloss. Right down to the marble-top island he hovers near as his nephew builds the world's tallest sandwich.

"Mikah," he says gently, "are you sure you want all that cheese?"

"Yes!"

"And no bacon?"

"Nooo." Mikah's kneeling on a chair so he's at the proper height to add another slice of Gruyère to the pile. Thank God he didn't inherit his mom's weak stomach. "It's better that way, Uncle Denzie!"

"It's fine," Braylon says from behind Denz.

He's busy whisking the batter. It's his first time in Denz's kitchen. In his *apartment*. And yet . . . he looks at home. As comfortable as being in a swimming pool again.

Denz is admittedly overwhelmed by the sight.

"However," Braylon begins, sidling up to Mikah's other side.

Mikah grins up at him. It's another thing Denz is processing.

When Braylon first arrived, Mikah hid behind Denz's legs. He's shy with unfamiliar faces. But Braylon just lowered himself to Mikah's level for re-introductions. He complimented Mikah's curly 'fro, then mentioned grilled cheeses for dinner. From there, he's become Mikah's new best friend.

As if he remembers that time Braylon hummed him back to sleep in Kenneth's office.

"If you add too much cheese," Braylon goes on, "it's harder to do the magic flip."

Mikah's eyes balloon cartoonishly. "Whoa, a magic flip?"

"You bet." Braylon relocates a slice of cheese from Mikah's bread to Denz's unfinished sandwich. "Even Uncle Denzie can't do it."

Denz fake scowls, poking Braylon's side.

"You're gonna teach me?" Mikah asks excitedly.

"Of course!"

Denz watches them, smiling to himself. His nephew helps Braylon remove more cheese. Braylon holds Mikah's tiny hand while helping him climb down from the chair.

It's the weirdest sensation. Like an emptiness in Denz's belly suddenly being filled.

He never imagined this: Braylon in his apartment. Not the one in Athens where they shared a hamper and bathroom counter space and so many secrets between sateen sheets. Here, where Denz spent two hours cleaning every surface, collecting all of Jamie's discarded work shirts and hiding his own sex toys before Braylon arrived.

Over the years, he's done so well preventing *anyone* from getting this close to him again. Threading barbed wire around the heart he pieced back together with Scotch tape and goals and a career. But here's tea-drinking, monochrome-wardrobe, bristly faced Braylon, and Denz wants him to stay.

He wants to live up to his dad's expectations as CEO.

He wants both, and picturing that future is so easy, it's like breathing.

While the bread browns, Braylon listens to Mikah's ramblings about *Kiki's Delivery Service,* the movie they're watching after. He asks silly questions. Laughs at Mikah's suggestion to add whipped cream to their sandwiches.

And Denz is right there, elbow-to-elbow with Braylon as he

teaches Mikah The Flip. The air's thick with melted cheese and smoky bacon. Underneath, a quiet layer of orange and cardamom that Denz can't seem to hate anymore.

Braylon holds the spatula out to him. "Your turn."

"Me?"

"You forced me to lie to my boss about being sick so we could—"

"'Forced' is a strong word."

"Uncle Denzie, lying's bad!" Mikah shouts.

"I didn't—" Denz huffs, glaring at Braylon. He turns to Mikah. "I told him to *pretend.*"

"Momma says that's lying."

"Yeah, well," Denz mumbles, "Momma's good at that, so . . ."

"Denz," Braylon says, admonishing, still holding up the spatula. "You're quite capable of doing The Flip."

Denz eyes the pan, then Braylon. "I haven't—" He swallows. "Not since . . . with you. I'm gonna mess it up."

He hates how pathetic he sounds.

But Braylon doesn't approach him like a sad, broken Muppet with some seriously unresolved hang-ups. Instead, he presses his chest to Denz's spine. He guides the spatula into his hand. Hooking his chin over Denz's shoulder, he says, "Can't hurt to give it another go, can it?"

Is Braylon talking about the grilled cheese or something else?

Mikah's "You can do it, Uncle Denzie!" stops him from asking.

Braylon's breaths sync with his. Denz remembers watching him do this dozens of times and, honestly, it's a fucking grilled cheese. If he can't do this, how the hell will he run a *Forbes*-ranked company?

"Just a sandwich," he whispers.

Braylon hums his agreement against Denz's temple. It's enough for him to angle the spatula, jam the blade under the bread, and—

Flip his sandwich onto the hardwood floor.

"Motherfu—"

Mikah's wild giggling and Braylon's low, deep laugh cut Denz off. For a brief second, he forgets about the greasy, splattered cheese at his bare feet. Or how he once again failed at the simplest task.

Denz steps back to let Mikah help Braylon clean up the mess. They share crinkle-eyed smiles while building a new sandwich. Warmth radiates on each side of him as they cook together.

On the living room floor, Mikah crammed between them, Braylon cues up the movie. Denz passes out the juice pouches. Maple syrup drips down Mikah's chin after his first bite. They leave the lights off. Only the bluish glow of the TV fills the apartment.

For an hour and forty-two minutes, Denz is out of his own head. He laughs with Mikah. Gets tangled in the way the art and music and emotion fuse with his bones. At his periphery, blurred but somehow still so crisp, Braylon grins.

When the end credits roll, Mikah's knocked out, drooling on Denz's chest.

After Kami, looking flushed and happy, picks him up, Denz washes the dishes while Braylon dries.

"I can't believe you don't have a kettle."

"We're not tea drinkers," Denz says, hip propped against the kitchen island.

"How uncivilized." Braylon dodges the wet sponge chucked at him. "What about when you're sick? Can't sleep?"

Denz runs a dry cloth across the spotless counters.

He doesn't want to talk about how he wakes up with a gasp, a corkscrew in his chest. His constant thoughts about what the aunties said the other day. About losing everything because he's not enough. The restless turning in bed. Echoes of *one of them better step it up* haunting him until his alarm goes off.

He doesn't want to ruin the moment.

"I don't have any trouble sleeping."

"Just 'cause you're great at lying to everyone else," Braylon says, "doesn't mean it works on me."

"I've got it under control."

Braylon eyes him for a beat. Denz doesn't flinch. He means it.

He'll figure things out. But he won't solve anything right now, especially not when Braylon peels his gray T-shirt away from his stomach, giving Denz a glimpse of his abdomen as he dabs at a maroon stain.

"How does opening *one* juice pouch make such a mess?"

Denz laughs. "Talk to Jamie about that."

"I should get this in the wash."

Braylon reaches for his phone and keys, and Denz shouts, "You can wash it here!" before he realizes what he's doing.

Braylon pauses, one eyebrow flexed.

Denz manages to lower his voice to a reasonable volume when he says, "It's a long drive home. The stain might set. All that cranberry concentrate in those juices. I have a . . . machine."

He waves a hand in the general direction of the laundry space.

The hem of Braylon's shirt is still gripped by one hand, exposing more skin. God bless a lifetime of swimming.

Uncertain, Braylon says, "You want me to take off my shirt so you can wash it . . . now?"

Denz thinks he nods. His brain's a little distracted by other body parts.

"And there's no other reason you want me to take my top off?"

"No?" Denz swallows so hard, his ears pop.

A taunting smile pulls at Braylon's mouth. He shrugs, then peels his shirt off in the most painfully slow way possible. He tosses the shirt at Denz.

"Well, what now?"

Well, first, Denz needs to remember how words work. Second, he wants to thank whoever designed this apartment, because the kitchen lighting against Braylon's smooth, honey-brown skin is Sistine Chapel worthy. Third, he should have a conversation with his erection, the one he hides behind Braylon's balled-up shirt.

"Thing is," he says. "I thought, like—"

In four steps, Braylon crosses to him. He grips the counter behind Denz, caging him in. His gaze drags from Denz's eyes to his mouth and back up.

"For someone who's so confident," he says in a deep, goading voice that leaves goose bumps across Denz's forearms, "so poised, so charming—" His tongue flicks over his lips. "—in front of a crowd, you're quite . . . *tentative* when it's just us."

"I'm not . . ." Denz struggles to remember what he wants to say. "That word."

Braylon dips his head. "Then tell me what you want."

Denz takes a beat to make sure he won't black out.

"What I want—" He drops the shirt. His hands move to Braylon's waist. "—is to give you a tour of my place."

He pops open the button of Braylon's jeans. Yanks at the zipper.

"Starting with my bedroom."

Braylon doesn't look away.

"I want—" Denz wiggles the denim down. Braylon's boxers are next. "—to show you my bed."

His fingers creep over the coarse hair on Braylon's belly. He watches him shiver. The tremble of his lower lip. He spits into one hand, gripping Braylon's dick with intent, with a need searing through his bones.

"I want," he continues, "to tie your hands above your head with your stupid gray shirt."

He strokes. Soft and loose, at first. Then, measured and firm.

"Spread your legs."

Braylon's forehead glows with sweat. His dark eyes are unfocused. Denz can map out every vein in Braylon's biceps as he struggles to hold on to the counter.

"I want to swallow you like you did me. Want your toes to curl. Want my name on your tongue."

Braylon inhales sharply, his cock throbbing in Denz's palm.

Denz leans up on his toes. "I *owe* you," he whispers against parted lips. "I owe you big."

"Th-this isn't a competition."

"You're right." Denz grins. "Because I'd win. Every fucking time."

Before Braylon can retort, his accent thickened, words clipped, Denz kisses him. It's quick and messy and perfect.

Braylon lifts Denz off his feet. A low swear leaves Denz's lips after Braylon's cock slides from his fingers. But it's fine. He lets Braylon kick out of his jeans and boxers. Carry him to his bedroom, ease him down onto the mattress.

He pulls Braylon apart with his hands. With teeth on taut nipples. With fingers on hips, then thighs.

With his mouth and tongue along an aching cock that happily responds to Denz's every motion like a snake to a charmer.

Every other gasp and moan from Braylon is punctuated by his squirming along the sheets. His muscles tightening. By Denz's name chanted until his throat's sore.

When Denz is finished, there's another first in this apartment: Braylon Adams, speechless.

Crema's remarkably empty for a Thursday. Only a few patrons huddled in their own worlds of laptops or phones. Denz grins at an unoccupied corner table, the same one he shared with Braylon months ago.

Planning the retirement party with both Kami and his dad has been time consuming. Braylon's hands are equally full. Their communication has whittled down to emails about their upcoming parties. Nothing else. Definitely not what happened at his apartment last week.

He's not saying today's lunch is because he *misses* Braylon. Because his pillowcase smells like oranges. Because he wakes in the middle of the night thinking about the inside of Braylon's thighs, the way Denz's name whispered in a British accent was like a secret prayer.

He's not saying when he stands in his kitchen, he imagines a future with Braylon.

Today is completely *work*-related.

For once, he's early. According to his last text, Braylon's ten minutes away. He studies Crema's new spring menu until a throat clears. Denz is greeted by a beautiful man around his age. Light sepia skin, tousled dark hair, a knowing smile.

After a beat, recognition settles: it's Jade Suit Guy from the Valentine's gala, from Elite Events.

"Javier," the man says by way of introduction. "Javi, preferably."

"Denzel Carter."

"Oh, I know." Javi's smile grows, revealing dimples. "Hard to ignore the competition when they look like you."

Denz half smirks. "Is that so?"

"Didn't mean to sneak up on you," Javi tells him. "We were supposed to meet at the gala. Your aunties—"

"Are nosey and aggressively wrong about things," Denz finishes.

Javi laughs. A rich, melodic noise. "Aren't all tías?"

"I guess."

Javi's brown eyes are piercingly attentive, as if he's reading Denz, no context needed. "They tried to set us up," he says. "Something about you being on the rebound?"

Denz frowns. "They were wrong."

Javi crosses his arms in a smooth, relaxed way that doesn't intimidate Denz. Or turn him on. "I'm in a relationship," he manages to get out. "We're very happy. I'm in a good place."

And he is. Sure, his "relationship" isn't real. There's a fifty-fifty chance he'll either be CEO of his dad's company or working for someone else next week. Someone who won't give a shit about his family's legacy like he or his sister does. But he's fine.

"That's . . . good," Javi says, then laughs again.

"And you?" Denz asks. "Life must be great at the *second-best* event planner in Atlanta."

"You're funny." Javi's lips curve upward, a twinkle in his eye. "Just like the client I had the other day. Said he wanted to commission 24 Carter *Silver* to host his engagement party and future nuptials. Unfortunately, you guys don't do weddings."

Denz's confident expression slips.

"That's a shame," Javi comments, even though he doesn't look disappointed.

"Yeah," Denz chews out. "Real shame."

"For the record—I'm always looking," Javi says. His eyes roam Denz's face, then lower, those dimples relentless. "In case you're ever *not* good."

He steps around Denz to get to the front counter.

Denz waits three minutes, enough time for Javi to order and walk away, before he tugs out his phone to call Kami. He can't let this continue. It's time for 24 Carter Gold to get back into the wedding industry. Prove to everyone they're still the best event company in Atlanta.

Turning, he almost slams right into Braylon.

"He-hi-lo," he stumbles out.

"'Ello." Braylon's gaze looks past Denz. To the bar where Matty's passing off a drink to Javi. "Another friend of yours?"

Denz doesn't know why his face blisters. Or why he's laughing nervously as he says, "Not like *that*. Just my aunties interfering in my life. Back when they still didn't like you."

Braylon hums.

"They won't shut up about you now," Denz adds. "My uncles too. Everyone's in love with you. You're doing a great job."

"A job," Braylon deadpans.

"And my dad's finally coming around."

An hour ago, after another meeting, Kenneth didn't make his usual judging face when Denz said he was meeting Braylon for lunch. That counts, right?

"He's nothing," Denz whispers as Javi exits the café.

"Like Matty?"

Denz fights a flinch. "Both. Nothing at all."

A beat. Braylon motions toward the counter. "Shall we?"

After ordering and avoiding eye contact with Matty, Denz leads them to the corner table. He licks sugar from his blueberry-lemon scone off his thumb. "This is a new look."

Braylon's in a soft hoodie, jeans, and sneakers. All black. "We were rearranging the furniture. Nora's hosting a movie night," he explains. "Whit's looking forward to your social media tutorial tomorrow."

"By which you mean she'll have an hour-long *Dateline* episode dedicated to her after she murders me."

"Strong possibility."

"I hope I don't disappoint."

"You won't," Braylon says. "You always try, Denz."

"History, according to my family, says otherwise." Denz does his best not to sound self-deprecating. It doesn't work.

Braylon sips his tea. "Have you ever considered their opinion of you is wrong?"

Tangentially? Sure. But it's hard to brush off what your family thinks of you. Hard to not let it bleed into everything you do.

It's why Denz chose UGA.

By senior year of high school, he wanted to get away. Be anyone other than Denzel, young face of the Carter legacy. It's not a coincidence that he waited until his acceptance letter arrived before he finally came out. His family wasn't—*isn't*—homophobic, but he knows how the public sees him. How his every move as a Black man is watched. Layering his queerness on top of that? No, thanks.

College was his escape from the unwanted spotlight.

Now he's back to being the only son of Kenneth Carter. Constantly proving himself. Not only as a Carter, but as a successful Black man. A capable queer man. He walks into every situation five steps behind most people because of who he is.

On the table, Braylon's fingers brush across his knuckles. He knows Denz is overthinking. He doesn't hesitate to let Braylon hold his hand.

"They're wrong," Braylon says, low and serious.

Denz wants so badly for that to be the only voice in his head, but it isn't. It never is.

"I didn't invite you to lunch to be my therapist," he jokes.

"You say that like it's a bad thing."

"Therapy? I don't think it is." Denz bites into his scone. "Never tried it."

"It saved my life."

Denz smiles, genuinely. "Then it's the best thing in the world."

He eats one-handed. Tells Braylon about the time Cheryl auditioned for *American Wonder*, a short-lived reality singing competition. How she met Tevin backstage, reconnecting years later after Jordan was born. He admits Kami *thinks* Mikah's first word was "Mom" when it was actually "shit" after a weekend of Denz babysitting. He gushes about better times with his family, when he felt like one of them instead of someone wearing a Carter face, trying to fit in.

Denz wants to ask Braylon about memories with his own parents but is scared to reopen a wound for either of them.

When Braylon finishes his tea, he pulls his hand away. "I bet loads of lads will be chuffed to see you back in the dating world. Once this is over, of course."

It comes out of nowhere. Denz didn't expect to have this conversation now. This thing always had an expiration date. But Denz is just learning Braylon again. The parts of him he never knew.

He's not *falling* for Braylon—he swears—but there's this unnamable, loud, fierce beating in his chest that he can't shake.

"What makes you think that?"

"The comments on your social media are—"

"Thirsty? Bold?" Denz offers.

"You'll have plenty of options."

Yeah, Denz really can't wait to update his profile: *25. Cancer. Loves muffins, rom-coms, and being your perfect fake boyfriend.*

He clears his throat, switching tactics. "What about you? I'm sure there are hot, eligible guys all over Atlanta eager to snatch you up."

"I wouldn't know." Pink spills across Braylon's cheeks like paint. "Work is my focus. I love what I do. I want to see Skye's the Limit expand."

"How'd you end up there, anyway?"

Denz isn't avoiding the dating interrogation. Part of him believes Braylon's full of shit. He can date *and* have career goals. Kami's doing it. But his fight or flight has kicked in. He doesn't want to hear about Braylon's future boyfriends.

A smile quirks Braylon's mouth. He launches into how Nora built Skye's the Limit in honor of her nephew Skye, who "needed somewhere where he was safe, loved, and always allowed to be himself." How she started paying attention to the lack of LGBTQ+ resources for teens in Atlanta. So she created her own. Hired people with the same mission.

"I stumbled on a video interview of hers after my dad's funeral," Braylon says, his voice a mix of sad and fond. "Nora had me in the first minute."

"Really?"

Braylon describes his last weeks in London. The unhappiness. Constantly feeling lost. Then, his dad passed and he "never went back." He emailed Nora for an interview a week after the funeral.

"Because of you," he admits.

"Me?"

"Yes, you." His laugh is endearing, unlike Javi's. "When I heard Nora speak, I thought about when we first met. You were always so intensely yourself. You made me want to be the person I hid from others. All I thought about were the hundreds of Denzes in this world. They deserve a space where people care and fight for them. Where they can be themselves." He pauses, eyes bright. "I thought about all the Braylons too."

Denz lets out a quiet breath. He's simultaneously weightless and grounded.

"I believe in what Nora's doing," Braylon says, beaming.

After listening to him, Denz does too.

Braylon's expression shifts. "I can't date anyone here. If I get this promotion, I'll be in Los Angeles."

"You're moving? *Again?*"

Braylon sighs as if he's been holding on to this one detail for a reason. As if he's been anticipating Denz's reaction. "Nora's expanding," he explains. "There's a new location in Santa Monica. I'd be helping with start-up."

Denz is going to scream.

Braylon kept this from him. He never had any intention for their arrangement to go past early April. They had a deal. Braylon helps him and, in turn, Denz helps Braylon break his heart for the second time.

The kisses, the sex—it was meaningless. They had fun, got off. The end.

It's the same thing Denz's done with every guy since college. It's what he's always after: a clean break. No repeats. No attachments. No falling in love.

This was never about them reconnecting. Braylon is his past, not a future. Denz's endgame is being the Carter everyone's expected him to be since day one.

And that emptiness behind his ribs? The place Braylon's not supposed to be anyway? He'll fill it with something else.

He's done that before too.

Five Years Ago
Senior Year—Spring Semester

"Minor crisis." Bray stands, pressing a peck to Denz's temple. "BRB."

Early February sunlight dusts the modest interior of One More Cup golden. They don't come here often. Usually, Denz will snag something from Jittery Joe's or Starbucks on campus. But neither coffee shop has the quiet, college-town normalcy of OMC. Or the triple-chocolate scones Emmanuel *inhales* whenever he visits.

He's across from Denz, savoring his extra-hot latte. Bray is the perfect mix of his parents. His mom's high cheekbones and rounded nose. His dad's chin dimple and wide, infectious smile. In his eyes too, Emmanuel's a shade lighter than his cool umber complexion, a rich contrast to his favorite pale blue button-down.

"That boy." Emmanuel nods to the café corner where Bray's pacing, phone to his ear. "Think it's the swim team again?"

"Probably," Denz agrees. "Lyle freaking out over his backstroke time. Keegan lost his earbuds. *Again*. Jake F. and Jake D. fighting over the same girl. Who's hosting the next pizza night . . ."

"He's always watching out for them." Emmanuel shakes his head. "I can't believe they didn't name him captain this year."

"Bray didn't want it," Denz mentions. "He doesn't like that kind of attention."

He smiles softly. He still has the video Nic sent him from New Year's Eve—the one of half-drunk Bray, washed in multicolored spotlights, doing the Wobble in the middle of all the guests. Denz is saving it for future blackmail.

"He'd rather be the heart than the brain," Emmanuel says. He chuckles. "Got that from his mother."

Denz's lips curve higher.

"He'll grow out of it," Emmanuel notes. "After graduation. You'll see."

Fuck, Denz hopes not. He loves this Bray. Thoughtful and observant and wanting nothing to do with being the focus of every room he walks in. Serenely confident when it's just the two of them. He can't imagine a different version.

"Life changes a lot of things once you're on your own," Emmanuel tells him.

Denz tears at his flaky croissant. "I guess."

"What about you?"

"Um, me?"

Emmanuel laughs fondly. "Yes. What are your plans?" He dips a piece of scone into his mug. "Graduation will be here sooner than you think. Are you thinking about the future?"

Denz has. But maybe not in the way Emmanuel's asking.

Some mornings, while Bray snores beside him in bed, Denz scrolls through his phone. He studies apartments near Atlanta. He's not thinking about *proposing*—though Nic's been messaging him ideas like a possessed Cupid—but a future.

A next step for him and Bray.

Can he tell Emmanuel that? They've long passed the awkwardness of their first meeting, though Denz habitually moves his latte to a safe corner of the table any time they come here, just in case. He feels a familiar comfort with Emmanuel now. Too many virtual Scrabble nights and long conversations over coffee like this one. During the school year, he sees more of Emmanuel than his own family.

But is this the right time? Before he's even talked to Bray?

Denz tears another section of croissant. "I don't know."

"There must be a million opportunities for you. You could get a job anywhere." Emmanuel eyes him. "Where would you go?"

A beat. Denz shrugs. "Atlanta."

"Atlanta?"

"Thing is—" Denz looks away from Emmanuel's heavy, skeptical stare. "—my whole family's there. Which, you know already. But, like. I'm so close to my sisters. And my nephew's barely two. I don't want to miss anything that happens in their lives."

"What about creating your *own* life?"

"I can do that. There." Denz is sweating. In February. Is this an interrogation? Is this what Bray felt like? "Atlanta's great. The weather's nice too."

"The weather's nice a lot of places, Denz."

"Yeah, but . . ." Denz rips another soft layer of flaky dough. "It's home."

Emmanuel's mouth twists into a frown. "What if that's not where Bray wants to be?"

"Why wouldn't he?" Denz blinks, confused. Bray loves his dad. It's been just the two of them since Elyse died. "You're there. He'd never leave you."

"Don't get me wrong," Emmanuel says, smiling sadly, "I'd hate for him to leave. But I wouldn't discourage him. I want the best for my son. Like my parents wanted for me when they came to America. To make sure I got all the best chances at a great life."

"I want that too."

Emmanuel rests a hand on his. "I know. You love him."

A smile tries to inch up Denz's mouth.

"And I want the best for you too," Emmanuel says, leaning back. "Which is why I wanted to know your plans."

Currently: he's trying to survive his stupid Communication Strategies in Social Movements course, remember to throw away that expired pizza in his fridge, and avoid the impending diarrhea from this conversation.

"I'm working on them."

Emmanuel nods thoughtfully. "Do me a favor: consider *all* your options."

Denz stares down at the shredded remains of his croissant.

"I will," he says, distractedly reaching for a napkin to clean up his mess. Which of course means his hand bumps into his iced latte. The cup teeters, wobbles, two seconds from ruining his only clean pair of joggers.

"Whoa!"

Bray's quick reflexes prevent Spillgate 2.0 from happening. He straightens the cup, then flops back into his seat. "Sorry. Drama solved. What'd I miss?"

Denz shares a cautious stare with Emmanuel. "Nothing," he whispers.

"Cool." Bray tosses an arm around Denz's tight shoulders, hauling him closer. "Oh, Dad, did I tell you? Denz has been studying his word lists. He might finally beat you on our next Scrabble night."

"Is that so? Planning for the future, Denz?"

Denz looks up sheepishly. He bites his lip, nodding.

"Wonderful." Emmanuel's next smile doesn't quite reach his eyes. "I can't wait."

-19-

Denz *hates* Jägermeister.

It tastes like black licorice and death. The smell alone makes him want to projectile-vomit. It's also led to him doing irrationally stupid things in the past. Things like eating two dozen hot wings in under fifteen minutes, making out with a crosswalk sign, streaking through the Arch on UGA's North Campus. Thankfully, none of it was caught on video and sold to TMZ.

He hasn't touched the stuff since college, which is precisely why he's pouring two shots for himself while Jamie sits on the floor, slurping from one of Mikah's juice pouches. It's nights like this where he wishes Jamie enjoyed drinking. That way he wouldn't be the only one looking for answers at the bottom of a dusty green bottle.

Does alcohol expire?

In front of Denz are two pub glasses—"borrowed" from one of Jamie's bars—half full of Red Bull. The classic Jägerbomb. Jamie eyes him suspiciously as he drops the first shot glass into the energy drink before downing it all.

"We had sex again."

"Me and you?" Jamie raises an eyebrow. "When was the first time?"

Denz belches. "Me and Braylon! The other night!" The alcohol hasn't kicked in, but the Red Bull certainly has.

"*Obviously.* Hard to miss Braylon sneaking out of our apartment in one of your shirts after midnight."

"Why didn't you say anything?"

"I like watching you squirm." Jamie reaches for a chicken burrito on the coffee table. When Denz texted him, EMERGENCY TALK, he stopped for supplies. "Besides, you're much nicer when you've got that I-just-got-dick face."

Denz groans into his hands. He's spent *days* trying to add up what's changed. Walked into numerous trash cans and doors while rereading Braylon's texts, analyzing their moments together. The night at Braylon's apartment. The hotel. Even what happened here, which he's admittedly jerked off to—just to clear his head.

Shredded cheese falls off Jamie's burrito. He scoops it into his mouth, then says, "Is that your big problem? Sex with your boyfriend?"

"*Fake* boyfriend."

"How's lying to yourself working out?"

Denz flips him off. "Doesn't matter. He's moving to California."

"He is? When?"

"I don't know. A few weeks? After the spring break event."

Jamie stands abruptly, pacing the living room, burrito in one hand. Beans fall on the carpet. He drags his other hand through his hair. "So, you're moving to California?"

"What? No. *Braylon* is."

"Yeah, but." Jamie's forehead wrinkles. "You're obviously going with him."

Denz tilts his head. "Why would I go with him?"

"Why *wouldn't* you?"

"Because he didn't ask me to." Denz stares at the dark brown liquor in the shot glass. He wills back the tears misting his eyes. "He's not making that mistake again."

"That wasn't his ch—"

"It was his choice," Denz argues. "Don't defend him. You're *my* best friend."

Jamie holds up his hands, burrito and all, in the universal sign of *calm the hell down.* "I'm not defending him. Just pointing out things weren't so black-and-white."

"Fuck, I know. I was there."

He plunks the shot glass into the Red Bull, chugging with minimal spillage. He wipes his mouth and says, "I wanted time, Jamie. I didn't know what to do and he—" The alcohol burns in his chest. "He didn't give me enough."

Jamie flops dramatically onto the sofa. He squeezes his hand hard as Denz relives everything in vivid brightness.

Braylon told him six weeks before graduation. The job in London. Leaving after graduation. His whispered, "Will you come with me?" in the crook of Denz's neck, like he was too shy to ask.

Like he already knew how big of a request it was.

Then, Denz's brain unwound. The threads unraveled all the way back to OMC, his conversation with Emmanuel. Could he leave his family? His home? The future he was supposed to step into the second his graduation cap was tossed in the air?

His "Can I think about it?" was followed by weeks of Braylon hinting about London and Denz avoiding the topic. He had finals and essays. An entire family expecting him to come out of UGA with a diploma and a plan.

Was he good at anything besides being a Carter? Could he move to another city, another *country* with no fucking clue about how to survive? What if, six months down the road, the world discovered he wasn't as great as everyone else in his family?

Four years of college and Denz still knew nothing about himself. But there was Braylon, who never made him feel like Denzel Carter, like his destiny was set in stone. Who made him feel . . . *normal.*

Could Denz leave everything behind for that?

Ten days before graduation, Braylon said, "I talked to my dad."

And: "He said I shouldn't stall my future waiting for someone to figure out theirs. I need to move on."

And: "I made a decision. I'm going to London. Without you."

And finally: "I love you so much, but I need to do what's best for me. For you too."

"I went into UGA so sure," he tells Jamie, now. "I knew my major. My goals. That's what you do, right? Spend every day dreaming about who you're gonna be. Then, you get to college and you just . . . *do it.* You become that person." He sniffles. "But I didn't think I'd fall in love. That everything would change, and I'd have no idea how to manage what's next."

"But that's the fun part," Jamie assures him.

"I didn't want to disappoint anyone," Denz whispers. "Disappoint . . . him."

"Denz, you haven't."

"Because he let me go before I could." A bitter laugh wobbles in Denz's throat. "Because I went right into working for my dad like a good son does."

Jamie smacks his knee. "Stop talking about my best friend like that."

Denz wipes his cheeks. Shit, when did he start crying?

"Braylon's still here," Jamie reminds him. "What if he wants you to come to California?"

"He doesn't."

"How do you know?"

"Because he would've mentioned it!"

"Bro, he fucked up royally in the past," Jamie says. "He made a big mistake. Big! Huge!"

Denz almost guffaws at the *Pretty Woman* reference, but his tears prevent him.

"Maybe he's scared?" Jamie suggests. "Just like you're scared to admit you're still in love with him."

"I'm . . . not."

"Don't lie, asshole."

Jamie knows him better than anyone. He knows Denz loves to shove things into a dark corner, hide all his insecurities and failures.

Sometimes, pretending the worst things in your life never happened is how you survive. But sometimes, you have to shatter in order to figure out how to piece yourself back together. So you can heal.

Jamie's phone pings on the coffee table. He releases Denz's hand but doesn't reach to check his notifications. "You're gonna let him go? Even though you're in lo—"

"Stop using that word!"

"After all this, you're not even gonna *try?*"

"What's the point? I'm still going after the CEO job," Denz says firmly. He stares at the Jägermeister, considers pouring another shot. "I have a chance to prove to everyone who I am."

"Making things work with a great guy is proving something too."

"Yeah? What?"

"That you care about yourself. That you're doing something for *you.*"

Fuck, Denz really hates that sympathetic tilt to Jamie's lips. The honesty in his voice. "How dare you." He laughs roughly at the wild parkour move Jamie does dodging the pillow he chucks at him.

"I'm just saying," Jamie says from the floor. "Why can't it be both?"

In all those dreams from Denz's childhood, the ones from college, he never considered having both. Being as amazing as his dad and managing a relationship with the man he loves.

Should he ask Braylon to try?

No. That's not fair. After seeing the light in Braylon's eyes while talking about Skye's the Limit, what this means to him, Denz can't propose him staying. He can't let Braylon rip his heart out again when he inevitably chooses California over Denz.

He knows what he *needs* to do: throw the best party Atlanta's ever seen. Impress his dad. Continue the family legacy. Dedicate the rest of his energy to making Braylon's event a success. Then let him walk away without a word.

The next morning, Denz wishes it was the sun waking him. Or Jamie blending one of his breakfast smoothies. Maybe his alarm, the one he forgot to set after that final Jäger shot last night. Perhaps a warm, sleepy man with scruff on his cheeks and jaw, strong hands, a tolerable British accent next to him in bed.

It's none of the above.

He's startled awake by his phone chirping noisily. It's like a jackhammer drilling through his skull. His mouth tastes like licorice and remorse. He either needs to pee or vomit in the next five minutes. Quite possibly both.

He peeks one eye open to check his phone. There are three missed calls. It's 10:12 A.M.

Fucking shit.

He's late. Dead-on-arrival late. As in, they'll never find the body because Kami will set his corpse on fire, bury his ashes, and salt the earth for good measure.

His phone rings again. Nervously, he answers.

"Denzel," his dad says. His voice is somewhat distant like he's on speakerphone. "I've been trying to reach you."

Denz clears the sleepiness from his throat. "H-hi, Dad. I was . . . at the gym?"

"At ten in the morning on a workday?"

Denz nods, then remembers Kenneth can't see him. "Wanted to make sure I looked, y'know, *fit*. In my suit tomorrow." He laughs weakly. "Can't have the press dragging me for looking a hot mess on my big—I mean *your* big night."

Kenneth lets out a deep exhale. Underneath that, Denz can hear the city's noise in the background.

"Is something wrong?"

"We have a major issue at Vista de Atlas," Kenneth says, frustrated.

Denz nearly slips off the bed trying to sit up. Vista de Atlas is the retirement party venue. Ten thousand square feet of pure luxury. Atlas has hosted movie premiere after-parties, the governor's birthday, Audrey Hudson's wedding reception. Tomorrow is a full-circle moment in Kenneth Carter's career.

"They've been conducting routine maintenance around the

facility in preparation," Kenneth explains. "Minor things, I was promised. But the room above ours sprung a leak during repairs." Another annoyed breath comes through the phone. "It's flooded."

Denz's stomach freefalls into his ass.

"Flooded," he repeats. *Shit. Fuck shit fuck.* He looks around his bedroom as if some magical answer is going to appear on his bedside table or underneath his wrinkled boxers on the floor. "Should we move to another location?"

"Less than thirty-six hours before the party?"

"Um."

"What's your plan? Email all two hundred guests? Inform everyone in a Facebook post?"

Denz was leaning more toward a less corrupt social media platform, actually.

"No, no," he rushes out, rubbing one eye. His hangover is mutating into a migraine. "Maybe I can—"

"Don't bother," Kenneth says, cutting him off. "I've been on the phone with management all morning."

It's another blunt reminder that his dad, *the CEO*, starts his mornings at 7:00 A.M. like a motivated executive while Denz sleeps off bad alcohol choices, naked.

"They're offering us the rooftop," Kenneth informs him.

Denz has only been to Vista de Atlas a handful of times. Once for a party hosted by a hot Netflix star who slid into his DMs with a personal invite to tour the VIP lounge. *Privately.* He vaguely remembers the rooftop space with its panoramic views of the Atlanta skyline. It's smaller than the space they reserved, but just as breathtaking.

A car door opens in Kenneth's background. Words are exchanged with the driver. The whoosh of a morning breeze comes and goes, replaced by more voices, urgent greetings and apologies.

"Dad?"

"I'm at Atlas to meet with vendors. We'll need to rearrange the layout and alter the menus . . ." His dad goes on like he's not upending *months* of work in a single breath. "You need to get down here. Now."

"*Me?*"

Denz struggles to keep up. His brain's a PC from the Stone Age still running Windows Vista, but Kenneth's communicating with him like he's a MacBook. It's too much.

"What about Kami?"

"Tied up," his dad answers. "She'll be here later. In the meantime, she's sending Jordan."

"Should I send Eric?"

"He's working on another project for me." Kenneth's next breath comes out agitated, bordering on dismissive. "This is what a real CEO does, Denzel. Drops everything. Ensures every event detail goes off without a hitch. He manages from the front line, not from his Peloton. Or his bedroom."

Denz winces. His dad always knows. He squeezes the bridge of his nose, the pressure building quicker than he can react.

"You need to be here," Kenneth reiterates, as if he needed it.

Denz rubs his goatee, which is in serious need of a trim. Vista de Atlas is on the other side of downtown. Traffic on a Friday is going to be hell, even at this hour.

"Give me, like, forty minutes?"

"Make it less. Time's essential, Denzel."

Kenneth hangs up.

Denz allows himself ten seconds to sag against his headboard. Ten seconds to scream into a pillow. Then, he's up.

He skips reading the other notifications, including the three texts from Braylon he's more than happy to avoid. He rolls out of bed. He stubs his big toe twice while brushing his teeth and searching for clean clothes. In the shower, he whispers a prayer to whatever god is listening. He desperately needs to sober up before seeing his dad.

Chaos greets Denz at Atlas's doors. The staff and vendors collide left and right. Jordan scrambles past him. Wild tendrils slip from the manager's messy bun, her cheeks flushed. At the heart of it all, Denz's dad has the sleeves of his Stefano Ricci shirt rolled to his elbows, a tablet in one hand, his phone in the other.

He's in boss mode. Denz approaches accordingly.

Within seconds, he's given a checklist and a small group of employees, plus Jordan. Denz sends Kami a Where the hell are you? text, and promptly hides his phone in the pocket of his jacket, leaving both at the front desk. He can only handle one shitshow at a time.

Jordan hands him a coffee. "What's the plan, cuz?"

Denz goes full Eric Tran, pushing up his own sleeves. He didn't come dressed for manual labor but fuck it. If his dad's doing it, he is too.

"Let's head upstairs."

Their "stage" is now a glass balcony ten feet above the main rooftop. After surveying the area, Denz decides to nix the "History of 24 Carter Gold" video they were going to show. He cancels the ice sculpture in the shape of the company's logo. Atlanta in March might as well be summer in hell. It's too humid outside.

He sits crisscrossed on the tiled stone floor to condense the seating charts. If he's lucky, they can fit all two hundred guests up here.

"We can overflow to the banquet area," Jordan shouts from the balcony.

"Good idea."

Denz makes a note. In all his reorganizing and overcommunication, he realizes something: he's calm, in control. Panic can kiss his future CEO ass.

"Mr. Carter," one of the staff says, startling him. "The other Mr. Carter's meeting with the head chef. Would you like to join them?"

Denz leaps to his feet. "Lead the way."

He misses lunch, making sure all the employees eat first. Without them, none of this is possible. When his dad sends up a turkey club from a local deli, Denz hands it to Jordan. He's too focused on mapping out where the live band will set up to stop. Around 4:00 P.M., he pauses for a handful of M&M's and a bag of spicy Cheetos, half a Coke bottle. Then, it's all adrenaline until past dinnertime.

"Damn," Jordan says, impressed. "You *might be* as good as Kami."

Denz flips him off, smiling.

It's not true. Through every step, he feels like he's missed an item. A detail Kami wouldn't forget.

At 6:30 P.M., as the staff files out, Kenneth thanks each of them by name. This is why he is who he is. People respect the eye contact, his genuineness.

Once everyone's gone, Denz watches his dad's shoulders drop. He sluggishly fixes his shirt. He can't hide his exhaustion anymore.

He stares at Denz: "Are you okay?"

The transformation is always a little jarring. How he goes from Kenneth Carter, million-dollar face of a company, to Dad, the man who raised Denz. From the person he looks up to career-wise to the man who taught him how to ride a bike.

"Y-yeah."

"Today was a lot."

Denz chuckles. "Understatement."

Kenneth grins. "I haven't had to put in that much work since I was your age." He stretches, wincing when his back cracks. But there's a light behind his eyes. "Felt damn good."

"Are you gonna miss it?"

"Hell no." Kenneth laughs, loud and shameless. "My body can't take it." He gives Denz another long look. "Are you good for dinner? You can join me and your mom—"

Denz waves him off. "I'm fine. I need a night in."

Kenneth tugs out his phone to call a car. On his way to the doors, he says, "Really impressive job today, son."

Denz blinks. He can't think of a single word that'll match the sincerity in his dad's tone. So, he says, "Thanks, Dad."

When Denz turns on his phone, dozens of notifications pour

in. Texts and missed calls and social media alerts. He sighs, fatigue wrenching his bones as he prepares to swipe through.

"You look like shit."

He glances up.

Kami stands near the lobby doors. She's wearing sneakers, yoga pants, an old Emory University T-shirt, curls pulled up into a lopsided bun. Meanwhile, Denz's button-up and slacks are sticking to his skin.

"You're late."

She ignores his flat tone. "I'm here now. Wanted to make sure y'all had everything handled."

"You mean, you wanted to make sure I didn't fuck it up?"

The lobby's fairly empty. A handful of evening staff linger, making last-minute calls for tomorrow. But it's just the two of them standing on the bronze Vista de Atlas logo carved into the marble floor.

"No," Kami says, jaw tight. The irritation in her eyes reminds Denz of their childhood. When "allergies" was to blame for the rare occasions they turned on each other.

He hated those days. He's not fond of this moment either.

"We're fine," he says, dismissive. "I don't need a babysitter."

Kami arches an eyebrow. "Really? You sound like you need a nap."

"Where were you?"

"This isn't just about you," she replies, deflecting. "I know we're not exactly Dad's number-one and number-two picks. Auntie Cheryl told me."

Denz wonders if he's "number two" in that scenario. "Then you should've been here," he reminds her.

"I sent Jordan. I did what I could."

"So did I!" He doesn't mean to raise his voice, to startle Atlas's manager as she passes. He can't help it. "I got here. Put in the work. I *impressed* Dad. You're not the only one who can do this job."

"I never said I was."

"You did," Denz argues. "In my office. When this all started. Remember?"

"Denz," she says with a sigh. "I don't want to—"

"Where. Were. You?" he repeats.

"In case you forgot, I have a *son*," Kami snaps. "Sorry I had to pick him up early from school because he was sick. Or that I had to find someone to watch him because our mom's on a campus tour with Nic. Because my brother is acting like a *dick* while doing the job he signed up for."

Denz stumbles a little. "Mikah's sick?"

Kami shakes her head, frowning. "It's nothing serious. He was fine when I left."

"I didn't need you to do all that to get here. I got this."

"Do you?" She cocks her head. "Like you handled the menu drama on Valentine's? Or how about something simple, like muffins for the staff meeting? Signing a venue contract?"

"You heard about that?"

"I'm not so focused on me that I don't notice what's happening with you." She bites her lip. "Your track record in high-pressure situations isn't—"

"God." Denz drags a hand over his face. "You sound like the aunties."

"I didn't mean—"

"No, you obviously did," he interrupts again. "Clearly, it's something you've thought for a while. Please, continue."

Outside, waves of pink melt the blue from the sky. Denz just wants to go home and shower. Destroy some Thai takeout while rewatching *The Best Man*. But he chooses to wait for his sister to elaborate.

"Fine," she huffs. "You're always late. You constantly forget things. At every opportunity, you either run from a problem or lie. How is anyone supposed to think that *this*—" She waves her hand at his disheveled appearance. "—isn't too much for you?"

A beat. He asks, "Is that everything?"

Gently, Kami says, "I want you to succeed. But you need to stop avoiding reality."

"Which is?"

"You're doing this for them. Not you."

It stings. Her words, her genuine expression. The way it sounds like what their dad said last month.

She's right. Denz wants to run. Or lie.

Instead, he laughs, short and joyless, then says, "Thanks, but I don't need advice from someone who can't admit she's too scared to share her personal life with her own family."

Kami steps away, blinking hard.

Fuck. He wants to take it back.

"Wow." The lobby's pendant lighting catches on the tears brimming in her eyes. She swallows. "Who sounds like the aunties now?"

"Wait, Kam—"

"What's going on here?"

Denz jolts at Kenneth's voice. He's in the lobby again, trading looks between them.

"Are you two really arguing," he says, low and steely, "right here, right now? In public?"

Denz tries to speak, but his throat tightens.

"No, Dad," Kami says, her voice steadier than Denz expects. "We're not."

"Then why do you look so upset?"

Kami fixes her gaze on Denz. "Allergies," she says, and walks away.

Kenneth follows her. Denz thinks to do the same. He should apologize, talk rationally to Kami instead of with emotions not meant for her.

But he can't. His phone vibrates in his palm with a notification.

Formerly Known As Bray
I can't believe you didn't show up.

Above the last text are several more. A thread of messages that starts with I can't wait to see you and Thanks for doing this before shifting to please be on time because Whit is restless today. Questions about where Denz is, how long he will be. Is your battery dead? It ends with the most recent text.

Shit, shit, shitty forgetful idiot.

It's the missing detail that's been haunting him all day. He was supposed to meet with Braylon's coworkers two hours ago. To work on social media content.

Denz calls Braylon's phone. There's no answer. He tries again. Nothing. Not even a read notification when he texts.

"Denzel," Kenneth starts as Denz double-times outside.

"Can't talk now, Dad!"

"You need to—"

"*Braylon* needs me," is the last thing he shouts while running to his car. He knocks into a potted shrub outside Atlas. His left loafer is barely hanging on, but Denz never stops.

There's only time for one thing. One person.

He hopes he's not too late.

-20-

When Denz approaches Skye's the Limit, he expects to find a disappointed but forgiving Braylon outside. Not an exasperated Whit wearing the facial equivalent of an ax murderer staring down their next victim.

To be fair, he should've expected both.

"I canceled dinner plans," she says through her teeth, "with *my wife* for this."

Denz raises surrendering hands, shielding himself. "I didn't even know you were married!"

"I went to FAMU," she says.

"Um, *sorry?*"

Whit points a sharp gold nail at him, her left eye twitching. Denz promptly shuts up.

"I have a bachelor's in economics. A minor in business," she continues. "I don't need to waste a Friday evening waiting for you to teach me which filter to use on a selfie."

Denz nods very slowly.

"I'm here because your boyfriend is a great guy who cares. Never asks for anything," she says. "He deserves better than my bitchiness over you being late."

He deserves better than me, Denz wants to add.

"But *you,* Atlanta's golden boy," Whit growls. "You don't get my kindness. My patience. Or my time."

"I—"

"Fix whatever you did to him. *Now.*" She walks away.

In her place: Braylon.

Denz takes him in. The tired posture. His gray button-down untucked from his black slacks. The pattern of his loose tie punching Denz in the throat—a navy-and-white design identical to the sweater Denz wore to dinner with his parents.

I'm sorry sits heavy in his chest. He can't get it out. Silence balloons between them as Braylon's jaw flexes, his eyes turning sharp and annoyed.

"You didn't answer my calls," Denz says.

"You drove all the way here to say that?"

"No." Denz rubs his jaw. "I'm sorry about today. I—"

He doesn't want to say "forgot." Or "failed." That's exactly what Kami said about him, and he hates how true it is.

"I didn't mean to miss this" comes out, another truth.

Braylon stares upward. Past the streetlamps that leave his complexion pale. To the mauve sky where the occasional blue-gray cloud sits. He whispers, "It's fine."

"It's not like this was the big party, right?" Denz steps closer. "The one that decides whether you get the promotion." *The one that's going to take you away from me,* he doesn't say. "It's a one-off. We can reschedule."

Braylon's chin drops. Anger pinches the skin around his eyes. "It's not a one-off to *them*." He waves a hand toward the building behind him. "They stayed after hours. Their lives aren't something you can just 'reschedule.' You *embarrassed* me."

"I didn't mean—" Denz cuts himself off again.

God, what *does* he mean?

"Sometimes, Denz . . ." Braylon exhales. There are so many little reminders in his appearance—the forehead wrinkles, dark stubble, stiff shoulders—that he's no longer the boy from college who easily forgave Denz's mistakes. Who'd rather kiss than argue. "I wish you didn't miss so damn much in this life trying to be someone you're not."

It's a kick to Denz's stomach. The only thing he thinks to say is, "Like the fact that you're leaving? Again?"

"This isn't about that."

"It *is*," Denz argues. He's shaking. "You dropped that fucking bombshell on me like it was a two weeks' notice at your job. Like I . . . we—"

His voice gives out.

They had a deal. Denz's stupid, unexpected feelings weren't part of it.

"You've always had it figured out," Denz tells him, the heaviness of the day finally pulling him under. "I wish I didn't fuck up. That I wasn't so worried about what the world thinks. What my family thinks."

"Then don't—"

"And I wish I would've had the guts to tell you the reason I wasn't sure about London is because I was *terrified* you'd figure out I wasn't good enough."

Braylon's eyes widen.

"I didn't get a chance to," Denz says, voice thick. "You took that from me. You let your *dad* take that from us."

Braylon swallows but doesn't speak.

Good. Denz isn't done yet.

"I've spent *my whole life* trying to be the right person," he says. "But I'm not sorry for everything else that's happened. I'm not sorry we ran into each other. Not sorry we made a deal. Not sorry I kissed you." He exhales, chest burning. "I'm not sorry for wishing you felt differently."

About me, another thing left unsaid.

The fists at Braylon's sides gradually uncurl. His shoulders sag. His features edge into something that's not quite sulking or pouting. More spulking.

Denz accepts it's the only response he's getting.

"Everything's set up for your party," he tells Braylon, switching on Work Denz. "The mayor's team has confirmed. The sponsors too. Donations will be ready for pickup. You don't need my help for the rest."

He knows he should leave it at that, but he can't.

"This is your home, Braylon," he whispers. "Those teens love you. Your coworkers love you. My family . . ." A shaky smile nudges his lips. "You fit in here better than I ever did."

He turns and walks toward the parking lot. He doesn't wait for a reply.

It never comes, anyway.

The evening starts with a succession of champagne corks flying.

With the bursting flash of cameras.

With a red carpet leading out to Atlas's rooftop bronzed by the setting sun.

The band revs up and their lead singer, Suki Firestone, an artist signed to Uncle Tevin's record label, breaks into Thelma Houston's version of "Don't Leave Me This Way" like a pro. Denz called in a second favor to his uncle after DJ Allegro's cancellation. From the guests' reactions, Tevin didn't disappoint.

In fact, everything about Kenneth Carter's retirement extravaganza seems to be a hit with this crowd. No complaints, not even about the last-minute change of venue. Denz tries not to be on edge about how well things are going.

Which means, of course, he nearly jumps off the rooftop when Nic taps him on the shoulder. She's striking in a Ralph Lauren blazer and cropped pants, pale pink to match her lip gloss. "My condolences," she says, smirking.

"Who died?"

"Your personality, apparently."

He side-eyes her. "Don't be a brat. I'm working."

"You look like Kami at these things," she says, folding her arms. "Where is she, BTW?"

Denz shrugs. He's only caught flashes of her metallic Badgley Mischka gown, the dipping sunlight giving the illusion she's wearing constellations. They haven't crossed paths. It's safer that way. Except . . .

It's strange to be at a 24 Carter Gold event without her by his side. Kami, who people-watches with him. Who drags him away from boring conversations with equally boring celebrities or politicians. Who laughs at all his tipsy jokes. Kami, who he was unnecessarily cruel to yesterday.

"Are you two still fighting?"

Denz's eyes narrow. "Who said we were fighting?"

"Your face. Just now," Nic says. "Is it about her secret boyfr—"

"Uh, I need to go check on the floral arrangements."

Denz weaves through the noisy crowd. He finds a spot under the spiral staircase leading to the balcony. From there, he observes the party. He forces himself to avoid checking his phone, to see if a new text from Braylon has arrived. He's overloaded with enough nerves, enough regret that every breath is like a fist trying to punch through his rib cage.

He's not coming.

Denz knows it, and still.

"How's The Final Word going to get a cover photo of you if you're hiding?"

Eric steps forward in a classic tux, a champagne flute in one hand and his wife, Julie, on his other arm. She's glowing—long, dark hair swept up into an elegant ponytail. Her pleated lilac tulle gown does nothing to hide a very pregnant belly.

Eric beams when Denz's mouth falls open.

"Sorry to greet and run," Julie says, rubbing her stomach, "but these two are treating my bladder like a trampoline. Everything looks beautiful, Denz."

"So do you," Eric whispers, kissing her temple, and then Julie's gone, moving toward the indoor restrooms.

Denz smacks his shoulder. "What the hell?"

"Ow!" Eric rubs his arm. "Surprise?"

"Why didn't you say anything?"

"Really, Denz? When was the last time we had lunch? Got coffee? Shared an elevator?" Eric rolls his eyes. "I've never been introduced to your boyfriend, even though we were at the same parties."

Denz frowns. "Fair point."

"She—*they* are the reason I pulled my CEO nomination." Eric sips from his glass, gesturing to where Julie once stood. "I didn't want to put in more work. I didn't have to. Financially, we're good."

"What about moving up? Making a name for yourself?"

Eric laughs, carefree. "You don't have to get promoted to make a name for yourself," he says. "*Love* what you do. Be great at it. That's the impact people see."

Denz bites the inside of his cheek.

"I wasn't ready to give up quality time with my wife or the twins," Eric adds. "Not for a position I'd only take because your dad invested so much in me."

"*Twins.*" Denz coughs, then collects himself. "That's smart."

"At the end of the day—" Eric motions to where Kenneth holds court, the center of a laughing group. "—I know he's proud I chose my happiness first."

Denz studies his dad. The ease with which he moves through conversations. Everyone surrounding him has their own Kenneth Carter story, a moment he created that changed their world. Just beyond that, Denz sees the wrinkles around his dad's eyes. The slumped posture behind closed doors. The way this job has aged and pulled from him. All the seconds, minutes, hours he's missed from his own life.

But this is what his dad loves. What he *wants* to do. Denz isn't sure if his own dedication is built on a foundation of want or obligation anymore.

"I should check on the missus," Eric says. "She's been eyeing that seven-tier chocolate cake since we walked in." He jostles Denz's shoulder. "See you on the big stage soon, boss."

Denz doesn't correct Eric as he jogs off. After a minute, he meanders over to the corner bar. The band's bouncing through "Single Ladies" and there's enough people dancing that he can claim a prime spot in front of Jamie.

"You're quite the hit," Denz comments.

The poco grande glass near Jamie is overflowing with cash

tips. He rubs his bare chin. Denz is proud his best friend shaved for the event. However, the top three buttons of his shirt are undone, revealing warm tan skin and dark chest hair.

Jamie leans forward, whispering, "I'm just trying to remember what's in a screwdriver."

"Orange juice and vodka."

"That's it?"

Worst bartender ever. Denz shakes his head. "Why are you showing so much skin?"

Jamie grins smugly. "These collarbones are going to pay next month's rent."

Denz rests his elbows on the bar, immediately regretting his decision when he notices how sticky the surface is. He'll have to get this Dolce & Gabbana jacket dry-cleaned before returning it to Auntie Eva.

"You look stressed," Jamie notes. He fixes a Long Island iced tea that's all alcohol and a drop of Coke for color.

"'M fine."

"Liar." Jamie passes off the glass to a waiter. "Want a drink?"

"Can't," Denz bemoans, even though he's proud of himself for maintaining some restraint. "Working, remember?"

He needs to be prepared for anything. Clear head, strong heart, keep calm and all that other stuff.

"I'll take that drink."

Jordan sidles up with an empty highball and a wicked grin. His jacquard blazer is multicolor and shimmery, a bold choice with Eva in attendance.

Denz elbows his cousin. "Aren't you working too?"

"Technically? Yes. Theoretically?" He winks. "I'm celebrating my uncle's long, successful career."

"Is that what you told Kami?"

Jordan makes a fart noise. "She's too anxious to even look me in the eye."

Something twists in Denz's chest. When they were much younger, Kami got the starring role in her middle school's spring play. She rehearsed religiously. On the night of the performance, Denz remembers standing on his tiptoes to lock the girls' restroom door so no one would walk in on Kami spewing her dinner all over the last stall. He didn't leave her side until Leena found them.

"Haven't you had enough, sir?" Jamie says to Jordan, shaking up a new cocktail.

"Have I?"

"Can't afford for you to be a mess during the big announcement."

"Jamie Noah Peters," Jordan says in a slow, teasing voice. Pink spreads across Jamie's cheeks as Jordan licks his lips. "You've never seen me a mess."

"What about that one summer when—"

"Don't you *dare*," Jordan half warns, half giggles.

Jamie's eyes lower as he pours Jordan's drink. A shy smile creases his mouth. He adds an extra cherry, then lets his fingers purposefully brush Jordan's as he hands over the glass.

What the fuck is happening?

Denz glares at his best friend. Then his cousin. He counts back the days and months. The strange conversations and casual mentions. Jamie going to a *fucking basketball game*.

All the jagged pieces fall into place.

Jamie's the first to notice Denz's *you little shit* expression. He knocks over a cup of ice. Stumbles into another bartender who swears while balancing two beers.

Jordan catches on next. "Thanks," he stammers to Jamie. "Uh, for the . . . yeah. Bye!"

He exits as quickly as he arrived.

Denz points an accusing finger at Jamie, mouthing *We'll talk later,* before legging it to catch Jordan. Too bad he walks right into Auntie Cheryl instead.

"Nephew," she says, squeezing his forearm, "whose idea was it to include those lobster mac and cheese bites?"

"Mine, actually."

Cheryl nods appreciatively. She looks every bit a Hollywood starlet in a strapless brocade gown. "Nice touch. You two went all out to impress your dad."

"Enough for him to pick one of us and not some random outsider?"

"Denzel," she says, a dark eyebrow rising, "are you prying for insider info?"

"Can't hurt, right?"

After scooping a glass of red wine off a passing tray, she cocks her hip, sizing him up. "You really pulled it off. I'm shocked."

Denz smiles civilly. *Respect your elders.*

"I wasn't one hundred percent certain you could be serious about something. Step up when things got hard. But you know what?" She tips her glass toward him. "You proved me wrong."

Denz gapes at her. "Say that again?"

"Well," Cheryl amends, "your *relationship* proved me wrong. It changed you. You're driven in a way I've never seen."

Yes, well, creating a fake relationship and having to jump through flaming hoops to keep that lie alive will do that, he wants to say.

Fighting off a frown, he says, "I suppose so."

"Despite what he's done in the past," Cheryl adds, slurping her wine, "that Bray's made you better."

And what was he before? Useless? Incapable and immature? The spare Carter?

His jaw tightens. "His name is—"

"To be quite honest, you're wrong, Aunt Cheryl."

The voice that comes from behind Denz is firm, but kind, coated in a warm British accent. A hand settles on the small of his back. The air around him is spiced in peeled oranges and cardamom.

Denz turns to confirm.

Braylon's breathtaking. Short, tight curls. Cheeks and jaw as bare as the night when they first met. His midnight-blue tuxedo that *coincidentally* complements Denz's rose-gold suit. A quiet smile tugs at his lips.

"Denz has always been serious about his goals. About the business. His family," Braylon says to Cheryl, something steady, unreadable in his expression. "He's perfect for the job."

Denz blinks. He wants to ask why Braylon's doing this. Why he's here. But he swallows all the whys and lets Braylon finish.

"He didn't need me or anyone else to make him better," Braylon asserts. "He just needs people to stop doubting him."

Cheryl's mouth hangs open, fishlike. Denz has witnessed her go toe-to-toe with refs at Jordan's pee-wee basketball games. He's seen her make a *pastor* cry for cutting her choir solo short. But now, face-to-face with the triumphant glint in Braylon's brown eyes, she's speechless.

Denz wants to laugh until it hurts.

Braylon tugs on his hip. "Shall we?"

And Denz goes.

Suki and the band have slipped into a stripped-down "Can't Help Falling in Love." It's a little too ironic for Denz. On the dance floor, Braylon takes the lead. Denz's arms circle his neck. Their bodies move in a slow, swaying figure eight.

"Did you see her *face?*" Denz says with a giggle. "I've never seen her like that."

"I wasn't too rude, was I?"

"Oh, fuck that. She's probably deeply in love with you now."

His phone chimes from his jacket pocket. The group chat, no doubt. He can only imagine what Cheryl's latest message says.

Braylon's lips quirk into a pleased grin.

In theory, this continues. The warmth in Denz's cheeks. The crinkles around Braylon's eyes. This one dance turns into a dozen more, at birthday parties, for anniversaries, every holiday and special occasion. Barefoot in Denz's kitchen under the halo of artificial light.

In theory, they never have to talk about what was said last night.

In reality, it's never that easy.

"I'm sorry about—" Denz pauses. "I didn't mean—" Again,

nothing feels good enough. His hand brushes over the silk of Braylon's shawl collar. "I'm glad you're here."

Braylon says, "I didn't show up to make either of us look good for your family."

"Why then?"

"Because I hated how yesterday ended."

"Oh?" Hope flickers like a firefly in Denz's chest.

"I don't want this to end like last time." Braylon clears his throat. "Without me saying what I really wanted to say."

Oh.

"Nora offered me the promotion. In two weeks, I'll be in LA."

It's as if the rooftop's disappeared. Denz is free-falling, *fast.* And the one person who's been around for months to catch him is the one pushing him off the ledge.

"You were right," Braylon says as they turn, "I didn't give you an opportunity to decide about London. I let my dad influence me. It wasn't fair to you. I'm sorry."

And there it is. The two words Denz wanted so bad when he first saw Braylon at the café. The two words he thought would heal the ugly wound in his heart.

They don't. Not when he can sense a *but* coming.

"But if I'm being quite honest," Braylon goes on, "I knew your decision long before I told you what my dad said. I knew you'd choose your family. Choose who you are *here,* instead of what we *could be* in London."

"It wasn't like that."

"Not to you. But it looked that way."

Denz doesn't argue.

"You want to know why I kept your sweatshirt?"

Denz's eyes squeeze shut. *No.* He wants to know why Braylon can't—*won't* stay.

"Sure," he says, exhaling.

"I was moving to a strange, new place. No bloody fucking clue what I was doing and . . ." Braylon sighs. "The last time that happened was in Athens. Then I met you. I *had* you. I was safe."

His fingers tighten on Denz's hip. "I kept it as a reminder that I'd be okay. Amazing how one silly sweatshirt can do that, innit?"

Denz sniffles. "I guess so."

A warm hand cups his cheek until Denz's eyes flutter open.

"I'm terrified to let people in my life," Braylon admits softly. "I always lose the ones I love. My mom. My dad." He inhales. *"You."*

Denz forces himself to look away.

"I'm a bloody mess," Braylon acknowledges, another laugh in his voice. "But I don't want to pretend to be someone good enough for your family. For you. I love who I am."

"I do t—"

"I'm better than *good enough*," Braylon interrupts. "You are too."

Tears bite at Denz's eyes.

"I'm really not."

Braylon leans down to press their foreheads together. "It kills me how wrong you are about yourself, Denzel Carter." His minty breath dances over Denz's face. "And you're wrong about one more thing—this isn't my home."

Denz stares into Braylon's sad brown eyes, unblinking.

"When I look at this city, all I see is my parents' grave," Braylon whispers. "The end of my first real relationship. Home isn't a place that constantly rips your heart out. Where you can't sleep at night. Where everything reminds you of how fucking terrible this world is."

They glide around laughing couples, tipsy guests, everyone oblivious to how bad Denz aches.

"Home is where you *want* to be," Braylon says.

"So, build a home here," Denz requests. He doesn't add the *with me.*

Braylon can do anything. Be with anyone. All Denz wants is for him to know he belongs.

"I'm still looking for my home," Braylon confesses. "My place."

The voice in Denz's head is shouting for him to say something, *anything.* But he can't. So, he's quiet.

"As stubborn as you are—" Braylon strokes Denz's jaw. "—I think you're looking for your home too. Your place."

"It's here."

"Of course it is." Braylon doesn't hide his disappointment.

Everything is threatening to spill out of Denz. His tears, hurt, remorse. He holds it together. He memorizes the fingers tracing his ear. The scent of oranges and cardamom.

This version of Braylon. The one he's no longer annoyed by. The one he might just be in love with.

"Promise me you'll never forget that Denzel Kevin Carter is pretty fucking amazing." He kisses Denz's temple. "I won't."

Then, Braylon breaks one final rule:

He leaves Denz behind before April sixth.

Hands shaking, Denz swallows the sour, smashed pieces of his heart. He stares out into the nothingness of an attachment he was never supposed to have.

"We're pausing for an intermission," Suki announces. "Please welcome the man of the hour, Kenneth Carter, to the stage."

Thunderous applause kicks Denz into autopilot. The speeches are next. Then, his dad's announcement. He beelines to his former spot under the staircase to prepare for the big moment. Problem is, you can't prepare to face the world after the person you love walks away. There's no cheat code. No five-step plan.

You can't do *anything*.

Denz doesn't realize he's hyperventilating, a hand thrown over his mouth to stay quiet, until someone says, "Sweetheart?"

It's Leena. She's camera-ready, a regal goddess in her black dress paired with a string of pearls. Always the perfect Carter matriarch.

But the second she sees his face, she's Mom.

"I just saw Braylon," she whispers, edging closer. "He didn't look . . . happy."

Denz tries to slow his breaths. "He's . . . he's g—" Bile races up his throat. He gulps it down. "He's gone."

"Okay," Leena says in that voice she used when Denz was

overwhelmed in college. When he was a boy, knees scraped raw from falling off his bike, his dad nowhere around because of another event. "Breathe."

"He's *gone*."

"Yes, I know. Sweetheart. Breathe."

Denz does. With fire in his lungs. A storm in his stomach.

"Once more," she requests. "Slow and easy."

He follows his mom's instructions. Feels the world coming into a gradual, vibrant focus.

"How'd you survive all of this?" Denz gesticulates behind her. To the party. At the empire his family helped Kenneth build. "How'd you make it work?"

His mom smiles empathetically, like she knows. Like she's asked herself those same questions a million times in the mirror.

"I remember that, before all of this came along—" She gestures widely just like Denz did. "—I was LeeLee. Mom. Auntie Leena."

Denz leans against the wall.

"Sweetheart, I stopped playing by their rules," she adds. "I'm still Leena from Sandy Springs. The Spelman graduate who eats pickles straight from the jar. I'm me, take it or leave it."

Denz would laugh if he could.

He knows what she's not saying. That there are people who look at her—a successful Black woman—and try to minimize how great she is. Qualify it not by how hard she's worked, but because of who she is. As if they gave her this. And they'll try to strip it away if they can.

"I love your dad with my *soul*," she says, a spark in her eyes, "but I love myself too. I'm more than 24 Carter Gold. I'm more than a name or a face. Even when it's hard."

"It's always hard these days," Denz says, choked.

"We make tough decisions because it makes us better. Because life doesn't always give us the easy answers."

Denz inhales once more. He holds his mom's gaze.

"If I would've known you and your sister were going to have

panic attacks on the same night, I'd never have let your dad re-tire," she jokes. "I'd keep him chained to that damn desk until Mikah graduates high school."

"He wouldn't mind."

"For the longest time, I thought the same thing." Leena grins. "But he's changed." When Denz raises a confused eyebrow, his mom doesn't elaborate. She says, "I need a drink. I'm too old for this shit."

And finally, Denz laughs.

Leena tugs his sleeve. "Ready to show everyone who Denzel Carter really is?"

He nods confidently. There's nothing left for him to do.

This is his moment, not theirs.

-21-

". . . and that's the day I realized this little dream of mine had become a reality. I—no, *we* were on our way to changing lives. Turning other people's dreams into realities."

Applause roars from below. Whistles and the occasional "Yesssss," champagne flutes raised high. Denz sees it all through a hazy fog.

He remembers the first time he ever heard a Kenneth Carter speech. Not the one in his office, for Audrey Hudson, for the cameras. It was at the very first 24 Carter Gold New Year's Eve bash his parents allowed him to attend. He was thirteen, giddy on adrenaline. Nauseous from the dozens of photographers snapping pics of him in an Armani suit, repeatedly calling his name.

He tripped on stage and forgot his line when introducing his dad, but he remembers his dad's swagger. The way he drew the crowd in. His energy and jokes. The little personal touches that started an echo of *awws*.

The part he recalls with such brilliant clarity is the Kenneth he saw afterward—pale, wide-eyed, wringing his hands as if worried he'd fucked up.

That day, Denz saw himself in his dad.

That day, he truly believed he could be Kenneth Carter.

Now, as his dad recites a speech he spent weeks composing, he feels farther and farther away from thirteen-year-old Denz.

Up on the glass balcony, his eyes flit over the guests below. The aunties in their gowns, the uncles in their tuxes. Eric holds Julie from behind. Jamie anxiously chews his nails behind the bar. A sea of excited faces for miles.

On stage, next to him, Nic smirks. Mikah's wearing a kids' version of Denz's suit, holding Leena's hand. To the left of his dad, Kami avoids eye contact with him.

He wishes she was closer. Wishes he would've found her sooner, asked if she's okay.

Sparkling smile on display, Kenneth says, "And now, I'm happy to introduce you to the new CEO of 24 Carter Gold—"

Holy shit, it's happening. His dad decided to keep the company in the family. Denz has a second chance to be the Carter he's supposed to be.

"—and that person is—"

Anticipation vibrates off the crowd.

Denz expected nerves, like his dad after that New Year's speech. But that's not what this is. It's not calmness either. It's an emptiness, stretched from his skull into his toes. Like he's finally realizing this one thing won't do what he hoped it would.

It won't make him feel worthy.

The part of him that wanted to win is tiny, microscopic by the time the crowd erupts. By the time his dad shouts, "Congratulations, Kamila Carter!"

It happens quickly. Nic hoists Mikah up on her shoulders. Balloons and confetti rain down on them. Camera flashes catch on the tears rolling down Kami's cheeks as Leena hugs her. Denz wants nothing more than to remind her that she's *earned* this moment, but the guests are rowdy and Kenneth's shouting, "Speech, speech!"

It's easy for Denz to step back. Disappear from the stage.

He hears Kami say shakily, "I'm not as great as my dad at speeches, but here goes . . ." as he descends the spiral staircase into the night.

The first person Denz runs into after the buzz from the announcement wears off isn't one of the aunties. Or a reporter from The

Final Word or By Invitation Only looking for a quote about losing. It's not Jamie, lemon drop martini in hand.

Or even Braylon with a change of heart.

It's a slightly taller man with rich ochre skin and thick, dark brown hair. He's got the kind of symmetrical face Denz is instantly jealous of, an endearingly lopsided smile. The frames of his rectangular glasses match his navy suit.

"Hey, Denz!"

His voice is deep, a stark contrast to his very boyish cheeks.

Inside Vista de Atlas's banquet area, guests come and go. Suki's ecstatic version of "Happy" is softened here. Denz could almost imagine the crimes against dancing Tevin's committing, if he wasn't so confused by the stranger in front of him.

Denz glares at him. "Uh . . . *who* are you?"

"Oops. Forgot we haven't formally met." The other man extends a hand. "I'm Suraj."

"No fucking way."

Suraj beams at him.

"Wow. Shit," Denz sputters, his brain ten steps behind his mouth. "You're here? Like, *the* Suraj?"

Suraj's laugh is nice, like hot cider in December. "In the flesh. That's a weird saying. Like, how else would I be here? As a ghost? Ooh, a poltergeist!"

Denz shakes his hand. "Actually, I was starting to believe Kami had an imaginary boyfr—"

He catches himself, eyes chasing every face that passes them. Suraj has been a secret for a reason. Denz might've been an asshole to her yesterday, but he's not going to fuck up whatever his sister has going on by inviting all of Atlanta into her relationship.

He lowers his voice: "You're *real*."

"I am." Suraj releases Denz's hand. "Been dying to meet you."

"Really?"

"Hell yes." Suraj pushes up his glasses. "Kami never shuts up about you."

Denz eyes him skeptically. "She talks about me?"

"All the time. In a good way!"

Denz smiles. Not in the charming, cover-of-*People* way he grew up memorizing. Or the one he uses for clients. The rehearsed one he gives his family when all he wants is to run away. It's genuine.

"She talks a lot about Nic too," Suraj says earnestly. "But you have no idea how highly she thinks of you."

No, Denz doesn't. He assumes Kami hasn't mentioned the fights. The absolute human trash fire Denz has been to everyone, including her, in the past twenty-four hours.

"Suraj? Babe? I've been looking for—"

At the soft, fond voice, Denz pivots ninety degrees, shocked.

The afterglow of being named CEO remains on Kami's face. But the edges are starting to fade. Exhaustion sits heavy in her eyes. She's carrying a sleeping Mikah. His tiny arms and legs cling to her like a koala's.

She stops short when she notices Denz.

"Hey, love," Suraj says. He's got that lovesick sweetness in his eyes, something Denz never saw in Matthew. "I was just—"

"Excuse me," Denz interrupts, aghast. *"Babe? Love?"*

Suraj's cheeks flush. Kami doesn't look opposed to yanking off one of her heels and stabbing Denz in the eye.

He'd deserve it.

Kami passes Mikah into Suraj's arms. Denz is thrown by how *easy* the transaction is, as if they've done it before. As if Mikah, who shies away from strangers, is suddenly comfortable snuffling his nose into Suraj's shoulder.

He's not sure how to feel about his nephew being held by the boyfriend he just met five seconds ago.

"Denzel." Kami snaps her fingers. His head jerks in her direction. "I'm tired. I need to get my son home. We can do *whatever this is* later, okay?"

You mean the whole officially meeting your secret boyfriend who's clearly spent time with my nephew and is actually kind of cute, in a dorky way, thing? Denz considers suggesting. The warning in her eyes stops him.

"Fine," he relents.

"Thank you." She sighs. "Text me when you get home."

Before Kami's too far, Denz blurts, "Congratulations."

She pauses. Denz registers the surprise in her eyes before she blinks it away. She smiles, grateful.

Suraj curls an arm around Kami's waist. Her head tucks into his chest. The three of them make a casual, if not quick, exit toward the elevators, leaving Denz with one thought:

His sister, newly crowned CEO of 24 Carter Gold, stubborn workaholic, is in full-on Sandra Bullock–rom-com love.

Another thought:

He's gonna drag her so hard for those tragic nicknames.

When the glowing embers of the party finally snuff out, all the guests climbing into their sleek black SUVs and limos and luxury cars, Denz shrugs off his suit jacket. He rolls up his sleeves. Pockets his phone. He marches over to where the staff is methodically disassembling things. Denz waves off anyone saying "No, sir, we've got it" to dig in and do his part.

"Rule number one," Kenneth told him after his first event with the company, "never make anyone feel like they're beneath you. Thank them. Help them. Be supportive. Then look everyone in the eye and thank them again."

And so, Denz does.

He hasn't seen his dad since the announcement. The aunties and uncles are gone too. It's just him and the Atlas staff.

At least, for the first ten minutes.

He's walking backward, carrying a box of clean wineglasses, when he collides with someone. A hand catches his elbow, steadying him before he topples over.

"I'm pretty sure," Eric says, grinning, "if you drop these, your dad will unretire just to fire you."

Denz guffaws, then remembers Julie. "Shouldn't you be at home?" It's close to 1:00 A.M., a nice chill descending on the rooftop.

Eric rubs the back of his neck, bashful. "Ever since she hit her second trimester, my wife says I've been a little . . . clingy?"

"Annoying?"

"Suffocating," Eric confirms, righting the box in his arms.

That's when Denz notices the others. Connor, yawning as he helps gather used glasses. Kim, who's changed from her pleated minidress into casualwear and sneakers, folding linen in a corner. The occasional intern wiping down surfaces, detangling lights.

"You don't mind a little help, right?" Eric picks up a box. "We've got your back, bos—I mean, Denz."

Denz shoulder-checks him, smiling. "Thanks, E."

While they work, he doesn't think about losing. What's happening between Kami and Suraj or Kami and him. He doesn't think about Braylon either.

Not much.

Denz watches the party they—*he*—worked so hard on vanish like Cinderella's dreams at midnight.

Somewhere after 2:00 A.M., the rooftop's clean and organized. Denz tells the staff to go home. He hugs Connor and Kim goodbye, calls a rideshare for a sleep-deprived Eric.

When Denz steps off the elevator, his breath catches. For hours, it feels as if he's been dragging an anvil everywhere. But the moment he sees them, his strength crumbles.

Waiting in the lobby are Nic, Jordan, Jamie, and his mom.

It hits him like a tsunami. He's not alone. *They're here.* And no one looks mad, annoyed, or disappointed in him. He doesn't have to deal with the weight of what's happened by himself.

At least, not yet.

He doesn't know how many seconds pass before they circle him. No questions are asked. It's as if they saw it in his red-rimmed eyes, how quickly he was breaking, and immediately caught the shards.

The night *finally* ends with his tears on Nic's shoulder. Jordan's hand rubbing circles on his back. His face buried in Jamie's neck.

With his mom whispering, "One breath at a time, sweetheart. Just one."

It rains the next day. And the day after. For three straight days, the sky is one heavy, gray weighted blanket over Atlanta, unleashing intermittent thunderstorms across the city.

All Denz can do is watch from his bed. He rarely moves from the ball-shaped lump in the middle of his queen-sized mattress. He doesn't talk to anyone. Only showers once, on the second day, when he permits Jamie to cuddle with him for an hour. He somewhat misses human contact but is too afraid to ask for it.

Jamie never comments on Denz's shaky breaths. He never asks where Braylon is. With his arms wrapped tightly around Denz from behind, he says, "Please don't punch me, but you smell like a middle school boys' locker room."

"Fuck off," Denz mumbles into a pillow.

"No, seriously," Jamie says. "You smell like the alley behind a gay club during Pride."

"And how do you know what that smells like?"

"I was curious."

Denz doesn't punch him. He *does* kick Jamie out of his bed, though.

"I'm being polite!" Jamie swears.

"By saying I smell like one of your sexcapades?"

"Don't kink-shame me," Jamie huffs. "I learned a lot of valuable techniques that night."

"Well, you smell like a very specific cologne my cousin wears," Denz accuses.

"We went for breakfast." Jamie scratches the shadowy stubble on his pinkening cheeks. "Are we talking about this now?"

"No," Denz moans, burying his face in the pillow. "I don't have the energy."

On his way out, Jamie says, "It doesn't have to be all or nothing, bro. You *can* have both."

Denz rolls to his other side. No, he *can't* have both. That's not how life works. At least not his. He watches raindrops streak across his window, waiting for his bedroom door to click shut.

An hour later, his tears swirl with soapsuds down the shower drain.

All his phone notifications pile up like a car wreck. The missed calls, unread texts. A couple of Snapchats from Nic, which he's certain are out of concern or death threats for ignoring her, depending on how she feels.

Underneath all the rubble, the social media alerts and family group chat rants, Denz knows what he won't find:

Braylon.

There won't be a new joke that he'll pretend to hate, but will secretly read over and over, laughing himself into a stomachache. Merely this prolonged nothingness that Denz has accepted as his new default.

On Monday, he emails 24 Carter Gold's offices. He CCs everyone of importance he can think of, including his dad. The subject line is simple: **Mental Health Week**. He doesn't go into details. Short and to the point:

I won't be in.

Five minutes later, a reply-all response from Kenneth L. Carter's official CEO account comes in:

Take as much time as you need.

In the dark, hands shaking, Denz scrolls through the thread of messages from Formerly Known As Bray. He starts, then deletes new texts. One after another. *Hello,* then *I miss you.* Finally, *I'd do it all over again, no regrets.*

He never sends any of them.

He flings his phone across the sheets. He sinks into the abyss of his comforter. With every movement, the shattered debris of his heart rattles around his chest.

Exhaustion pulls him under every few hours before thunder startles his eyes open. Each time, he finds his pillow damp from more tears. He flips it over.

Denz stares out at a cement-gray Atlanta that still looks more colorful and promising than the void growing inside him.

He waits for the ache to start all over again.

It's never late.

By Wednesday morning, after the sun finally peels the charcoal gray off the sky, Denz decides he needs *real* food: a blueberry muffin from Crema.

"Uh, Denz?"

It's after 11:00 A.M., and the café's reasonably empty. Which is good, considering he put zero fucks into his outfit choice: a faded University of Georgia T-shirt, black joggers, and old Nikes. What he didn't sign up for is the weird, surprised look Matty's giving him from behind the bar. He managed to shower without crying today. Denz is taking every win he can get.

Matty rereads the name on the drink he just finished. "You ordered a—"

"Don't start with me," Denz grunts. He grabs the cup, then pauses, sighing. "Sorry. Thanks, Matty. For the drink. And putting up with my shit."

He walks away before Matty can reply. Or spontaneously combust.

Denz pointedly avoids that one corner table, settling for a circular one in the middle of the café. Within seconds, the tightness in his chest returns. This used to be *his* place. Monday muffin runs, afternoons taking photos for the company's socials or client meetings near the picturesque windows. Now it's the bar where he ran into Braylon. Weird stares from the barista he hooked up with. The scent of blueberry-lemon scones he can't stomach.

Denz rips into his muffin.

Whatever. One silly pretend relationship isn't going to ruin him. He can go back to Unattached Denz. The man he was before

January. But when he sips from his cup, he realizes asking Mindy to surprise him with a drink of her choice was a horrific mistake.

At the back of his throat, he tastes notes of citrus. The sweetness of honey. He turns the cardboard cup around to read what's written on it:

DARJEELING TEA.

Tears mist his eyes. He considers tossing the cup. Or hugging it close, just to have a piece of Braylon still. Denz does neither. He's too distracted by who slips into the chair across from him.

"So," Kenneth says, unbuttoning his suit jacket as he sits, "this is where the cool kids spend their lunch hour."

Denz stares at his dad like it's been weeks, not days, since they last saw each other. He seems different. Denz decides it's the relaxed shoulders, no longer carrying the weight of his company's future.

Kenneth pushes his glasses up, inspecting Denz. "Eva would have a lot to say right now."

"Doesn't she always?" He winces. That was harsh, even for him. Evidently, he's too miserable, too depleted to filter his thoughts. "Sorry, I—"

"No, you're right. She's always been like that," Kenneth interjects. "Did you know she tried to dress me for prom? Like I don't have taste."

"Didn't you wear a powder-blue tux?"

"Damn right."

Denz snorts. Absently, he takes another sip of tea. "Maybe, just that one time, you should've listened."

Amusement tweaks the corners of his dad's mouth. "What're you drinking?"

"Oh. Tea?"

Kenneth leans forward, conspiratorially whispering, "Is this a cry for help? Are you being held hostage? Is this why you're hiding in a coffee shop instead of coming to work?"

"I'm not—" Denz stops short. He very much *is* hiding. "How'd you know I'd be here?"

"Kami," Kenneth says matter-of-factly. He clocks Denz's frown. "You two on radio silence?"

"It's complicated."

"I can relate." Kenneth laughs. After Mindy drops off his cup of dark roast coffee sprinkled with cinnamon, he says, "I grew up with twin sisters. We fought more than we talked."

"Can you? Relate?" Denz asks.

His dad replies with a *try me* expression that Denz would've been hesitant toward years ago, but today? Today he's bold.

"Why'd you pit us against each other?"

"I didn't," Kenneth says. "You had the same opportunity as everyone. You nominated *yourself*. You chose to—"

"Was it a choice?" Later, Denz might regret his decision to interrupt his dad. Not now. "I heard the aunties that day. After the meeting. I know the pressure the company's been under."

"I don't need you to fight my battles, son."

"It's not *your* battle," Denz says. "It's our family's. We've all put something into 24 *Carter* Gold. Kami and me. Nic. Mom."

Kenneth sighs. "Trust me, I know."

"Then why were you so hard on us?" Denz's voice grows thick. Into his tea, he whispers, "Why are you *always* so hard on me?"

"Because the world's gonna be hard on you. No matter how great you are. What you have to offer." Kenneth pauses, clearing his throat. "They'll always see you as a Black man first. Someone who hasn't *earned* his place."

"I know that."

"Do you?" Kenneth asks, genuine and concerned. "It doesn't matter how many magazine covers, TV interviews, or red carpets I'm on. I still get a million questions from a potential client about who I am. How many hoops am I willing to jump through for the job? Meanwhile, they hire my mediocre, unaccomplished white peers to host their events because I didn't 'fit' the vision they were going for."

Denz watches anger pinch the skin around his dad's eyes.

"Because of who *we* are"—Kenneth gestures between them—

"we'll always have to be twice as good as the next person. I've worked hard to prepare you and your sisters for that."

"You sure did," Denz mumbles, sniffing.

"Clearly, I failed to do it the right way." A deep frown reaches into every wrinkle along Kenneth's face. He takes off his glasses. "Do you know why I didn't choose you?"

Part of Denz knew this was coming. A formal discussion between boss and employee about decisions made. The thing is, Denz isn't sure he wants to hear it.

He says apprehensively, "Because I'm not Kami?"

"Almost." Kenneth sips his coffee. "Because you're gonna turn into another me. I can't let that happen."

"Wow, that's kind of fu—"

Kenneth holds up a hand. "I don't mean I'm worried about you outshining my success. I want that!" He smiles. "What I don't want is for you to destroy your future trying to replicate my past. It'll ruin you, son."

Denz shakes his head. "What does that even mean?"

"Your mom swears you're just like her and Kami's like me. But she's wrong." Kenneth snorts. "You care *too much*. Like me. You want the company to succeed more than you want yourself to."

He pauses for another sip.

"I almost lost her," Kenneth confesses. "Your mom."

There it is. His dad finally said out loud what no one in their family talks about.

"I put everything into the business. Long nights. No days off. And it nearly cost me everything. Neither you nor your sister ever asked *why* I was retiring early."

Denz picks at his muffin. "I thought—"

"It was for your mom," Kenneth finishes, a cheek-aching grin blooming. "I love her. Since the day we met. But I suck at work-life balance."

"You're a *Carter*, Dad. We're great at everything."

"Oh, please." Kenneth guffaws. "With Nic heading to college, I knew it was time. It'll be just me and your mom. I'm not spending the rest of my life celebrating everyone else's best moments and not my own."

Denz's index finger traces the rim of his cup. "You're not worried about Kami becoming another you?"

"I *was*," Kenneth says, leaning back. "That's why I wanted to go public with the job. I didn't want either of you to make my mistakes. Even after the amazing events you both hosted, I still wasn't sure."

"What changed?"

"The flood."

Denz's forehead wrinkles. "But she didn't show up until we were done."

"When I called Kamila, she had her hands full with Mikah. To my surprise, she also told me all about this Suraj fella and their relationship."

Denz slurps more tea to prevent himself from admitting he knew.

"She told me flat out she wasn't leaving Mikah's side until she knew he was comfortable with her boyfriend," Kenneth adds.

"Wow."

"She did what I never did when one of you were sick or going through something," Kenneth tells him. "She delegated. Sent Jordan in her place. She prioritized her son and her relationship while still making sure the job got done."

Denz thinks back to that day. All the work he put in, thinking he made a difference by choosing the company first. By putting his promise to Braylon second.

"She chose both," he says low, awed.

"Denzel—" Kenneth reaches across the table to touch the back of his hand. "—I saw everything you did to win the job. The late evenings. Extra hours. The lunches you skipped. I saw the old me. But I never saw my son."

Denz didn't either. He saw the Carter he thought he was *supposed* to be.

"When Braylon came back," Kenneth says with a sly grin

instead of a scowl, "you were happy. Passionate. *In love.* It took me a while to forgive him, you know."

"Yeah, Dad." Denz chuckles derisively. "You didn't hide that at all."

"What? Am I not allowed to have beef with the man who broke my son's heart?"

Denz swallows the lump that's been clogging his throat like the world's largest jawbreaker. "No, you are."

"He left you. I couldn't just let him off the hook."

"I know."

"But the more I saw him with you—I could tell he wasn't who he was in college. Neither are you." Kenneth pats his hand. "Don't repeat my mistakes, son."

"Too late for that."

"Your mom told me it's over."

"Something like that." Denz's face wrinkles. Is this really how he's going to tell his dad? In the middle of a café on a Wednesday? "Actually—"

Kenneth waits patiently.

"I lied about things with Braylon." Denz sighs. "We were never back together. It was all fake."

Kenneth blinks, the wheels turning behind his eyes. He nods slowly, maintaining a steady gaze as he says, "No, it wasn't."

"Um, Dad, I'm pretty sure I know when I'm in a fake relationship."

"No, no. I knew about that part."

"You did?!"

Denz ignores Matty's hostile stare the moment he raises his voice.

Kenneth rolls his eyes. "Denzel, I changed your shitty diapers. You thought I wouldn't figure out you were lying about your relationship?"

"Maybe?"

"We knew you were lying. Me *and* your mom," Kenneth concedes.

Denz flails, knocking his muffin over. "Do the aunties know?" Fuck, does that mean he needs to check the cursed family group chat? "Oh God, is Uncle O the one who figured it out?"

Kenneth shakes his head, laughing lowly. "I love my sisters and their husbands, but they all missed this one. Even Auntie C.C."

Despite the urge to throw himself through Crema's glass front door, Denz smiles.

His dad reaches into his jacket pocket. He slides a Polaroid on the table. A gasp rushes up Denz's chest. It's the Polaroid from four years ago. From the New Year's party.

"Where'd you get this?"

"Nic's corkboard," Kenneth admits. "I was helping her clean her bedroom. To make packing easier. It was right there."

Denz hasn't visited Nic's room in a while. He remembers the fairy lights and peach walls he helped paint. All the K-pop posters. Over her desk is a corkboard with all her favorite photos. Including this one, apparently.

"This face"—Kenneth points at Polaroid Denz—"is the same one I saw every time you two were together. Then and now."

Denz tentatively brushes his fingers over the photo. Two lovesick boys unprepared for what was next. "It's really over," he whispers.

"Didn't look that way Saturday."

"Yeah, well." Denz isn't in the mood to explain the rest.

"I didn't recognize the Denzel I saw every day at work, but I know the man I saw with Braylon," Kenneth says, covering Denz's face on the photo. "That was my brilliant son. He was in love. *Is* in love. Those feelings are real."

Tears line Denz's eyes. No surprise. His dad gives him space to think, a minute turning to three, before Denz says, "I'm not ready to go back. To work. I need more time."

"Okay."

"I want to take a leave. Figure out who I am. Effective immediately."

"*Technically,* I'm not your boss anymore, but—" Kenneth

fishes out his phone. He slips his glasses on, typing. A new email wooshes. He grins. "Done."

Denz sags with relief. It's time to be honest with himself. Discover what makes him happy. What he wants for the future, professionally and personally. And how to balance it all.

"Now," Kenneth says, standing, "stop being a pain in the ass and answer your mom's calls. She's threatened to kick me out if I've ruined your life by choosing Kami."

Denz face-palms, laughing. "Sorry, sorry. I'll call." Peeking through his fingers, he adds, "And Dad? You didn't ruin my life."

The softest, most Denz-like smile emerges on Kenneth's mouth.

Before leaving, his dad unearths one last item from his jacket: a business card. "A gift." He rests it next to the Polaroid. "Someone asked to meet with you. Maybe it'll help you figure things out."

Then, his dad's gone.

Denz forgets about his tea, the upside-down muffin. He grabs the card. His eyes scan over the Helvetica font. Above an email and telephone number, it reads:

NORA BRIDGER
FOUNDER & CEO
SKYE'S THE LIMIT

-22-

Surprisingly, Denz doesn't spend two weeks waffling over what his next move is. It only takes one Will Thacker Night with Jamie. They demolish two large pizzas while watching *Forgetting Sarah Marshall*. When Jason Segel's character starts working on his Dracula puppet opera, Denz has an epiphany. After, in a fit of adrenaline and insomnia, finally cleaning his room and discovering a cranberry-stained T-shirt under his bed, Denz knows for sure.

It's Braylon's T-shirt. The one he wore while cooking French toast grilled cheeses with Denz and Mikah. A soft, gray reminder of a man who left behind the job he was expected to work for a place he loves. Somewhere he makes a difference. A position he would've never gone after had it not been for Denz.

Well, the Denz that Braylon saw, anyway. Someone who was unabashedly himself. Who made Braylon believe he could be that way too.

He sits with the T-shirt in his lap. With the edges of a white business card digging into his fingers. With his dad's words in his head. With hundreds of social media messages he's collected over the years from young queer followers thanking or praising him in his phone.

He sits with a sudden lightness in his chest, like he knows what he's meant to do.

Like he's always known where he belonged, but never thought it was good enough for a Carter.

But it doesn't have to be. He's never had to meet anyone's expectations. Just his own.

After hours of research, Denz composes an email.

He does something he's never done before: he takes a leap, knowing there might not be anyone there to catch him.

👑 the Carter Family Group Chat 👑

Today 9:09 A.M.

Aunt Cheryl Carter
EMERGENCY!
Whos this man holding hands with Kamila THE
NEW CEO and Mikah at the park??
ITS ALL OVER TFW!

Nic Carter
I FACKING KNEW IT!
*FUCKING! damn autocorrect

Uncle Orlando Rivera
That is so fetch.

Nic Carter
Uncle O stop with the white girl teen comedy
references!

Aunt Cheryl Carter
Leena did you know about this?

Leena Carter
That's my daughter's boyfriend. He's wonderful.
She loves him just like I love all my children,
including the ones with potty mouths.

Nic Carter
lol srry mom

* * *

Nothing's different about 24 Carter Gold's offices. There's constant chatter about upcoming events. Interns running around with frantic energy. Connor, on his third cup of coffee, walking into a wall while texting. The only change is Denz, stepping off the elevator in a check-sleeve Burberry T-shirt, dark denim jeans, and running shoes.

For once, he's not here to work.

But he has a checklist and plans.

His first stop: Eric's office with a lunch invite.

"*Lunch?* With the new boss's foot so far up my ass about the mayor's birthday party, I can taste her Jimmy Choos every time I swallow?" Eric asks flatly. He cleans his glasses before adding, "Does noon work for you?"

Denz laughs, accepting Eric's calendar invite when it pops up.

His next stop: an office he's seen too many times since the age of six. Before he can knock, the door swings open, and someone almost crashes into him.

"Whoa, cuz!"

Jordan blinks owlishly.

Denz flexes an eyebrow. They haven't talked since the retirement party, a recurring trend with everyone important in his life. "So . . . what's new?"

And this one question is what undoes Jordan.

"Nothing! Nope. There's no me and Jamie." Jordan cringes, then lowers his voice. "I mean, we're *friends*. We hang out. We do stuff—but not, like, *that stuff*. Because . . . I'm still figuring things out?"

"Okay. Stop."

Denz isn't here to press Jordan on the topic. Not like Auntie Cheryl would.

He sees a tiny bit of himself in Jordan. Being the only queer person in their family has always been . . . *hard*. Constantly feeling like the odd one out. A feeling he knows no other Carter will ever understand or experience. But that doesn't give him any right to ask Jordan to come out.

He thinks about College Braylon, who wasn't out when they met. The thousands of teens and adults still learning themselves, at their own pace. The ones who don't have a label yet. The ones who don't *want* a label. All the ones who need time and space and safety first.

Jordan deserves that same respect.

"If you ever want to talk, I'm here, okay?" Denz offers. When Jordan nods, he adds, "And if you don't want to talk, that's cool too."

Jordan releases a slow, relieved breath.

"Thanks, cuz."

Denz pats him on the shoulder, then slips into the office.

It's weird, seeing Kami behind the large desk opposite the lavender love seat where Audrey Hudson cried. Where Denz laid the foundation for his dreams at 24 Carter Gold. The ghosts of Kenneth Carter still linger here. From the bookcase stuffed with awards to the ebony leather chair Kami's sitting on. But there are pieces of her filling up the spaces too: a giant whiteboard with Pinterest ideas. Mikah's Spider-Man LEGOs on the coffee table. A glass bowl loaded with green M&M's on the desk's corner.

It's not weird, he thinks. *It's right.*

She belongs on that side of the desk, living her dream. And he belongs here, on the opposite side, figuring out what his is.

"Out of curiosity," he says, flopping onto the love seat, "where'd *this* energy come from?"

He shows off his phone screen. The group chat. Her last message reads: His name's Suraj. I love him. That's all you need to know.

Kami rests both elbows on the desk, fingers forming a bridge for her chin to sit on. "Someone said I was too scared to share my personal life with my family," she says, "so I did something about it."

"I didn't mean let the whole world in."

She shrugs. "Go big or go home, right?"

Denz's hands fidget in his lap. "Sorry. I was an ass."

Kami considers her aquamarine nails. They match her silk bow blouse. "Is that it?"

"Do you want the ten-minute Taylor version?" Denz grins. "Monologues are Dad's thing."

A beat.

"God, Denz." Her eyes are shiny when she glares at him. "For months, I thought the aunties were right. That I couldn't handle this. Balancing work and Mikah. And then you—*my rock*, who always drags me kicking and screaming to be great—confirmed their words."

Denz's stomach knots. "I'm really sor—"

"Don't be." She exhales. "What you said was bullshit, don't get me wrong, but it made me think. So, I called Mom."

"You narced on me?"

"We talked about *family stuff*. Love stuff too."

"Did she talk about her and Dad?"

Kami nods, frowning. "I know everyone thinks I'm just like him—"

"Well, you are both Leos."

She chucks an M&M at him. "As much as we're alike, I don't brush things off like he does. And I'm definitely not tough like Mom."

Denz holds up a small space between his thumb and index finger. "A tiny bit."

"I talked to her about all the pressure," Kami explains. "Trying to manage my career while being a mom and girlfriend."

"So," Denz says, "pretty much everything?"

"And you know what? She said I'm right." Kami laughs, a breathy noise like she's still surprised. "That I'm allowed to make mistakes. That her and Dad made a ton over the years. But I'm not him. I'll never let a company mean more to me than Mikah or anyone else in my life."

A soft grin teases Denz's lips.

"We're not failures if we do things differently than they did," she tells him. "We can choose different paths. A different way of getting there."

Denz grabs a handful of M&M's. He lets the quiet linger for a second. "Mikah likes Suraj," he says, chewing. "How'd that happen?"

"I needed a babysitter the day of the flood. No Mom, no Nic, no you."

"And you asked him?"

"I was so nervous. I wanted them to eventually meet. Just—"

"Not like that?"

Kami nods. "Suraj wouldn't shut up about how long he'd been looking forward to it."

Denz can almost picture that weird introduction.

"When I got back, I found them sleeping on the couch," Kami says fondly. "Mikah was drooling on Suraj's chest."

An unexpected laugh leaps out of Denz. For some reason, he thought he'd be jealous. Other than Kenneth, Denz was always the male figure Mikah's been comfortable with.

(And Braylon, but he's not going there.)

But now there's Suraj. Denz is okay with that. He can tell Suraj cares about Mikah.

He says, "I'm putting in my notice, Kam."

"I figured." She leans back. "There's no way you were showing up in my new office, in clothes Auntie Eva wouldn't approve of, just to chat."

"I came to apologize," Denz whines.

"Congratulations, you could've done that over text," she says, smirking. "Does this mean you've figured your shit out?"

"Maybe?"

Nora responded empathically to his email with a date and time. It's just a meeting for now. But he *hopes* it develops into something more.

"How long do I have?" Kami asks, plucking M&M's from the bowl.

"A month? Whatever it takes to train Jordan."

Kami levels him with a skeptical look. "Train him to do what?"

"Be the next me, asshole!" He dodges the candy thrown at him. "Come on. You can't have a Kami Carter without her wingman. Her right-hand guy. Her rock."

"Denz . . ." She offers him sincere eyes. "You'll always be my rock. Whether you're here or somewhere else. It's mandatory, got it?"

He nods, overwhelmed by the warmth in his chest.

"And what about Braylon?"

"What about him?"

"I saw him leaving the party. It's pretty obvious things aren't great between you two."

"Yeah," Denz draws out, lowering his chin, "about that—"

"It was fake."

"It was fake," he agrees. His head snaps up, mouth agape. "Wait, *you knew?*"

"I knew from day one. You're an awful liar." She cackles. "You have a serious tendency to run from things that, if you just saw them through, might change your world."

Denz blinks. "I don't see how a fake relationship is gonna change my world."

"Maybe it's not as fake as you think."

"It's over," he says, aggressively crunching on M&M's. "He's leaving. It's London all over again."

"Stop being so stuck on the past," Kami growls, looking ready to toss the whole bowl of candy at him. "What happened in college. What the aunties said. How weddings changed the company—"

"They did!"

"Exactly. *Did,*" Kami emphasizes. "People change. Things change. That's not bad. It's different, but not bad."

Denz sniffs. "What does this have to do with me and Braylon?"

"This isn't UGA or London. Tell him how you *feel* this time."

"It's too late."

"Denzel Kevin Carter," Kami says in that firm mom-tone he heard growing up, the one he still hears when Mikah's done something wrong, "it's only too late if you keep going about this the old Denz way. By running. Or lying. Or not doing a damn thing about it."

"Maybe I *don't* know what to do."

He's built walls for a reason. Kept anyone who wasn't family or Jamie at a distance. He refuses to repeat history. But here he is, discovering how bottomless that hole in his heart is because he let Braylon crawl back into it.

"Tell him the truth," Kami suggests.

Denz closes his eyes, swearing under his breath. So much of his life has been stacking lie after lie, one on top of another. He's perfected a likable persona for the public. Walked toward the future while dragging his past with him. But he doesn't want to continue like that.

He *can't*.

"Where do I start?"

"*Jesus.*" Kami snatches her phone off the desk. Her thumbs blur across the screen. "You're the goddamn king of rom-coms. You live for that shit. How do you not know how to tell the love of your life what's in your heart?"

Denz scowls. "Sorry, I'm not Jane Austen or Garry fucking Marshall."

"Or Nora Ephron," she huffs.

Okay, Denz didn't come here to be ridiculed for his inability to Will Thacker his own life. He came to apologize. Mission accomplished.

"*Sit!*" Kami demands when he goes to stand. He flops back down. "I ordered you something. It'll be at your apartment in four hours. Jamie's meeting you after work. Once I feed Mikah, I'll FaceTime you two." She types. "Groceries will be at your place around six-ish."

"*Groceries?*"

When she looks at him, Kami's excited grin is on levels Auntie

Cheryl could never reach. "Denz, you're a fucking Carter. We don't do anything small."

Leaving this entire operation in the hands of a Pinterest mood board fanatic was a massive mistake.

First, it's seventy degrees outside and he's in full cosplay.

Second, it's not even the right character. When Kami explained the plan to him, Denz figured he'd be dressed as Captain America. Maybe the Winter Soldier. Instead, he's trapped in an Iron Man suit made of ethylene-vinyl acetate, from eBay. He can barely see out the helmet.

Third, he's in public, at a downtown park overflowing with screaming children, loud music, and way too many witnesses for what he's about to do.

"Are you sure—" Denz sighs, yanking the helmet's faceplate up. "—this is necessary?"

"Absolutely." Jamie grins euphorically. "This is your Will Thacker moment. It's gonna be bigger than Heath Ledger singing 'Can't Take My Eyes Off You.' Better than the boom box scene in *Say Anything*. Sweeter than Henry Golding—fuck, he's hot— proposing on the airplane while helping everyone with their luggage."

Denz stares down at himself. "None of them were cosplaying as a superhero."

"None of them have what you and Braylon do."

"Which is *nothing* last time I checked."

Jamie turns to look out at the park. With a lot of effort—as nice as the suit looks, it's impossible to move in—Denz does the same.

Pavilions and benches dot the green, flat land. Skye's the Limit's staging area is a white tent with food and drinks. Nearby, barbeque pits exhale trails of smoke. A van parked on the grass pumps out Muna's "I Know a Place," and a drag queen Denz called a favor in to lip-syncs for her life to the crowd of families and teens and adults.

It's a strong turnout.

Denz spots the mayor and her team, the only group in Ray-Ban aviators under giant umbrellas, but no Braylon. What if he didn't come? He already has the promotion. What's left?

Jamie, sensing his hesitation, says, "Remember what I told you—you *can* have both."

Fear catches in Denz's throat. "What if he doesn't feel the same?"

"Bro, life is full of what-ifs," Jamie tells him. "What if it rains? What if the burgers are undercooked and everyone gets food poisoning? What if you fall on your face and—"

"Not. Helping."

"We can't live in fear of worst-case scenarios," Jamie says with a sincere smile. "So what if he doesn't feel the same? You'll live. But never doing anything, living with the regrets—that's the shit that kills us."

Denz tilts his head. (Well, as best as he can.) He surveys Jamie and wonders when the hell he became the love expert in their friendship? Maybe he always was? Maybe all those relationships where Jamie fell fast and hurt hard gave him a wealth of wisdom neither one of them could ever find in the movies they've watched.

Maybe sometimes you just have to jump headfirst into the water to know whether you'll drown or swim.

"Here." Jamie shoves an aluminum foil–wrapped sandwich into Denz's gloved hands. "Don't forget this."

How could he? Denz spent *hours* this morning making it. It took him four tries. Two were burnt. One fell on the floor. None of that's relevant now because he has this and an iron suit and a heart lodged in his throat, ready to either leap into the hands of the man he's hopelessly in love with or slip back down into the abyss of his stomach acid.

"You can do this," Jamie assures him. He lowers the faceplate.

Denz takes ten wobbly steps in the direction of the white tent, chest high, ready to find Braylon and—

Someone steps in front of him.

No, not *someone*. Whitley.

She glares, crossing her arms over her white Skye's the Limit T-shirt.

It's enough for Denz to stop short. Or, at least, he *tries* to, but the stupid suit. Stupid wet grass from a water balloon toss earlier. His heel catches. His arms pinwheel as he falls backward with a muffled "Fuck my life!"

Mud soaks into his costume. In the background, he hears laughter above the shocked gasps. A pair of hands yank his helmet off. He blinks against the sunlight before honey-brown skin and confused, dark eyes come into focus.

Frowning, Braylon helps him up.

"Are you okay?"

"Yes," Denz lies. He squeezes his hands into fists by his sides, then realizes he's missing something. His eyes flit to the muddy grass. To where shiny aluminum foil is splattered an ugly brown. "*Fuck.*"

"What're you doing here?"

Denz forces his eyes away from the ruined sandwich, back to Braylon. He's in the same T-shirt Whit has on, a nice pair of dark gray joggers, running shoes.

"I—" Denz tries, but he's not as prepared as he thought. "Hi. Um. Hey."

Braylon's full lips purse, unimpressed. "What have you got on?"

Denz says unironically, "I'm Iron Man."

Braylon snorts.

"And I came to—"

"Braylon?" Mayor Reynolds appears, eyebrows raised. She tilts her head at Denz. "Denzel? Why're you dressed as a Marvel hero? Is this for the kids?"

"Yes," Braylon begins, but Denz interrupts with, "No. It's for *him.*"

The mayor and her team trade stares, confused. Braylon steps back, surprised at Denz's boldness. His honesty too.

"Can we talk?" Denz whispers.

"Braylon, the speech," Mayor Reynolds says, tapping her wrist in a *hurry up, my time is precious* motion.

"Of course." Braylon pinches the bridge of his nose. "Could Denzel and I have, like, five—no, *ten* minutes? Whit can get you set up on the stage. We have chilled waters. For the heat. Just, please, Your Honor? Or madame? Your Mayorship?"

"Tiffany's just fine," Mayor Reynolds replies, smirking. "Eight minutes. I have another appointment after this."

Once the mayor and her team are out of sight, Braylon sighs. He motions to a shaded area nearby. "We can talk over there."

Denz does his best to walk side by side with him. But, again, the suit. Pair that with the mud in places it shouldn't be and his squishy shoes and Denz barely manages to keep up with Braylon's long strides.

Fucking tall people, he thinks with hostility.

Under the cool shade of a maple tree, Braylon says, "Well?"

Denz hates himself for wanting this to be easy. Confessing your feelings isn't easy. Going out on a limb isn't easy. *Love* is never, ever easy.

"I had a plan." He gestures toward the costume. To the swamp devouring the sandwich he worked so hard on. Frustrated tears bite at his eyelashes. "I was gonna dress as your favorite rom-com hero—"

"Tony Stark?"

He groans. "No, Captain America. But they didn't have his costume. Or the Winter whatever he's called."

"What about Carol Danvers?"

"I don't know who that is."

Before Braylon can launch into a feverish rant that'll surely cost Denz more of the short time he's been given, he says, "I wanted to dress up as *your* version of romance. And I made you a French toast grilled cheese." He hates the tremble in his voice as he adds, "I even did The Flip. It took four tries, but I did it."

"You . . . cooked? For me?"

"Yes."

"Why?" Braylon asks.

If there were ever a moment in his life where Denz truly wished he was his dad, it's now. Because he sucks at speeches. He's terrible with words, which is why he loves social media. There, he can disguise his inability to think of clever or vulnerable things to say with artistic and gorgeous photos. Or just go shirtless.

But here . . . Denz has to strip all that away. No smoke and mirrors. Once he says what's in his heart, there's no edit button. No deleting and trying again later.

This is *final.*

"The moment you walked back into my life, I hated your accent," Denz says. "Your obsession with tea. Your god-awful wardrobe."

"If this is—"

"No, wait," Denz pleads. "I hated that you didn't look the same. That you didn't smell like coconut bodywash. Or that you owned a *cat* in London when you used to always talk about getting a dog."

Braylon's eyebrows raise in a *where is this going* way.

"I came up with at least ten other things to hate about you because . . ." He inhales shakily. "Because I loved you the second I saw you again."

Braylon's mouth opens, but nothing comes out.

"I loved you the moment we met at that silly party," Denz goes on. "I loved you all through college. Loved you when you left. Damn it, I loved you even after you broke my heart."

His throat is so tight. But Denz doesn't quit.

"I'm sorry I ever wanted you to be someone different, someone from the past, just to impress my family. Because—" Denz smiles nervously. "—how could anyone not instantly fall in love with you?"

Braylon rubs the back of his neck. "I could think of a few reasons."

"If someone can't love every version of you—amazing *and*

annoying—then they don't deserve to love any version of you."
Denz swallows. "Including me."

"Denz," Braylon starts, face falling. "You—"

"You said I made you want to be honest with yourself," Denz
interrupts, voice thick and overwhelmed, "but that's not true."

"It's . . . not?"

"No." A wobbly laugh. "We made each other honest. It just
took me longer to see it."

The corners of Braylon's mouth inch up.

"I'm so fucking tired of lying and pretending," Denz confesses.
"I'm tired of being the Carter people expect. I'm tired of trying to
be the Denzel everyone loves when—when the one person who's
loved me as plain old Denz is you, and I have no clue why."

A retort is forming on Braylon's lips. Denz gets there first.

"I quit my job."

"You—*what?*"

"It's okay!" Denz grins. "I have a plan: freelance work. I'm
starting up my own social media business. I have a meeting with
Nora on Monday about it."

Something like pride crinkles Braylon's eyes.

"It's a start," Denz says.

"Not a bad one, if I'm being honest."

The humor behind Braylon's voice gives Denz a rush of dopamine. That and the strains of music—a deep bass melody, sweet
vocals—coming from somewhere nearby. It's the song they
danced to at the engagement party. Holding a wireless Bluetooth
speaker over his head, looking like a young John Cusack, is
Jamie.

Denz wants to laugh, but tears spill out instead.

"You were right. I don't have a place here," he says. "All my
life, I've lived in a world my family built for me. The only time I felt
like I made a home for myself was with you." He pauses, wiping
his cheeks. "You were my home. You *are* my home."

Braylon scrubs a hand down his own face, exhaling.

"I know you're scared to let people in," Denz quickly says.

"That the universe is going to take one more thing from you. But fuck, I want to be your home, wherever that is."

Silence.

Braylon's mouth is a thin line that looks a lot like doubt. Like this is one more time where Denz is saying the right thing at the right time to impress someone instead of letting Braylon see him for who he really is: simply Denz.

Too many beats pass. Tears slice hotly down his cheeks. But Denz refuses to walk away.

Not until Braylon says something. *Anything.*

He doesn't. He pulls out his phone. Swipes a few times, and turns the screen for Denz to see. It's a Delta eCredit. A one-way, nonrefundable ticket.

Destination: LAX.

"I was waiting until after your dad made his announcement," Braylon admits. "Just in case." Now, he looks nervous. "I wanted you to come with me. But I wasn't sure you'd say yes. And then you—"

Reality smacks Denz in the face.

"Then I said what I said the other night," he fills in.

Braylon squares his shoulders. "None of it was fake for me either. Not a second. But I got so scared. Ironic, innit?" He laughs sadly. "That I'd be afraid of *you* turning *me* down when I'm the one who didn't give you a chance last time."

"I wouldn't have."

"Even now?"

Denz smiles. "You know, there's no Varsity in LA."

"But there's In-N-Out." Braylon blinks back tears. Hopeful, he adds, "And there's you. If you want? Will you come with me?"

Denz pauses. He never thought he'd hear those five words again. The ones from college. This time, Denz doesn't need weeks to decide. He doesn't need a minute.

He already knows. He's *always* known.

Clumsily, Denz strides forward. He tugs Braylon down until

their foreheads press together. Until Braylon can taste the salty tears on his lips when he whispers, "Yes."

He kisses Braylon. Soft and achy. Quiet like a thunderstorm passing. Loud like Julia Roberts's laugh in every rom-com. Memorable like Athens and London and Atlanta.

Like everywhere they've been, together or apart.

Denz has never cared about the place. The destination.

Because this is them.

This is *home*.

Epilogue

Seven Months Later

"I hope you know," Jordan is saying via FaceTime, his voice low and earnest, "I'm risking my life getting you this info. This is treason."

"It's *one* ingredient," Denz argues.

"That Auntie Leena hasn't shared with *anyone*!"

"But she clearly shared it with your mom."

Jordan and Auntie Cheryl might not be exactly alike—mainly because Jordan can *keep a secret*—but their ability to extract classified information from a reliable source is god-tier.

"Cuz," Denz says, lifting his phone from where it was propped against a mug with a Union Jack design, making sure Jordan has a clear view of his face, "remember when you were fourteen? At the Sedwicks' first wedding? When you—"

"Don't you finish that story." Jordan's warm brown cheeks are glowing. "Extortion? Seriously, who are you?"

Denz grins arrogantly. "I'm a Carter."

Jordan lets out a long, low breath. "Lemon extract."

"Sorry, what?"

"The secret ingredient to your mom's sweet potato pie is—" Jordan pauses. His eyes dance around his surroundings, as if there might be trained mercenaries hiding in the shadows, waiting to kidnap and subject him to sleep deprivation or waterboarding for uttering two words again. "—lemon extract."

"You're fucking kidding. That's *it*?"

Denz is offended. Years and years of failed pies. Cheap replicas of his mom's greatest bake. A lifetime of secrets for . . . *lemon extract?*

"If you narc on me," Jordan warns, pulling at the collar of his Ralph Lauren wool sweater like he can already imagine Leena's hands around his neck, "I'll lie. I'll disavow. I'll—"

"Blah, blah, blah. Your secret's safe with me."

Denz returns his phone to its former position on the quartz kitchen countertop. Afternoon sunbeams flood through the apartment's windows. It's a sharp contrast to the green sofa in Jordan's background.

He *knows* that sofa.

"Gotta go, cuz," Jordan says. "I have—um. Things to, yeah."

Denz squints, waiting for Jordan to elaborate.

Instead, Jordan shouts, "Bye, Braylon!"

Off camera, to Denz's left, comes an enthusiastic "See you soon, Jordan!"

Denz rolls his eyes. He says, "Jordan? Tell Jamie he owes me a text." The face on the other side of the screen freezes: wide-eyed, mouth hanging open. "And for the love of God, please don't fuck in my old bed."

Jordan ends the call.

Braylon says fondly, "He's gonna retaliate when we go back to Atlanta next month."

"I know." Denz's mouth quirks upward. "I can't wait."

Two weeks in Atlanta for the holidays. They've been planning the trip for months. Dinner with the Carters. *All* of them. Spending way too much time on his parents' sofa as Mikah forces them to rewatch every Studio Ghibli movie they've missed. Visiting Braylon's parents' graves.

It's a rare Saturday off for them. Braylon's not working tirelessly on a new project or awareness campaign for the LA branch of Skye's the Limit. Denz isn't spending another weekend advising new clients to grow their online platforms.

It's just them. They're standing barefoot in the kitchen—*their kitchen*—wearing matching aprons. An early Christmas gift from Nic. Embroidered on Denz's is MUFFIN. Braylon's says SWEETEA.

Braylon peels the boiled sweet potatoes over the sink while Denz gathers all the dry ingredients.

The open patio door lets in a warm mix of city and ocean scents. Of earth and salt. The apartment is another gift, this one from Denz's parents. It's not a top-floor unit like he shared with Jamie. Just a one-bedroom studio in Culver City. Seven hundred square feet of space with their shoes by the door. Braylon's electric kettle on the kitchen counter. A walk-in closet divided between monochromes and designer looks Auntie Eva insisted Denz pack.

"If you leave that Dolce sweater here, I'll disown you," she told him tearily.

Denz never thought he'd see the day Eva would cry *happy* tears for him.

He's been in LA for four months now. Braylon arrived first, in April, apartment hunting and logging hours at the youth center while Denz set up his brand in Atlanta. Skye's the Limit was his first client.

Those first few weeks apart were . . . a trial of errors. Missed calls. Time zone issues. Denz tried to surprise Braylon with a semi-naked FaceTime that was supposed to involve a toy or two, but instead ended with Braylon mortified on the other end. He was in the middle of a charity dinner.

But they survived.

They found ways to communicate and laugh and *schedule* sexy video calls.

In hindsight, Denz wonders why they never considered long-distance dating before. When Braylon left for London. Maybe they weren't ready then? Maybe you have to lose something before you realize how strong you are? The lengths you'll go to keep it?

He hasn't mentioned any of that to Braylon, though.

One day, he will.

Now, it's weekend mornings down at the farmers' market.

Afternoons discovering new queer neighborhoods. Holding hands on Santa Monica Pier. It's Braylon insisting In-N-Out is inferior to The Varsity and Denz pretending to disagree. It's Sundays playing Scrabble while Braylon tells Denz old stories about growing up with his dad.

Now, it's Braylon curling around him from behind, hooking his chin on Denz's shoulder to ask, "What's next?"

Denz walks him through dumping the peeled sweet potatoes and melted butter into the stand mixer's bowl.

"Sugar, vanilla, nutmeg," he instructs.

"Bossy," Braylon teases.

They've done this dance so many times before. But it's never been Denz leading their waltz. He's never been the one with the recipe and deft hand, helping to bring everything together. He warns, "Too much cinnamon."

"Coming from you?" Braylon lifts an accusing eyebrow. "Is that a joke?"

Denz laughs, elbowing him aside.

This isn't the life he dreamt about in college. It's a lot less Hugh Grant happily-ever-after, more Netflix adaptation of a Jane Austen novel—clumsy and sometimes chaotic. Charmingly flawed.

He loves every second of it.

He loves the café two blocks from their place with the mint-green interior. Their dedicated corner table where Braylon steals bites of his muffin and Denz sips his way through the entire tea menu until he finds the right one.

For the record: it's *not* Darjeeling.

He loves his new job. He finally gets what Kami was saying. Being 24 Carter Gold's CEO was a fantasy. The kind of thing that's so big and untouchable, it only exists in your head because you know it'll never happen. But this? Taking on queer clients who want their content to impact others in the community? It's his *dream*, the thing you think about over and over until you have no choice but to make it a reality.

He loves finding balance between work and his relationship. The fights with Braylon that end in the most enthusiastic make-up sex. The little reminders that they're imperfect.

Turns out, he loves those quiet, achy five minutes after ending a FaceTime call with Mikah too. When he's hugging himself, trying not to cry. When he's missing his family so much, it aches down to his toes. Because Braylon always finds him. Always folds his long arms and legs around Denz, face buried in the side of his neck, never speaking.

Just holding Denz. Letting him ride the wave until he's okay again.

Even now, he loves Braylon watching him fill the crust. Slide the orangey pie into the oven. Set a timer. There's a look in his deep brown eyes like he wants to say something. The same words Denz stumbled over in an Athens apartment he almost set on fire.

Denz tries to beat him to it.

"I love you," he says just as Braylon says, "I want you on this counter right now so I can su—"

Braylon freezes, cheeks darkening.

Denz bursts into lung-aching laughter.

"I mean, I love you too," Braylon stammers.

"Sure. Sounds great," Denz says, already guiding Braylon backward until the edge of the counter digs into his spine. He unties Braylon's apron. "But I think it's my turn."

"It's hardly a competition."

"Then why am I always winning?"

"I really do, you know," Braylon says, overwhelmed by Denz gripping his hips, lifting him up, tearing off his own apron. "Love you, I mean."

Denz stands on his toes to kiss him, quick and fierce.

"Love you too."

He's almost figured out the annoying drawstring on Braylon's joggers when a pair of warm hands grab his face.

Braylon drags him back to eye level. He whispers, "I love you, Denzel. All of you. All the time."

Something swells underneath Denz's ribs. It's lightning and

thunder. This time, he kisses Braylon slow and deliberate. Soft, then suffocatingly deep. He buries his fingers in Braylon's curls. Their clothes are half tugged off, hearts synchronized.

"I love you, Braylon Adams. Silly accent and all."

Braylon laughs. Mumbles "We're gonna burn the pie" against his lips.

Denz doesn't fucking care. For the most part, anyway. He doesn't want to explain losing the security deposit to his dad.

His hands map out Braylon's skin. He discovers new places to press: "Can I kiss you here?" He ignores that the balcony door is open, and the neighbors can hear Braylon's deep groans.

The thing that *does* distract Denz from mouthing his way down Braylon's tense abdomen is his phone vibrating on the counter. He turns his head. Usually, he wouldn't care. It's probably just social media notifications. But he peeks at the string of texts lighting up his screen.

"Fuck," Braylon grunts impatiently. "If you bloody stop what you're about to do for a fucking email, I'll—"

"It's the group chat."

Braylon's head thunks against a cabinet. "Is it about our trip?"

Denz snorts. "Of course."

Lately, his family's messages have been less about which Carter made a headline and more about Denz's plane arrival. What airline is he flying? Why are they staying at a hotel instead of at his parents' or Kami's new house—the one only he knows Suraj is living in too.

"God," Braylon says, still somewhat breathless. "Tell Auntie Eva that a jumper from *the mall* is a perfectly acceptable dinner outfit and—"

"No, no." Denz laughs again. "It's not that."

"Then what?" Braylon asks incredulously. "Is your dad on about my choice in restaurant? Is it because I don't celebrate Christmas? Is that what's finally going to get me permanently kicked out of this family's good graces?"

Denz smirks. "No, but how long has *that* been on your mind?"

"Too long."

If Denz is being honest, watching Braylon ranting about the Carters while shirtless, his joggers around his knees, is turning him on even more. But he can't get to that part yet. Not without turning his phone screen around for Braylon to read.

Aunt Cheryl Carter
I can't wait to see him!

He's gonna teach me about tea! not the gossip kind!

Nic Carter
auntie stop trying to be besties with my bestie!

Aunt Eva Carter-Rivera
I hope he likes the mcqueen sweater I got him for the family xmas photo!

Leena Carter
If you're reading this Braylon . . . I promise we're not this embarrassing 🖤🖤🖤

The light in Braylon's eyes is irresistible. So is the sweet, affectionate grin unrolling across his mouth.

"You have nothing to worry about," Denz promises, brushing his lips to Braylon's. "I think they love you."

Acknowledgments

As with all stories, the journey from idea to fully formed book is always different. Some journeys are long and winding roads. Some are short, fun skips through the park. This idea has lived inside of me since 2015. Actually, longer. Since I was a little boy swooning over every Meg Ryan and Julia Roberts and Reese Weatherspoon rom-com available, wishing I could exist in those love stories and find the queer happily ever after I longed for.

Getting here—where I got to tell my own version of those rom-coms I obsessed over—feels like living in that happily ever after. I wouldn't be at this moment without so many people who helped and guided and stood by me on this journey.

Special thanks to my agent, Thao Le, who encouraged me to write this silly little idea at the end of 2019 and then spent almost a year with me as we revised and tweaked and polished it. Thanks for saying, "Julian, it's time to write an adult book." This wouldn't exist without you.

To my incredible editor, Vicki Lame, who just *might* love Denz and Braylon more than me. I've never been so grateful for an editor asking me to add "more" of these two clueless goofballs. Thank you for having a vision and a killer sense of humor.

Biggest thanks to the amazing team at St. Martin's Griffin, for loving this book so deeply: Anne Marie Tallberg, publishing director; Chrisinda Lynch, managing editor; Lisa Davis, production editor; Meryl Levavi, designer; Olga Grlic, jacket designer and creative director; Soleil Paz, mechanical designer; and Janna Dokos, production manager. Thank you, Sandra Chiu, for bringing Denz and Braylon to life with your gorgeous illustration—you're a gift to the book world.

Huge shout-out to Vanessa Aguirre, the most amazing assistant editor; Kejana Ayala and Brant Janeway, marketing geniuses; and my publicist, Zoë Miller—I'm so lucky to have all of you on Team Julian.

To Adib Khorram, who's probably read every draft of this story and never once said you hated it. You told me to write this book when I was scared no one would want it. You're a friend, a lifeline, a heartbeat in the darkness.

Thanks to Ashley Poston, my geeky, bighearted, day-one inspiration and Denise Williams, the most brilliant light in this world, for their lovely blurbs.

Immeasurable gratitude to Julie Murphy, who *refused* to write this book for me when I asked. Sierra Simone, who gave me confidence when I had none. Leah Johnson, who makes me want to be better in every facet of life. To Susan Lee and Ali Hazelwood, who've been fiercely supportive. To Natalie C. Parker, Tessa Gratton, and the entire Madcap Discord community—thanks for the sprints, the banter, the motivation. To Anjanette Harper, who has been with me since my first novel and, miraculously, *still* wants me to write more.

To every romance writer who has come before me: thank you for writing books that I squeeze tightly to my chest long after reading "The End." My deepest love to Beverly Jenkins, Rebekah Weatherspoon, Denise Williams, Alyssa Cole, Kristina Forest, Jasmine Guillory, Farrah Rochon, Elise Bryant, Adrianna Herrera, Taj McCoy, Kennedy Ryan, Kosoko Jackson, Tia Williams, Ebony LaDelle, N.G. Peltier, Nicola Yoon, Krystal Marquis, and every Black romance writer who's ever dared to give us the kind of love stories we've desperately needed.

My family and friends, who are no doubt tired of my excuses for not hanging out more when I'm on deadline: sorry and I love you.

To every reader who picked up this book in search of a laugh, healing, hope, and a safe space to exist in—I wrote this for you. We deserve big, unapologetic love stories. Strong support systems. Moments of joy and sadness and every messy second in between.

Most of all, we deserve second chances. I hope you find yours here.

About the Author

Vanessa North

Julian Winters is the author of the award-winning young adult novels *Running with Lions, Right Where I Left You, How to Be Remy Cameron, The Summer of Everything, As You Walk On By, Prince of the Palisades,* and his adult romance debut, *I Think They Love You.* A self-proclaimed comic-book geek, Julian currently lives outside of Atlanta, where he can be found swooning over rom-coms or watching the only two sports he can follow—volleyball and soccer.